**This book is to be returned on or before
the last date stamped below.**

RENEWALS   Please quote: date of return, your ticket number
and computer label number for each item.

The Sinister Man

HOUSE OF
STRATUS

Copyright by Edgar Wallace

The right of Edgar Wallace to be identified as the author of this work has been asserted in accordance with sections 77 and 78 of the Copyright, Designs and Patents Act 1988.

This edition published in 2001 by House of Stratus, an imprint of Stratus Holdings plc, 24c Old Burlington Street, London, W1X 1RL, UK.

www.houseofstratus.com

Typeset, printed and bound by House of Stratus.

A catalogue record for this book is available from the British Library.

ISBN 1-84232-706-2

CONTENTS

A PROPOSAL

"You have beauty," said Mr Maurice Tarn carefully, "you have youth. You will in all probability survive me by many years. I am not the kind of man who would object to your marrying again. That would be sheer selfishness, and I am not selfish. When I die you will have great property; whilst I live you shall enjoy my wealth to its full. Possibly you have never looked upon me in the light of a husband, but it is not unusual for a guardian to marry his ward, and the disparity in our ages is not an insuperable obstacle."

He spoke like one who was reciting a carefully rehearsed speech, and Elsa Marlowe listened, stunned.

If the old-fashioned sideboard had of its own volition stood on end, if Elgin Crescent had been suddenly transported to the suburbs of Baghdad, she could not have been more astounded. But Elgin Crescent was in Bayswater, and the gloomy dining-room of Maurice Tarn's maisonette remained undisturbed; and here was Maurice Tarn himself, sitting on the other side of the breakfast table, an unshaven, shabby man of fifty-six, whose trembling hand, that went automatically to his shaggy grey moustache, was an eloquent reminder of his last night's carouse (there were three empty bottles on the table of his study when she looked in that morning), and he was proposing marriage.

She could only gaze at him open-eyed, scarcely believing the evidence of her senses.

"I suppose you think I am mad," he went on slowly. "I've given a lot of thought to it, Elsa. You are heart-free, as I know. There is no reason in the world, except – except the difference in our ages, why this should not be."

"But – but, Mr Tarn," she stammered, "I had no idea…of course it is impossible!"

Was he still drunk? she wondered, without a tremor of apprehension, for fifteen years of association with Maurice Tarn had not tended to increase her awe for him; if she had not been so staggered by this proposal which had come like a bolt from the blue, she might have been amused.

"I don't want to marry you, I don't want to marry anybody. It is very – very kind of you, and of course I feel" – she could hardly bring her lips to say the word – "honoured. But it is too ridiculous!" she burst forth.

His tired eyes were watching her, and he did not even flinch at the word.

"I'm going away to – somewhere. I've got to go away for – for my health. Since Major Amery has come into the firm it is impossible to continue."

"Does Ralph know this – that you're going away?" she asked, curiosity overcoming her amazement.

"No!" He almost shouted the word. "He doesn't, he mustn't know! You understand, Elsa? Under no circumstances must Ralph know – what I have said to you is confidential. Think it over."

With a gesture he dismissed the subject, to her great relief. For fully ten minutes she sat staring out of the window. Mr Maurice Tarn's dining-room looked out upon the garden of Elgin Crescent, a garden common to all the houses that backed upon it. It was not a garden in the strictest sense of the word, being no more than a stretch of worn grass, intersected by brown paths; and its chief value was best appreciated by the parents of very young children. On sunny days the shade of the big tree in the centre of the garden was a favourite resting-place for nursemaids and their tiny charges. At this hour the garden was deserted. The pale yellow sunlight, slanting through the big window, lit a diagonal patch on the table, and gave to the spring flowers that, by a movement of her chair, mercifully hid Mr Maurice Tarn from her view, the glory which belonged to them.

She stole a glance at him past the flowery screen. He was wearing yesterday's collar – he invariably made a collar last three days; and his rusty black cravat was fastened behind with a tarnished buckle. The lapels of his ancient frock-coat shone with much wear; his cuffs showed ragged threads. Speculatively and, for her, cold-bloodedly, she examined him in the light of a possible bridegroom and shuddered.

Elsa had preserved toward her guardian and his habits an attitude of philosophical patience. She had grown tired of urging the purchase of clothes. He had a fairly good income, and once she had surprised the information that he had a substantial balance at his bank. But by nature and habits he was miserly. She owed him something…but not much: an education at the cheapest boarding-school he could find; a dress allowance reluctantly given; an annual holiday at Clacton – a fortnight in a crowded boarding-house; and a post-graduate course in shorthand and typewriting which was to fit her for the position of a private secretary to old Amery. In addition to these things, Maurice Tarn gave her what he was pleased to call "a home."

She had often wondered what freak of generosity had induced him to adopt the orphan child of a distant cousin, but the nearest she had ever reached to explaining that fit of altruism was when he told her, one evening, that he hated complete loneliness and preferred a child in the house to a dog.

He was apparently absorbed in the devilled chicken he was cutting into microscopic pieces, for presently he asked: "Is there anything in the paper?"

He himself never read the newspapers, and it had been part of her duty for years to supply him with the principal items of the morning's news.

"Nothing," she said. "You know about the parliamentary crisis?"

He growled something under his breath, and then: "Nothing else?"

"Nothing, except the drug scandal," she said.

He looked up suddenly.

"Drug scandal? What do you mean?"

She picked up the newspaper from the floor where she had dropped it.

"It is about two gangs that are importing drugs into this country – I didn't think you'd be interested in that," she said, searching for the paragraph.

She happened at that moment to look across at him, and nearly dropped the paper in her surprise. Mr Maurice Tarn's complexion was one of consistent sallowness, but now his face was a deathly white. His jaw had dropped, his eyes were staring.

"Two gangs?" he croaked. "What do you mean? Read it, read it!" he commanded huskily.

"I thought – " she began.

"Never mind what you thought, read it!" snarled Tarn.

Masking her astonishment, she found the item. It was a half column on the top of the principal page:

Yesterday morning Detective-Inspector Bickerson, accompanied by half a dozen police officers, made a raid upon a small warehouse in Whitechapel, and, after arresting the caretaker, conducted a search of the premises. It is understood that a considerable quantity of opium and a package containing 16 pounds of cocaine were seized and removed, and it is believed that the warehouse was a distributing centre used by one of the two gangs which are engaged in putting illicit drugs upon the market, both here and in America. The police believe that one of these nefarious associations is conducted by a Japanese merchant named Soyoka, who, however, is the merest figurehead in the business, the operations being carried out by a number of unknown men, said to occupy good social positions, and two of whom are believed to be officials in the Indian Civil Service. The composition of the second gang, which during the past two years has amassed a considerable fortune, is not so well known. Behind these two organisations are hundreds of agents, and a small army of desperadoes are employed to cover the gangs' workings. The recent arrest of a Greek in Cleveland,

Ohio, and his confession to the Federal authorities has enabled Scotland Yard to get a line on the British branch of the 'business.' From the statement of the Greek Poropoulos, it is believed that the heads of the second gang include an English doctor and a leading merchant of the City of London –

"Ah!"

It was not a groan, it was not a sigh, but something that combined the quality of both. Elsa looked up and saw her guardian's head sinking over the table, and sprang to her feet.

"What is the matter?" she asked.

He waved her aside.

"Get me some brandy – in the cupboard of my study," he mumbled, and she hurried into the stuffy little room, returning with a tumbler half-filled, the contents of which he swallowed at a gulp.

Slowly the colour came back to his face, and he could force a smile.

"You're responsible," he grunted, with heavy pleasantry. "A fellow of my age doesn't propose at this time of the morning without feeling the effects – eh? A little too old for love-making, I guess. Think it over, Elsa. I've been a good friend of yours."

"Do you want me to read any more?"

He stopped her with a gesture.

"Stuff! A newspaper invention: these fellows are always out for sensation. They live on it."

He rose to his feet with an effort.

"I shall see you at the office," he said. "Think it over, Elsa!"

The door of his study slammed behind him – he was still in his locked room when the girl boarded an eastward bound bus that carried her almost to the door of the Amery Corporation.

THE HOUSE OF AMERY

The house of Amery & Amery stands where it stood in the days when its founder marshalled his apprentices and clerks to fight the Great Fire of London, so that, when the holocaust had smouldered to ashes, the cramped old house alone raised its head amidst the blackened ruins of Wood Street. Improvements had come with the years, an exigent City Council had demanded certain structural alterations, but in appearance the Amery building remained what it was in the days when the "Mayflower" set forth from Plymouth Harbour and narrowly missed fouling the "Pleasant Endeavour," the first of the Amery Brothers' fleet of East Indiamen.

The centuries had seen many fluctuations in the fortunes of the house. One evening at White's, in the days of the Regency, an Amery had diced the fleet out of existence; later, another Amery had won back its equivalent in the tea trade; but the narrow-fronted house, with its uneven floors, its poky little cupboards and presses, its low ceilings and tortuous stairways, defied the passage of time.

Above the thick green glass window panes that admitted light and distorted vision the faded inscription "Amery & Amery, Shippers & Importers," appeared in the identical lettering that an Amery had chosen on the day George the Third went to his rest. The little room where Elsa Marlowe attended to the private correspondence of the newest proprietor had been furnished in his youth by a chief clerk who, as an old man, had seen the first policeman on the streets of London.

Elsa, sitting before her worn writing-table one morning in late spring, when the sunlight poured into the room, seemed as much out of place in the grim setting as the bunch of lilies of the valley she had arranged in a cheap glass vase beside the typewriter.

There was a sculptor in Paris who specialised in dainty statuettes of slim Parisiennes, and she might have posed for M. Millière, a straight-backed, long-limbed girl, with the tilted chin, the straight nose, the large, enquiring eyes and the confusion of spun gold hair he loved.

She had that complexion which made wise and sceptical women look twice at her; yet her pink and white owed nothing to artifice, and the rich red of her mouth was as everlasting as the deep grey-blue of her eyes.

Her forehead was puckered as she listened to her voluble companion. She was never quite comfortable when Miss Dame came to her favourite topic of discussion, though the gaunt woman expressed much that she thought.

Elsa Marlowe was not prepared to accept Miss Dame's judgment on any other subject than stenography. Her views on human affairs were inclined to be coloured by the peculiar brand of romance she had absorbed overnight. But when she described the house of Amery & Amery as "creepy," and spoke of Paul Roy Amery as a "sinister figure," Elsa found herself ranged on the side of Romance.

"You can laugh about the pitchers," said Miss Dame earnestly, "but you get ideas of Life out of 'em…types, characters, if you understand me? It's experience to a young girl like me. The villains I've seen!… My Gawd! But I've never seen anybody like the Major. Sinister! You've only to look at him, Miss Marlowe. And why your dear good uncle, the finest gentleman that ever breathed – more like The'dore Roberts 'n anybody I know – should let you stay in this place, is more'n I can understand. See what I mean?"

Miss Dame glared fearfully through her big rimless spectacles. Her large mouth was grotesquely open, her little button of a nose redder than ever. She was tall, round-shouldered, awkwardly made. Her hands and feet were large; her bobbed hair, refusing to behave as bobbed hair should, spread fan-wise from her head.

"I wouldn't call him 'sinister,' " said Elsa thoughtfully; "he is certainly unpleasant. I don't think he is used to dealing with white people – "

"That's what I say," broke in Miss Dame. "Niggers and black people an' Injuns! I'll bet he lashes 'em to death. I've seen it done. Do you remember the 'Monster of the Marsh'? Anna Conseuello was in it. Oh, it was perfectly marvellous! This monster took her to an 'ut and tied her up, and Frank – that was her fiancy, that was misjudged by her owing to her seeing him kiss his sister that she didn't know anything about – he rode all night with a sheriff's possy – the way they flew across the hills was perfectly marvellous – "

Elsa's soft laughter interrupted her.

"Anyway, he's sinister," said Miss Dame firmly, "and so is this building. Hundreds of years old – there ain't a floor that's level or a door that fits; and look at the poky little windows and the beams over the ceiling. And there's no proper washing place, and in the heart of the City too! Where did he come from, anyway? Old Mr Amery never said he had a nephew, and your dear uncle was that surprised when the will was read that he could have dropped. He told me so himself."

For the moment her "dear uncle" was as unpleasant a subject as the sinister Mr Amery. It was accepted by the employees of Amery's that Mr Tarn and she were uncle and niece, and she never attempted to correct that erroneous impression.

"We shall get used to him," she said with a half sigh. "New people are always awkward at first. And probably he isn't used to business. He had an official position in India. I know that – "

She stopped. Here she was going beyond the bounds of propriety. She could not tell of the mysterious letters which Paul Amery dictated, letters in which whole lines were made up of unintelligible code words.

"Mr Tarn knows something about him," Miss Dame nodded vigorously. "They were together hours yesterday – I heard 'em! Gee! The noise they made!"

Elsa turned startled eyes to the other.

"Quarrelling?" she said incredulously.

"Quarrelling!" repeated Miss Dame triumphantly. "You never heard anything like it! It was when you were out at lunch. When I say 'hours' I mean twenty minutes. I never saw your dear uncle so upset in my life."

Elsa was not impressed. Mr Maurice Tarn was easily upset in these days. Was she responsible for that? she thought whimsically. But a quarrel! Why should Amery quarrel with his general manager? They hardly knew one another, for Paul Amery had not occupied the presidential chair a month as yet, was new to the business and scarcely acquainted with its routine.

"Are you sure?" she asked.

Before Miss Dame could answer, a bell shrilled and Elsa hastily gathered her notebook and pencil and passed into the lair of her ogre.

It was a pleasant room, carpeted in a dull blue that showed the polished black panelling to advantage. Over an old fireplace, a solemn-faced clock ticked sedately. The leaded windows were curtained with dark blue velvet; the only touch of gay colour in the room was the scarlet leather of the fender and seats.

The man at the big writing-table was glowering at a letter on his blotting-pad, and, seemingly oblivious to her presence, was reading it over to himself, his thin lips moving silently as he assimilated every line, every word. A minute passed, and then.

Paul Amery looked up with that expression on his saturnine face which never failed to rouse in her breast something that was akin to fury. Not that he was consciously offensive – her resentment would have been excusable if he were.

There was just the faintest hint of a sneer, a downward droop of the corners of his mouth that coincided with the lift of his upper lip, and a something – a cold, appraising something in his blue eyes that was altogether and yet indefinably insulting.

She had surprised that expression before – invariably followed upon the interruption of a reverie. And Paul Amery's day-dreams were not pleasant. Only for a second did that twisted smile disfigure his thin dark face. In another second, it set like a mask of fate; except that the black brows had met in a frown that hardened and almost dehumanized him.

"Yes?"

His voice had the quality of granite. Instantly he had passed through the stage of transition between dreams and reality, and his eyes were searching hers suspiciously. There were people who would think he was good-looking, she thought, and was sufficient of a woman to concede this advantage to him. The hot sun of India had tanned his face to a permanent brown; it had given him, too, something of the character of the jungle beasts he had stalked – she never saw him come noiselessly, almost furtively, through the outer office without thinking of a cat – and she loathed cats.

"Yes?"

He never raised his voice; he did not display his impatience, but his "Yes?" was like the flick of a whip in her face.

"You rang for me and you wished to see the bills of lading… Chi Fung and Lee, Mr Amery," she stammered, and despised herself for her deference.

Without a word he reached out his hand and took the papers she had brought to him. Silently he examined them and then put them aside.

"Why are you afraid of me?"

The question stunned her; it was so unexpected, so utterly unanswerable that she could only stand and stare at him until, before the masterful blaze of his eyes, she lowered her own.

"I'm not afraid of you, Mr Amery," she said, and tried hard to keep her voice level. "What a queer thing to say! I'm – I'm not afraid of anybody." This defiantly.

He did not speak. His very silence gave her the lie as plainly as if he had spoken.

"Besides," she went on with the ghost of a smile, "isn't it the proper attitude of a secretary toward her employer? A wholesome respect…"

She finished lamely, feeling a fool. He was looking through the window into the dusty sunlight of Wood Street. Apparently his attention was absorbed in the laden trucks that lined the narrow road;

in the red-faced City policeman who was engineering a passage for a steam trolley; in the drab fascia of the office block opposite – in anything but one pink and white girl with a mop of fine, browny hair that defied regulation.

"You are five feet three inches," he said, going off at a tangent. "Sixty-three inches! The little finger of your left hand is crooked – you must have broken it when you were a child. You live constantly in association with somebody who is deaf: your voice is just a little too strong. Of course, Mr Maurice Tarn! I have noticed that he is deaf."

Elsa drew a long breath.

"Shall I leave the bills of lading, please?" she asked.

His eyes were no longer on her face. They had dropped moodily to the blotter.

"No… I wanted you. Take this letter to Fing Li T'sin, 796 Bubbling Well Road, Shanghai – 'Tang chiang chin ping ch'ang – ' I beg your pardon, you do not understand Chinese, of course?"

He was not joking. She saw him flush with annoyance at his mistake – at the possibility that she might think he was being funny at her expense.

"He reads and speaks English better than you – or I, for the matter of that," he added hurriedly. "Take this. 'I am looking for a trustworthy man to cover the Nangpoo province. Feng Ho has arrived – you may send letters to him here. When you see the Long Sword of Sun Yat tell him – "

Here he paused, and passed a slip of paper across to her. Carefully pencilled in capital letters were the words:

Barrow Tendency Makeshift Warlike Candle Stencil Pendant Maple Crest Hamlet Desire.

He was looking at her as she read, a thin hand caressing the little black moustache that covered his upper lip, and as she raised her head she met his glance and went hot.

"Nice job, this?" he asked absently. "Not too much work? Wages good?"

It was the first time he had displayed the slightest interest in her. Hitherto she had had the feeling that he had regarded her as part of the movable fixtures of the establishment.

"Yes, it is a good job," she said awkwardly, and added (fatuously, as she told herself): "I hope my work is satisfactory?"

He did not answer, and she added boorishness to his sins.

"You knew my great-uncle, Bertram Amery, of course?"

He was not looking at her; his eyes were still on the street below. "Slightly," she said. "I was here during the last few months of his life. He only came in for a few minutes each day."

He nodded slowly.

"The ancient ran the business, of course?"

"The ancient?" She frowned, and then realised that his flippant reference was to Mr Maurice Tarn. "Mr Tarn has always helped to run the business," she said, a little stiffly, though heaven knew she was in no mood to feel offended because he spoke slightingly of her very distant relative.

"Mr Tarn always helped to run the business," he repeated absently, and then jerked his head round to face her. "Thank you, that will do," he said.

She was at the door when his voice arrested her.

"How much does the Stanford Corporation pay you?" he asked.

She turned round, staring at him in wonder.

"The Stanford Corporation, Mr Amery?"

His keen eyes searched her face.

"I'm sorry," he said simply. "I see you do not know that enterprising business."

He nodded to the door, and she was back at her desk before she realized the indignity of her dismissal.

THE MENACE OF SOYOKA

Stanford Corporation! What did he mean? Did he suggest that she was secretly working for some other house? If she had been on better terms with her uncle, she might have solved the puzzle; but for the moment their relationship was more than a little strained.

She was typing the letter when she heard the door of her room opened and closed, and, looking up, saw the tall, hollow-eyed man whom she had particularly wished to avoid that day.

He stood for a while, fingering his bristling grey moustache, his small, faded eyes fixed moodily upon her, and then he came slowly across the room and towered above her. He was an unusually tall man, and, for the general manager of a prosperous business, shabbily attired. His cuffs were ragged at the ends, his black cravat rusty with age.

"Where's Amery?" he asked, lowering his voice.

"In his room, Mr Tarn."

"Humph!" He fingered his bristly chin, "Did he say anything?"

"About what?"

"About anything," impatiently.

She shook her head. It was in her mind to tell him about Major Amery's enquiry, but she could not bring herself to the point of taking him into her confidence.

"Have you thought over the matter I spoke about this morning?" He stole a quick glance at her, and read her answer before she spoke.

"No, it – it doesn't bear thinking about."

He blinked at her, and his face twisted to an expression of pain.

"Too old, I suppose? I'll make any arrangement you like, only... I want company. I hate being alone. I want somebody I can talk to – a wife. Somebody I know I can trust. I've got to get things off my mind. They can't make a wife tell – you understand? Any arrangement," he emphasised the words and she grasped his meaning. But he was not looking at her as he spoke. That "any arrangement" promise was a lie. He wanted more than a trustworthy listener.

She drew a long impatient sigh.

"We needn't go back to that, need we?" she asked. "I wish you wouldn't, Mr Tarn. It worries me terribly, and it is going to make life insupportable."

He was still fingering his chin nervously, his eyes straying to the door of Paul Amery's room.

"Is anything wrong?"

He shook his head irritably.

"Wrong? What should there be wrong?" He glanced apprehensively toward the door. "I'm going in to see him."

There was a note of defiance in his voice which surprised her. She had not seen this side of Maurice Tarn's character. She knew him best as a most self-possessed business man without imagination. At his worst, he was a slovenly domestic tyrant, with a passion for secret drinking. Yet here he was, bracing himself as for a great ordeal, the hand that touched his moustache trembling, his eyes fearful.

"I've got to go away." His voice was lowered. "I don't know where, but – but – somewhere."

He heard the turn of the handle and looked round affrighted. Paul Amery stood in the doorway, that hateful smile of his upon his thin lips.

"I – I wanted to see you, Major Amery."

Without a word, Paul Amery opened the door a little further and his general manager went in. Amery closed the door behind him and walked slowly to his desk. He did not sit down but stood, his hands in his pockets, his head slightly bent forward, his cold eyes scrutinising the man.

"Well?"

Twice the lips of the older man moved, and presently, in a half-unreal voice, he spoke.

"I feel I owe you an apology for that – that scene which occurred yesterday, Major Amery. I fear I lost my temper; but you can quite understand that one who has held a trusted position in the house of Amery, who was respected, I venture to say, by your uncle – "

"Sit down."

Mechanically the man obeyed.

"Mr Tarn, I'm new to this business. I ought to have come over eight months ago, when my uncle died and the property passed into my possession. There were certain things that I did not realise, but which I realise now. I looked upon Amery & Amery as a corporation that could get along very well without me. I never looked upon Amerys as – an enemy I should have to fight."

Maurice Tarn stared at him.

"Fight? I don't understand you. An enemy, Major Amery?" he said tremulously.

"Who is the Stanford Corporation?"

The question rang out like a pistol shot, and Mr Tarn winced, but did not answer.

"There is a business being carried on in a block of offices in Threadneedle Street," said Amery slowly; "not a very flourishing business, for the Stanford Corporation occupy one large room and employ no clerks. All the work is done by a mysterious individual who comes after most of the other offices are closed, and leaves just after midnight. He types his own letters, of which he keeps no copies; he has interviews with strange and disreputable people; and although the name of the Stanford Corporation does not appear in the books of Amery & Amery, I am satisfied that our very reputable business" – his lips curled again – "built up by the labour of years, and founded on the honesty and integrity of my dead relatives, is a screen behind which a certain traffic is in progress."

"Major Amery!" For a second Maurice Tarn's pose of virtuous indignation held, and then, before the glittering eyes of the other, he wilted. "If you feel that," he mumbled rapidly, "the best thing I can do

15

is to get out. I've served this firm faithfully for thirty-five years, and I don't think you're treating me well. What traffic? I know the Stanford Corporation: I've just remembered them. They're a perfectly straightforward firm…"

The lifted lips, the hard, smiling eyes silenced him.

"You'll bluff to the last, eh? Well, so be it! Tarn, you're doing something of which I do not approve, and that is a mild way of putting it. And I'm going to stop you – I'm going to stop you if it means killing you! Do you get that? You know what I am – you guess a whole lot more than you know! You're in my way, Tarn. I didn't expect to find this obstacle here." He pointed to the floor, and Tarn knew that he was speaking about the house of Amery. "I'm going to put the matter plainly to you," he went on. "Fortunes are to be made, and are being made, by two gangs, who are running a dope industry. Maybe you saw something about it in the morning paper. Two gangs! There isn't room for two – is that clear to you?"

Tarn's face had gone ashen; he was incapable of speech. The man by the writing-table was not looking at him: his eyes were fixed on the street below – he seemed to find in the life and hurry of Wood Street something of overpowering interest.

"Not room for two – hardly room for one," he repeated. "The second gang had better shut up business and get out whilst the going's good. There are many dangers – Soyoka's crowd aren't going to take competition lying down. I am telling you this as a friend."

Tarn licked his dry lips but did not answer.

"The girl isn't in it?"

"No." The older man blundered into this partial admission.

"You're… Soyoka!" he breathed. "God! I didn't dream…! I knew they were working from India and the East…but I never guessed…"

His voice sank to an indistinguishable rumble of sound.

Amery did not answer him: with a sideways jerk of his head he dismissed the man. Elsa saw him stagger through his office like one in a dream, and wondered what was the reason for his white face and trembling hands.

Left alone, Amery walked slowly to his desk and sat down, his chin on his hands. Facing him on the wall hung a picture in an old-fashioned gilt frame – a portrait of an elderly man in a long, flowing wig; he wore a coat of homely brown, lace ruffles swelled under his ample chin, and in his hand was a half unrolled map of the world. The first of the Amerys! The last of the race looked up into the hard grey eyes of his ancestor, and he nodded.

"Illustrious forbear" – with mock gravity – "the crooked house of Amery salutes you!"

DR RALPH HALLAM

It was the custom of Amery's, and had been the custom from immemorial times, to allow the staff an hour and twenty-five minutes for luncheon. Nobody knew why this extra twenty-five minutes had been granted. It was a tradition of the house, and was a very welcome one to Elsa Marlowe that day, for she had decided to take counsel of the only man in the world who could help solve her problems.

On the stroke of one o'clock she was out of the office and was hurrying toward Cheapside. Taxis there were in plenty, and within fifteen minutes she was alighting at the door of a small house in Half Moon Street. Scarcely had she paid the driver than the door was opened and a good-looking man of thirty was halfway across the sidewalk to meet her.

"This is a miracle! Has the noble house of Amery gone bust?"

She preceded him into the house, and not until she was in the sedate little dining-room did she answer.

"Everything has gone bust, Ralph – no, my dear, I couldn't eat. Go on with your lunch and I will talk."

"I have had my lunch – bring something for Miss Marlowe," ordered Dr Ralph Hallam, and, when his man had gone, he asked anxiously: "What is wrong?"

She had known Ralph Hallam in the days when she was a lank school-girl. A friend of her "uncle's" and a frequent visitor to their house in Bayswater, they had grown up together. He was, by his own confession, so inefficient a doctor that he had never practised since the day he left hospital. A keen business man, he had employed the small fortune which his mother had left to him to such advantage that he could afford to dispense with the problematical income which might have come to him from his profession.

A fair-haired, clear-eyed man of something over thirty, his boyish, clean-shaven face and irrepressible good-humour gave him the impression of one who had not left his teens very far behind.

"You're not ill, are you?" he asked, and when she shook her head smilingly he sighed his relief. "Thank heavens! I should be obliged to call in a real doctor if you were."

All the time he was speaking he was disposing of her fur, her gloves, her handbag, in his helpless way.

"You know that Mr Tarn isn't really my uncle?"

"Eh?" He stared at her. "Oh, yes – your cousin or something, isn't he? Queer old devil – doesn't he bore you?"

"Ralph – he wants to marry me!" she said tragically.

He had taken a wine-glass from the sideboard and was putting it on the table when she spoke. The glass dropped from his fingers and splintered to a thousand pieces. Looking at him, she saw his face go suddenly white.

"I'm a clumsy fool." His voice was very steady. "Say that again. He wants to marry you – that – that – ?"

She nodded.

"Exactly – that! Isn't it hideously unbelievable? Oh, Ralph, I'm worried. Something queer has come over him in this past week. He has quarrelled with Mr Amery – "

"Steady, steady, old girl. Sit down. Now tell me all about it. Quarrelled with Amery – that's the Indian fellow?"

She told him as coherently as she could of the scene that had occurred that morning. Ralph Hallam whistled.

"The old villain!" he said softly. "But what is the idea? Why this sudden desire for matrimony? He never struck me as a marrying man. And to be mistress of the menage at Elgin Crescent is not the most pleasant of prospects – "

"He is going abroad," she interrupted. "That is why he wants to marry in such a hurry – oh, I ought not to have told you that!"

Too late, she remembered her guardian's injunction. But if Ralph Hallam was surprised by the news he did not betray himself.

"You'll not marry him, of course. That kind of December doesn't belong to your kind of May, Elsa."

It seemed to her that he was going to say something but checked himself. For a second she had a spasm of fear that the day would bring her a second proposal, for a meaning light had kindled in his expressive eyes. She liked Ralph Hallam…but not that way. He was so good, so kind, such a good pal, and it would spoil everything if the unspoken message was delivered. To her intense relief he spoke of Amery.

"What kind of man is the Indian?" he asked. "Wasn't he in the Civil Service?"

She shook her head.

"I know very little about him," she said. "None of us do. He was in India for years. They say he isn't even English – he belongs to the American branch of the Amerys, and it was old Mr Amery who found him his position in India. He is so strange."

Ralph Hallam smiled.

"Mad, probably – most of these Indian fellows go daft. It is the sun…"

She shook her head.

"No, he isn't mad. His manners are awful – he is abrupt to the point of rudeness. And yet – Ralph, there is something queerly fascinating about him. I find myself wondering what his life must have been, what his recreations are: he seems to move in an atmosphere of mystery. I can't tell you what happens at the office – that wouldn't be fair – but his correspondence is so unusual. And he's magnetic. When he looks at me sometimes, I have the feeling that I'm…out of control. That sounds alarming, doesn't it?"

"It certainly does," smiled her puzzled companion. "Does he hypnotise you?"

"Ye-es," she hesitated. "Perhaps that is it. He reminds me of some beautiful sleek animal, though he isn't at all beautiful! Sometimes his eyes are so cruel that I shudder, and sometimes they are so sad that I could weep – and generally he is so hateful that I loathe him." She laughed softly at her own inconsistency. "Jessie Dame calls him 'the sinister man,' and perhaps she is right. Sometimes I feel, when I am in his presence, that he has the burden of some terrible crime on his mind. He is so suspicious, so horribly unbelieving. When he asks you a question he gives you the impression that he is prepared for you to tell a lie. You feel that he is watching you all the time. Everything about him is that way. He wears shoes with thick rubber soles, and when he moves it is with a sort of stealthiness that makes you jump. Mr Tarn hates him."

"A singularly unpleasant person," said Ralph with a chuckle, "but impressive – don't lose your young heart to him. As to Tarn, I think it would be a good idea if you went away for a while. You have never met my sister-in-law?"

"I didn't know that you had one," she said, and he smiled.

"You will like her," he said simply. "I'll get her to invite you over for a few days."

The servant came in with a tray at that moment and, until they were alone, neither spoke. She had finished her lunch and had risen to go, when the sound of a taxi stopping at the door brought his eyes to the street.

"Wait."

She followed his glance, but from the angle at which she stood she could not see the figure that was paying the cabman.

"Who is it?" she asked.

"The admirable Tarn," he said. "I don't think he'd better see you here. Go into the library – you know your way. When I show him into the dining-room you can make your escape. I'll take care that he doesn't see you."

There came the sound of the doorbell and she hurried into the little study and presently heard Maurice Tarn's deep voice in the passage. She waited a second, then, tiptoeing along the passage, opened the door and let herself out.

Tarn, his nerves on edge, heard the thud of the closing door and looked round suspiciously.

"What was that?"

"My man going out," said Ralph coolly. "What is your trouble?"

For a while the other man did not answer; then, with a groan, he dropped into an easy chair and covered his face with his hands.

"As bad as that, eh?" Ralph Hallam nodded.

"He knows," said the muffled voice of Tarn.

"Which 'he' is this? The Indian gentleman? And what does he know?"

"Everything. Hallam, he is Soyoka!"

Hallam looked at him open-mouthed.

"You're mad – Soyoka?"

"He's either Soyoka or he's somewhere high up in the gang. Why shouldn't he be? The profit of Amery's isn't eight thousand a year. We know what profit there is in Soyoka's – they're making millions whilst we're making thousands. He's been living in India, not guessing that old Amery would leave him this business. We've always known that Indian officials were hand in glove with Soyoka's gang. Otherwise, how would he have known where to look in the books for the consignments we've had? The first thing he did was to put his finger on a case of fancy goods we had from Stein of Leipsic and ask for particulars. He told me to get, and I'm getting. Hallam, it's death to fight Soyoka! They'll stop at nothing. I can't stand any more, Hallam. I am too old for this kind of business."

"Not too old to marry, they tell me."

Tarn looked up quickly.

"What do you mean?"

"Just what I say. I understand that you contemplate making a getaway with a lady, who shall be nameless."

Maurice Tarn shrugged his shoulders.

"I don't know what I'm going to do. I'm scared."

"Scared you may be." There was nothing pleasant in Ralph Hallam's voice; his face had hardened, the underlip pouted ominously. "And if you feel like getting away, why, you can go. You've enough money to get your nerves in order. South America, of course? I thought so. Go and be blessed! You've lost your nerve and so far as

I am concerned you're valueless. You're worse than that – you're a danger. We'll have a quick division and then you can go – to the devil if you like."

Slowly he crossed to the broken man and stood looking down at him.

"But you go alone. I want a partner."

"Elsa?" gasped the other.

"Elsa," said Ralph Hallam. "I can talk her into my way of thinking. That will be easy. I want her, Maurice. She is altogether adorable. I don't blame you for wanting her. She is divine! But I want her too. There is a world of happiness in that slim lady, Maurice!"

"But – but – " Tarn was looking at him, horror-stricken. Some solitary cell in his brain, where decency had once dwelt, was operating powerfully – " but you can't, Ralph! You're married – I know that you're married. You can't marry Elsa!"

"I said nothing about marriage," said Ralph Hallam testily. "For God's sake don't be so respectable!"

THE MAN IN THE ROOM

In the drive back to the office Elsa was in a quieter frame of mind and could think clearly. She had not told Hallam everything: he knew nothing (she thought) of her nightly ordeal, when, his study table littered with the bottles he had emptied, Maurice Tarn had talked and talked until her head reeled. She used to think his oblique references to matrimony, its advantages and compensations, were efforts of sheer loquacity. She understood now. Muddled and bemused, he was trying to prepare her for his monstrous proposal. Something was wrong – badly wrong. He did not drink so heavily in the old days. She checked a sigh as the cab turned into Wood Street, and she tapped at the window to stop the machine before it reached the door of Amery's.

It was half past two when she hurried up the narrow stairs, hoping that her unpleasant employer had not rung for her. As she opened the door of her room she saw a man sitting on a chair by the window. Though it was a warm day, he wore an overcoat, over the collar of which his black hair flowed. His back was toward her, for he seemed absorbed in his contemplation of the street below, and not until he heard the click of the closing door did he turn round suddenly and stand up. For a moment Elsa stared at him open-mouthed. It was a Chinaman!

He was dressed in the height of fashion. His smartly-cut overcoat was wasp-waisted, his striped grey trousers were rigidly creased, and over his enamelled boots were a pair of white spats. The fashionable cravat, the neat gloves, all these things were European. But the face! The fathomless black eyes, set behind lashless lids, the yellow face like wrinkled parchment, the bloodless lips, the protruding under jaw – she had never seen anything quite so hideous; and, as though he read her thoughts, he said, in perfect English: "Handsome is as handsome does – Feng Ho, Bachelor of Science – my card!"

And with a little bow, he handed her an oblong of pasteboard, which she took mechanically.

At that moment she became aware of a strange and lovely sound. It was the glorious note of a bird in song. Perched on a shelf was a cage of exquisite workmanship. Gold wire and coloured glass combined to make the palace of the little songster a thing of rare beauty. Standing on the perch was a lemon-yellow canary, his thick throat throbbing in the song of his kind.

"How wonderful!" she breathed. "Where did it come from?"

Feng Ho grinned.

"I brought him here. Pi always accompanies me. In the street many people look round, thinking it remarkable that a Chinese gentleman, a bachelor of science, should carry a common birdcage in his hand. But Pi needs the air. It is not good for a little bird to live all the time in rooms. Pi, unworthy and ugly little crow, sing your stupid song for the beautiful lady."

The bird had been momentarily silent, but now he burst again into a flood of melody that filled the drab room with golden sound.

"He is wonderful!" said Elsa again, and looked from the bird to his owner.

The inscrutable eyes of the Chinaman were watching her. "I am afraid I gave you rather a shock," he said, in his queer, mincing way. "You are probably not used to meeting Chinamen, Miss Marlowe."

She gasped. How did this creature know her name? "You – you want to see Major Amery?" she said, recovering her equilibrium.

"I have seen him. He asked me to wait a little while and to introduce myself when you came. I am afraid I shall be a frequent visitor."

She forced herself to smile.

"You need not be afraid of that, Mr – "

Should she call him "Mr Feng" or "Mr Ho"? Again he must have read her thoughts.

"Feng Ho is a compound name," he said, "and the 'Mr' is unnecessary, unless you would feel more comfortable in the employment of that prefix."

He was looking complacently at his brand-new gloves as he spoke, and then: "Major Amery has just come in."

She looked up at him quickly.

"I didn't hear him," she said.

He nodded rapidly.

"Yes, he is now walking across the room; he has stopped by the fireplace." He held his head erect in an attitude of listening. "Now he is at his desk and he has picked up a paper. Did you not hear the rustle?"

She looked at him suspiciously. Was this wretched man, who had so easily assumed terms of equality, being amusing at her expense?

"I hear everything," he said. "Now he is sitting in his chair – it creaked."

She walked to the door of the Major's room and opened it.

He was sitting at his desk; his hand was out-stretched to touch the bell that summoned her when she looked in.

"Come in," he said brusquely. "You've met Feng Ho?"

He saw her flushed cheeks, and his lip lifted in that hateful smile of his.

"He has been giving you a demonstration of his hearing? That is his one vanity."

He looked round at the Chinaman. Feng Ho displayed the immense cavity of his mouth in a grin that stretched from ear to ear.

"Close the door, please," he said, and then, as she was about to obey, shutting the Chinaman out, a string of unintelligible words came from his lips and she saw Feng Ho hide his hands in his sleeves and bow.

"You may see a great deal of Feng Ho. On the other hand, you may not. Take this letter."

For the next quarter of an hour her fingers were flying over the pages of her notebook, for when Amery dictated, he spoke at a speed that tried her ability to the limit. His words came like the staccato rattle of a machine-gun, and the sentence ended as abruptly. She looked up, expecting to be dismissed, and found him looking at her.

"Feng Ho is Chinese," he said unnecessarily, and added, with a look of annoyance when he saw her smile: "So many people mistake the Chinese for a neighbouring nation." He paused, and then went on slowly: "Soyoka, on the other hand, is a Jap. And Soyoka is a very good paymaster."

The name seemed familiar to her, but for the moment she could not remember where she had seen or heard it.

"A very excellent paymaster," he went on. "I think you might do better if you served him instead of this amateur crowd. Soyoka pays well."

His eyes did not leave her face, and he saw that she was still puzzled.

"Do you want me to leave you – Amery's?" she asked. "Who is Soyoka? I seem to have heard the name."

"Soyoka is a Japanese – gentleman," he said, a hint of primness in his tone, "and a very powerful Japanese gentleman and a very rich Japanese gentleman. There are no" – he paused – "flies on Soyoka. And his friends are always willing to enlist the services of people who are likely to be of help. Soyoka would not object to engaging one who had been working for his competitors; in fact, he would welcome the opportunity. And, as I say, he is a very excellent paymaster."

She shook her head.

"You bewilder me, Major Amery. I really don't know who Soyoka is, and I don't think I should care to work for – Eastern people."

He made no reply. Then: "You can trust Feng Ho," he said unexpectedly. "He has all the virtues and none of the vices of the East. Most Chinamen are amiable souls with a passion for song-birds. If Feng Ho ever walks into this office – however, you may like Feng Ho. He improves upon acquaintance. A river pirate killed his father," he went on in his inconsequent way. "Feng Ho followed him into the mountains of Ningpo and brought back seven pirates' heads in a Gladstone bag. A queer fellow."

She was speechless with horror and amazement.

"That – that little man?" she said incredulously. "How dreadful!"

"It's rather dreadful to have your father's throat cut," said the strange man coldly. And then, again going off at a tangent: "Feng Ho is death to Soyoka's rivals – remember that."

"Who is Soyoka?" she asked, a little exasperated. "You've made three references to him, Major Amery, and I may be dull, but I really can't see their application."

He did not reply: that was his most maddening and most offensive trick.

"What do you do with yourself on Sundays?" he asked abruptly.

For answer she rose and gathered up her notes.

"You will want these letters before the afternoon post, Major Amery," she said.

"You haven't answered me."

"I don't think that is a matter which really concerns you, does it?" she said with a touch of hauteur which she felt was absurd.

His fingers were beating a rapid tattoo upon his blotting-pad. "The private lives of my employees are a matter of considerable interest to me," he said. "But perhaps it isn't the practice in this country to be too closely concerned. Only it struck me that your cottage was rather isolated, and very near the river; and there should be bars on the window of your room. It is rather too close to the ground, and any active man could jump up to the portico and be in your room before you could say 'knife'."

Elsa sat down suddenly. How did this man know of Maurice Tarn's little week-end cottage on the upper reaches of the Thames? And yet he not only knew, but had examined the place so carefully that he had located the room in which she slept on her weekend visits; had even made calculations about the height of the window – it was unbelievable.

"I really don't understand you, Major Amery. There is something behind all these questions, and frankly, I am not very easy in my mind about – about things."

She hated herself for this failing of hers: there was always a lame end to her sentences when she was speaking to this man. And then to her amazement, he laughed. She had never seen him laugh before, and she gazed, fascinated. His whole aspect was changed, and for a second he was human; but as suddenly as he had begun, he stopped, and his face was frozen again to a graven inexpressiveness.

"You must ask Feng Ho for one of his canaries; he has several. But unless you promise to take the little bird for a walk every evening, as the Britisher takes his dog, he will not give you one. Thank you, that will do."

Elsa came out of the office, her face flushed, her mind disordered, hesitating between anger and amusement. Feng Ho had gone. She wished he had left the canary behind; she needed some antidote to the sinister man.

MRS TRENE HALLAM'S CONSIDERATION

Few people who visited Mrs Trene Hallam's expensively furnished flat in Herbert Mansions associated her name with that of the prosperous young doctor of Half Moon Street; and those who, by coincidence, were acquainted with both, never for one moment dreamt that this pretty, golden-haired woman, with her pale blue eyes and tight, hard mouth, was in any way related to that very popular and pleasant man.

For a consideration Mrs Hallam lived apart from her husband and claimed no relationship. She bred Pekinese dogs, was a member of two bridge clubs, and apparently was a lady of independent means. It was not likely that people would think of Dr Hallam in her connection, for she was a daughter of the people, whose lack of education and refinement was sometimes only too painfully apparent.

She had married Ralph Hallam with the object of getting away from the tiny villa where he had lodged with her mother during the days when he was a student at St Thomas'. The marriage had not been a happy one. Louise Hallam, to other failings, added a somewhat erratic conception of common honesty. She was a born pilferer, and not even her changed circumstances eradicated the habit. Twice Ralph Hallam had to pay heavily to avoid a scandal. Once this kleptomaniac had narrowly escaped arrest. Thereafter they had lived apart, and for the "consideration" she now enjoyed, she was quite willing to remain in her present state for the rest of her life.

He was the rarest of visitors at Herbert Mansions, and the surprise she displayed when he was shown into the drawing-room where she was taking her rest, with a cup of coffee by her side and a cigarette between her lips, was not wholly assumed.

"Welcome, stranger!" she said genially. "This is a sight for sore eyes. What's up?"

His expression was one of pain.

"I wish you'd get out of that gutter habit," he said wearily.

She was eyeing him keenly and unresentfully. The taunt of her humble origin had not aroused her anger in years.

"What do you want?" she asked bluntly. "A divorce?"

He took out a cigarette and lit it before he answered.

"No. Thank God I've recovered from that folly! When I think of the fools I should have married if I'd divorced you when I wanted, I am grateful to you. You're my safety, Lou. Never divorce me!"

"You needn't fret," she said complacently; "I shan't. If I wanted to marry again it would be different, but I don't. One marriage is enough for little me! Ralph, what are you doing nowadays?"

"What do you mean – what am I doing?" he demanded.

"You're making money. I'm not complaining about that; but you're making big money, and I'm wondering how? You've increased my allowance, bless you! And when I asked you to buy me that little place in the country, you bought it without a kick. You're not doing that out of momma's money. What is the dope?"

He started and looked at her suspiciously.

"I'd like to know what you mean by that?" he asked.

She struggled to a sitting position, laughing.

"You're getting touchy, Ralph! What I meant was, how are you getting it? I can't imagine you committing a burglary, though I've always known there was nothing crooked you wouldn't do. It must be a safe swindle, because you don't look a day older than when I left a good home to marry you. Worry ages."

"Never you mind how I get my money," he said shortly. "I want you to do something to earn yours. I've made life pretty agreeable to you, haven't I, Lou?"

She shrugged her shoulders, and the tight mouth became a straight red line.

"I mistrust you when you start in to tell me all the things you've done for me," she said truthfully. "At the same time, I'll admit that you've never stinted me of money. What is the hook to this bit of bait?"

"You're a suspicious woman!" he said. "All I want from you is information. A few years ago you wanted to see the world and I sent you to India."

She nodded, watching him.

"Well?"

"You had a chance of meeting the very best people in India, and apparently you did. You came back with more jewellery than you took out – a diamond sunburst was one thing." She did not meet his eyes. "A rajah gave it to you – you were there a year. Did you ever meet a Major Paul Amery?"

She knit her brows.

"Amery? Why, yes, I think I met him. One of those reserved people who never speak, and you get an idea they're thinking a whole lot, until you know them better, and then you discover that they're worrying about their overdraft. Paul Amery? Why, of course! He was rather nice to me, now I come to think of it. Attached to the political service, isn't he?"

"That I don't know," said Ralph; "but if he was 'rather nice' to you, and you're friendly with him, I'd like you to improve his acquaintance."

"Is he in London?"

He nodded.

"What do you want? Are you stringing him?"

"I'm not stringing him," said the other with elaborate patience, "if by 'stringing' you mean – " he paused for a simile.

"Kidding," suggested his wife, lighting one cigarette from the glowing end of another. "I'm out of practice with that work, though I'll do anything to oblige a loving husband. Which reminds me, Ralph, that my car has reached the museum stage. That Boyson woman has got a cute little Rolls, one of the new kind – "

"We'll talk about that later," said her husband, with a touch of irritability. "The point is, will you go along and see this fellow? I have an idea he's engaged in a – er – unpleasant business. At any rate, I want you to get acquainted with him – that's one thing."

"And the other?" Mrs Hallam's eyes narrowed. "In my experience of you, Ralphie, it's 'the other thing' that's most important. You always make a fuss about the least important job, and pass the other over careless like. What is it?"

Ralph rose with a laugh.

"It is nothing really. Only Tarn's niece is having a little trouble with him. Tarn is the City man I've told you about. The old fool wants to marry her, and I think it would be rather doing the girl a service to get her away for a day or two. I want you to invite her to come and stay with you – you can be my sister-in-law for the occasion."

"Pretty?"

He nodded.

"I'll bet she is. And she thinks you're the wonderful boy – handsome Alec! And when she comes here, what happens? Do I go out when you visit? Or am I called away into the country, like I was when that girl from the Stores – "

"Keep your damned mouth shut about that girl from the Stores." There was an ugly look on his face. "You get a little too fresh sometimes, Lou. I don't keep you to amuse me. There are four good theatres in town that I can go to when I want to laugh."

She waved him down.

"Don't lose your temper: tempers worry little sister! Write down her name and address. Have you spoken about me?"

He nodded.

"Yours to command," she said lazily. "Now what's the consideration, Ralph?"

"You can have your new car," he growled. "But I'm serious about Amery: it is necessary that you should see him. You can't miss the place; it's in Wood Street – the Amery building. And you'll see the girl: she's working in the office – her name is Elsa Marlowe. You can't very well mistake her either – she's a peach! And be careful with Amery: he's sharp!"

She smiled contemptuously.

"I've got a new gown from Poiret's that would take the edge off a razor," she said. "When do you want me to go?"

"Today. You can speak to the girl; tell her you're my sister-in-law."

"And a widow. My departed husband will have to have been dead for a year or so, for that gown of mine is slightly on the joyous side."

She made no further reference to the girl, her future or her fate. That was not the kind of "consideration" that ever troubled Mrs Trene Hallam.

AN INDIAN ACQUAINTANCE

There was a tap at the door, and, without moving her eyes from the notebook from which she was typing, Elsa said:

"Come in."

The faintest whiff of an exotic scent made her look round in surprise. The lady who stood in the doorway was a stranger to her. Elsa thought she was pretty in her thin and dainty way. The dress, she saw with an appraising woman's eye, was lovely.

"Is this Major Amery's office?"

The voice was not so pleasing; there was just the faintest hint of commonness. But she had no time to form an impression before, with a sweet smile, the woman came forward, her gloved hand extended.

"Isn't this Elsa Marlowe?" she asked.

"That is my name," said Elsa, wondering who this unknown might be.

"I am Louise Hallam – Mrs Trene Hallam. Ralph told me about you."

A light dawned upon Elsa.

"Oh, yes, of course, you're Ralph's sister-in-law?"

"Yes – I married his dear brother – such a sweet man," murmured Mrs Hallam. "But much too good for this world!" She sighed and touched her eyes daintily with a little handkerchief, providentially at hand. "The good die young," she said. "He was thirty. A few years younger than Ralph, but oh! such a sweet man! What a dear little office!" She beamed round approvingly, raising unnecessary gold lorgnons to survey the uninspiring scene. "And how do you get on with Major Amery? I always thought he was such a perfectly lovely man when I met him in India. My dear husband took me there for a holiday."

She sighed again, but this time perhaps with a little more sincerity, for India held memories which were at once dear and dour.

"You know Major Amery?" said the girl eagerly. "What sort of a man is he – to meet, I mean?" and grew hot as she realized that her eagerness might be misunderstood.

"A sweet creature," said Mrs Hallam, and the description was so incongruous that Elsa could have laughed.

"I've called to see him, and I was killing two birds with one stone," Mrs Hallam went on, and, with a roguish little smile and uplifted finger: "I know a little girl who is coming to stay with me for a whole week!"

Elsa flushed, and for some reason which she could not fathom, hesitated.

"I don't know whether it will be possible, Mrs Hallam –" she began.

"It must be possible – I'm going to give you a really nice time. It was very stupid of Ralph not to tell me that he had such a charming friend. I would have asked you over before. We'll do some theatres and concerts together, though concerts certainly bore me stiff – I mean, they bore me" she corrected herself hastily. "I will not take 'no' for an answer. When can you come?"

Elsa thought rapidly.

"Tomorrow?" she suggested.

She could not understand her own reluctance to accept an invitation which sounded so enticing.

"Tomorrow I shall expect you."

Mrs Hallam took a card from her jewelled case and laid it on the table.

"You shall have the dearest little room of your own. I'm all alone, and you won't be bothered with servants; it is a service flat. If you want anything, you just ring for it. I think you'll be very happy."

"I'm not so sure that my uncle can spare me," said Elsa, more loth to go than ever, now that she had practically accepted.

"Your uncle *must* spare you. And now I must see dear Major Amery. Would you tell him I am here?"

Elsa tapped at the door and her employer's sharp voice answered her.

"Mrs Trene Hallam to see you, Major Amery," said Elsa.

He stared up from his writing.

"Mrs Trene Hallam to see me. Now, isn't that nice of her? Shoot her in!"

Elsa opened the door for the woman and closed it behind her, as Major Amery rose slowly to greet the visitor who sailed across the room.

"You don't remember me, Major Amery?" she said, with a hint of coquetry in her pale blue eyes; a smile at once pleased and reproachful.

"Indeed, I remember you very well, Mrs Hallam. Won't you sit down?"

"It was in Poona, I think," said Mrs Hallam when she had settled herself. "Do you remember that delightful ball the Governor gave? Those glorious roses everywhere. Don't you remember what a terribly hot night it was, and how they had great blocks of ice on the stairways?"

"Are you sending back Lady Mortel's diamond brooch?"

At the sound of that metallic voice the smile left the woman's face and she sat up.

"I – don't know what you mean," she faltered "I – I really don't understand you."

"Whilst you were the guest of Lady Mortel, a diamond sunburst was missed. A servant was arrested and tried for the theft – he went to prison for three years. The other night I saw you at the theatre – I saw the brooch too."

She went red and white.

"I really do not understand you, Captain – "

"Major," he said laconically. "I have been promoted since. Hallam sent you here, of course?"

"Hallam? My husband is dead – "

"That's news to me," he broke in. "He was alive when he left your flat at Herbert Mansions this afternoon. Street accident?"

"I think you're very horrid," she whimpered. She was no longer the urbane woman of the world. Under his merciless glance she seemed to cringe and shrink. It was as though the meanness of her had worn through the veneer that modiste and milliner had overlaid upon the hard and ugly substance of her soul.

"I thought you were a friend of mine... I would never have called on you if I'd known you could be so horrid..."

"I'm not being horrid, I'm being truthful, though I admit that truth is pretty beastly," he said. "Why did you come here?"

"To call on you," she said. "Just to renew...to meet you again...I didn't expect..."

Again he checked her.

"Tell Hallam from me to find a new occupation. Tell him I am after his blood, and I mean it! I want that amateur dope-running corporation out of my way."

"Dope-running?" she gasped.

He nodded.

"You didn't know? I wondered if he had told you. My last word to him is – git! You'll remember that?"

He had not resumed his seat, and now, leaning across the table, he jerked out his hand.

"Goodbye, Mrs Trene Hallam. Trene is your maiden name, if I remember rightly? Your mother lived in Tenison Street, Lambeth. Don't forget the message I have given you for your husband – git!"

It needed all her artistry to compose her face into a smile as she passed into the outer office, pulling the door behind her.

"Such a dear, sweet man, but a little changed," she murmured, and took the girl's hand in hers for a second. "You will remember, my dear?"

"I will try to come, but if I can't – "

"You must come," said Louise Hallam, and there was a sharp quality in her voice. "I will not take 'no'."

She seemed in a hurry to leave, did not linger for another second; and all the way home she was wondering whether Major Amery and his secretary were on sufficiently good terms for him to take her into his confidence.

She had hardly left the room before Amery turned quickly and opened a door that led to a tiny room, which served as a clothes press and wash-place. Its solitary occupant, who was sitting on an old trunk, rose as the door opened, and came out into the office. The major held Mrs Hallam's card between his two fingers.

"Go to this address some time tonight. Search the flat thoroughly. I want every document that you can find."

He spoke in the sibilant dialect of Canton, and Feng Ho was sufficiently Europeanized to nod.

"You must use no force, unless it is absolutely necessary. You may find nothing. On the other hand, you may get some valuable information. If necessary, you may be able to use the name of Soyoka to advantage. Go!"

THE EXPLOIT OF FENG HO

Elgin Crescent was singularly unattractive to Elsa that night. She came by bus from the City to Trafalgar Square and walked the remainder of the way through the three parks. The crocuses were blooming; the trees were shooting out emerald-green buds; the early bushes were in full leaf; here and there she saw the beginning of rhododendron flowers, hard little sticky masses of an indescribable colour that would presently set the park aflame. But wherever her eyes roamed, her mind was completely absorbed, even to the exclusion of Maurice Tarn and his amazing proposal, in the strange man who had suddenly come into her workaday life. She did not even resent the companionship of the voluble Miss Dame, who, against her will, had insisted upon coming home with her. Miss Dame lived at Notting Hill Gate, and her company could hardly be refused.

The speech might have been all on one side but for the fact that Jessie Dame chose for her discourse the subject of Elsa's thoughts.

"What I hate about him," said Miss Dame, with typical energy, "is his slinkiness. Have you ever noticed, Miss Marlowe, how he slinks around, wearing sneakers too?"

"Sneakers? Oh, you mean his rubber shoes?"

"Sneakers is the word for them, and a very good word," said Miss Dame. "He's like that fellow in 'The Horrible Night.' You know the one I mean – Ethel Gilbey was in it. You remember when those mysterious hands came out of doors and the lights went out? And then another hand came up and caught her by the throat. Oh, it was perfectly marvellous. Well, that's him," she added incoherently.

And yet, thought Elsa, the sinister man did not "slink." He was furtive, but not meanly furtive. You could not imagine a mean leopard or a mean lion stalking his prey... The thought startled her. Was that the reason for his queer secretiveness? Was he stalking somebody? She dismissed the possibility with a smile.

"I'm getting romantic," she said.

"You *are* romantic," said Miss Dame decisively. "I've always said that you're wasted in an office; you ought to be on the pictures. You're svelte – that's the word, svelte. I believe in a woman showing her figure if she's got any to show."

"Do I show my figure?" asked the alarmed Elsa.

"Of course you do," said Miss Dame derisively. "And why shouldn't you? What's a figure for? You'd be perfectly marvellous on the screen. I thought of going in for it myself, but only as a comic," she said with a sigh. "I'm not svelte enough."

Out of the corner of her eye Elsa caught a glimpse of the ungainly figure and agreed.

Mr Tarn had not returned when she got to the maisonette. They kept no servants; two daily helps came in, in the morning and in the evening, and from one of them she learnt that he had telephoned to say that he would not be home until late, and that she was not to wait dinner for him. For this she was grateful, for she was not inclined to resume the conversation of the morning.

No. 409, Elgin Crescent, consisted of two maisonettes, a lower, comprising the ground floor and basement, and an upper, which her guardian occupied, comprising the remainder of the house. The study and dining-room were on the first floor; she had the back room on the second floor, above the dining-room, for a bed-sitting-room; and to this safe harbour she retreated just as soon as she had finished her dinner.

It was a pleasant little apartment, with a writing-table, a dozen well-filled bookshelves, a cosy chair that she could draw up before the gas fire, and a tiny wireless set which had filled so many long and dreary winter evenings with amusement.

She tried to read, but between her eyes and the printed page came the face of the sinister man, and the lifted lips sneered up at her so vividly and so insistently that presently she closed the book with a crash. She wondered what a man like he did in the evenings. He had a club perhaps. She remembered Ralph had told her he had seen him there. Perhaps he went to theatres. What sort of plays would arouse him from his ingrained cynicism? Had he any relations or friends? In a way she felt a little sorry for him, just as the sight of a prison would arouse sorrow and tenderness for its undeserving occupants.

She fitted the headphones and heard part of "Aida" relayed from the Opera House, and found herself speculating as to whether he would be in the audience. At this evidence of imbecility she viciously tugged off the headphones and prepared for bed. She was undressing when she heard the blundering steps of Mr Tarn on the stairs, and the bang of his study door as he closed it. At any rate, he could not bother her that night. She said her prayers, turned out the light and jumped into bed, and in a few minutes fell into the sweet, sound sleep which is youth's greatest but least appreciated blessing.

She was not a heavy sleeper, but, if she had been, the sound would have awakened her. The room was in complete darkness. She could hear the ticking of the clock on the mantelshelf, and, for the rest, silence reigned in the house.

What was it? She sat up, trying to recall the noise that had awakened her. It came again, but this time it could not have been so loud – a faint, snapping sound, which came from the window.

Slipping out of bed, she pulled aside the curtains. The fading moon still bathed the world in its eerie radiance, and reflected evilly from a glittering something that lay on the window-sill.

She threw up the window and, with a cry of astonishment, took the thing in her hand. It was a dagger, and the handle was inscribed in Chinese characters!

"MAYFAIR 10016"

A knife! Who left it there? She had to remove the wedge which kept the upper sash of her window in place, before she could lift the lower and look out. For a second she saw nothing, and then...

A builder's long ladder had been reared against the wall, and the explanation of the midnight visit was now clear. The top of the ladder reached within two feet of her window, and as she looked she saw a dark figure slide down to the ground, pause for a moment and look up before it vanished in the shadow of the big tree. In that space of time she saw the face distinctly – it was Feng Ho!

What should she do?

"I ought to scream, I suppose," she said to herself, but never felt less like screaming although she had had a bad scare.

She turned on the light and looked at the clock. It was half past three. Mr Tarn would be in bed, and he was the last person she wanted to arouse. Pulling on her dressing-gown and slippers, she went out of the room and down the dark stairs to the dining-room, the windows of which were shuttered and barred. Here she made herself tea with an electric kettle, and sat down to consider what she should do next.

Feng Ho! She frowned at the thought. "You will see a great deal of Feng Ho," Amery had said, and her lips twisted in a smile. At any rate, she did not wish to see a great deal of Feng Ho in circumstances similar to those in which he had made his appearance that morning.

And then came to her a wild and fantastic idea. It was the sight of the telephone on the sideboard that gave it to her. Major Amery occupied his uncle's house in Brook Street...

She put the thought from her, only to turn to it again. Presently she went in search of the telephone directory and found it in her uncle's study. The place reeked with the smell of brandy, and for a moment she felt physically sick, and hurried out with the thick volume under her arm.

Yes, there it was – "Amery, Major P, 97b, Brook Street. Mayfair 10016." He would be in bed and asleep. The prospect of rousing him filled her with malicious joy, and she lifted the hook and waited. It was a long time before the operator answered, but within a few seconds of his answering her signal, she heard a click and a sharp voice demanded: "Who is that?"

Elsa's lips twitched.

"Is that Major Amery?" she asked sweetly.

"Yes. What do you want, Miss Marlowe."

He had recognised her voice! The discovery took her breath away, and for a moment she was unable to proceed.

"I – we've just had a visit from a friend of yours," she said, a little wildly. "A least he didn't come in!"

"A friend of mine? You mean Feng Ho?"

His coolness was staggering.

"Of course I mean Feng Ho. He was trying to get in through the window of my room," she said, her anger rising.

"Your room?" came the quick response. "You mean your bedroom?"

"That is the only room I have," she added, and there was a silence at the other end of the 'phone.

After a while he spoke.

"You must have been mistaken. It could not have been Feng Ho," said his voice. "He is with me now. One Chinaman looks very much like another to the uninitiated eye. I'm sorry you have been frightened."

The last words came in a different tone. He had explained her error hurriedly, which was not like him. She knew it was useless to argue the matter on the telephone.

"I'm sorry I got you out of bed," she said.

"Are you scared?"

Was she mistaken in imagining an undercurrent of anxiety and concern in his voice?

"No, I was startled."

Another silence.

"Does Mr Tarn know?"

"No, he is asleep; I haven't awakened him, unless I'm waking him now. I'm sorry I bothered you. Goodnight."

"Wait," he said sharply. "You are sure you're not frightened?"

"Of course I'm not frightened, Major Amery. You're for ever thinking that I'm frightened," she said with a smile, remembering the conversation of the morning.

Was it a quiet laugh she heard? Apparently not, for there was no laughter in his voice when he said, with his customary brusqueness: "Good night. Go back to bed."

How like him to finish that strange conversation with a peremptory order, she thought, as she hung up the telephone. At that moment Maurice Tarn, with an old dressing gown huddled about him, came blinking into the light.

"What's wrong?" he asked harshly. "What are you doing here, telephoning at this hour of the morning? Whom were you talking to?"

"I was talking to Major Amery."

"Amery!" he squeaked. "Major Amery? What were you telling him?"

He was terrified, and in his agitation gripped her wrist with such force that she cried out.

"I'm sorry," he muttered. "What is it all about, Elsa?"

"I was merely telling Major Amery that I caught a friend of his tonight, trying to get in through my window."

For a moment he could not grasp her meaning. "Who was it?"

"I don't know. A Chinaman – "

"A Chinaman!" he screamed. "A friend of Amery's trying to get in!"

In as few words as possible she told him all she had seen, and he listened, his teeth chattering.

"Oh, my God!" he said, his hand on his brow. "A Chinaman...! Had a knife, had he? You're sure about the knife?"

"He may have only been using it to open the window," said the girl, astounded at the extraordinary effect which the news had upon her relative. She had never seen a man in such an abject condition of fear. By the time she had finished his pallid face was streaming with perspiration.

"You 'phoned Amery?" huskily. "What did he say?"

"That it wasn't Feng Ho."

"He's a liar! It was the Chinaman who came into the office today...I just saw him...Feng Ho! Elsa, that's my finish! They'll be watching for me now – every port..."

"What is the matter, Mr Tarn?" she asked, frightened in spite of herself by the terror of the man. "Have you done something – "

"Don't talk, don't talk." He waved her to silence. "I don't want to discuss it, I tell you. I was expecting this." He waved his hand into the pocket of his tattered dressing-gown and drew out a long-barrelled revolver. "But they'll not catch me, Elsa, by God!"

The hand that held the pistol shook so violently that she was in some fear that it would explode by accident, and was relieved when he put it back into his pocket.

"Paul Amery, curse him! I could tell you something about Amery...not now, not now... I'm going into my study."

He rushed out, and she heard the key turn in the lock, and then, through the thin partition which separated the dining-room from the study, there came the clink of glass against glass. Mr Tarn was fortifying himself against the terrors which the remaining hours of darkness might hold.

MR TARN MAKES A WILL

Mr Tarn was not at breakfast the next morning: she would have been surprised if he had been. His door was still locked, and only after repeated hammerings did his sleepy voice growl an intimation that he would be out in a few minutes. Elsa hurried her breakfast and was successful in leaving the house before Tarn made an appearance.

She was anxious to get to the office, and curious as to what explanation Amery would offer. She might have guessed that he would offer none. When, at half past nine, his bell summoned her, she went to a man who certainly bore no appearance of having spent the night out of bed. He met her with his characteristic lack of greeting, and plunged straight away into his letters, firing across the table magazine after magazine of words, to be caught and recorded. It was not until she was leaving that he made any reference to their conversation of the early morning.

"Didn't you call me up in the night? I have a dim recollection of the circumstances."

"I had almost forgotten," she said coolly, and his face twitched.

"Possibly you were dreaming," he said. "But it is a dream which will never come true – again. When Feng Ho comes, ask him to tell you the story of his finger."

"His finger?" she repeated, surprised in spite of herself.

"His little finger. You broke yours at school, playing hockey. Ask him how he lost his."

"I didn't know he'd lost a finger."

"Ask him," he said, and his head jerked to the door.

She wished he would find another way of telling her that she could go.

It was nearly lunch time when Feng Ho came, as dapper as ever, his coat spotless, his trousers even more rigidly creased, his white spats exchanged for articles of bright yellow leather; his umbrella and his hat were in one hand, and in the other the gilded cage with a dignified canary balancing himself on the central perch.

He greeted the girl with a grin.

"My unworthy little bird has been sick all night. I have been sitting by his side, feeding him with sugar – from midnight till six o'clock this morning. And now he is better and will sing for us. Pi" – he addressed the yellow songster – "open your hideous little beak and emit unmusical noises for this honourable lady."

"Feng, you are not telling the truth," said Elsa severely. "You weren't sitting up all night with your bird."

The little man looked at her, blandly innocent. Then he turned his melancholy eyes to the bird.

"Little Pi, if I am lying, do not sing; but if I am speaking the truth, then let your ugly little throat produce contemptible melody."

And as though he understood, the loyal little bird burst into a torrent of sunny song. Mr Feng Ho smiled delightedly.

"It is a peculiar and noteworthy fact," he said, with his best European manner, "that has been observed by every seeker after truth, from Confucius to Darwin, that the animal world – by which I refer to the world of vertebrate mammals – are the living embodiment of truth and the chief exponents of veracity. I will now, with your gracious permission, sit down and watch your vivacious fingers manipulate the keyboard of your honourable typewriter – to employ the idiom of our neighbours, but not friends, the Nipponese."

He sat patiently, practically without a movement, except to turn his eyes from time to time to the bird, and there seemed some strange understanding between these two, for no sooner did Feng Ho's slit of a mouth open in a smile than the bird seemed to rock with musical laughter.

Miss Dame came in while she was typing, dropped her jaw at the first view of the Chinaman, but graciously admitted that the canary was the best song-bird she had ever heard.

"It must be a gentleman bird," she said. "Gentlemen birds always sing better than lady birds. And why shouldn't they? They've got less responsibility, if you understand me."

She glanced coldly at the Chinaman as he nodded his agreement.

"If you've got to lay eggs, you can't find time for keeping up your singing. Excuse me, do you know Sessuekawa?" This to Feng Ho, who expressed his grief that he had never heard of the gentleman.

"He's the model of you," said Miss Dame, glaring at him. "Slightly better looking, if you'll excuse my rudeness, but that's probably the paint and powder he puts on his face. You've never seen him in 'The Bride of Fuji Yama' – that's a mountain?"

The explanation was necessary because Miss Dame pronounced it "fujjy yammer."

"You've missed a treat," she said regretfully when he shook his head. "He was simply marvellous, especially when he committed – what's the word? – haki raki?"

Elsa refused to assist her, and paused in her work with such point that Miss Dame was conscious of the interruption she had produced, and retired.

"A very pretty young lady," said Feng Ho, and Elsa, who thought he was being sarcastic, was prepared to snub him, but his next words demonstrated his sincerity. "The Eastern view differs considerably from the Western view. I can tell you that, speaking with authority as a bachelor of science."

She wondered what special authority this particular bachelorhood conferred when it came to a question of judging looks, but wisely did not pursue the topic.

When she got to the office she had found a note from Mrs Trene Hallam. It would have been a letter from anybody else, for it occupied two sheets of notepaper; but Mrs Hallam's calligraphy was not her strong point. The lettering was enormous, and ten words a page was a generous average.

You will come tonight at seven. I will have dinner ready for you, and I will drive you every morning to your office. (*She spelt "office" with one "f" Elsa noted.*)

There was a postscript:

Please don't tell Major Amery that you are staying with me. He may think I have some reason.

The postscript annoyed her, though why she did not know. Perhaps it was the assumption that she would tell Major Amery anything about her private affairs.

She saw her uncle only for a few minutes. Coming in from luncheon, she had to pass his door, which was open, and she saw him sitting at his table and would have gone on if he had not called her back.

"Shut the door," he growled. "I've been to see my lawyer on a certain matter – and I've made my will."

This was rather surprising news. She had never thought of her uncle as a man of means, or having property to dispose, and she could only utter a commonplace about the wisdom of taking such a precaution.

"He's a shrewd fellow is Nigitts," he said, "very shrewd. And remarkably well up in the matter of" – he cleared his throat – "criminal law. The most one can get in this country for a certain offence is two years, and Nigitts says one would probably get away with less – if a statement was made voluntarily."

She wondered what on earth he was talking about. Had he been drinking? His face was flushed, his eyes heavy with want of sleep, but from her own experience she thought he was sober.

"I've had to give the matter a whole lot of thought – there are other people besides me involved in this…business," he said; "but I thought you'd like to know that I'd improved the shining hour" – his attempt to be jovial was pathetic – " and I've left you a little bit of money, although I don't suppose you will touch it for years. Would you like to be rich, Elsa?"

He looked at her from between his narrowed eyes.

"I suppose everybody would like to be rich," smiled the girl.

"You'd like to be good and happy, eh? Like the girl in the story-book?" he sneered. And then: "What has Amery been doing all the morning?"

"Working," she said.

"Nothing unusual?"

She shook her head.

"I'd like to take a look at some of his letters, Elsa. Anyway, I'm in the business, and Major Amery has no secrets from me. Where do you keep the copy file?"

"Major Amery keeps his own copies in the safe," she said.

He played with a blotter.

"I don't see why you shouldn't slip in a second carbon?" he suggested.

There was no profit in discussing the matter with him.

"I can't do that – you know very well I can't. It would be dishonest and mean, and I'd rather leave Amery's than do it."

"You like him, eh?"

"I loathe him," she said frankly, and his face brightened.

"That's the kind of talk I like to hear, little girl. He's a swine, that fellow! There's nothing anybody could do to him that could be called mean."

"I am the 'anybody' concerned, and there are some things I will not do," she said, and walked out.

THE SYNDICATE

There were times when Ralph Hallam's mind went back to the days of romance, and conspirators, cloaked and masked, met in underground cellars to plan their dark deeds. Certainly there was the advantage of safety in that picturesque method – and Ralph played safe all the time. Such meetings gave to the leaders an anonymity which must have been comforting.

This thought occurred to him as he went slowly up the stairs that led to No.3, the largest of the private dining-rooms that the Café Fornos had to offer to its clients. For luncheon these rooms are very seldom bespoke, but once a month Dr Hallam gave a little party where business men could meet, discuss politics, theatres, the contemporary events of sport, and when the coffee and liqueurs were served and cigar cases came to light, and when, moreover, the waiters had withdrawn, the peculiar business which brought them together.

As Ralph stood in the doorway, smiling and nodding to the waiting guests, he decided that he had never seen an assembly that looked less like a meeting of conspirators. They were stoutish business men, lovers of good living, middle-aged, slightly or completely bald; men in the sober habiliments of their class. Jarvie of Birmingham greeted him warmly and looked past him, seemingly expecting a companion.

"The old man couldn't get away," said Hallam easily. "He's not particularly well."

He shook hands with the half-dozen of guests and took his seat. No.3 had an outer and an inner door, and when at last the waiter had placed his cigar-boxes and liqueur bottles on the buffet and had withdrawn, Hallam walked to the doors, turned the key in both and came back to his chair.

Instantly the company relaxed and the atmosphere changed. It was as though, for the past hour, everybody had been playing a part, and all that had been said and done was an act from a dull comedy.

Without preamble Hallam spoke.

"There are three new consignments, the largest in London, the second largest at Hull – "

"Bonded or through the customs?" somebody asked.

"Out of bond, of course," replied Hallam. "Jarvie, you will arrange the distribution. It is consigned to Stanford's Birmingham address. The second came into Avonmouth yesterday and goes forward to Philadelphia."

"What about this Greek they caught at Cleveland?" asked Jarvie, and it was clear that this question was on the lips of the whole company, for there followed a babble of questions.

"You need not worry about him, and the story of the American police tracing a doctor and a City merchant is all bunk. Some imaginative reporter invented that. No, that isn't our trouble. Bickerson – "

"Hasn't anybody tried to straighten Bickerson?" asked a voice. "A couple of thousand would put him quiet."

Ralph shook his head.

"I know Bickerson: he's not that kind. And if you straightened him, he'd slack down, and the higher up people would put another man into the case, and he'd have to be straightened," said Hallam. "The only man you need worry about is Tarn, who is getting cold feet. And Soyoka," he added.

There was a glum silence at this. Soyoka was the spectre that walked at every man's elbow, the terror of the unknown. They were business men, each with his little bolt hole, his alibi, his ready explanation if the police by accident hit upon his story, and behind each was a reputation for commercial integrity that could not be gainsaid. Moral considerations did not concern them. That they were marketing a vile poison that wrecked men and women and drove them to insanity, hardly counted. They were marketing a commodity which paid enormous profits and for which there was an increasing demand.

"Soyoka?"

Jarvie took his cigar from his mouth, looked at it thoughtfully and put it back. He was a heavy-browed man with a fringe of hair above his collar and a shining head.

"There's room for Soyoka," he said.

"So I think," nodded Hallam, "but he doesn't share the view that there is room for two. Now I'm going to tell you fellows something. Old Tarn is certain that his boss is either Soyoka or Soyoka's leading agent!"

"His boss? Who is he?" asked Jarvie, scowling at his chief.

"Major Amery."

Ralph saw the eyes of the beetle-browed man open wide.

"Amery?" he said incredulously. "Not Paul Amery?"

"Why, do you know him?" demanded the other.

Mr Jarvie was whistling softly.

"Paul Amery! I wonder if it's the same? It's not Paul Amery of the Indian Political Service, by any chance? The man who got into trouble at Shanghai?"

In his excitement Ralph pushed back his chair from the table.

"Let us hear this," he said. "You've got the man right enough. Do you know him?"

Jarvie shook his head.

"No, I don't know him, but one of my managers knew him very well. We have a branch house in Shanghai: we export Brummagem goods and that kind of truck; and my manager, who came back a year ago on sick leave, was full of him – he is not by any chance connected with Tarn's firm, is he?"

"He *is* Amery & Amery," said Ralph. "His uncle left him the business some time back."

Again Mr Jarvie whistled.

"I only know what my man told me. It appears that Amery was lent by the Indian Government to the Board of Control, or whatever they call it, in Shanghai. In Shanghai, as you probably know, there are three or four millionaire families that have made their money out of opium smuggling and running guns to the rebels. He was sent up to keep an eye upon the arms gang but got into the opium commission and had to leave suddenly. I don't know the rights of it, but my man says he was caught in the act of passing out opium. There was a tremendous scandal. There was a veiled reference to the case in the Shanghai press, but of course no reference to Amery, because these Europeans in Shanghai are pretty clannish. All that was known was that his name was taken off the roll of members of the French Club, and he disappeared by the first mail-boat. It was the gossip of the place that he was working with Soyoka, who has a pretty vivid reputation in the China Sea. There was also talk of his having knifed a Chinese policeman who was going to give him away. They say he's better than the best knife-thrower that ever starred in a circus. Learnt it up in Nepal, and never carries any other weapon. What makes Tarn think he's Soyoka?"

"Something he said to him," replied Ralph, "some threat of his. If he is Soyoka's man – "

"If he is Soyoka's man," interrupted Mr Jarvie, "he's more dangerous than a bagful of rattlesnakes." He looked meditatively at Ralph. "Isn't there a way you could fix a fellow like that?" he asked.

"How do you mean – 'fix'?" demanded Ralph bluntly, conscious that the curious eyes of the party were on him.

"I don't mean anything illegal," said Mr Jarvie virtuously, and he again examined his inspiring cigar. "But I think, if a fellow like that had a bit of a shock…well, he'd go carefully and probably save us a few uncomfortable minutes."

This was evidently generally agreed. Somebody at the far end of the table murmured: "Not illegal, of course," though his tone hardly convinced.

"There is only one way to stop Soyoka – if he is Soyoka," said Ralph coldly, "and that is to put him beyond the power of troubling us. Does anybody mean that?"

Nobody apparently did mean that, for the company murmured a soothing denial.

"No, what I mean," said Jarvie, who hesitated so long that apparently he was not quite sure of what he did mean, "is that, if he can't be straightened, he ought to be – frightened."

He puffed at his cigar and looked up at the ceiling.

"I don't know much about London: I'm a provincial man myself: but I'm told that there are places in this town where you could hire a man to beat up your own grandmother for a ten-pound note. Personally, I do not approve of violence: it is foreign to my nature. But there must be people who – ah – could scare – that is the word, scare – Amery."

It was four o'clock when the luncheon party broke up, and Ralph went downstairs alone. In the vestibule he saw a very plump pleasant-looking gentleman being helped on with his greatcoat. At first he could not believe the evidence of his eyes, and then, glancing through the doorway, he saw a very sedate Rolls draw slowly up to the kerb, and a footman alight and open the door.

"Why, Tupperwill," he said, "you're in a strange part of London!"

Mr Tupperwill, proprietor of Stebbing's Banking Corporation, looked round leisurely. Every movement of his was deliberate, and his round blue eyes lit up in a stare of recognition.

"My dear doctor," he murmured, "extraordinary – most extraordinary! A queer place for Stebbing's indeed, a very queer place!"

In the City of London, Stebbing's Bank was respected without being considered. A survival of one of those private banking corporations that had come into existence in the early part of the eighteenth century, its business was comparatively small and its clientele extremely select. Stebbing's had resisted the encroachments of the great joint stock companies and maintained its independence largely on the tradition established by its founder, who in the early days of the firm had gone to prison for contempt of court rather than produce books which would have incriminated one of his clients. For generations men with great names put private accounts at Stebbing's – accounts which their confidential secretaries never scanned; for even the owners of great names have affairs and businesses of a peculiarly private kind, and Stebbing's flourished by its very secrecy.

Mr Tupperwill, its present proprietor, was wont to boast that he had not an employee under the age of fifty, though he himself was on the breezy side of thirty-five, a stout, youthful looking man, with a large face, many chins, and hands of exceeding plumpness.

"Heavy luncheons are anathema to me." He put his hand in his pocket, pulled out a little pile of silver and, selecting sixpence, handed it to the unsatisfied cloakroom attendant with a benevolent smile. "*Anathema maranatha!* But some of my clients are rather sybaritic. 'Sybarite,' as you probably know, is the name given to the people of Sybaris, an ancient town of Greece, the citizens of which were given to self-indulgence and luxury."

He said this with an air of revealing a mystery which hitherto had not been made public. This passion for passing on information was one of his characteristics, and it may be said that, in nine cases out of ten, he really did convey information to the City men with whom he was mostly brought into account.

Ralph had his private account with Stebbing's, and in a way could claim a sort of friendship with the banker, who was a member of two of his clubs. If he had one drawback it was his mild interest in medicines – a source of embarrassment to Ralph, who had almost forgotten his early training.

The fat man sighed heavily as he pulled on his gloves.

"A glass of milk and a few crackers constitute my normal lunch, and I shudder to contemplate the effect that lobster mayonnaise would have upon my system. You're not coming my way?"

Ralph was walking with him to the open door of his car.

"No, I'm not coming your way, though I shall be in your neighbourhood tomorrow or the next day."

Mr Tupperwill shivered.

"I commiserate with you," he said. "The City lacks aestheticism – a cult which, as you may know – "

He stopped suddenly, looked along the crowded sidewalk, and his fat chin wagged downward.

"The cosmopolitan character of our streets at this period of the year is always to me a fascinating and interesting feature."

Following the direction of his eyes, Ralph saw a man standing on the edge of the kerb; a slim little man, in a grey felt hat and violent yellow gloves. His face turned at that moment.

"A Chinaman!" said Hallam in surprise.

"A Chinaman," agreed the other soberly, "one Feng Ho, the body-guard and *fidus achates Asiaticus* of one Major Amery, an astonishing gentleman."

Before Ralph had recovered from his astonishment sufficiently to ask what the banker knew of Paul Amery, the glistening car was threading its way through the traffic, on its way to the unaesthetic purlieus of Old Broad Street.

The Chinaman was looking steadfastly toward him, but made no move to approach, and presently, when Ralph began to walk in his direction, he turned and moved swiftly away and was lost to sight in the crowd.

Feng Ho, Amery's man! It was the first time Ralph had heard of the Chinaman, and he wanted to get a closer view of him. If all that he had heard that day was true...

But Feng Ho had disappeared, and, looking at his watch, Ralph remembered that he had promised to make a call on his wife. He was paying the cabman at the entrance of Herbert Mansions when, looking round, he saw another cab stop a little distance down the road. A man got out. It was Feng Ho!

Ralph did not hesitate. He went toward the second cab, and the Chinaman awaited his coming with an expressionless face.

"I want a word with you, my friend."

Feng Ho's head bent slightly.

"When I came out of the Fornos a quarter of an hour ago, you were standing on the sidewalk, obviously watching me. Not content with that, you have followed me here. Now what is your little game?"

Feng Ho's grin was as expansive as it was unsightly.

"Little game? I have no little game," he said blandly. "I merely come this way; perhaps tomorrow I go some other way."

"You're making a call – where?" asked Ralph roughly. Feng Ho lifted his thin shoulders in a shrug.

"That is not good English politeness," he said. "There is a policeman," he nodded in the direction of a patrol. "Perhaps you will send for him and say: 'Take this Chinaman and put him in the cooler. His name is Feng Ho, he is a Bachelor of Science and he has followed me.' Mr Hallam, you cannot go anywhere in London without following somebody."

"Why do you follow me?" asked Hallam, ignoring the logic of the statement.

Again that little shrug.

"I am bachelor of science, interested in phenomena. My speciality is – crime! Not only do I like to attend the court whetn a man comes up before the judge and hear the story, but I wish to see the crime when it is committed. A depraved and morbid ambition, Mr Hallam, but you as doctor of medicine will understand."

"What crime do you expect to see here?" asked Hallam, watching him narrowly.

"Murder," was the startling reply.

"Murder!" Ralph wondered if the man were joking, but there was no trace of a smile on his immobile face.

"Murder," repeated Feng Ho, his face beaming. "When Soyoka kills you, I desire to be near, so that I may see ingenious methods employed. That he may kill antediluvian gentleman Tarn is possible, or sprightly Miss Marlowe, but that he will inevitably and completely kill *you*, you shall find!"

AMERY KNOWS

For a second Ralph Hallam experienced a wild sense of panic. The very matter-of-factness of the man's tone sent a cold chill down his spine. Fighting hard against the eerie sensation which for the moment overwhelmed him, he presently found his voice.

"I see," said he between his teeth. "I am to accept that as a warning from Soyoka, eh? Now listen to me, Chink! You can take this to Soyoka with my compliments – that if he starts anything in this country, he's going to get hurt. You understand that? And the next time I catch you shadowing me around, you will be kicked. Is that clear to you, Mr Bachelor of Science?"

Feng Ho grinned.

"To be kicked will be no new experience, learned sir; for when I was a poor Chinese boy many men kicked me. But now I am a man it is different, and people who kick me lose their toes – so!"

Quicker than eye could see, he had stooped. There was a swish of steel and the point of a knife, which had appeared as if by magic in his hand, scraped a straight white line that missed the toe of Hallam's boot by an infinitesimal fraction of an inch. He was erect again, the knife had disappeared, and he was his urbane, grinning self when Ralph stepped back with an involuntary cry.

"Too quickness of hand frequently deceives optical observation," said Feng Ho complacently. "How rapidly could a kicking doctor of medicines become a 'late,' with wreaths and suitable adornments of a post-mortem character!"

And then, as though he himself recognised the futility of further argument, he turned back to the astounded cabman, gave him instructions, and, stepping quickly into the cab, was whisked away before Ralph could recover from his amazement.

Lou was out. Keeping appointments was not her strongest suit, and, having heartily cursed her, he went back to Maida Vale in search of another taxi. He was hardly home before she rang him up. She had been out to make some purchases in view of the coming of her guest that night.

"And I might have saved myself the trouble, for she's just telephoned to say that she won't be able to come tonight, as she has some work to do at home."

"You saw Amery?" he asked, and noted the acid that came into her voice.

"Yes, I saw the pig! Do you know what he had the nerve to say to me?"

Ralph raised his eyebrows and smiled to himself.

"Can you guess?" she asked impatiently.

"I guess he referred to your unfortunate habit of acquiring other people's property," he said coolly. "Lou, one of these days your intelligent kleptomania is going to get you into serious trouble. I've heard one or two oblique references to the coincidence of your presence in India with the disappearance of movable property. You're a fool! You have enough money to live on, without indulging in that vice of yours. I never open a paper and see the headline 'Woman Shoplifter Charged' without wondering whether you're going to scandalise me."

"You needn't worry!" she snapped. "And if you think I am likely to help myself to this girl's jewels, you'd better not send her to me."

"She hasn't anything worth stealing," said Ralph coolly. "What else did Amery say?"

"Nothing," she exploded, "except, of course, he knows that I'm your wife. And what's the use of swearing? I didn't tell him."

"How did he know unless you betrayed yourself?"

"I tell you I didn't! He knew. He must have been having Herbert Mansions watched, as he told me exactly the minute you'd left the flat. Which reminds me," she said, in a changed voice. "I had a burglar in the flat last night, when I was at the theatre."

"A burglar?" he repeated. "Did you lose anything?"

"No, that is the curious thing. He opened my jewel safe, but nothing was missing. The janitor thinks he must have been disturbed. I'm quite sure he searched my little writing-desk, because I distinctly remember leaving my address book on top of some papers, and when I looked this morning it was underneath."

There was a long pause. Ralph Hallam thought quickly. Was that the explanation of Feng Ho's presence near Herbert Mansions? Was he watching Mrs Hallam as well as her husband, occupying his spare time by a closer inspection of her belongings? "Did you report it to the police?" he asked.

"No, it wasn't worth while," she replied. And then, impatiently: "When is that girl coming? She's a bit shy, isn't she?"

"I'll let you know," he said, and hung up.

Paul Amery had assumed a new significance.

THE SCANDAL OF SHANGHAI

It would have been unnatural if Elsa Marlowe had not her conception of the ideal man. And he had no face, figure or dimensions, being mainly character and behaviour. Her ideal man did not order girls about as though they were machines; he did not resent a civil "Good morning," or scowl, or fire out interminable letters; he did not dismiss the humblest of his employees with a curt nod; and, whatever kind of face he had, it most certainly was not disfigured by an ugly sneer.

That morning at breakfast Mr Tarn had made a brief reference to his conversation of the previous day, but happily had not pursued the subject. She would have to leave him: that was clear. But it was not going to be easy. The association of many years could not be lightly broken; and somehow the more she thought of Mrs Trene Hallam's offer, even as a temporary measure, the less she liked the idea.

Maurice Tarn seemed to grow more and more depressed as the days progressed. Though she was not feeling any too friendly toward him, she added his misery to the account of her uncouth employer.

Just before lunch Amery sent for her and dictated instructions to be followed if a telephone call came through for him during his absence. She noted, with feminine interest, that he was wearing a new grey suit, and thought it was an improvement, though by contrast with the light material his face looked darker and more forbidding than ever.

When he had finished dictating, he leant back in his chair, and his eyes wandered to the window. Not least of his unpleasant practices was to talk without looking at her.

"Have you any friends in Shanghai?" he asked.

"I, Major Amery? No," she said, surprised by the query.

"Queer place – full of scandal. I suppose you hear fragments of gossip – yes?"

"No. I know there is such a place as Shanghai, and of course we have letters from our agents there, but I've heard no scandal or gossip. About whom?" she asked daringly.

"Me, mostly… I wondered," he said.

She was fired with a natural curiosity. What kind of scandal or gossip could touch this inhuman man? Yet he must be human on some side.

"Queer place, Shanghai. You know why the bandits held up the blue train? I suppose you don't."

The colour and the mystery of the East were comprehended in that short question. She remembered reading something about bandits wrecking a train, robbing the passengers and holding them to ransom, and she wished now that she had given the item of news a closer study.

If she had expected him to refresh her memory, she was to be disappointed.

"There is a lot of money to be made in Shanghai – straight and otherwise," he said, "but mostly otherwise. That will do!"

As her busy fingers flickered above the keyboard of the typewriter, she found herself wondering which method of making money most appealed to the sinister man, and supposed that he was not very particular, for the acquisition of money seemed to be his principal occupation just then.

A few weeks before, he had begun to institute a system of economy. Superfluous clerks had been discharged; new printed warnings had appeared above every electric light switch. He was in the habit of making unexpected appearances in the lower office, where row after row of clerks stood at their high desks, and there had been summary dismissals. Once he had surprised a flushed, dishevelled girl, her eyes bright with anger, and had instantly discovered the cause. She had come from one of the little offices which housed the various sub-managers of departments, and, without a word to the girl, Amery had walked into the bureau and with a crook of his finger had summoned to him its middle-aged occupant.

"You tried to kiss that girl, I think?" he said.

"If she says that, she's a liar – " began the manager.

"*I* say that," said the sinister Amery, his lip up. "See the cashier and draw your salary up to today: you're fired!"

Lawyers' letters had followed this incident, and Elsa had typed a few of the acrid replies. The matter had come up when she was called in to take a letter to the sub-manager's legal representative, and she ventured to put in a word for him.

"Mr Sturl has been ten years in the firm," she said. "He's a married man with a family. Don't you think you're rather hard on him?"

He transfixed her for a second with that granite look of his, and then:

"I am not in need of advice," he said.

She was so furious that she could have thrown her book at him.

It was characteristic of the change which had come over the business that Mr Tarn had not been consulted about this dismissal, and even more remarkable that he was too far gone in gloom to resent his overlooking.

She met him as she was going out to lunch. It was so unusual for him to leave the office until he left it in the evening that she almost asked him where he was going. She checked herself in time, though he could not have been ruder to her than Amery had been. On one thing she was determined: she was leaving this establishment at the earliest opportunity. The man had so got on her nerves that she loathed the very sight and sound of him.

Mr Tarn would have been glad to have such definite views. His mind was in a whirl. Plan after plan occurred to him, only to be rejected, and there seemed no pleasant prospect in life but the quiet of a remote ranch in a foreign country, and the solace of mind that obscurity would bring.

Ralph Hallam had telephoned to him to come to lunch, and it was to the little house in Half Moon Street that his steps were directed.

"I've had a talk with the crowd," said Ralph, when Tarn was seated before a luncheon which would have choked him to eat, "and they agreed that it would be best if you got away. Your nerves are gone, and this fellow Amery looks like smashing up one side of our organisation."

"It's smashed," groaned Tarn. "Not another ounce can come in through Amery & Amery. I wish to God I'd never come into the game! Look at this: it was left for me this morning."

His trembling fingers dived into the inside of his frock coat and brought out a letter, which he handed across the table to the other. It was written on very thick and very cheap notepaper, in a hand obviously disguised. Without preliminary it began:

You are poaching on our preserves, and thanks to your blundering folly, the police are working double shifts. We are willing to give you £100,000 for the business, you to hand over your agents and agree to dissolve your organisation. If you do not accept this offer, we will find a way of clearing you out.

It was signed with a capital "S".

Ralph handed the letter back with a smile.

"If it's worth a hundred thousand pounds to them, it may be worth a million to us. Why did they send it to you, do you think? Because they knew you were the one scared chap in the organisation! When did you get this?"

"I found it on my desk this morning when I arrived at the office. Nobody seems to know how it got there."

"Perhaps Amery could explain," said the other drily. "Did he arrive before you?"

The old man nodded.

"I'm going to quit," he said. "We'll cut up the money: there's enough to make us both rich."

"You've got it in ready cash, of course?"

"How else?" said the other impatiently. "If I'd followed your advice, I'd have put it in that fool Stebbing's Bank, and when we went to draw it we'd have found two Scotland Yard men waiting on the doorstep. The money's all right," said Tarn, cheerful for the first time that day. "We'll divide up at the end of the week. I've booked my passage."

"You're a queer old devil." said Ralph, something amused, "and you're sacrificing a fortune. But I think – we all think – that you're wise to take this step."

He got up from the table, lighting his cigar, and blew a ring to the ceiling.

"You'll go alone, of course?"

Tarn shifted uncomfortably.

"I suppose I shall," he growled, "but that's no concern of yours."

"It is a very big concern of mine. I've already explained to you, my dear fellow, that Elsa is necessary to me. To be biologically exact, you have more brains than she; but she's smarter than you, and, with a little instruction, will more than take your place. Now kill that crazy May-and-December bug that's tormenting you. Go away by all means; you'll be a happier man the moment the Lizard's astern; and if you are serious about your matrimonial project, why, South America is still full of very beautiful young ladies who would jump at the opportunity of marrying a man with your wad. And honestly, Tarn, I think you'll be a lucky man to get away alive."

"What do you mean?" demanded the other, startled.

"I mean this, that Soyoka is going to be very busy, and you're better out of it."

SCREENING MAJOR AMERY

All that afternoon Maurice Tarn sat before his writing-table, his hands thrust deep in his pockets, his shoulders bent, his eyes half-closed, Hallam's warning in his ears. He was fifty-six, and life and liberty were very dear to him. And he wanted – very badly he wanted – to think singly. That was a term he invented himself. And all the time he was thinking trebly, three lines of thought running parallel, only to come together at short intervals into one confused, embrangled mass, until they so interlaced and overlapped, and ran one into the other, that he could not extricate them for an eternity of time.

And then, in the blackest hour of his gloom, came the discovery which was destined, though this he could not know, to bring catastrophe in its train.

"A cablegram, sir," said a clerk. "I think it is in the private code."

"Eh?" He gazed gloomily at the paper that had been laid before him. Looking absently at the signature, he sat up with a jerk.

The sender was a Japanese merchant with whom he had had some dealings on behalf of his nefarious syndicate. Soyoka had discovered this, and that source of supply had suddenly stopped. But it was the presence of a name in plain English in the very middle of the cablegram that left him gasping, and he hastened to find his secret code-book and write out the message.

And then he saw what had happened. By some aberration of memory the cable that was addressed to him was intended for Soyoka's principal agent. The discovery left him shaken... The name in plain English! Soyoka! He had his rival in the hollow of his hand,

and his soul was filled with a wild, savage sense of exhilaration which he had not known in years. That was what had happened: the message had been sent to his private telegraphic address...in error.

He sat back in his chair, his breath coming quickly, his face flushed; and thus Elsa found him when she came in to mention that she might be away that night. He did not even reply to her and her very natural conclusion, drawn from his flushed face and bright eyes, was that he had been drinking.

Soyoka...in the hollow of his hand! So they would threaten him, would they? He would show them.

Elsa was going home that night, and had turned into Cheapside, when she saw a familiar figure crossing the road toward her.

"Why, Ralph!" she said. "What are you doing in this industrious quarter of London? I never associate you with the City."

"I had to come East to see a man," he said, falling into step by her side. "Are you taking a lordly taxi, or are you being democratic and boarding a bus?"

"I'm being healthful and walking," she laughed. They passed along Newgate Street, turned into the Old Bailey, and stopped to admire the pompous face of the Central Criminal Courts. To Ralph the building had a peculiar interest, and he pointed out where Newgate Prison had stood, the place where the little narrow wicket, festooned with irons, had opened into the gloomy gaol.

"It makes me shiver," she said, and turned away.

"I'll bet it makes Maurice shiver too," he said incautiously, and she stopped and faced him.

"What is wrong with Mr Tarn?" she asked. "He has done something terrible, hasn't he? Do you know what it is?"

But he turned the discussion with a laugh. He was glad enough to reach Elgin Crescent, for he was no pedestrian.

"You're staying at Lou's place tonight – you promised her yesterday when you put her off. Have you told the old man?"

She had spoken to Tarn that afternoon, but doubted if he had taken in what she had said. For some reason which she could not define, she dreaded this coming visit.

"I'm not sure that Mr Tarn understood me," she said.

"Need you tell him?" he asked quietly. "Maurice is sore with me, for some reason, and I have an idea that, if he knows that you're going to Lou's place, he'll raise objections."

"But what can I say?" she asked in astonishment. "I can't tell him a lie."

"Tell him you're going to spend a week with a friend. If I know him rightly, he won't bother to ask you who it is."

It did not seem entirely to her liking, but she agreed.

"I'll lend you my moral support," he said gaily, and, changing his original intention, which was to leave her at the door, he went in with her, to find, as she had expected, that Maurice Tan had not yet returned.

She left him in the dining-room while she went upstairs to pack a bag. Again that little doubt entered her mind. She did not like Mrs Trene Hallam; but she disliked her no more than she would any other stranger, and possibly she would improve upon acquaintance. And there was a very excellent reason why she should go away for a little time. Instinctively she knew that the moment of Maurice Tarn's crisis was at hand, and what might be involved in its culmination she dared not let herself think.

She took longer over her packing than she had intended, for there had arisen a new and preposterous consideration. Would Paul Amery approve? Preposterous indeed! She laughed at herself and resumed her packing. When she came downstairs, Ralph, stretched in the big armchair by the window, was looking out upon the youth of Elgin Crescent at play.

"The noise these young devils make must get on Maurice's nerves," he said. "What does he do in the evenings – drink?"

She nodded. It was distasteful to her to discuss her guardian.

"He hasn't changed his habits," she said.

"No – not if I know him. I'll tell you what he does," said Ralph slowly. "You can check me if I'm wrong. He finishes his dinner at half past eight, goes to his study at a quarter to nine, has his usual four brandy liqueurs, and then starts in seriously to increase the liquor consumption."

Elsa sighed.

"He wasn't always like this. It is only during the past few years that he has been drinking," she said.

He nodded.

"A queer devil is Maurice. I wish to heaven he'd go to South America."

"With me?" she smiled.

He shook his head.

"Certainly not with you. I'm not going to let him take you away."

She very hastily changed the subject.

At eight o'clock Mr Tarn had not arrived, and he went away, after vainly trying to persuade her to let him accompany her to Herbert Mansions.

"I can't do that," she said, shaking her head. "It wouldn't be fair to him to go away only leaving a message with the servants. I must see him and explain."

"Loyal lady!" he said with a smile. Somehow she did not like his tone.

After he had gone, it occurred to her that, with every opportunity and every inducement, she had not told him about Feng-Ho's midnight visit. It was curious that she had not done so. And it was not because she had forgotten that she had not told him. Twice it had been on the tip of her tongue to narrate her midnight adventure, and something had stopped her. And then later, as she heard the unsteady hand of Maurice Tarn put a key in the lock of the lower door, the explanation came to her and left her wondering at herself. She had not told him because she was screening Paul Amery!

THE MAN IN THE ROOM

Inspector William Bickerson had written the last line of a very long report to headquarters; he blotted, folded and enclosed the document, and, looking up at the clock, saw it was a quarter to nine. It was at that moment that his clerk came in to ask him if he would see Dr Ralph Hallam.

"Dr Hallam?" said the inspector, in surprise. "Why, surely!"

He greeted Ralph as an old friend.

"It is a hundred years since I saw you last, doctor," he said warmly. Again his eyes wandered to the clock. "And I wish I had time to have a chat with you, but I've an appointment at nine. Did you want to see me about anything particular?"

"If you consider the dope gangs are something particular, then I did."

The inspector whistled.

"The dope gangs? Do you know anything about them?"

"I know very little, but I guess a lot; and I suppose you can do some guessing for yourself."

The inspector did not reply.

"You're a friend of Mr Tarn's, aren't you?"

Ralph nodded.

"Yes, I am a friend. We have been much greater friends than we are at the present moment."

"What's the matter with him?"

Ralph shrugged.

"I don't know exactly. Booze, I should imagine. He has taken it rather badly. Why do you ask if I am a friend of his?"

The officer considered a moment.

"Because he's the fellow I'm going to see at nine. He asked me to come round, said he had something very important to say. In fact, he gave me to understand that he had an important statement to make. Do you think that was booze?"

Ralph was cautious here.

"It may be," he said, and bit his lip. "What kind of statement?"

The inspector shrugged his shoulders.

"I don't know. Are you his doctor?"

"I have been, though I'm afraid my medical knowledge isn't worth boasting about. At nine o'clock, you say? Would you mind if I went with you?"

Again the officer glanced at the clock.

"No, you can come along, though if it is serious, I don't suppose he'll want to say much before you."

"In which case I can go," said Ralph.

Bickerson had arisen when the telephone bell rang, and he took up the instrument.

"Hullo!" he called, and Ralph saw his eyebrows rise. "It's our friend," said the detective in a low voice, putting the receiver out of range.

"Is that you?"

It was Maurice Tarn's voice, thick and slurred, almost indistinguishable.

"That you, Bickerson?...You coming round to see me? They tried to get me tonight...yes, tonight!... She's in it...I wouldn't be surprised. She's ungrateful, after all I've done..."

"What are you talking about, Mr Tarn?" asked the detective sharply. "I'm on my way now."

"Come as quickly as you can. I can put you right about Soyoka – I know his principal agent!"

He whispered a word, and Bickerson's jaw dropped.

73

There was a click as the receiver was hung up. The inspector turned to his companion.

"He's drunk," he said.

"What did he say?"

But Bickerson was so overwhelmed by that whispered word that he did not answer.

"I shouldn't take a great deal of notice of what he said," suggested Ralph, concealing his anxiety. "The old fool is pickled! Why, he wants to marry his niece!"

"Humph!" said Bickerson, deep in thought. "I've found some drunkards remarkably talkative. Will you come?"

From the police station to Elgin Crescent was ten minutes' walk, and the detective had an opportunity for adding to his knowledge.

"Where is the girl – does she live in the same house?" he asked.

"Usually, but tonight she's staying with a relative of mine. The truth is, she has had a fairly bad time with him," said Hallam, "and Tarn's getting worse. He's scared of Soyoka's crowd."

"What's that?"

The officer checked his step and stared at the other in wonder.

"Soyoka – what do you know of that gang anyway?" he demanded.

"Nothing," said the other promptly. "That is one of his crazy delusions. I came to see you especially to tell you about that, and to warn you as far as Tarn is concerned. It is his obsession that he has offended Soyoka."

Every police officer has had experience of that kind of delusion. Never was a great crime committed but some lunatic produced a confession, and his enthusiasm for the interview was a little damped. Dr Ralph Hallam desired that it should be.

"I don't know why," said Bickerson as they turned the corner of Ladbroke Grove, "but I had an idea all the time that Tarn wanted to see me in connection with the drug cases. No, he never said so; it was just a hunch. And here we are. You go first – you know your way."

Together they mounted the steps, the inspector following through the broad, open portal. Half-way up the passage they were confronted by the doors, one of which led to the lower part and the other to the upper-floor flat which Mr Tarn and his niece occupied. Ralph pressed the bell, and when no answer came, pressed it again.

"It looks as if it is open," said the inspector suddenly, and pushed.

To his surprise, the door swung back. They passed to the foot of the stairs, and Ralph felt for the switch. After a while he turned it down, but no light appeared.

"That is queer," he said. "The lamp must have burnt out." Feeling their way by the wall, they mounted to the first landing "This is his study," said Hallam, as he touched a door-knob and turned it.

The door opened. The only light in the room was the dull glow of a small fire, which gave no illumination whatever.

"Are you there, Mr Tarn?" called the inspector.

For answer came a deep snore.

"Is there a light anywhere?"

The detective's hand swept along the wall, and Ralph heard the click of a switch. But again the lights failed to show.

"That's queer – where is he?"

It was easy to locate the snorer. Presently Ralph's hand rested on the back of a big armchair and, reaching down, he felt bristly face.

"He is here," he said.

At the touch of the Visitor's hand, Maurice Tarn moved uneasily. They heard his drowsy grunt, and then, like a man speaking in his sleep, he spoke thickly.

"They tried to get me under…I know…but I'm too strong…got the constitution of a horse…"

The words died away in a rumble of sound.

"Wake up, Tarn," said Ralph. "Mr Bickerson has come to see you."

He shook the man by the shoulder and the snores ceased.

"I'm afraid you're going to have a difficulty in rousing him."

"Is he awake?"

"I don't think so. Tarn! Wake up!"

Then, suddenly:

"*There's somebody else in the room!*" said the inspector sharply. "Have you a match, doctor?"

He had heard the thud of a falling chair, and strained his eyes to pierce the darkness. Even as he looked, he heard a rustle near the door, lurched out and caught the shoulder of the unknown intruder. There was a sibilant hiss of sound; three Chinese words that sounded like the howl of a dog; a bony fist caught the officer under the jaw; and in an instant the stranger had jerked from the detective's grasp, slipped through the door and slammed it. They heard the patter of his feet on the stairs.

"A light, quick!" cried Bickerson hoarsely.

From Ralph's direction came the rattle of a matchbox, a light spluttered and flared. As if in answer to his cry, the electric lights suddenly blazed up, momentarily blinding them.

"Who did that –?" And then: "Hell – look!" hissed the detective, and gaped in horror at the sight.

Maurice Tarn lay huddled in his chair, his head thrown back. His soiled white waistcoat was red and wet, and from the crimson welter protruded the black handle of a knife.

"Dead!" breathed Hallam. "Killed whilst we were here…!"

He heard the detective's cry and saw him glare past him.

"What – ?" he began, and then he saw.

Crouched in the farther corner of the room was a white-faced girl. Her dress was in disorder, her white blouse was torn at the shoulder; across her face was a red smear of blood…

It was Elsa Marlowe!

ELSA'S SECRET

Bickerson gave one glance at the girl, hesitated a second, and then, running to the door, flung it open and flew down the stairs. The street was empty, except for a woman who was walking toward him. Far away, at the corner of Ladbroke Grove, he saw a bored policeman standing, and he raced across the road toward the officer, who did not seem aware of his presence until he was on top of him.

"Go to 409, Elgin Crescent," he said breathlessly. "Hold the door and allow nobody to come in or out. A murder has been committed. Blow your whistle: I want another constable. You saw nobody come out of 409, Elgin Crescent?"

"No, sir; only one man has passed me in the last few minutes, and that was a Chinaman – "

"A Chinaman?" said Bickerson quickly. "How was he dressed?"

"He was dressed in the height of fashion, as far as I could see, and I noticed him because he wore no hat. But a good many of these Easterners don't wear hats – "

Bickerson interrupted the dissertation on the customs of the East. "Which way did he go?"

"Down Ladbroke Grove. He took a cab: I was watching him getting into it just before you came up, sir. There it goes."

He pointed to the hill leading to Notting Hill Gate, and Bickerson looked round for a taxi to pursue, but there was none in sight.

"Never mind about the house: go after that cab. Sound your whistle and see if you can get it stopped. There's another man on point duty farther along, isn't there?"

"Yes, sir," said the constable, and went off at a jog-trot in pursuit of the taxi, which had vanished over the brow of the hill.

Bickerson hurried back to the flat. Whoever the intruder was, Elsa Marlowe would have to account for her presence.

When he got back, he found Elsa in the dining-room. She was very white but remarkably calm. The blood smear that had been on her face was gone, and the handkerchief in Ralph Hallam's hand explained its absence. She turned to him as she came in.

"Is it true?" she asked. "Mr Hallam says that my – my uncle has been murdered."

The detective nodded slowly.

"Didn't you see?"

"No." It was Ralph who answered him. "I turned the light out. There are things which I shouldn't want her to see, and that was one of them. I switched off the lights before I brought her out. And thank God she hadn't seen it!"

Bickerson looked again at the girl.

"Yes, Miss Marlowe, your uncle has been killed."

"That – that man did it," she said.

"What man?" asked the detective sharply.

She struggled hard to control her voice, but the experience of the last two hours had brought her as near to hysteria as she had ever been in her life.

"I'll tell you everything from the start," she said. "I was going away tonight, to stay with – with a friend; and I waited at home to tell Mr Tarn that I should not be returning for a week. And then he asked me where I was going. I hoped he would not, because there was a possibility that he might object; but I told him, and from that moment he behaved more like a madman than a rational being. He raved and screamed at me, called me the most terrible names, and in his fury he threw a glass at me."

She lifted her hair and showed a cut which, slight as it was, had matted the hair with blood.

"This happened in the dining-room; and then, suddenly, before I realized what was happening, he grasped me by the arm and pushed me into the study. I think he must have been drinking before he came in. He sometimes stops at an hotel on his way and spends hours there.

" 'You sit down and wait till I tell you to move,' he said; 'you are not going out tonight.' I tried to reason with him, but he was like a man demented, and I could only sit patiently, watching him pour out glass after glass of brandy, and wait for an opportunity to make my escape from the room. Once I thought he was sleeping, and got up softly to go. He opened his eyes and sprang up, and flung me back on the settee in a corner of the room. I was terrified. I don't think I have been so frightened in my life. I thought he must have gone mad, and I really believe he had.

"Presently he went to sleep again, and then I hadn't the courage to move. He was talking all the time of what he was going to do to somebody. And then, suddenly – this was about ten minutes ago – the lights went out. There are heavy curtains before the windows of Mr Tarn's study, and these were drawn. Except for the very small illumination that the fire gave, there was no light at all in the room. I sat still, dreading his waking up, and hoping that presently he would be far enough under the influence of drink to make my escape possible. Whilst I was thinking this, I heard the door creak, and had a feeling that there was somebody in the room. I was sure of it a second later, for quite unexpectedly a bright ray of light shot out and focused Mr Tarn."

She shivered.

"I can see him now, with his head rolled over on to his shoulder, his hands clasped on his chest. The light half woke him and he began to talk."

"Did you hear Mr Tarn telephone?" interrupted the detective. The girl nodded.

"Yes, that was more than a quarter of an hour ago. I heard him speak to somebody – it was you, I think. You're Mr Bickerson, aren't you?"

The detective nodded.

"Go on, please," he said. "When the man put the light on your uncle, did it wake him up?"

She shook her head.

"No; he stirred in his sleep and talked. Then the light went off. I dared not move, thinking it was a housebreaker. And then I heard your voice coming up the stairs…that is all I know."

"You didn't see this unknown man stab your uncle?" She shook her head.

"It was impossible to see anything."

The detective rubbed his chin irritably.

"He was quick: I'll give him that credit. The poor old chap must have been killed whilst I was within a few feet of him. This will be a fine story to make public!"

He looked suspiciously at the girl.

"I shall want your evidence of course. I'd like you to be somewhere where I can get you at a moment's notice. Why not go to an hotel?"

"I'll get a room for you at the Palace Hotel," said Ralph.

He had no especial desire that Herbert Mansions should be a place of call for the police in the next few days; he wanted, if possible, to keep his wife's name out of the case, for fear that the connection between her and himself became public. Perhaps Elsa understood that he did not want to bring his "sister-in-law's" name into the case, for she made no comment, and was very glad of the suggestion: she was not in the mood to meet a strange woman that night.

By the time the detective had re-examined her, the policeman had returned, and with him a comrade. A small crowd had gathered in front of the house, attracted by that instinct for tragedy which is the peculiar possession of crowds. By telephone Bickerson notified the murder to headquarters, and whilst he was waiting for the photographers and finger-print experts to arrive, he made a quick examination of the study.

It was poorly furnished. A faded green carpet on the floor, a worn knee-hole writing-table, two or three chairs, and a large bookcase comprised the principal furniture of the room. On the walls hung a few old and apparently valueless oil paintings, of that variety which it was the mid-Victorian artist's pleasure to paint. There was, too, a piece of furniture which looked at first like a pedestal gramophone, but which proved, on inspection, to be a well-stocked cellarette.

On the table near the chair where the body was found was a full bottle of brandy, that had not been opened, and an almost empty bottle, from which, he guessed, Maurice Tarn had replenished his glass that night. With a tape-measure he jotted down a few exact particulars. The chair on which the wretched man was lying was three feet from the fireplace, a foot and a half from the table where the bottles were resting, and nine and a half feet from the door. It was obvious that the murderer could not have passed between the table and his victim, for Bickerson had occupied that space. But there was ample room to pass between the fireplace and the chair, and it was in this direction that the detective at first heard the noise, and an overturned chair on the other side of the fireplace practically located the murderer's movements to the satisfaction of the officer.

There were no documents of any kind visible, except a few unpaid bills, which were on the table where the bottles stood. He began a tentative search of the dead man's pockets, but found nothing that could throw any light upon the crime.

His rough search concluded, he went downstairs, past the door where Elsa and Ralph Hallam were talking, and out into the street. The little knot of people had increased in size to a fairly large crowd, and as he came out to the top step, casting a glance along the Crescent for a sight of the police car, he saw a man elbow his way through the press and advance toward the steps. The constable on guard stopped him, and Bickerson watched the brief colloquy.

The stranger was a tall, spare man, slightly bent. He looked, thought Bickerson, a soldier; the tanned cheeks suggested that he had recently returned from a hotter sun than England knows; and then the identity of the stranger dawned upon him, and he went down the steps to speak to him.

"Are you Major Amery?" he asked.

"That is my name," said Amery. "Tarn has been murdered, they tell me?"

The detective shot a glance at him.

"Who told you that?" he asked suspiciously. "Are you a friend of his?"

"I am his employer," said Amery; "or rather, I was. As to the other question, why, I suppose everybody in the crowd knows that a murder has been committed. I happen to be aware that the occupant of the house is Maurice Tarn. There are only two people who could be murdered in that flat, and Tarn is the more likely."

"Will you come in?" asked the detective, and showed the way into the passage. "Now, Major Amery," he said, "perhaps you can tell me something about Tarn. Had he any enemies?"

"I know nothing of his private life."

"You were a friend of his?"

Amery shook his head.

"No, I wasn't," he said coolly; "I disliked him intensely, and trusted him not at all. May I see Miss Marlowe?"

"How do you know Miss Marlowe is here?"

The detective was glancing at him under lowered brows.

"She lives here, doesn't she?" asked Amery. "Really, Mr Bickerson – oh, yes, I know your name very well indeed – you have no reason to be suspicious of me."

Bickerson thought quickly, and when he spoke again it was in a milder tone.

"I am very naturally looking upon everybody within a radius of three miles as being under suspicion," he said. "I'll ask Miss Marlowe to come down to you, but you're not to take her away under any circumstances. You understand that, Major Amery? I need this lady for further information. She was in the room when the murder was committed: I'll go so far as to tell you what I would tell a reporter."

Amery inclined his head gravely, and seemed in no way surprised by what the detective told him. He waited in the hall, staring gloomily out upon the morbid crowd, and presently heard a light step on the stair, and, turning, saw Elsa.

"You've had pretty bad trouble, they tell me?"

His voice was entirely without sympathy: that was the first thing that struck her. He was making a plain, matter-of-fact statement of an incontrovertible event, and she wondered why he had troubled to see her.

"I happened to be in the neighbourhood," he said, "and I heard of this happening. I wondered if I could be of any assistance to you or to the police – though I admit that I know much less about Mr Tarn than you or any of his acquaintances. Who is with you?"

"Mr Hallam," she said. "He was a great friend of poor Mr Tarn's, and he is a very dear friend of mine."

"Dr Hallam?" He nodded. And then, with his usual unexpectedness: "Do you want any money?"

She looked at him, astonished.

"No, thank you, Major Amery," she said. "It is very good of you to ask – "

"There is some money due to your uncle, and if it were necessary I would advance your wages," he said. "You will be at the office tomorrow at the usual hour, if you please. It is mail day and I have a great deal of work to do. Good night."

She could only stare after him as he walked down the steps, utterly aghast at his callousness. What had mattered to him was that she should be at the office at her usual time. For a second a wave of anger and resentment swept over her, and her eyes flashed toward the disappearing figure of the Major.

"The brute!" she murmured, and went back to the waiting Hallam.

"What did he want?"

She shrugged her shoulders.

"As far as I can gather, he wanted to make sure that I would be at the office tomorrow at my usual time, because it is mail day and he has a lot of work to do."

"A perfect gentleman," said Ralph Hallam sardonically. "Of course, he sympathized with you?"

"No, he didn't say a single kind word. He's just a – a brute!"

Now that the strain had relaxed, she was on the verge of tears and wanted to be alone, far, far away from that grisly, sheet-covered thing in the study, from Ralph, from everybody who knew her. "Be at the office early!" The man had no heart, no human feeling. It was unthinkable that she should go to the office at all, and she doubted if she would ever go again. And she had done so much for him. She had wanted to tell him then, but had lacked the courage, just what she had done, how she had lied for him, how she had become almost a party to her uncle's murder, that he might be saved embarrassment. But he should know!

There came the sound of many feet on the stairs. The Scotland Yard men were going into the room; the handle of the door turned and Bickerson entered.

"Do you know this?" he asked.

He showed her a new soft felt hat.

"I found this in a corner of your uncle's study," he said. "Have you ever seen it before?"

She shook her head.

"No, my uncle never wore that kind of hat," she said.

Bickerson was looking at the inside. It bore the name of a popular store. It was grey, with a black ribbon. If, as he believed was the case, this hat had been purchased by a Chinaman, it was not going to be very difficult to trace the owner.

"You are perfectly sure that the man who came into the room, the man with the flash-lamp, did not speak?"

"No," she said, "he did not speak."

"And you didn't see him?"

"No, I didn't see him."

"Not even by the reflected light?" persisted the detective. "It is impossible to throw a ray from an electric torch upon any light surface without some reflected glow revealing the holder."

She shook her head.

"I saw nobody; I only saw the light, and that for a second." Why was she doing this? Why, why, why? she asked herself in despair. She was shielding a murderer – the murderer of Maurice Tarn. She was lying to save a cruel and remorseless villain from the hand of the law, and she was horrified at her own folly. For she knew the man in the room – had seen him, as the detective suggested, in the glow which had come back when the light had fallen upon a newspaper. And the man was Feng Ho!

AT THE USUAL HOUR

Elsa spent a very sleepless night, though she occupied a comfortable bed in one of the quietest of the West End hotels. No sooner did sleep come to her eyes than the memory of that horrible night intruded itself upon her, and she awoke trembling, expecting to see the parchment face of Feng Ho leering at her in the darkness.

And Feng Ho was Paul Amery. Their acts were interdependent…as were their responsibilities. Once she got up and paced the room, striving to calm her mind and sort her values. She must see Mr Bickerson and tell him the truth. On that point she was decided. As to Amery, she never wanted to see him again, never wanted to mount those narrow crooked stairs, never answer that shrill bell and go fluttering into his presence, like a rabbit to the fascinations of a snake.

There was a little writing-table in her room, and, putting on the light, she sat down, took out a sheet of notepaper and began to write.

DEAR MAJOR AMERY, (*she began*),
After this terrible happening I do not feel that I can come back to the office again; and whilst I am very sorry if my sudden departure puts you to the least inconvenience, I am sure you will quite understand –

He wouldn't understand at all. He would be very annoyed. That lip of his would lift in a sneer, and possibly he would sue her for breach of contract.

She read the letter again, frowned and tore it up. There was no justification for beginning so familiarly. After all, she was not on such good terms that she should call him by his name. She started another letter "Dear Sir," and sat staring at it blankly, until the church clocks chimed four, and a sudden sense of utter weariness made her put the light out and go back to bed.

She was dressed at eight and had rolls and coffee in her room. Again she sat at the writing-table, playing with a pen, her mind torn in many directions. The quarter-past chimed, the half past; she began another letter. There would be time to send it by district messenger. But the letter was never written. At a quarter to nine she tore up the paper, put on her hat and her fur and went out.

At five minutes past nine, Miss Dame, waiting in her room, a newspaper under her arm, her brain seething with excitement, saw her come in and literally fell upon her.

"My dear," she said, "how perfectly awful! It's in all the newspapers! I wonder you didn't die with fright. *I* should! I can't even see a murder on the screen…"

"My dear woman," said Elsa wearily, "for heaven's sake don't talk about it! If you imagine that I want to discuss it…I'm not staying anyway; I've just come to see Major Amery, and then I'm going."

"Did you faint?" demanded the seeker after sensation. "I'll bet you did!"

And then the merciful bell above Elsa's desk rang long and imperiously. Before she knew what she was doing, she had slipped off her coat, hung up her hat, and seizing her notebook and pencil, had opened the door of the private office.

Amery sat at his desk, his hands clasped on the edge, his stern eyes watching the door. He did not express any surprise, either by look or word; seemed, indeed, to have taken it for granted that she would be within reach of the bell when he pressed the button.

"I'm early," he said.

That was the only human speech he made, and began immediately a long letter to a firm of Indian merchants at Delhi. He did not give her any opportunity of telling him that she had only come for a few moments to explain why she couldn't come again. She had no time even to be annoyed at his assuredness. It was as much as she could do to keep pace with him. He never gave her a chance to question. When he came to a difficult or a native word, he spelt it rapidly, three times in succession, so that it was impossible she could miss it, or that there should be any excuse for a break.

From the Delhi merchants he switched instantly to a letter to Bombay, but this time he paused midway through to hand her a slip containing a number of meaningless words printed in capital letters, which was to go in at the place he indicated.

"That'll do," he said.

She rose and stood waiting.

"Major Amery, I want – " she began.

"Get those letters out quick. I want to catch that mail via Siberia. It closes in an hour."

"I don't care if it closes in two minutes," she was stung to retort. "There is something I want to say to you, and I'm going to say it."

He put down the newspaper he had taken up, folded it with exasperating leisure, placed it on the side of his tidy desk and put a paper-knife on top of it.

"Well?" he asked.

"My uncle was murdered last night, by a man who broke into our house – a man who had tried to break in before. I haven't told the police – I recognised him. I saw him as plainly as I see you. But I haven't told the police – "

"Why not?" His eyebrows went up, his voice was wholly unconcerned. "It is your duty to give the police all the information that lies in your power," he said.

"I didn't because – because I am a fool, I suppose," she said wrathfully.

Looking up quickly, he saw the unusually bright eyes and the flushed cheeks.

"Who was he?"

"Feng Ho," she blurted. "You know it was Feng Ho. You know it was, you know it!"

He lowered his eyes to the blotting-pad, and for a little while made no answer. She saw the white teeth gnawing at the lower lip, and went on.

"I did not want to – involve you – or your friends in this. It was a distorted sense of loyalty to Amery's. But I've got to tell."

He looked up again.

"An excellent resolution," he said. "But I think you are mistaken. Feng Ho – "

"Was with you!" She made an heroic effort to sneer, but failed lamentably.

"If he had been with me," he said quietly, "your story would hold good, because I was in the neighbourhood when it happened. No, Feng Ho was many, many miles away from London. Believe me, he has a complete *alibi.*"

"Perhaps his hat has one too," she said tartly. He was on his feet in an instant.

"His hat?"

"I ought not to have told you that, I suppose," she said ruefully, "but the police found a hat. And a bareheaded Chinaman was seen coming away from the house."

The ghost of a light showed in the expressionless eyes fixed upon hers, flickered for a second and was gone.

"Is that so?" he said slowly. "Well, in such a case, Feng Ho will have to have a double-plated *alibi.* That will do."

A few minutes later she found a word in her notes that she could not decipher, and was reluctantly compelled to go back to him to secure an elucidation. The room was empty. Major Amery had gone out, and did not return for another hour, during the greater part of which time he was waiting at a district messenger office for the return of a boy whom he had sent to the Stores to purchase a soft felt hat, size 6½, and it was a special instruction that it should be grey, with a broad black ribbon.

THE STANFORD CORPORATION

Dr Ralph Hallam spent an unusually busy day at his house in Half Moon Street. Ever since his partner's death he had been realizing, with gathering force, the immense source of embarrassment, not to say danger, which Maurice Tarn's death might well be. If he had only had a chance of a heart-to-heart talk with the dead man before a murderer's knife had cut short his life, he could have made sure of many developments which were now problematical.

He waited impatiently for the hours to pass, and for darkness to come: and though his waiting was enlivened by at least three visits from Bickerson and a telephone call from his wife, the time passed all too slowly.

Ralph Hallam had been reminded how precarious was his position by a letter which had come to him that morning from the bank, pointing out the excessive amount of his overdraft. Ordinarily, this would not have disturbed him, for there was a big accumulation of profits from the illicit business in which he had been engaged with Tarn. Neither man favoured banks; the money had been kept in dollar currency. There was nearly £200,000, of which half belonged to the dead man and to his heirs.

His mind went immediately to Elsa Marlowe. Unless Tarn had left his money elsewhere, she would be as rich a woman as he was a man – if he made the division. That was a nice reservation, for he had not the slightest intention of sharing with her, and the mere possibility only entered his mind to be as instantly rejected. All the money that was deposited in the big green safe of the Stanford Corporation was his for the taking. No heir of Maurice Tarn had a legal right to it. He might perhaps give her a thousand or two in certain eventualities; but the idea of dividing this no man's property never entered his head.

And yet – suppose the old man had left particulars of his nefarious interests, and a legal claim arose? Ralph Hallam had spent his life keeping on the safe side, and it would be in his best interests if he made the girl an unconscious partner to the removal of Maurice Tarn's effects.

Elsa had just returned from the office when his telephone call came through.

"I want you to come and dine with me, Elsa. There are a few things about Tarn that I think you ought to know."

She welcomed the diversion, for the day had been a trying one, and her employer had reached a point where she needed sympathy.

"I will come along straight away."

"Have you seen Bickerson?" he asked, with a half-smile.

"Seen him! He has haunted the office. And oh, Ralph, I'm so sick of it all, and I've got to go to the inquest – stand up and tell all the awful things he said to me! And did you see the evening newspapers? Ralph, they've published a picture of me coming out of the office for lunch!"

He chuckled.

"I've lived with reporters all day," he said. "Come along and we'll curse them together!"

He put down the receiver with a thoughtful expression. That was a good move on his part. There could be no question now of his stealing Maurice Tarn's property. They would go together and recover the fortune which his industry had accrued to him.

He was glad Tarn was dead – in a way. The man's nerve had failed; he had betrayed himself to Amery. Ralph laughed softly. Soyoka! Tarn had reached a condition of nervousness where he saw Soyoka at every street corner, and identified the mysterious head of the dope traffic in every unlikely individual. And yet…he frowned at the thought. Who sent the Chinaman to Maurice Tarn's house? What object would he have had in…

He stopped suddenly. Soyoka would have excellent reason for smashing his rivals.

That combination of which Ralph Hallam and Maurice Tarn were the heads had come into existence as the result of an accident. Five years before, Ralph had found himself broke and pursued by a host of creditors, who threatened to bring him into the bankruptcy court. And then one night, as he and Tarn had sat in a fashionable West-End saloon, an acquaintance had drifted in – the wreck of a man, who pleaded to him for a prescription that would enable him to stave off the cravings of his unholy appetite. Ralph had scribbled the prescription, and then a word dropped by the drug victim led him to pursue enquiries from his borderline friends, and he had learnt of the existence of a powerful organisation which, despite the efforts of the police, was engaged in what was known as the "saccharine trade." Saccharine was at that time the principal article smuggled; and the new and more sinister industry was only then beginning.

Tarn had unrivalled opportunities for engaging in the traffic. He was practically at the head of one of the oldest-established importers in the City of London, for the nominal chief was a sick man and seldom came to the office. When Hallam made the suggestion, he had shown a little hesitation, but after the enormous profits of the "trade" were demonstrated, he had fallen, and there had been founded an underworld corporation which had its agents in every part of the kingdom and its biggest branch in an American city.

Ralph was a doctor, but he was also a keen businessman. His title gave him certain privileges, and helped cover the local operations of the gang. A muddled success had been theirs at the start, and then, profiting by their mistakes and tightening their organisation, the "amateurs" had come into the market, to the serious inconvenience of the older-established Soyoka.

Soyoka! It might not have been a delusion on Tarn's part…and the murderous Chinaman…

"Soyoka!" said Ralph Hallam aloud. "I wonder?"

Elsa came half an hour later, a very tired and a very unhappy girl.

"I think I shall go mad if this lasts much longer," she said. "Tomorrow is my last day at Amery's."

"Have you told him you are leaving?"

She shook her head.

"I haven't had a chance to tell him anything," she said. "I don't think you know what he's like – he's inhuman! When you remember poor Mr Tarn served the firm for over thirty years, you would imagine that Major Amery would be distressed. But he isn't. He had a new manager in uncle's room today! Ralph, the man is indecent! And he hasn't given me a second's peace. 'I don't want you to take more than half an hour for luncheon,' he said. I wish I hadn't taken any, because those wretched newspaper photographers were waiting outside to snap me."

"You had better cut out Amery's as soon as you can. Has he any idea you're leaving?"

She shook her head again.

"He takes me for granted," she said viciously. "I'm a part of the furniture. But don't let us talk about him; I want to forget the sinister man, I want to forget Amery's, I want to forget everything! What did you want to see me about? Something pleasant, I hope?"

"I'll tell you after dinner," he said cheerfully.

When his man brought the coffee and had discreetly closed the door on them, Ralph told her what was in his mind.

"Have you ever heard of the Stanford Corporation?"

Her eyes opened wide.

"Yes; Major Amery asked me if I was engaged by them."

Ralph whistled.

"The devil he did! When was this?"

She told him of the surprising question that the head of the house of Amery had put to her.

"And of course you said you knew nothing about them? And quite rightly."

"Did uncle know?" she asked, as the idea occurred to her.

He nodded.

"Yes. The truth is that your uncle was running a little business of his own. As a matter of fact" – he spoke very reluctantly, as though he were loth to betray the dead man's secret – " he was trying to build up a trade connection for himself in his spare time; something he could go to when Amery became impossible. I'm not saying that it was a strictly honourable thing to do, because obviously he was coming into competition with the firm that employed him. But be that as it may – and I tried to persuade him against the project, but he was so keen that I didn't like to oppose him – he carried out his plan."

"Then he was the Stanford Corporation? What is it, Ralph?"

"It is a firm of importers or something of the sort," he said carelessly. "I've been to the office once, and the only thing I know is this: he told me that in his safe there were a number of documents that he would not like to come to light. I've been thinking about it all day, and it seems to me that the best service we can render to the poor old chap is to go along and get those papers before the police find a clue. I don't want the old man's name to be soiled, and Amery is certain to paint his double-dealing in the blackest colours."

She looked at him with a troubled frown.

"It doesn't seem a very dreadful thing to have done," she said. "Besides, will they know that he had anything to do with Amery's?"

"It is pretty certain to come out," he said promptly. "Now the question is, Elsa, will you come along with me to Threadneedle Street – "

"But if the documents are in the safe, how can you get at them?" she asked, logically.

For answer he took out of his pocket a small key.

"Tarn and I were very good friends, in spite of the disagreement we've had of late, and he gave me this key, as the only man he could trust, so that, if anything happened to him, I should have access to the papers."

Threadneedle Street by night is a howling wilderness, and the building in which the Stanford Corporation was housed was in the hands of the cleaners when they climbed the three flights of stairs that led to the floor where the secretive Mr Tarn had operated. Half-way down a narrow corridor was a door, inscribed "Stanford Corporation," and this Ralph opened. She wondered whether it was with the same key that opened the safe, but did not ask him any questions.

Switching on the light, he ushered her into a medium-sized room and closed and bolted the door behind them.

"This is the sanctum sanctorum," he said.

It was an unimpressive office. The floors were innocent of carpet or covering; one rickety table, a chair and a handsome safe in a corner of the room were the sole articles in view. Even the electric light that dangled from the ceiling was without a shade.

"It's a pretty mean-looking apartment, isn't it?" said Ralph, who, thought the girl, had evidently been there before.

He put down the bag he had brought on the table, crossed to the safe, inserted the key and turned it twice. The great door swung open and the girl saw him peer into the interior.

Suddenly she heard him utter a strangled cry of wrath.

"The safe is empty!" he said hoarsely. "Nothing...nothing!" She looked round quickly. Something was tapping on the glass panel.

"Ralph" – instinctively her voice lowered – "there is somebody at the door."

She could see the shadow against the panel – the shadow of a man.

For a second Ralph Hallam was so dazed by his discovery that he could not understand what she was saying. She seized his arm and pointed.

"At the door?" he said dully. "One of the cleaners." And, raising his voice, he shouted angrily: "Go away...!"

"I'd like to see you first," said a voice, and the girl nearly dropped. It was the voice of Paul Amery!

MAJOR AMERY LOOKS IN

It was Elsa who unbolted the door, and she stood back to let the man come in. He was wearing a dinner-jacket, and over his arm he carried an overcoat. He looked from the girl to Ralph, and she saw that half-contemptuous, half-amused twitch of lip, and hated him.

"You've found your way to Stanford's, after all, Miss Marlowe?" he said. "And do you know that I almost believed you when you told me you had never heard of this enterprising establishment?"

Ralph Hallam had been taken aback for a second, and then the memory of Tarn's warning came to him. This man was Soyoka!

"I brought Miss Marlowe here to recover some money, the property of her uncle," he said, looking the other straight in the eyes. "But it seems that I'm rather late; somebody has been here before me."

The intruder glanced carelessly at the open safe, and then looked at the girl. Genuine astonishment was in her face.

"Money?" she said. "You didn't tell me about money, Ralph!"

For a second he was nonplussed.

"There was money here as well as documents," he said glibly. "The point is that it's gone! Perhaps Major Amery will be able to tell us how it was taken?"

"By Tarn, I should imagine," was the cool reply. "Who had a better right?"

Again he looked at the girl and she flushed under his searching scrutiny.

"I should keep out of this if I were you, Miss Marlowe," he said. "There are certain occupations that are not good for little girls."

His patronage was insufferable. She trembled in her anger, and if eyes could have struck him down he would not have stood before her.

"You know a great deal about Stanfords, Amery," said Ralph, bottling down his fury with a great effort. "Soyoka wouldn't be superior to a little burglary, I guess?"

"Continue guessing," said Amery. Then, to the girl: "Now, I think, Miss Marlowe, you had better go back to your hotel."

She could contain herself no longer.

"Major Amery, your dictatorial manner with me is unbearable! You have no right whatever to instruct me as to what I should do and what I should not do. Please don't call me 'little girl' again, because it annoys me beyond endurance. This is my uncle's office, though I was not aware of the fact until tonight, and I shall be glad if you will go."

With a shrug, Amery walked through the door into the corridor and in another instant Ralph Hallam had followed, closing the door behind him.

"Now see here, Amery, we're going to have this thing right," he said. "I understand there isn't room in England for both of us, and I think it is fair to tell you that, if any crowd cracks, it will not be ours! There was money in that safe – a lot of money. It was there a few days ago; it's gone tonight. You know all about Stanfords, you've known about it for a long time. That means you've been able to get in and out as you liked."

"In other words, I've stolen your money?"

There was a look of quiet amusement in the grey eyes.

"I'll pass one word of advice to you. It has already been offered to your dead confederate. Keep away from Soyoka. He's dangerous."

Without another word, he turned on his heel and walked down the corridor.

Ralph went back to the girl, livid with fury.

"Has he gone?" she asked.

He tried to say something, but his anger choked him.

"So that's Amery, is it?" he breathed. "I'll remember the swine!"

"Ralph, was there money here? You didn't tell me."

"Of course there was money here!" he said impatiently. "I wanted to give you a surprise. There was a whole lot of money. I know it was here, because Tarn told me the other day."

He searched the safe again, examined a few papers that were in there, and presently she heard him utter an exclamation.

"What is it?"

"Nothing," he said, concealing the sheet of pencilled writing he had taken from one of the two little drawers at the back of the safe. "I thought I'd found – something."

He seemed to be in a hurry to get out of the office, almost pushed her into the passage before he closed the door.

"Not that it is much use," he grunted; "if this fellow is what I think he is, a little thing like a lock is not going to stop him."

"You mean Major Amery?" she said in wonder. "What did you mean, Ralph, about there not being room enough in England for you both? And about taking the money? Ralph, you don't imagine that he would have taken it, do you?"

She had a confused idea that the money belonged to Amery's, had been stolen perhaps, and that the sinister man's interest in its existence was the proper interest that the robbed have in the proceeds of the robbery. Had Maurice Tarn been engaged in speculation on the grand scale? Her heart went down at the thought. If this were the case, all her vague suspicions were confirmed, and Mr Tarn's behaviour was revealed in a new light.

"Was it stolen…the money?" she asked jerkily. "Did Mr Tarn…?"

"For God's sake don't ask questions!"

Ralph wanted to get away somewhere by himself and read the memorandum. His nerves were so on edge that he could not even simulate politeness.

Elsa was silent all the way back to the hotel, and was glad when her cavalier made his excuses and left her hurriedly at the entrance. She, too, needed solitude and the opportunity for calm consideration.

Hallam reached Half Moon Street, scarcely noticing the two men he overtook just before he reached his house. His key was in the lock, when a sudden premonition of danger made him turn quickly. The blow that was intended for his head just missed him, and, striking out, he floored the first of his opponents, but the second got under his guard, and this time he saw the flash of steel and felt the rip of the cloth where the point struck.

"That's for Soyoka!" hissed the man as he stabbed.

Hallam kicked wildly, and in the brief space of time that his advantage gave to him, he had jerked his automatic from his pocket. In another second his assailants were flying toward the Piccadilly end of the street…for a second his pistol was raised, and then, realizing the commotion that would follow a shot, he put the gun back in his pocket.

Ralph Hallam came to his little study, white and shaken, Soyoka had struck his second blow!

TUPPERWILL TALKS

Early on the following morning, Ralph Hallam made a call at Stebbing's Bank, Old Broad Street, and, after the usual mysterious conferences and scrutinies which invariably accompanied a call upon the general manager and proprietor, he saw shown into the handsome board-room where Mr Tupperwill presided.

Mr Tupperwill, settling his wing collar, offered him an expansive smile, a large soft hand, and the Louis Quinze chair he kept for distinguished visitors.

"I had your letter, Tupperwill, and I thought it best to come along and see you. I have some money coming to me – a large sum – in the course of the next few days, so you'll have to let my overdraft run."

Mr Tupperwill pursed his lips as though he intended whistling but had thought better of it.

"You can have an overdraft, of course, my dear fellow, but – "

"There is a but to it, then?" said Ralph, a little irritated.

"There is a slight but," said the other gravely. "We run on very conservative lines – from *conservare*, to keep together – in our case to keep together our – er – assets; and when the scale goes down with an overdraft we like to have a little collateral on the other side to balance it up again. But in your case, my dear Hallam, we'll let the scale drop down without a balance! How much do you want?"

Hallam told of his requirements, and the proprietor of Stebbing's Bank jotted it down on a tablet.

"That's that," he said. "And now I want to ask you a question. In fact, I thought of ringing you up the day before yesterday, after I saw you, but I thought you would not want to be bothered. Who is Amery?"

"Amery? You mean Paul Amery? I thought you knew him?"

Mr Tupperwill nodded.

"I know him; I know also his erratic henchman. Hallam, I'm breaking all the rules of the bank when I tell you that he has an account with us, a fairly big one. He came very well recommended and" – he pulled at his long upper lip – "I don't know what to make of him. My own inclination is to close his account."

"Why?" asked Ralph in surprise.

Mr Tupperwill seemed to be struggling with himself.

"With our clientele," he went on slowly, "we cannot afford to be associated, even remotely, with dubious projects. My directors would never forgive me if I allowed the bank to be used – er – for purposes which are outside the ordinary channels of commerce."

Ralph Hallam thought of the number of times the bank had been used to further his own peculiar devices, and smiled inwardly.

"Why are you suspicious of Amery?" he asked.

"I'm not suspicious of him," said the banker reproachfully. "Suspicability does not enter into the question. I merely point out that Stebbings is essentially a family bank. We have no commercial houses on our books, and there hasn't been a bill of lading in this office for fifty years."

He looked round as though he were afraid that some sacrilegious eavesdropper might have concealed himself in that chaste apartment, and then, lowering his voice: "Hallam, you are a friend of mine, or I would not tell you this. Yesterday he deposited a very large sum of money. I am not at liberty to tell you the amount, but it was – "

Ralph gasped.

"Two hundred thousand pounds?" he suggested eagerly. "In American bills?"

Mr Tupperwill stared at him.

"How on earth did you know that?" he asked.

His visitor drew a long breath.

"Is that the amount?"

"Well, it was very nearly that amount, and, as you so shrewdly guess, it was in American currency. When I say he deposited that amount, I am in error. What he did was to put into our safe keeping a box. I may tell you – and I would not tell my own wife, if I were blessed with one – that we do not like these, what I would call, 'secret deposits.' We have a means, which I will not disclose to you, of discovering their contents. There are many things which happen in banks of which you are not aware, but your description of the amount and the nature of the money is very nearly correct – very nearly correct. How did you come to guess?"

Here Ralph was not prepared to enlighten his friend.

The banker rose and began to pace the room slowly, his chubby hands behind him. For a time he did not speak.

"You wonder why I asked you if you knew Amery, and now I'm going to complete my confidence, and you have the fate of the bank in your hands. I've been troubling about this matter ever since I made the discovery, and worrying myself to death as to whether I should tell you. In the box was something besides money. There was a large sealed envelope inscribed 'Evidence against Hallam, to be employed on behalf of S. if necessary.' Those were the words – 'Evidence against Hallam' – and who is 'S'? I am not an inquisitive man, but I would have given a lot of money, a lot of money, to have broken those seals!"

Ralph went a shade paler.

"This morning he came and took the envelope away. Why, I do not know. He mentioned that he had taken it, quite unnecessarily. 'It will be better in my own study,' he said. But where did all that money come from? I don't like it, I don't like it at all. I like money to have a label. I like money able to announce the place it came from and how it was earned. That may sound curious to you. Two hundred thousand pounds – a million dollars, almost to a cent! Why doesn't he put it to his account? Why keep it locked up, earning nothing? Fifty thousand dollars, ten thousand pounds' worth of interest lost per annum! That is a crime."

He shook a podgy finger at Ralph as though he were responsible.

"That is not good business. And I do not like a client who isn't a good business man. Now, Hallam, you must tell me where that came from. You must know, because you mentioned the sum and the currency. Tell me."

For once Ralph was not in an inventive mood. He offered some lame explanation, which obviously did not convince his hearer.

Then, most unexpectedly, Mr Tupperwill changed the conversation.

"One of these days I should like to have a talk with your friend, Mr Tarn – " he began, and Ralph stared at him incredulously.

"Didn't you know? Haven't you read?"

"Read what? I have seen nothing but this morning's financial newspapers. Has anything happened to him?"

"He was murdered the night before last – murdered in my presence," said Ralph.

Tupperwill took a step backward.

"Good God! You are surely not jesting?" he said.

Ralph shook his head.

"No, he was killed the night before last – as I say, in my presence. It is remarkable that you should not have heard of it."

On Mr Tupperwill's boyish face was a look of almost comical concern.

"Had I known, I would not have troubled you with that wretched letter, my dear friend." He shook his head, almost humbly. "But I never read the newspapers, except those devoted to my own profession, and my valet, who usually keeps me *au courant* with contemporary happenings, is away visiting his sick mother. This is terrible, terrible! Will you tell me what happened?"

Ralph told the story in some detail, and the banker listened, without comment, until he had finished.

"Have they any idea as to who was the man in the room?"

"A very good idea. But unfortunately, the fellow we suspect, and who I'm pretty sure is the murderer, has proved an *alibi*. He was arrested late last night, on his return from the Midlands. Unfortunately for the police theory, he was wearing the hat which they expected to find he had lost, and his *alibi* was very complete."

He did not tell how the bewildered Bickerson had put through a call to the Birmingham police, and from them had learnt that they were satisfied that at the hour the murder was committed Feng Ho was at the police station, registering his visit under the Aliens Act.

"One Chinaman looks very much like another," he said, unconsciously paraphrasing Paul Amery's words; "and I imagine that the *alibi* was very carefully faked, and the person who was with the Birmingham police wasn't Feng Ho at all."

"Feng Ho! Not Major Amery's Feng Ho?" said the other, aghast.

"Do you know him? Yes, I remember you pointed him out to me."

Mr Tupperwill's agitation was now complete.

"I know him because he has come to the bank on one occasion with Major Amery, and we cashed one of Major Amery's cheques in his favour. Feng Ho! That is most surprising, most alarming! What of the poor young lady?"

"I think she will be well provided for," said Ralph, anxious to pass that topic.

Mr Tupperwill seemed profoundly affected by the news of Tarn's death. He stood, his lips pursed, his eyes vacant.

"I remember seeing a newspaper poster: that, of course, must have been the murder. Extraordinary!"

And then he became the business man again.

"So far as your overdraft is concerned, my dear Hallam, you may draw, without any further reference to me, to the extent of your needs. No, no, I will not be thanked. Having expressed the caution which my directors would wish me to express, I have done my duty, and will of course give my own personal guarantee. The inquest will be – ?"

"Today," said Ralph. "I am on my way now."

Again the banker appeared lost in thought.

"Would you object greatly if I accompanied you to this inquisition? Such tribunals are infinitely depressing, but...well, I have a reason."

Ralph wondered what that reason might be, but in his relief that a very difficult financial crisis had been overcome, though the relief was tempered by the news he had heard, he was prepared to endure the company of his ponderous friend. They arrived at the little court in time to hear his name called.

Until he was taking the oath at the witness-stand he did not see the girl, but when his eyes fell upon her face he guessed from her expression that she had already given her evidence. The proceedings held him until nearly five o'clock, when the inquest was adjourned. During this time it was impossible to get near her, and not until they were outside the court did he have a chance of speaking.

"I was rather a bear last night, Elsa, and I want you to forgive me. But my nerves were on edge."

"Mine were too," she said, and saw Mr Tupperwill hovering in the background.

"I want you to meet my friend Mr Theophilus Tupperwill," he said, introducing the stout man. "This is Miss Marlowe…"

The banker took the girl's hand in his, his countenance bearing that expression of melancholic sympathy for which the occasion called.

"I knew your poor uncle," he said in a hushed voice. "I will say no more. 'Sorrow breaks seasons and reposing hours, makes the night morning and the noontide night' – Shakespeare."

And with the delivery of that profound sentiment he took his farewell.

"Who is he?" she asked.

"Tupperwill: he's the head of Stebbing's Bank and a good fellow," said Ralph. He had never suspected the banker of sentiment. "Are you going to Lou's tonight?"

She shook her head.

"No, I can't go tonight; I have to go back to the office."

He looked at her in astonishment.

"You don't mean to tell me that Amery expects you back there tonight?" he said incredulously.

"Not only expects, but demands," she said, with a tightening of her lips. "I am resigning on Saturday: I left him a note telling him so. He has given me no consideration whatever. But please don't talk about him. You can drive me a part of the way, can't you?"

"All the way," said Ralph indignantly.

His indignation was largely assumed. He did not expect any consideration for man, woman or child from Soyoka's representative, and it would have been inconsistent with his mind picture of the man if Amery had shown the slightest evidence of humanity.

She thought he was a little *distrait* on the journey to the City and put it down to the natural reaction from the inquest. In truth Ralph Hallam's mind was considerably occupied by the knowledge that, somewhere in Amery's study, was a heavily sealed envelope ominously inscribed. His mind went back to the letter that Tarr had received on the morning of his death. The offer of £100,000 was considerable, if Soyoka knew where he could lay his hand on twice that amount of money, and probably had already extracted the bills from the safe.

At her request, he left the girl at the end of Wood Street, and in spite of her wrath at her employer, she hurried back to the office in a flutter, and was quite ready, when she saw him, to excuse herself for being late.

He was waiting in his room, standing with his back to the fireless grate, his hands clasped behind him, staring moodily at the floor. On his desk she saw, open, the letter she had left for him, and such was the power he exercised over her that she felt a little spasm of unease at the prospect of the reception which he would give to her resignation. The first words he spoke were on that matter.

"So you're leaving us, Miss Marlowe?" he said. "You have saved me the trouble of dismissing you."

At this, all her fears fled.

"You might at least have had the decency to spare me that offence," she retorted hotly. "I am leaving you for no other reason than that it is impossible for any self-respecting girl to work with you; because your manners are deplorable, and your attitude to women, so far as I am able to judge from my own experience, is so unmannerly and boorish that it is degrading to be at your beck and call!"

He was staring at her as she spoke, and she thought she saw in his eyes a look of astonishment.

"Is that so?" was all he said. And then: "You told me you knew nothing of Stanfords?"

"And neither did I," she said angrily. "Twice by inference you have called me a liar, and I hope that you will not repeat your insult."

He was taken aback by her vehemence, and before he could speak she continued: "I went to Mr Tarn's office without being aware that the Stanford Corporation had any existence except in your imagination. I haven't the slightest idea of the business my uncle was conducting, but I suppose, from your attitude, that it was an improper one. As to how he got his money, and how much money he had, I am equally ignorant. I had no idea that there was money at all there. Dr Hallam told me there were documents – it was your money, of course? My uncle stole it – is that the mystery?"

He shook his head slowly.

"No, your uncle stole no money from Amery's," he said, to her amazement. "So far as I know, he was a trustworthy man – where the firm's money was concerned."

He licked his lips. He had gone back to a contemplation of the blue carpet.

"I'm sorry," he said, though there was no quality of sorrow in his tone. "I seem to have fallen into an error. Of course you knew nothing about Stanfords. He wouldn't have told you."

"Mr Tarn never discussed his business affairs with me."

"I'm not thinking of Mr Tarn," he said deliberately. "I am thinking of the excellent Dr Hallam, who, unless I am greatly mistaken, is scheduled for a very troublous time."

Another long interregnum of silence, during which a little of her old discomfort had returned, and then: "I'm sorry. I withdraw the statement that I intended discharging you, although I did. If you wish to stay on in this post you may."

"I have no such wish," she said briefly, and, sitting down at the desk, opened her notebook.

Still he made no move.

"A chubby man," he said, apropos of nothing, "and a lover of good things. His boast of abstemiousness is part of his vanity. The cracker and milk come at eleven, but he lunches royally a two."

She was gazing, stupefied.

"Mr Tupperwill," he said, and explained, "I was at the inquest. You would not think Hallam could make friends with a man like that? But Hallam has unsuspected charms."

Was he being sarcastic? She gave him no excuse for discussing Ralph, and waited patiently, her pencil poised.

"Feng Ho thinks you are wonderful." He broke the silence with this gratuitous remark, and she flushed.

"His good opinion of me is not reciprocated," she said tartly "and really, Major Amery, I am not interested in Feng Ho's view about me. Do you wish to dictate any letters? I should like to go home as early as possible: I have a headache."

She saw his lip curl.

"You think I have been a brute, eh? Keeping your nose to the grindstone? But I'll tell you something, young lady. I haven't given you time to think! I have invented work for you, to keep your mind off a certain dark room in Elgin Crescent, where Tarn got what was coming to him for a long time. He had been warned."

"By you?" she asked quietly.

"By me and by others."

And then, with an effort, he tore himself from his thoughts which were obviously unpleasant, and began, without preliminary, the dictation of what promised to be an interminable letter. This, however, it was not. Halfway through he stopped is suddenly as he had begun.

"I think that will do for tonight," he said. "You need not make the transcript until tomorrow morning."

He followed her into the outer office, his coat on his arm, his hat and cane in his hand.

"You are at the Palace Hotel, aren't you? I may want you to come to my house tonight."

"I'm afraid I have an engagement tonight," she answered coldly.

At that moment the door opened and Jessie Dame came in. She was incoherent in her embarrassment at the sight of the forbidding face, and would have withdrawn.

"Miss Dame! I may want some work done tonight, in which case I would like you to accompany Miss Marlowe to my house – 304, Brook Street. Will you keep in touch with her?" Elsa opened her lips to protest, but before she could speak he was gone, with no more acknowledgment of her presence than if he had been the desk against which she leant, stricken dumb with anger.

"I'll not go, I'll not go! I told him I was engaged, and I refuse to go to his house."

Miss Dame glared sympathetically. But at the same time – "I'd rather like to see his house," she said. "I'll bet it's full of trap-doors and secret panels. Have you ever seen 'Sold for Gold'? Amery does remind me of the husband! He used to keep his real wife tied up in a cellar, and pretended he was single. And then, when he was leading the other girl to the altar, a strange figure appeared at the vestry door, heavily veiled, you understand – and, mind you, he still thought she was in the cellar – and just as the parson was going to say 'Who will take this woman to be his wedded wife?' up she springs, takes off her veil and it's her!"

"Who?" asked the bewildered Elsa, interested in spite of herself.

"The wife – the real wife!" said Miss Dame triumphantly. "The one that was in the cellar. She got out owing to the butler, who'd been stealing money from the man, leaving the door open."

"Anyway, I'm not going to his house," said Elsa.

"There'll be Indian servants there perhaps," said Miss Dame hopefully. "Dark, noiseless men in spotless white. He claps his hands and they appear as if by magic from secret doors. And idols too! And incense – incense comes from India, doesn't it Miss Marlowe? I'd like to see that house." She shook her head sadly. "I'd go if I were you, Miss Marlowe."

"I'll not do anything of the sort," said Elsa, banging down the cover of her typewriter viciously.

"I'll be in the same room with you," encouraged Miss Dame "There's always trap-doors in those kind of houses. Do you remember 'The Rajah's Bride'? Ethel Exquisite was in it – I don't think that's her real name, do you? What's your telephone number?"

"You needn't bother to call me, because, if he sends for me, I shall not take the slightest notice."

"304, Brook Street," mused Miss Dame. "A House of Mystery!"

Elsa laughed in spite of herself.

"Don't be absurd. It's a very ordinary West End house: I've passed it heaps of times, and I went there once, when the old Mr Amery was alive."

"He has probably transformed it to suit his Eastern ideas," said Miss Dame, loth to relinquish the picture she had formed "There'll be carpets that your feet sink into, and divvans – "

"Divans?" suggested Elsa.

"Is that how you pronounce it?" asked Miss Dame in surprise "Dy-van? Well, there'll be those. And joss-sticks, and music. I know these kind of people. Lord! I'd like to see it."

Elsa saw her wistful eyes and was as much amused as she could be.

"One would almost think you were in league with him," she said good-humouredly. "And now you can walk with me to the hotel, for fear I'm kidnapped in the streets of London and carried off to Major Amery's secret harem."

"Even that has been done," said Miss Dame cheerfully.

It was not a pleasant evening for Elsa. She had scarcely arrived at the hotel before the girl rang her up and asked her whether she had changed her mind. At intervals of half an hour she heard the anxious voice of the seeker after romance.

"Don't be silly, Jessie," she said sharply. This was after the fifth time; she had had her dinner and gone to her room. "He hasn't sent for me; and if he sends, I shall not go."

"I shall call you up every half-hour till half past eleven," said the determined female at the other end of the wire. "You can trust me, Miss Marlowe!"

Elsa groaned and hung up the receiver.

It was a few minutes before eleven when the telephone rang, and, thinking it was Jessie Dame, Elsa was in two minds about answering the call. When she did so, the voice that greeted her was Amery's.

"Is that Miss Marlowe? Major Amery speaking. Get a cab and come round to my house, please. I have sent my housekeeper to fetch Miss Dame."

"But, Major Amery, I am going to bed – "

Click! The receiver was hung up.

Here was her opportunity for asserting her independence. She had been a feeble, weak-kneed creature, deserving the contempt of every self-respecting woman. He should not order her about as though she were a slave. She would show him that he could not force her will.

She sat determinedly on the bed, her eyes fixed on the telephone bell, and when it rang, as it did after a quarter of an hour's interval, she jumped.

"Is that Miss Marlowe?" The voice was impatient, almost angry. "I am still waiting for you. Miss Dame has already arrived."

Elsa sighed wearily.

"I'll come," she said.

She tried to persuade herself that it was only because she could not leave Jessie Dame in what that imaginative lady had described as "The House of Mystery" that she was going, and because she was humouring the gaunt girl in her desire for sensation. But she knew in her heart that she was yielding to the domination which the sinister man had established, and she hated him more than ever.

A very prosaic butler opened the door to her, and a little, middle-aged woman, eminently respectable, took her up into the drawing room, where she found Jessie Dame sitting on the edge of a chair, her lips tightly pressed together, her magnified eyes looking disapprovingly upon the extremely Western character of the room.

It was very large and a little old-fashioned, with its cut-glass chandelier converted for the use of electric current, its high backed Chippendale chairs and ancient cabinets. The carpet, tortured with floral designs, scrolls and coarse-skinned Cupids was distinctly Victorian. Elsa could well understand Miss Dame's disappointment.

The sinister man was nowhere in sight, and they were left alone together.

"Have you seen him?" hissed Miss Dame.

"No."

"He's nothing much to look at," deprecated Miss Dame, "but there's a Chinese servant here. You've got to be careful!"

She put her finger to her lips as the door opened and Amery came in. He was in evening dress, and, from the scowl that puckered his forehead, she guessed that he was in his usual mood.

"I didn't expect to send for you tonight," he said brusquely "but something has happened which has given a very serious aspect to my little joke."

His little joke! She gasped. Was that his idea of humour to suggest he might send for her at any moment? Apparently it was for he went on: "I am relying upon you girls to treat this matter as strictly confidential. You will hear things tonight which certain people would be very glad to know, and which they would pay a large sum of money to learn."

He clapped his hands twice, and Miss Dame's eyes glistened eagerly as a door at the end of the room opened and a Chinaman came in. It was not Feng Ho, but a little man in a blue silk coat and a sort of white petticoat. He stood with his hands concealed in his sleeves, his head bowed respectfully, and there was a rapid exchange of question and answer in some hissing language, which the girls guessed was Chinese. When they had finished: "Will you come this way?" said Amery, and walked toward the open door.

The Chinaman had disappeared, and, after a second's hesitation, conscious that Miss Dame's hand was clutching her arm with bruising tightness, Elsa followed the head of the house of Amery into a smaller room, from which opened three doors. Amery turned the handle of the first of these, opened the door and stepped in, holding up his arm to warn them to remain. Presently his face reappeared round the edge of the door.

"Come in, please," he said, and Elsa, with a wildly beating heart, walked into the well-lit room.

To all appearance a servant's bedroom, its dimensions were limited, and the furniture consisted of a bed, a strip of carpet and wardrobe. On the bed lay a man, and at the sight of him the girl was speechless with amazement.

His face white as death, his head and one hand heavily bandaged, he stricken man greeted her with a cheerful smile.

"Extraordinary!" he murmured.

"Meet Mr Theophilus Tupperwill, the eminent banker," said Amery.

THE SIGNED STATEMENT

Mr Tuppwill greeted the girl with a pathetic smile.

"We have met under happier circumstances," he said. "This is the young lady who – ?"

"We will take your statement," interrupted Amery characteristically, and turned to the girl. "Our friend has had a very unpleasant turn, and is anxious – or rather, I am anxious – to see his experience recorded in black and white."

"Very business-like," murmured Mr Tupperwill.

"And signed," added Amery, and the girl noted the extra emphasis he gave to the word.

The sinister man was touching the bandage on the man's head, and she saw Tupperwill wince.

"Not bad for an amateur," he said, with a pride which was almost human. "Now, Mr Tupperwill. Have you brought your book, by the way?"

Elsa nodded. What was the meaning of this strange scene? Out of the corner of her eye she could see that Jessie Dame was shivering with excitement. At last this lover of the sensational had been brought into actual touch with a happening out of the ordinary.

Amery went out and returned with a chair, which he planted down with unnecessary noise near the wounded man's bed.

"Now, Miss Marlowe," he said curtly.

The banker turned his head with a grin of pain.

"Very business-like," he murmured again. "You would like me to make this statement? Now where shall I begin?"

She thought, from the position of his lips, that he was trying to whistle, but Amery, who knew him better, guessed the meaning of the grimace.

"I think I had better start with my dinner," said Mr Tupperwill slowly. "I dined at home – a devilled sole, a little chicken grandmère, and a soufflé – I don't think there was anything else – oh, yes, an entrée, but the composition of the dinner has nothing to do with the matter. I had my coffee and then, at a quarter past ten, I took my evening stroll, three times round the block – an exercise which is necessary to me, for I am a poor sleeper. Usually I take my little dog for a walk, but this evening poor little Tamer was suffering from injuries inflicted by a large, undisciplined dog that he met in the park, and I walked alone. I did not in consequence deviate from my usual route, but went my customary round, passing along Brook Street to Park Lane, and returning by the same route.

"I was half-way along the street, which at that time of night is a very quiet thoroughfare, when I saw a car drive up to the kerb and two men alight. A third man now appeared upon the scene, and suddenly, to my horror and amazement, all three began to fight! Though not of a pugnacious nature, I made my way quickly to the spot, with the idea of inducing them to desist. It was, in all the circumstances, a very hazardous decision for a man who is not especially athletic, and I have very good reason for regretting my action. I saw that the two assailants were powerfully built men. The third, whom they were attacking, I could not see, because they had wrapped his head in a cloth of some description, though he was still struggling violently. No sooner did I appear on the scene than somebody struck me, and I lost consciousness, and did not wake until I found myself in the hands of Major Amery and passing pedestrian, who kindly assisted the Major to bring me into his house, at the door of which I had been attacked."

"You have forgotten the letter," said Amery drily.

"Oh yes, oh yes! All my ideas are at sixes and sevens. Please put in your statement that after dinner my footman brought me a letter, which he said he had found in the letter-box. I opened it and discovered a sheet of paper with four words – 'You talk too much.' Those were the words: the original may be seen. Exactly what they mean, and to what act of loquacity they refer, I cannot guess. I am habitually and by nature a – a person extremely reserved. That I could talk too much in any circumstances, is unthinkable. Now, are there any questions you would like to ask me, Major?"

"The car was gone, of course, when you were found?"

"Yes, and the man also – you saw nothing of them?"

"Yes, I saw them," said the other carelessly. "At least, I saw a car. Have you got that, Miss Marlowe?"

Elsa nodded.

"You will find a small typewriter in my study. Mrs Elman will show you the way. I would like that statement typed and signed."

She went out with Jessie Dame, the latter so thrilled that her voice was a squeaky twitter of sound.

"What do you think of that?" she asked, when they were alone together in the plain little study to which the housekeeper had taken them. "Have you ever heard anything like it? Doesn't that beat the pictures? As I always say, there's more villainy happens in real life than people know – who do you think it was, Miss Marlowe?"

Elsa was sitting before the typewriter, her mind in a turmoil.

"I don't know whether Major Amery has a grudge against this man," she said slowly, "but I have heard and read about these sham street fights, which are intended to bring innocent people within reach."

Miss Dame gasped, and flopped down on a sofa, which was the nearest to a "divvan" she had seen.

"You don't mean that the sinister man got up this quarrel to catch Mr Tupperwill?"

Elsa shook her head.

"I don't know what to think," she said.

For some reason she did not wish to discuss Amery with the girl, but as she recalled Amery's callous indifference and his eagerness to have a signed statement which obviously would exculpate himself, her suspicions grew.

Why did he not go to the police? It was unthinkable that he should have any quarrel with Tupperwill. There seemed no grounds, except that he was a friend of Ralph. But if that were the case, and Tupperwill could be regarded as an enemy who had 'talked too much,' how easy it would be to engineer that scene in Brook Street! He must have known something of Tupperwill's habits. Probably at the same hour every night the stout man took his constitutional along Brook Street. A creature of habit, playing into the hands of these men.

She shivered. It did not bear thinking about.

Searching the table where the typewriter stood for a sheet of blank paper, she saw there was none suitable, and did not like to open any of the drawers. Then, glancing quickly round the room, her eyes rested on a small cupboard of unpainted pine. It was evidently a new fixture. Miss Dame intercepted the look.

"Do you want paper, dear?" she asked, and half rose. But Elsa was already on her feet.

"It may be here," she said.

The door of the cupboard was ajar. She pulled it open and found, as she had expected, a number of shelves with library requirements. She found something else: a short length of material which she recognised as rhinoceros hide and which the South Africans call 'sjambok.' Mr Tarn had had a walking-stick made of the skin. In length it was about twenty inches, and was almost as thick as her wrist. She would not have noticed it, but for the fact that it lay upon a package of paper which was sprinkled with some dark stain. She opened the cupboard wider. The stain was blood, and, repressing her desire to announce her find, she picked up the thing gingerly and brought it to the light. And then she saw that the end was red and still wet!

THE TRUTH ABOUT TARN

The mystery of Mr Tupperwill's injury was a mystery no longer. This was the weapon that had been used, and the hand that had struck him down was the hand of Paul Amery. He must have come straight into the study, which was the first room off the hall, thrown the stick into the cupboard and forgotten about it, and then gone out to pretend he was assisting the unfortunate banker. Probably the presence of that pedestrian saved Tupperwill's life. She shuddered, and, clutching at the package of paper, came back to the table.

"Why, Miss Marlowe, what is the matter?"

Jessie Dame stared in stupefaction at the change in the girl's colour.

"I don't know. I'm a little upset perhaps," said Elsa unsteadily.

She tore open the package, fixed a sheet in the machine, and, biting her lip, concentrated upon the statement. While she typed, the hideous thing became more clear. Her theory was substantiated.

She had just finished when Amery came into the room. He took the paper from her hand, corrected two typing mistakes, and went out of the room again.

"One of you girls come," he said; "I want a witness."

Jessie Dame followed him before she realized that she was unattended. She came fluttering back a few minutes later with the announcement that she had "witnessed the deed," and that Mr Tupperwill was sitting up and had expressed his intention of going home.

"And I'm certain as certain can be," said Miss Dame dramatically, "that your theory as to how the murder was committed is true. When

I say 'murder,' I mean it might have been murder. They were waiting for this poor dear man – "

"Jessie Dame, you are to forget what I have said."

Elsa was surprising herself by her fatuous defence of the man.

"It is much more probable that Mr Tupperwill's theory is correct: that the two were strangers, they were attacking a third person, and that, thinking he was interfering, they struck him down…"

Through the open door she heard footsteps in the passage, and presently Mr Tupperwill, looking very wan and limp, came in.

"A little brandy, I think, will do you a whole lot of good," said Amery. He opened a cellarette and poured out a small brown potion.

"Brandy…yes, thank you," muttered the banker. "There's one other statement I should like to have made. I ought to have described the man they were taking away, but I forgot that part."

"You didn't see his face, I understand?"

"No, I didn't see his face. As far as I could tell, he was a shortish man, dressed in a yellowish kind of tweed. The trousers," said Mr Tupperwill soberly, "I could swear to."

"I am seeing Mr Tupperwill home." Amery was addressing the girl. "I don't think I have any further need for you tonight. Thank you for coming."

It was on the tip of Elsa's tongue to retort that she hoped her wasted evening would count as overtime, but so many things came to the tip of her tongue and went no further in the presence of this forbidding man.

She got rid of Jessie Dame as quickly as she could, and, going straight to the hotel, called up Ralph and told him what had happened.

"You're not in bed yet?" said Ralph quickly. "I mean, can I see you if I come round?"

"Why, yes," she said in surprise, "but I can see you in the morning."

"No, I must see you tonight. I can't talk over the 'phone. Will you be waiting for me in the vestibule?"

She looked at the watch on her wrist: it was then half past eleven.

"Yes, I'll risk my reputation. Come along," she said.

He was with her in a remarkably short space of time, and learn in detail the story of Tupperwill's alarming experience. Elsa had thrown discretion to the wind. She felt that in this case at any rate she need show no reluctance in relating her employer's business. When she had finished, Ralph was looking at her strangely.

"So that is it! He talks too much! The devil must have learnt what Tupperwill told me this morning, though how on earth they overheard beats me. First Tarn, then the money, and now Tupperwill. Soyoka stops at nothing."

"Soyoka? Why, that's the drug man, isn't it? Oh, Ralph!"

At that moment was revealed in a flash the mystery that had puzzled her.

"Soyoka! The drug gangs! There are two – one Soyoka, the other – not Mr Tarn!" she breathed.

He nodded.

"You've got to know sooner or later."

"And you?" she asked, in a voice scarcely above a whisper.

"And me also," he said coolly. "There's no sense in being shocked, Elsa. It is a commercial proposition. You wouldn't object to meeting a distiller or a brewer, just because a few fellows couldn't hold liquor and behave like gentlemen?"

"Soyoka!" she said again. "Major Amery?"

"He's either Soyoka or his big man."

"And Mr Tupperwill?"

"He's nothing," said Ralph impatiently. "Tupperwill is just my banker, and he happens also to be Amery's banker. He told me that he didn't like the account on his books – that was one of the things he said. Amery has come to know, and tonight the gang went out to teach Tupperwill a lesson. And I can prove it," he said. "Tomorrow Amery will close his account at Stebbing's Bank, and bring away all his deed-boxes. By gad! If I only knew!"

His eyes were bright, his voice quivered with excitement. As for the girl, she felt physically sick at the revelation.

"It is too dreadful, too dreadful!" she said in a low voice. "I can't believe that men could be such brutes! Was that money, Ralph – the money that" – she hesitated – "uncle earned, and you…?"

Her look of hardly concealed disgust irritated him.

"That's not the way to look at it," he said. "I tell you that it's just a commercial proposition. Against the law, perhaps, but then, many things are. It is no worse than rum-running, and I know of some decent people who are making money – "

"Not decent, surely!" she said, with a sudden revival of her old self. She rose.

"I'll have to think this over," she said, and went up to her room, her mind all ways.

PERFECTLY HORRIBLE

One very definite conclusion she reached, when she was putting on her shoes preparatory to going to that hateful office: her connection with Amery's was practically finished. Why she did not proclaim the man's infamy from the housetops puzzled her. Was her moral code so loose that she could condone one crime at least of which she had proof, and another which she now suspected?

How would he appear to her now, she wondered, now that she knew him for what he was, a man who was living by debasing humanity, a cruel, brutal thug, who could strike down an unoffending man because he had dared break some rule of the bank?

Her way eastward led her past the great newspaper offices, and obeying an impulse, she turned into the publisher's department and began a search of the files. Presently she found the paragraph she had read to her uncle that morning, and which (now she well understood why) had thrown him into such a state of agitation.

A stray reporter who drifted in, *en route* to the cashier's desk saw a pretty girl turning the pages, and, noticing that she was not scanning the advertisement columns, sidled up to her.

"Can I help you?" he asked. "I'm on the staff of the paper."

Her first inclination was to decline his assistance. But she had recalled something Major Amery had said, and she was debating whether it would be too long a job to find the news she wanted when he appeared on the scene.

"I'm trying to find an account of the holding up of the Chinese train."

"Oh, the Blue Train outrage? You won't find it on that file. It happened months ago," he said.

"Do you remember why it was held up?"

The youthful reporter smiled.

"To get a little easy money, I guess," he said. "There were one or two wealthy opium smugglers on the train."

Opium again! She drew a long sigh.

"Thank you very, very much," she said, and hurried out, to the disappointment of the young connoisseur of feminine elegance.

It was curious, she thought, when the bell called her to his presence, that Amery did not look any different. She thought that in the light of her knowledge and a keener scrutiny, she would detect some evidence of his callousness. There must be that in his face which would betray his evil mind. But no: he was just what he had always been, and for his part, neither his manner nor his tone revealed the slightest difference in his attitude towards her except that for once he was gracious.

"I am much obliged to you for coming to me last night," he said. "You will be delighted to learn that Mr Tupperwill passed an excellent night, and the doctor thinks that he will be able to go to business in a few days."

Was there an undercurrent of mockery in his tone? She thought there was, and could only marvel at his cool brutality.

"And what comfort had Dr Hallam to offer to you?" he went on immediately.

"You watch me rather closely, Major Amery," she said quietly. "I did not ask the doctor to come to comfort me."

"Oh, you *did* ask him to come, did you? I thought you might have done," he said. "Was he impressed by the news of Tupperwill's sad fate? I see that you don't feel inclined to discuss the matter. We'll get on with the letters."

The matter was still in his mind at the end of half an hour's dictation, for he asked: "Was there anything you did not tell him about last night's happenings?"

Quick as a flash came the reply: "I did not tell of the blood-stained sjambok I found in the paper cupboard."

She could have bitten her tongue. The sentence was half out before she tried to stop herself, but it was too late. Not a muscle of his face moved; the grave eyes did not so much as blink.

"I wondered where you'd found the paper, and hoped I had left some on the desk. I suppose you think I am a pretty tough case?"

"I think you're perfectly horrible," she said. "May I go now?"

"You think I'm perfectly horrible, do you? And so do others, and so will others," he said. "As for Tupperwill, he should have been a little more discreet."

"Oh!" she gasped. "Then you admit it!"

He nodded.

"The lesson will not be lost on him," he said.

She hardly knew whether she was asleep or awake when she got back to her typewriter, and was absurdly grateful for the unmusical click and crash of the keys, which brought her back to the mental position of a rational being.

She hoped, as she banged savagely at the keys, that Major Amery's new secretary would have sufficient spirit to shake his self-conceit. She prayed that the unfortunate female (no man would endure him for a week) would break every one of his rules – open his letters and unfasten the strings of his parcels; two of his eccentricities being that he would allow no one to open either except himself. She pictured a steely-faced Gorgon with a heart of stone, who would freeze him to humbleness. As Major Amery had the choosing of his own secretaries, she reflected ruefully, he would probably find some wretched, broken spirited girl who would accept his insolence as a normal condition of her employment.

She was engaged in inventing a special type of secretary when the bell rang sharply and she flew in to the tyrant.

"I forgot a letter when you were in here before," he said. "Take this:

To the Managing Director, Stebbing's Bank.

Sir,

I am this day closing my account with Stebbing's Bank, and have to request that my balance be transferred to my credit at the Northern & Midland. And this further authorizes you to hand to the bearer the steel box held by the bank in my name. The receipt of the bearer, Mr Feng Ho, B.Sc., should be accepted as mine.

Yours faithfully.

She went back to her machine, finally convinced that all that Ralph had prophesied had come true. Amery was closing his account at the Stebbing Bank.

Paul Amery was the subject of another discussion between two men, one of whom had reason to hate and the other to suspect him. Mr Tupperwill lay in the centre of his large bed, a picturesque figure; one white-clad hand gripped a golden bottle of smelling salts, for his head ached vilely. Nevertheless, he had not been unwilling to receive Ralph Hallam and to give him a first-hand account of his misfortune. And Ralph had been most sympathetic and enquiring. But at the very suggestion that his assailant was none other than Paul Amery himself, Mr Tupperwill had been as indignant as if his own *bona fides* had been attacked.

"Nonsense, my dear man, nonsense!" he said, as sharply as his throbbing head would permit. "Amery was nowhere near the place. I distinctly saw the men who attacked me. There may have been a third person, but I very much doubt it. There was not even a chauffeur on the box of the car. Why on earth should Amery attack me?"

There was excellent reason, thought Ralph, but this did not seem the moment to make a disclosure.

"It struck me as possible," he said. "Amery is a wildish kind of fellow – "

"Rubbish! Stuff! Excuse the violence of my language, my dear Hallam, but it is too fantastic to discuss the two wretched assassins – which, by the way, comes from the word Hassan, the old man of the mountains who first employed murderers to settle his private feuds. Neither of these two was Amery, I'll swear."

Very wisely, Ralph did not press the point.

"At the same time," Mr Tupperwill went on, "I confess that I do not like Major Amery as a client, and I shall seize the very earliest opportunity of getting rid of his account."

"I think he'll save you the trouble," said Ralph drily.

"Why?" Mr Tupperwill's eyes opened wide.

"Because – well, because – " Ralph picked up the letter that Mr Tupperwill had shown him, read the four words and smiled.

"Do you connect this warning with the piece of information you gave me yesterday morning?" he asked.

"About Amery? Good heavens, no!"

"It is the same kind of letter-paper, the same kind of writing, that poor Tarn received before his death. Evidently written by the same man. And to what other indiscretion, if it were an indiscretion, can this note refer? You have not talked about anybody except Amery and his account?"

Mr Tupperwill was silent for a moment, stupefied by the suggestion.

"Pshaw!" he said at last. "He could not have known of our conversation. It took place in my private office, where it is impossible, absolutely impossible, that we could have been overheard."

"You have a loud-speaking telephone on your desk: was that switched off?"

"I think so," said Mr Tupperwill slowly. "It is almost second nature to make it dead. I can't say that I am exactly comfortable with that wretched American invention, and I've thought once or twice of having it removed. It is very useful, for I have only to stretch out my hand and turn a switch to talk to any of my departments, but it is dangerous, very dangerous. Now I wonder!"

He pulled at his lip for a long while, trying to remember. "It is unlikely," he said, "but there is just the possibility that the switch may have been down. Even in that case, which of my staff would betray me? No, my dear man, you must get that idea out of your head. It isn't possible. There is nothing wrong about Amery. I am almost sorry I expressed my doubts to you, if by so doing I have sown the seeds of suspicion in your mind."

Ralph chuckled quietly.

"In my case they're already in flower," he said. "I admit I'm prejudiced against Amery, and would go a long way to do him a real bad turn."

Then, seeing the shocked expression on the other's face, he went on: "Not that I shall."

"Thank goodness for that!" said Mr Tupperwill fervently. "I have always disliked violence, and now I have a greater antipathy than ever." He touched his head tenderly.

Ralph said no more than the truth, that the thought in the foreground of his mind was an opportunity for getting even with the man whom he now hated with unparalleled intensity; and that afternoon opportunity took shape.

THE POISON TEST

"You're determined to go on Saturday, Miss Marlowe?"

"Yes, Major Amery."

Amery stood at the window, his hands in his pockets, glooming into the Street.

"You will be rather difficult to replace," he said. "Could you overcome your very natural reluctance to serve me for another week?"

She hesitated and was almost lost. If he had ordered her to remain, she might not have had the courage to deny him.

"I'm afraid I cannot stay after Saturday, Major Amery."

Somehow she did not expect him to press her to stay then, nor was any further reference made to the attack on Mr Tupperwill. Though she had nothing but the kindest feeling for Jessie Dame, she ventured to suggest that the girl should take her place when she had gone, for the position was a coveted one and carried a salary twice as large as the highest wage earned by the most expert stenographer in the firm.

"She can't spell," was his only comment, and in a way Elsa was glad.

If she expected him, knowing his pertinacious character, to renew his request later in the day, she was – "disappointed" was about the only word which exactly described her feelings when the day wore through and the matter was not brought up. At four-thirty the office caterer brought two tea trays, and one of these, as usual, she carried into Amery's room. She put the tray down on his desk and he nodded, lifted the lid of the teapot and smelt it – a practice of his she had noticed before. This time he looked up before her faint smile had completely vanished.

"That amuses you, eh? I'll show you something else that will amuse you more."

He took a little flat case from his pocket, opened it, tore off a narrow slip of sky-blue paper, which he dipped into the milk. When he brought it out, the paper was red.

"Wait," he said, poured the tea into the cup, and this time produced a thin pink slip.

Looking, she saw that the interior of the case held nothing but hundreds of these pink and blue slips. The pink paper he dipped into the tea, held it for a few seconds, and then drew it out. Where the tea had touched, the paper was a bright lemon yellow.

"A rough test, but reliable. Arsenic turns the milk paper green and the tea paper purple. Strychnine turns them both black, so does aconite. Cyanide, on the other hand, bleaches the blue paper white and turns the pink paper to a deep red."

Elsa listened, open-mouthed.

"You – you were testing for poison?" she said, almost unable to believe her ears.

"Something like that," he said, and, replacing the case, put the milk and sugar in his tea. "By the way, that is one symptom of insanity – the notion a man gets that he's being poisoned, or that somebody is attempting his life."

"But poison here!" she said sceptically.

"Well, why not? I have many enemies, and one, at least, is in the medical profession."

At any other time she would have resented this reference to Ralph Hallam, but now the relationship in which these men stood, the knowledge of Ralph's terrible business, silenced her.

Crook against crook – diamond against diamond! Surely he did not dream that Ralph would do so horrible a thing! That he should judge other men by himself was a human weakness. Perhaps he was mad, after all. He did not act like a normal being. And yet she saw none of the symptoms which she associated with an ill-balanced mind. He was a mystery, inscrutable. She had read stories of criminals who were endowed with a greatness which distinguished them from the rest of mankind, wonderful mentalities perverted to base use. Perhaps the sinister man was one of those, an object for compassion rather than contempt. On the whole she was very glad that her term of employ-ment was coming to a rapid close.

After tea some letters and a parcel came for him. She put the letters on the blotting-pad (he was out) and placed the parcel within reach of him. It had come by hand and was addressed: "Major Amery, DSO." It was the first intimation she had had that he held the Distinguished Service Order – she was constantly finding out new things about him, she thought whimsically, and, absorbed in the discovery, she took up a pair of scissors and cut the string that fastened the parcel. Invariably she had done this for old Mr Amery, and never realized that the scissors were in her hand, till a snarl of anger made her spin round, affrighted. Amery stood in the doorway leading to the corridor.

"What in hell are you doing?" he roared.

She fell back before the blaze of his eyes. He was so menacing, his mien was so savage, his voice so harsh that he terrified her.

"How often have I told you not to open my parcels?" he growled. His hand had dropped on the top of the cardboard box she had exposed.

"I'm – I'm awfully sorry. I had forgotten."

The brown face was sallow. Was that his way of going pale?

"Do as you're told," he said, and lifted the box carefully in his hand, waited a second, and then rapidly took off the lid.

Reposing in a nest of white cotton wool was a round object, covered with white tissue paper. He did not touch it. Instead, he took up the scissors she had put down, snipped gingerly at the paper, and pulled a large piece aside.

"Fond of apples?" he asked in a changed voice.

It was a very small apple, but like no apple she had ever seen, for it bristled with steel needle points.

"That's medical, I'll swear," and she saw his lip lift. "He used a hundred needles, and there's death in every point! The cute cuss!"

There was genuine admiration in his voice.

LAUDANUM

"Rather ingenious," said Amery. "Not heavy enough for a bomb, and when one opened the package, what more natural than to seize this paper-covered little ball?"

"But are they poisoned?" she asked, bewildered. "With what?"

He shook his head.

"I don't know. An analyst would find out if I took the trouble to send it to an analyst. Anthrax, probably – or one of a dozen other diseases. There is enough venom in the sac of the average cobra to supply all those little points with a fatal dose."

He carefully put the lid on, tied a piece of string round the box, and, opening a cupboard, locked it away.

"Who sent it? Not Ralph – not Mr Hallam? You don't for one moment imagine he would do such a thing?"

"Hallam?" He bit his lip thoughtfully. "No, probably not Hallam."

"Are you Soyoka?" she blurted, and he brought his gaze round to her.

"Do I look like a stout and middle-aged Japanese gentleman?"

"I know you're not a Japanese," she said impatiently, "but are you Soyoka's agent?"

He shrugged his shoulders and looked toward the cupboard. "Apparently there are people who think I am. Dr Hallam? No, I don't think it was Dr Hallam. If I did" – he showed his teeth for a second in a mirthless grin, and she shivered involuntarily.

"You look dreadful."

Again she had no intention of speaking. She had surprised herself when she had asked him if he was Soyoka.

For a second she thought he would resent her comment, but he accepted it without offence.

"I *am* dreadful – 'perfectly horrible' was your remark, if I remember rightly. And there are horrible things in this world, Miss Marlowe, things you do not guess and cannot know; things I hope you never will know. 'Horrible' is a word you should never apply to a plain, straightforward dope smuggler – nay, even to a murderer. The real horrors are things that newspaper men do not write about; and when you come into contact with these, why, you find you've been wasting a whole lot of superlatives, and you're stunned for an exact description."

It was quite a long speech for him, and she had an odd sensation of pleasure. She felt almost as if she had been taken behind the steel doors of his reserve.

"I don't want you to think that either murder or drug smuggling is an admirable pastime. You're pretty safe in believing that the things your mother taught you were wrong, and not all the gilding, or high-class thinking, or toney philosophy in the world can make them right. I suppose you think those are queer sentiments coming from Soyoka's right-hand man?"

There was a peculiar glint in his eye, which she chose to regard as threatening. Perhaps he was unbending because he wished to persuade her to remain with him, but apparently this was not the case, for he did not follow up the advantage which his unusual geniality had created.

For yet another night she postponed her removal to Herbert Mansions. By the weariness in Mrs Trene Hallam's voice when she telephoned her, Elsa gathered that the good lady was as anxious to get the visit over as she. Elsa slept better that night and went to the office without any preliminary searchings of heart.

She had been at work five minutes when Miss Dame came flying into the room, and from her flushed appearance and her startled eyes, Elsa guessed that something unusual had happened.

"Have you heard the news?" hissed the girl melodramatically.

Elsa had heard too much news of a startling character to be wildly excited.

"Who do you think is the new manager?"

One of the sub-managers had been temporarily appointed to fill Mr Tarn's position. That it was only a temporary appointment Elsa was now to learn for the first time.

"He's in the office, sitting there as large as life, giving orders to white Christian people."

"Not Feng Ho!" gasped Elsa.

"Feng Ho," said Miss Dame impressively. "That's the last straw! If Amery expects well-educated young ladies to take their orders from a savage, well, he's got another guess coming. I know what the Chinese are, with their opium dens and their fan-tans and other instruments of torture. Not me, my girl!" Miss Dame shivered in her indignation. "I'm going to tell his nibs."

"Tell him now," said Amery's cold voice.

Elsa always jumped at the sound of him, but Miss Dame literally leapt.

Paul Amery stood in the doorway, his hands in his pockets.

"Tell him now. I gather you object to Feng Ho as general manager. I regret that I did not call you to the board meeting which decided upon the appointment, but I like to be alone when I make these momentous decisions. What is your objection, Miss Dame?"

"Well, sir," stammered Miss Dame, going red and white, "he's Chinese and foreign."

"Don't you realize that you're Chinese and foreign to him? As to his being an ignoramus or a savage, as you suggested a little time ago, he is a particularly well educated gentleman. At least he can spell," he added significantly.

Elsa thought this was cruel.

"He may be able to spell in Chinese," said Miss Dame with dignity, "but that's neither here nor there. I'm not much of a speller myself, I admit. Only you can quite understand, Major Amery, that we girls have got to look out for ourselves."

Miss Dame's attempt to drag Elsa into the argument amused the girl. Apparently it amused the sinister man also, for his lips twitched.

"Feng Ho will not bother you, or interfere with you in any way. He will deal entirely with the Chinese trade, which is by far the most important department of our business."

When he had gone:

"Wasn't he mild?" said Miss Dame. "He must have seen by my eye that I wasn't going to let him start something without my being there to ring the bell. Put a man in his place once, and he stays there. And listen, Miss Marlowe: I had my horoscope cast this morning – at least, the letter came this morning. I was born under Pisces, and I'm supposed to be highly emotional, imaginative, observant, artistic, musical, precise and prudent!"

"In those circumstances," said Elsa, "I think you may be able to cope with Mr Feng Ho as general manager. You seem to have all the qualities that a girl should possess in those difficult circumstances."

Miss Dame scratched her head with the end of her pencil.

"It never struck me that way," she said, "but perhaps you're right."

Elsa did not go out to lunch: she had not forgotten her encounter with the press photographers, and until the case was settled she decided to lunch in the office.

It was fortunate that she did so, for Bickerson called to ask, with variations, the same wearing string of questions that he had asked at least a dozen times before: the names of Tarn's relatives, particulars of his friendships, his animosities, his likes and dislikes, his habits, his houses of call, his clubs.

"Is it necessary to ask me all this again?" said Elsa wearily. "I think I've told you this before." And then, as though the thought occurred to her but, was too preposterous to entertain:

"You're not expecting me to vary my story? Oh, Mr Bickerson, you are!"

The stolid Bickerson smiled innocently.

"A witness sometimes remembers fresh incidents," he said; "and you can well understand, Miss Marlowe, that everybody in that house when the murder was committed has to be questioned and cross-questioned. It is part of our system of detection."

"Did you cross-question Feng Ho?" she asked.

The smile came off his face.

"I certainly cross-questioned him to a degree, but he had his alibi all done up in silver paper; we couldn't have broken it with a steam hammer. Major Amery in?"

"No, he's gone out," she said. "Did you want to see him?"

"No," he said carelessly, "I don't particularly want to see him. If he's there I'll stroll in."

"I'll see," said Elsa.

As she expected, Amery was gone. But Mr Bickerson was not content, either with the view he had of the room through the doorway, or with his earlier and closer inspection of the apartment. He strolled in past the girl, humming an aria. (He was something of a baritone, and had a reputation in amateur operatic circles.)

"A very nice little room this," he said. "An extremely nice little room. Would you be so kind as to go downstairs and tell my man at the door that I'm waiting for Major Amery?"

She looked at him squarely.

"Yes, I will, if you'll be so kind as to come out of the room and let me lock the door," she said.

He laughed.

"You think I'm going to conduct a quiet little search on my own eh, without the formality of a warrant? Well, you were right, only I've got the warrant, you see."

He produced a blue paper and handed it to her.

"It would have been ever so much better if I could have done this quietly, without Major Amery knowing anything about it, but I respect your scruples, and if you'd rather I waited until the Major came in, I will do so."

They had talked ten minutes when Elsa heard the door of Amery's room close, and went in to him.

"A search warrant, has he? I wondered when that would come. Tell him to step in. Good morning, Bickerson. You want to have a look round, Miss Marlowe tells me. Sail right in."

"I've got a pro forma warrant," said Bickerson with a shrug, "but that means nothing." And then: "Bit of a tough case, that of Mr Tupperwill's the other night?"

"Oh, you've heard about it, have you? Who squealed – Mr Tupperwill?"

Bickerson scratched his chin.

"Nobody exactly squealed," he said. "It came to me in the ordinary way of business."

"Was it Mr Tupperwill or the excellent Dr Hallam?" persisted Amery.

"Know him?" asked Bickerson, his keen eyes on the other's face.

"I am acquainted with him, yes."

"It is a queer thing, that case of Tupperwill," drawled Bickerson. "I wonder you didn't report it to the police straight away, Major Amery?"

"You mean Tupperwill's beating?"

Bickerson nodded, and saw the thin lips twitch.

"Oh, well, there's nothing to that, is there? Those things happen every day."

"Not in London. They may happen in Calcutta, and they may happen in Shanghai, where the sight of a Chinese policeman half beaten to death doesn't create so much of a scandal as it might in, say, Regent Street or Piccadilly Circus."

"I get you," said Amery.

He opened a box on his table, took out a thin black cigar and lit it.

"I suppose I ought to have reported it to the police, but it's up to Tupperwill. After all, he was the aggrieved party."

"Humph!" The detective was inspecting his *vis à vis* earnestly. "Curious that dust up should happen outside your house."

"Very curious. Equally curious that it should happen outside anybody's house," said Amery coolly.

136

There was a little pause in the conversation. Bickerson was evidently turning over certain matters in his mind.

"There is a feud between two gangs that are operating in London – two dope gangs: the amateurs, and Soyoka's crowd. I have reason to believe that Tupperwill has offended one of the gangs in some way."

"So I understand."

"Do you know how?" asked Bickerson quickly.

"I only know what he told me, that he had had a letter saying that he was talking too much. It seemed to me rather an inadequate reason for beating his head off, for I think you will agree that, if every man who talked too much was flogged for his sins, there would be few people in London, or New York for the matter of that, who could wear hats with comfort."

Another interval, during which the sinister man puffed steadily at his cigar and watched the windows on the opposite side of the street with curious interest.

"You have travelled extensively in the East, Major. Have you ever met Soyoka?"

"Yes. Have you?"

He pushed the cigar-box toward the detective, and Bickerson helped himself and was now holding a match to the end. He waited until he had most carefully and deliberately extinguished the flame, and put the stick in a copper ash-tray before he answered.

"I've seen members of the gang, but I've never seen Soyoka. Met them in town. They're a slippery little crowd to hold. The amateurs may be easy, because we've got a line to them. There are one or two men in the Midlands who ought to have received that warning about talking too much – "

"You have met some members of the Soyoka gang?" interrupted Amery with polite interest. "You interest me. What are they like?"

"They are very much like you" – a pause – "or me. Very ordinary, everyday people, whom you wouldn't suspect of pulling down a comfortable income out of filling the psychopathic wards. There's thirty thousand pounds a week spent on drugs in this country – on illicit drugs, you understand – which is considerably over a million and a half a year. There's eighty per cent profit, and the trade is in a few hands. You understand, Major Amery?"

Amery nodded.

"Which means," the detective continued, "that it is worth the while of really swell firms to take up this trade, because it's growing and the million and a half this year is going to be three millions next year unless we find the man who will turn King's evidence – State's evidence they call it in America, don't they?"

"So I understand," said Amery. "In other words, unless you get a real valuable squeak, you don't think you'll catch Soyoka?"

"That's what I mean. I don't think we'll catch him this year. We may have a stroke of luck; we may break the gang by finding the man who murdered Maurice Tarn, whether that man is white or yellow."

"I see: you've still got poor Feng Ho under suspicion?"

"I've nobody under suspicion," said the detective calmly. "Feng Ho had his alibi in good order."

He rose to go.

"Pretty smart girl, that – Miss Marlowe, I mean. I was going to take a quiet look round your place, but she wouldn't have it."

"Is she under suspicion too?"

The detective carefully flicked off the ash of his cigar into the fireplace.

"No, she isn't under suspicion; she's all right, unless…"

"Unless what?" asked the other sharply.

"Unless we were able to prove that, at some time before the murder, she purchased from a chemist some two ounces of laudanum."

"What!"

"I am referring to the laudanum that was found in the nearly empty bottle of brandy that stood by Maurice Tarn's side, and from which he had been drinking all the evening," said the detective. "Good afternoon!"

AN IMPULSIVE QUESTION

Elsa heard him going down the passage, humming his aria, little dreaming of the onus which this officer of the law was attaching to her.

After the luncheon hour she was usually very busy, but the sinister man did not send for her, though he was still in his room. She had to take a file into the office that had been her uncle's, and it was with a little twinge of pain that she knocked at the door and heard Feng Ho's soft voice bid her enter. She need have been under no apprehension, for nothing remained to remind her of Maurice Tarn. The office had been completely cleared; there was not an article of furniture, not so much as a hanging almanac, to remind her of the man who had passed in so mysterious, so dreadful a fashion. Instead, the carpet had been removed, the floor scrubbed, and in the centre of the room was a square of grass matting.

Feng Ho sat cross-legged at a little table which was not more than a foot from the floor, and seemed wholly inadequate, since the gilded cage occupied more than half the available writing space, and his ink and brushes took up most of the remainder. He had discarded some of his modern garments: she saw his coat and hat hanging up on a hook behind the door: and he wore, instead, a little black silk jacket, buttoned closely to his neck and braided in most unexpected places.

"Good afternoon, miss." He gave her his usual grin. "Pi has missed you excessively."

And, as though corroborating his master's statement, the little canary burst forth into a wild jamboree of song, which ceased as suddenly as it began.

What made her ask the question, she did not know. Nothing was farther from her thoughts when she had come in. But these seemed days of impulse.

"Feng Ho, did you kill Mr Tarn?" she asked, and stood aghast at her own fatuity.

The little man was neither disconcerted nor hurt.

"Miss, I have not killed a gentleman for a very long time," he said, "not intentionally, with malice aforethought, according to law. Some time ago – yes. It was vitally essential to decapitate certain Chinamen who had been rude to my papa, viz., cutting his throat with a sharp instrument."

"I really don't know why I asked you," she said.

She could have cried with vexation at her own stupidity.

"It seems to me, if you will pardon me, miss, curiously inept. For if I had decapitated or otherwise destroyed my aged predecessor, it is extremely improbable that I would make an official statement for the titillation of official ears. Even a bachelor of science is not so scientific as to tell the truth when same leads to intensive hanging by the neck."

Which was logical and true. Because she guessed that Feng Ho would tell the Major, she seized the earliest opportunity of forestalling him.

"It was a silly question, and I don't know why I asked," she said ruefully.

"I'm glad you did," he said. "You still think Feng Ho was with him when he died?"

"I am sure."

"And yet you never told the police? It was only by the discovery of the hat that they were able to connect him with the crime – and, of course," he added as an afterthought, "the policeman saw him."

"And you saw him," she accused.

He raised his eyes and looked at her through half-closed eyelids.

"What makes you say that?" he asked.

"You were on the spot when the murder was committed. If it were Feng Ho I saw in the room, he would go straight to you. Of course you saw him!"

"Of course I saw him." His voice was almost mocking. "And yet, curiously enough, no policeman has connected my visit with Feng Ho. You ought to be at Scotland Yard. By the way," he said, "do you ever have toothache?"

She looked at him in wonder.

"Toothache, Major Amery? No; why?"

"I don't know. It occurred to me that you might suffer that way; most young people do. If you did, I have a much better medicine than laudanum, which is dangerous stuff to handle."

He saw her brows meet in a frown.

"I don't know what you're trying to say," she said. "I know nothing about laudanum; I've never seen it. What do you mean?"

For the second time she saw the quick flash of his teeth in a smile. "What a suspicious person you are, Miss Marlowe! I'm almost glad you're going," was all the explanation he offered.

ELSA PACKS

On the Saturday morning, when her pay envelope came, Elsa opened it with mingled feelings of relief and regret. Though the sinister man had reverted to his normal condition of taciturnity, he had been a little more bearable, and she found some new characteristic every day; something which, if it could not be admired, was so far out of the ordinary that it was interesting.

Without counting the money, she looked at the pay slip and found that she had received a substantial addition for her "overtime." Inconsistently, she wished he had not paid her this money: she would have preferred to give that extra piece of service, though why, she did not know.

At one o'clock, the hour at which she was to leave, she tidied her desk, emptied the drawers of her personal belongings, and at last, with a queer feeling of dismay, which had nothing to do with the fact that she was now out of employment, for Tarn's lawyer had hinted to her that the dead man had left her a substantial sum of money, upon which she might draw, she knocked at the door of Amery's room and went in.

He was pacing the floor slowly; stopped and turned as she entered, and raised his eyebrows enquiringly.

"Yes?"

"I'm going," she said.

"Yes, of course, it's Saturday. Thank you, Miss Marlowe. I will deal with the Nangpoo correspondence on Monday morning. Will you remind me, when the Chinese mail comes in, that – "

Elsa smiled faintly.

"I shall not be here to remind you, Major Amery," she said. He looked at her, puzzled.

"Why won't you be here?"

"Because – well, I'm leaving today. You knew that."

"Oh, of course!"

He had forgotten! And then: "When is the adjourned inquest?"

"On Monday."

He bit his lip, and she wondered whether that little pucker of brow had to do with her, or such inconvenience as the sudden death of Maurice Tarn had caused.

"You had better postpone your resignation till next Saturday," he said, and for some absurd reason she could have thanked him.

Her self-respect, however, called for a protest.

"I've arranged to go today," she said, in a panic lest he should agree to that course.

"And I've arranged for you to go next Saturday. I cannot be left at the mercy of a woman who spells 'India' with a 'y.' Thank you."

With a nod, more gracious than usual, he sent her back to the outer office with mixed feelings. She agreed, as she returned her belongings to their places, that one week more or less did not count; that on the whole it would be more satisfactory to remain at Amery's until the inquest was ended.

Although she was not to be called as a witness, she dreaded the renewal of the enquiry, but the adjourned proceedings lasted only two hours, at the end of which time a bored jury returned the usual verdict of "Murder against some person or persons unknown."

Ralph she did not see in court, though he was there for half an hour, standing at the back of the public gallery; and she was back at the office in time to take in Major Amery's tea. Apparently he did not object to her overlooking the rapid immersion of the little slips in tea and milk.

"What happened at the court today?" he asked as she was going.

"The jury returned a verdict," she said.

He nodded.

"Major Amery," she asked, "do you think they will track the murderer?"

He looked up slowly.

"There are an average of fifty-six murders committed in London every year. Twenty-eight of the murderers are captured and sent for trial; twenty-seven decimal something die by their own hands, and the other fraction escape the processes of the law. The odds are fifty-six multiplied by about three hundred that the murderer will be caught. By the way, did you see friend Hallam?"

"No, I haven't seen him,' said Elsa, before she appreciated the impertinence of the question. "He telephoned me yesterday to ask me something."

He nodded.

"You didn't by any chance mention my little toothache jest?"

"Toothache? Oh, you mean the laudanum? Why, no, of course not. Why should I?"

He was looking down at his tea and did not look up.

"I shouldn't if I were you. Are you staying on at the hotel?"

She shook her head.

"No, it is much too expensive. I am staying with a – friend for a week, and then I am finding a little flat. The police have given over Mr Tarn's maisonette to me, and I am going to sort out my belongings. After that the lawyers are putting the furniture in the hands of an auctioneer. I wanted to go early tonight, if you do not mind."

"Certainly, you can go at once. Does Hallam know you are making your farewell visit to Elgin Crescent?"

She frowned at him. This man asked the most offensive questions.

"Why should he be there? He is certainly a friend of ours, but I do not find Dr Hallam so indispensable that I cannot do without him. Why do you so persistently speak about him, Major Amery?"

"He amuses me," said the other.

She had certainly never found Ralph very amusing.

The lawyer's clerk was waiting for her when she arrived at Elgin Crescent, and she was glad to have somebody else in that house of death. The place looked dirty and forlorn, and it was a most depressing task to gather her little belongings. Her search for a missing book took her into Tarn's study. This room had evidently been the object of a very thorough search, for the books had been removed from the shelves, tables and chairs had been set back against the wall and the carpet was rolled up. She was glad. In its present state of disorder there was little to remind her of the home she had shared for so many years.

She filled one trunk and went to the lumber-room in search of a big wooden case that was hers, and which, as a girl, used to accompany her on her annual holidays. It was really a series of boxes within a box, for its interior consisted of five wooden trays that fitted one on top of the other. With the assistance of the servant, who had come in to help, she carried the box back to her room, opened it and took out the top three trays. The fourth, however, refused to budge.

"Don't worry about it, Emily," said Elsa. "There's room enough in the top three for all I want to take away."

She finished her packing quickly, for it was growing dark and she had no wish to be in the house after night had fallen. Her packing finished, she took a last look round, and then, with a feeling of thankfulness that she was leaving behind her so much that was mean and sordid and altogether unhappy, she went downstairs, handed the key to the lawyer's clerk, and submitted to the tearful farewells of the daily help, who, in virtue of the publicity which she had acquired, had assumed the style of an old family retainer. Elsa was very glad when the cab turned into Colville Gardens, and the drear thoroughfare was lost to sight, as she hoped, forever.

Leaving the largest and the least necessary of the boxes in the hotel store, she paid her bill, and, with the remainder of her baggage, went on to Herbert Mansions. Her promised visit to Mrs Trene Hallam could no longer be postponed, but she went in the spirit of one who had before her an experience both unpleasant and inevitable.

THE VISITOR

Ralph Hallam opened the window for the sixth time and looked out. There was no cab in sight, and he returned to his armchair before the fireplace, already littered with the ashes of his cigarettes.

"It is many years since you waited for me like that, Ralph," said Mrs Hallam, without resentment.

"I fail to remember that I ever waited," he snapped. "Don't get funny, Lou."

The woman laughed softly.

"What is he like, the old boy?" she asked. "Am I supposed to be on my best behaviour, or do I treat him as one of ourselves?"

"The 'old boy' is my banker, one of the leading men of the City of London, who will jump out of his skin at the first sound of anything raw."

Mrs Hallam sighed heavily.

"Whenever you fix a dinner party for me," she said in despair, "you always bring the dead ones! If this is the kind of life you live, Ralph, I wonder you don't grow old! Personally, I like a party that starts with cocktails and finishes with breakfast."

He made a little grimace of distaste.

"That's vulgar, I suppose," she said, watching him closely. "Put it down to my gutter training – you haven't mentioned the word 'gutter' for a week. And here's your young and beautiful lady." She rose, as the distant tinkle of the bell came to her.

Until Elsa had been shown her quarters, a beautifully furnished bedroom and a tiny sitting-room, she had no idea that Ralph was in the flat.

"I thought I'd come and see you installed," he said, as he shook hands.

She was not sorry he was there, for she felt a little ill at ease in the presence of his "sister-in-law."

"We have a very dear friend of ours coming to dinner tonight, and a friend of yours too, I think," said Mrs Hallam archly. "You know dear Mr Tuckerwill?"

"Tupperwill," said Ralph loudly.

Elsa observed the slip, and wondered how dear a friend he could be that she had forgotten his name.

"He isn't exactly a friend of mine. I've met him twice – poor man!"

"He's quite recovered," said Ralph.

Then, seeing that his wife was in the dark as to Tupperwill's injury, and was likely to betray the fact that she had never met him before in her life, he made some excuse and took her out of the room.

"Tupperwill was held up the other night by thugs. And remember his name, please," he said unpleasantly. "That girl is as sharp as needles – there was no need whatever for you to call him your dear friend; you've never met him."

"What is he coming for, anyway?"

"He is coming," said Ralph deliberately, "in order mainly to counteract any bad impression which you may make. I want this girl to feel a little more confidence in you than she does. At the moment she is nervous, and unless she gets more comfortable, you'll find she has an urgent message calling her back to the hotel, and I don't want that. In the next few days I'm giving her an insight into my profession."

"Which is –?"

"Never you mind what it is. She will be helpful. Now do you understand?"

147

Already Elsa was wishing she had not come, or that the ordeal was over, for ordeal undoubtedly it was. She did not trust Mrs Trene Hallam. Her sweetness was superficial and insincere. There was no disguising the hardness that lay beneath that all too ready smile.

Mr Tupperwill arrived a little later, just after she had changed for dinner and had returned to the drawing room. He looked none the worse for his adventure, and was, if anything, a little more talkative. The solemn eyes lightened at the sight of her and he hurried across the room to offer a very warm, soft hand.

"This is indeed a delightful surprise," he said. "We meet in circumstances which are a little more favourable to polite conversation!"

"You know my sister-in-law," said Ralph, and Mrs Hallam who could recall previous acquaintances on the spur of the moment, was at her gushing best.

Nevertheless, as a social event, the dinner was an abject failure. Lou was bored to extinction; the girl's face wore a strained look as her uneasiness increased; and the only person thoroughly satisfied with things as he found them was Mr Tupperwill, who, having got on to his favourite topic, which was the derivations of the English language, was prepared to do all the talking, and would have continued his discourse on philology until the end of the evening, if Ralph had not brought him back to a less gentle theme.

"No, the police have made no discovery," said Mr Tupperwill shaking his head mournfully. "I was rather annoyed that the police knew anything about it, and I can't understand how, unless Major Amery told them. I am sure you would not have taken that step, my dear Hallam."

"Of course I told them," said Ralph promptly.

Mr Tupperwill looked pained.

"It was my duty. I suppose Bickerson came to see you?"

"He has seen me twice," said Mr Tupperwill. "An extremely pleasant man, but immensely inquisitive. By the way" – he dropped his voice and leant over toward Ralph, and his tone became confidential and beyond the hearing of the rest of the company – "what you expected has happened. A certain person has closed his account!"

Ralph glanced significantly at the girl, and Mr Tupperwill showed signs of momentary confusion.

"He has, has he? I thought he would – I could have betted on it!"

Mr Tupperwill did not bet, and said so.

"I would like to discuss the matter later," he added, with his eyes on Elsa Marlowe.

The opportunity came when Mrs Hallam carried her away to see the photographs of her prize dogs.

"He has closed the account, you say? And taken away the box also?"

Tupperwill nodded.

"This is the first and last time I shall ever be guilty of discussing the business of the bank, even with my best friend," he said soberly. "Without accepting your theory, which I dismissed rather hastily as preposterous, that Amery had anything whatever to do with my terrible experience, I am satisfied that a business man is on the safest side by keeping a quiet tongue."

He delivered this sentiment with the air of one who had made a great discovery, and swayed back to observe the effect.

"Yes, he has closed the account without giving any explanation, and I can only assure you that I am very, very happy about it. You can have no conception of the state of mind I have been in for the past week or so, at the thought that Stebbing's held an account of a man who, although to outward appearance is a respected member of society, may – I only say may – be connected, directly or indirectly, with an enterprise which, possibly inoffensive in itself, would be looked upon with disfavour by my directors."

Having stated this reserved opinion, Mr Tupperwill waved his hand as though to dismiss the subject.

The door opened and Lou came in. Ralph Hallam saw by her face that something disturbing had happened.

"A man wishes to see you, Ralph. He says he would like to speak to you alone."

"Who is it?"

"Mr Bickerson."

The two men exchanged glances.

"Are you sure it is Mr Hallam and not me?" asked Tupperwill.

"No, he wants to see Ralph. Perhaps, Mr Tupperwill, you will come along and see my photographs?"

The fat man was apparently only too glad of an excuse to join the girl, on whom he had cast many furtive and admiring glances in the course of the meal, and in his haste preceded his hostess from the room. A few seconds later Bickerson came in and closed the door behind him.

"Do you want to see me particularly? Has anything turned up?"

"Yes, something has turned up," said Bickerson. His voice was cold, his manner a little distant. Uninvited, he took the chair that Tupperwill had vacated. "At the end of the garden in Elgin Crescent," he said, "there is a line of railings running parallel with the sidewalk, and a clump of laurel bushes, into which anybody passing along Ladbroke Grove might toss something and be pretty confident that it would never appear again. Unfortunately, the gardeners have been at work on trimming the bushes, and they found this."

He took out of his pocket a small fluted phial with a red label and put it on the table. Ralph gazed at it steadily, and did not betray by so much as a flicker of eyelid his interest in this damning piece of evidence.

"When it was found it contained about four drachms of tincture of opium, which is the medical name for laudanum," Bickerson went on. "It was purchased at a chemist's in Piccadilly a day before Tarn's death. The name in the poison book is yours, Hallam. Now I'm going to tell you something."

He shifted the chair round to face the other squarely.

"Part of the medical evidence at the inquest was suppressed, at my request. It was that laudanum had been found in the body of old Tarn, and that the brandy bottle at his elbow was also heavily doped. You can take your time to explain, but I warn you that anything you may say may be taken down and used against you in a certain event."

"What event is that?" asked Hallam steadily.

"In the event of my charging you with Tarn's murder," was the reply.

PACE

Ralph took up the bottle and examined it with an amused smile.

"Perfectly true," he said coolly. "I purchased this tincture of opium at Keppell's – on behalf of Tarn. As a matter of detail, I prescribed laudanum for him – he suffered from insomnia. The fact that the bottle was found in the bushes makes it look suspicious, eh? In the ash-can it would have been damning, I suppose? And is that the new police theory, that Mr Maurice Tarn died of opium poisoning? I seem to remember a small blackhandled knife: had not that something to do with his lamented death?"

"Do you suggest that Tarn put the laudanum in his own brandy?" demanded Bickerson.

"I suggest nothing," said Ralph with a shrug. "It is not my business to make suggestions. For the moment, I am rejecting certain innuendoes which connect me with Tarn's death."

He looked at the detective thoughtfully.

"If it were my business I should suggest how remarkable it was that you did not make any reference at the inquest to the telephone conversation you had with Mr Tarn."

The detective's face flushed an angry red.

"That wasn't necessary," he said stiffly. "The telephone conversation which occurred in your presence involved the name of a third person. There was a whole lot of evidence not produced at the inquest, Hallam – for example, I thought it wise not to refer to the fact that two hours before Tarn's death you were in the house – "

"With Miss Marlowe," interrupted Ralph.

"You were in the house, and had ample opportunity for going to his room and doping the brandy he drank, and which you knew he would drink, having a good idea of his habits."

Ralph laughed.

"Then you suggest that Miss Marlowe was a party to my doping the brandy? I tell you she was in the house all the time, and I left her there. And why should I want to dope him?"

The detective did not answer this last question immediately. Instead:

"I have cross-examined Miss Marlowe very thoroughly, and I know that she left you on the study floor and went up to her room to pack. She intended spending the night with a relation of yours. She left you alone for ten minutes. And as to the other matter, I'm going to speak straight to you, Hallam. I have every reason to believe that you were associated with Tarn in his dope-running business. If that is so, and by some means you got to know that the old man had asked to see me at nine o'clock that night, there is a possibility that you may have suspected that he intended making a statement which would incriminate you. I'll tell you frankly that I do not believe the story that you procured this laudanum for Tarn and at his request."

Ralph stiffened. He was alert now. The danger he had thought was past had reappeared in its most alarming form.

"I don't like your tone, Bickerson," he said. "If you believe that I was running dope, or that I am in any way connected with Tarn, or responsible, directly or indirectly, for his death, your course is a very simple one."

Bickerson's face was expressionless, and Ralph saw that he was not prepared to accept the challenge which had been thrown out.

"Maybe it is," said the detective, "but I am pretty certain just what I shall find if I go farther into this matter. The laudanun will be in your prescription book, under Tarn's name."

Suddenly he laughed and held out his hand.

"I'm afraid I've annoyed you, doctor, but this murder has rather rattled me, and the dope gang has got me thoroughly at sea. In a few days I shall know much more about them than I know now."

He picked up the laudanum bottle from the table, looked at it with a little grimace, and put the phial in his pocket.

"I want to get just a little more information, and there will be sad hearts in dreamland!" he said cryptically.

Ralph showed him to the door, and the man stood outside for a while, cogitating, before, with a brusque "Goodnight," he passed down the wide stairs into the street. As Dr Hallam closed the door on him, the tension relaxed and he sat down heavily upon a hall chair and wiped his streaming forehead.

What a fool he had been! It would have been a simple matter to carry the phial home and put it in the furnace; but a moment of over anxiety had led him to commit a folly which might well have proved his undoing. Bickerson was right in one respect, the prescription book in Half Moon Street would show the destination of that small bottle. Strangely enough, it had been an act of precaution, taken as an after-thought, and he blessed the inspiration which had led him to scrawl a bogus prescription in a volume which nowadays was very seldom used.

It was fully five minutes before he had composed himself and strolled into the drawing-room. Lou looked up with an anxious, enquiring glance as he came in, but could read nothing from his face. Elsa was playing at the piano, with the stout Mr Tupperwill, one podgy finger on the leaf of the music, ready to turn the page at her nod.

"Anything wrong?" asked Mrs Hallam in a low voice.

"Nothing," said Ralph. "He wanted to see me about Tarn."

He glanced at Tupperwill and smiled again.

"Almost looks as if he's fallen," he said.

Mrs Hallam nodded.

"He's certainly got it bad," she said, and for some perverse reason Ralph Hallam was pleased.

Yet he had no thought of influencing the banker when he had invited him to that informal dinner. His sole object had been to create a little confidence in the unquiet mind of the girl. Sensitive to her moods, he realised something of her uneasiness, and had played Tupperwill for respectability.

"A beautiful piece, a very bee-u-tiful piece!" sighed Mr Tupperwill, turning the last page reluctantly. " 'Peace, perfect Peace!' It is the motto on which my house is run. It is the keynote of my life. My private safe opens to the combination 'Pace' – a root word – er – um…" He saw Mrs Hallam's eager eyes fixed on him and shifted uncomfortably. "Do you sing, Miss Marlowe?" he asked, turning to the girl.

Elsa laughed.

"I sing behind locked doors," she said solemnly. "Which means that I realize my limitations."

Mr Tupperwill sighed again.

"It is a great pity." His eyes were full of undisguised admiration. "A very great pity. I can imagine you charming vast audiences, or, shall I say, bringing ecstasy to the heart of an audience – of one! You have great gifts, Miss Marlowe."

Elsa laughed aloud.

"It is very pleasant to hear that," she said drily. "I will set your compliment against the many unflattering things I hear in the course of the day."

"Which means that Amery has the manners of a pig," said Ralph. "Amery?" Mr Tupperwill looked round with a start of surprise. "Surely you are not associated with Mr Amery?"

"I work in his office, if that is an association," said the girl, a little nettled.

Why she should resent even the oblique disparagement in Mr Tupperwill's tone she did not know exactly. But she did.

"It is a mistake to think that I hear many uncomplimentary things from Major Amery," she said; "and if all the stories I hear from office girls are true, then it is a great advantage to have an employer who is neither soft-spoken nor too friendly!"

Mr Tupperwill pulled at his lip

"That is true," he said, "that is very true. You will quite understand that I am not saying a word derogatory to Major Amery," he hastened to protest. "It would indeed be a most improper act on my part to detract (from 'de,' away, 'trahere,' to draw or pull – in other words, to take away) from his merits. That indeed would be unpardonable."

Elsa changed the subject somewhat gauchely, and a few minutes later found herself being initiated into the mysteries of bridge.

At ten-thirty Mr Tupperwill glanced at his watch and uttered a note of alarm.

"I fear I have overstayed my welcome," he said, "but I have had a most delightful evening, a perfectly delightful evening! I can never thank you enough for giving me this opportunity of getting out of myself, my dear Hallam."

He looked from one to the other, his smooth brow bent.

"Would it be regarded as an impertinence if I invited you to dine with me tomorrow night – would that interfere very much with your arrangements?"

Elsa had no arrangements, and no particular desires except, at the earliest possible moment, to find a small flat and bring her visit to the earliest possible conclusion. Ralph saved her the embarrassment of replying by a prompt acceptance of the invitation. He accompanied Mr Tupperwill to his car, and when he returned the girl had gone, and Mrs Hallam was sitting on the hearth-rug, smoking a meditative cigarette before the fire.

"Who is he?" she asked, looking up.

"My banker. Where is Elsa?"

Mrs Hallam jerked her head in the direction of Elsa's room.

"Am I supposed to go to this party of his tomorrow night?" she asked. "That old man is certainly the slowest thing that has happened since horse buses went out. And you're a fool to let her go, anyway, Ralph. The old boy is dippy about her."

"About Elsa?" Ralph chuckled. "Yes, I thought he was rather smitten."

"He's married, of course?" said Mrs Hallam, blowing a ring of smoke at the fire.

"He isn't married: that kind of man won't marry, either."

"Won't he?" said the woman sardonically. "Tupperwill is the kind of man that keeps himself single and solvent till he's sixty, and then hands over his latch-key and principles to the first fluffy chorus girl who tells him the story of her sad life. Look out for your Elsa, my boy. Is he rich?"

"Beyond the dreams of actresses," said Ralph cynically.

She gazed moodily into the fire, and then:

"Are you rich, Ralph?"

He looked down at her quickly.

"What do you mean?"

"That's not a particularly difficult question to answer, is it?" she asked impatiently. "Are you rich?"

"Not so rich as I shall be," said Ralph softly. "In a week's time I hope to be one million one hundred and seventy-four thousand dollars richer than I am today."

That was the amount that had been pencilled on the little memorandum he had found in Tarn's safe. And the money was somewhere. He had a shrewd idea that, given the opportunity for making a careful examination of Paul Amery's study, he would have no difficulty in locating the stolen property.

Mrs Hallam made no comment, and they sat in silence until she threw the end of the cigarette into the fire.

"You're an optimist, both in love and finance," she said; "and I've an idea that it is going to be more trouble to get that girl than it is to get the money. What does 'Pace' mean, Ralph?"

A LETTER TO KEEP

Elsa slept more soundly than she had done in weeks, and felt almost reconciled to her stay when she was summoned to the pretty little dining-room to eat a solitary breakfast. Mrs Hallam had warned her that she did not rise before midday, and the girl was by no means sorry to have her own company for breakfast. The flats were service apartments: cleaners came when summoned, meals were procured from the kitchen in the basement, and Mrs Hallam's one maid was quite sufficient to serve the needs of this economical lady.

Major Amery had not arrived at the office when Elsa took the cover off her typewriter, and he did not come in until nearly eleven o'clock. Ordinarily, he went straight to his own bureau through the private door, but on this occasion he came through her office and, glancing up to bid him good morning, she thought he looked unusually tired and haggard.

"Morning," he said gruffly, before he disappeared into his room, slamming the door behind him.

A few minutes after, Feng Ho came in, greeting her with his typical grin.

"Has Mister Major Amery arrived?" he asked, dropping his voice when she answered. "Nocturnal peregrinations produce morning tardiness," he added.

Something in his face attracted her attention.

"You look as if you've had nocturnal peregrinations yourself, Feng Ho," she said, for she noticed the deep lines under his eyes.

"As a bachelor of science I consume unlimited midnight oil," he said calmly, "first placing Pi in a condition of obfuscation."

"What on earth is that?" she asked, startled.

"In a dark room," said Feng Ho, "where the actinic rays cannot delude into a similitude of daylight and create singings when silence is desirable."

He looked anxiously at the door of Amery's room.

"Do you want to see the Major?"

"No, miss," he said hastily, "not until contemplation has eradicated suspicion of a fantastical imaginativeness."

She detected an uneasiness in his manner which was unusual in this serene man, whose calm no circumstances had ever ruffled to her knowledge. She had noticed before that Feng Ho's agitation was invariably betrayed by his speech. In normal moments his English was unimpeachable; it was only when he was perturbed that he disdained simple language, and expressed his thoughts in words of four syllables.

"Yes, I will see him," he said suddenly. "Grasping nettles firmly destroys virulence of poison stings."

And before she realised what he was doing, he had tapped at and opened the door, slipping through and closing it behind him. Listening, she heard Amery's sharp voice raised almost in anger. He was speaking in Chinese (she guessed this) and she heard the murmur of Feng Ho's reply. Presently the voices were lost in the clatter of her typewriter, for Elsa was not by nature curious, and whilst she could wonder what the Chinaman had done to annoy her irascible employer, she was not especially anxious to know.

It was fully half an hour before Feng Ho came out, his face beaming, and, with a wriggling little bow, disappeared to his own den. The bell rang, and she took her book into the sanctum, to find Major Amery sitting on the fender seat, his chin on his breast, a dejected and dispirited-looking figure. He looked up sharply as she entered, fixed her for a moment with his steely eyes, and then:

"I think you'd better stay on at Mrs Hallam's" he said. "She's a kleptomaniac, but she won't steal anything from you."

"Major Amery!" she gasped.

"I want to say nothing against the woman," he continued, unmindful of her amazement and indignation. "She'll let you stay there as long as you want. If I were you, I'd get my traps and settle down for a week or two, at any rate. After that, nothing matters."

"I really don't understand you. Mrs Trene Hallam has been very kind – "

He interrupted her with an impatient gesture.

"Mrs Hallam you can forget; she's just – nothing. Ralph. I don't think you need worry about Ralph either."

"Dr Hallam is a great friend, and a very old friend of mine," she said, with what, she felt, was a ludicrous attempt to stand on her dignity.

His tired eyes were searching her face.

"A very great friend? Of course…a very great friend. Still – you need not worry about Ralph." Then, abruptly: "I want you to do something for me."

She waited, as he walked to the desk, took out a sheet of paper and began to write rapidly. Seven, eight, nine lines of writing she counted, then he signed his name with a flourish, blotted the sheet and enclosed it in an envelope, the flap of which he covered with a wafer seal. She saw him write a name on the envelope, and when he had blotted this he handed the letter to her. To her amazement it was addressed to "Dr Ralph Hallam," and was marked "Private."

"I want you to keep this letter. Have it where you can reach it at any hour of the day or night," he said, speaking rapidly. "Hallam may not be as bad as I think he is, but if he is any better I am a greatly mistaken man."

"What am I to do with the letter?" she asked blankly. "Keep it to your hand," he said, with a touch of his old irritability. "If Hallam gets…difficult, if any situation arises which you find impossible to handle…give him this letter."

"But, Major Amery, I really don't know what you're talking about. What situation can arise?" she said, holding the letter irresolutely, looking from him to the scrawled address.

"Tuck it away in your handbag by day and under your pillow by night. If Hallam ever forgets what is due to him…let me put it clearly: if you are ever afraid of him, give him the letter."

She shook her head smilingly and held the envelope toward him. "I shan't require this," she said. "I tell you, Dr Hallam and I are very old friends. He was a friend of poor Mr Tarn's – "

"I asked you to do something for me," he interrupted her sharply, "and that is all I want you to do. I am not in the habit of asking favours, but I'll break my practice and ask this: keep the letter and use it if an emergency arises. Will you do this?"

She hesitated, and then: "I think it is very unnecessary and highly mysterious," she smiled in spite of herself; "but if you wish me to do it, I will."

"Good," he said briskly. "Now we will initiate a business-like correspondence with our American friends of the Cleveland Police Department – I am anxious to know something about a gentleman who is at the moment in durance. Take this:

> To John L Territet, Chief of Police,
> Cleveland, Ohio.

SIR,
Yesterday I cabled asking you if you would kindly inform me whether the man Philip Moropoulos –

She looked up in surprise.

"I thought I knew the name! He was a man arrested in connection with the drug traffic. I read it in the newspapers."

He nodded, and went on:

– whether the man Philip Moropoulos, now under arrest in your city, is known to have any English alias. For a special reason I am trying to identify him with a man named –

There came a tap at the door. It was a girl clerk from the lower office, and she held a cablegram in her hand. Elsa took it and passed it across the table to Amery.

"Humph!" he said, and tore it open. "That is a coincidence. You needn't bother about that letter."

Absent-mindedly he pushed the message across toward her, and she read:

Amery Co., London. Charge against Moropoulos fell through. Released and now on his way to England.

It was signed "Police Chief."

"Humph!" said Amery again. "Released, is he? That is bad news for somebody."

Elsa did not ask who that "somebody" was, and indeed was surprised that he had shown her such unusual confidence. Apparently he realised for the first time that he had given her the cable to read, for he almost snatched it back.

"That will do," he said curtly. "I'll ring for you when I want you, which won't be for some time."

A CUSTOMER OF THE BANK

Mr Tupperwill's house in Grosvenor Place was a model of what a banker's establishment should be. From garret to cellar it was a pattern of order, neatness, and quiet luxury. It was a house where everything went according to schedule, from six o'clock in the morning, when the under-housemaid kindled the kitchen fire and stoked the furnace, to eleven-thirty, when the butler carefully bolted the front door, locked the pantry and turned out the last of the hall lights.

At any moment Mr Tupperwill, by consulting a neat typewritten time table, which was invariably kept in the top right-hand drawer of his table, could tell exactly what every servant was doing, the condition of every room, and the amount of petrol in the tanks of each of his motor-cars. On Thursday afternoons at five o'clock Mr Tupperwill received the exact time from the telephone exchange, and, checking his watch to the second, made the round of the rooms and wound up and set his innumerable clocks, for the collection of clocks was not the least pleasurable of Mr Tupperwill's hobbies.

He breakfasted at eight-thirty every morning, on two devilled kidneys, a crisp slice of bacon, three pieces of toast and two cups of coffee. He never had more and he never had less. When he had breakfasted, he glanced through three financial newpapers, folded ready at his elbow, and read *The Times* financial article. At nine-twenty-five, almost to the minute, he went out into the hall, was helped on with his fur-lined coat, and usually the half hour was chiming as he walked down the steps to his waiting car. Taking leave of him at the door, his butler was wont to remark that it was a cold day, a wet day, or a fine day, according to the meteorological conditions; and it was Mr Tupperwill's practice to agree entirely with all that his butler said. It was the only point on which they met as man to man, all other items of news than the weather being communicated to Mr Tupperwill by his valet.

On this particular morning, however, the banker broke his habits by ringing for the butler before he had finished his breakfast.

"Weeks, I am having a party tonight."

"Yes, sir," said Weeks, wondering which particular party was in Mr Tupperwill's mind.

"There will be four to dinner, including myself. Arrange with one of the maids – a trustworthy maid – to look after the ladies. My bedroom may be used as a retiring room – yes, I think so," said Mr Tupperwill thoughtfully. "And you will see that such things as ladies may require are placed on the dressing-table – powder and that sort of thing. You will consult the housekeeper as to the colour and quality, and purchase whatever receptacles are required."

"Yes, sir," said the wondering Mr Weeks.

"The dinner had better be a little more elaborate than usual," the banker went on. "Soup – Julienne, I think; sole mornay; poulet a la reine; a bombed glace and a savoury; I think that will be excellent. A good champagne and a light German wine for the ladies – that also will be admirable."

"At what hour sir?"

"At half past eight. Have a bridge table placed in the drawing-room…"

He gave a few other minor instructions and went to the bank five minutes late.

Though by nature lethargic, he spent a very busy morning, for, like Major Amery, he opened and usually answered all letters addressed to himself, and seldom requisitioned the services of the anaemic young woman who acted as his secretary.

The business of Stebbing's Bank was, as has already been explained, a peculiar one. Many of the names of Stebbing's clients were unknown, even to the nearest and dearest of their possessors. Great merchants, and small merchants for the matter of that, professional men, and even the leading lights of other banks, found it extremely convenient to have an account which was not identifiable with their better-known names.

Often it was the case that there was nothing discreditable in this desire for anonymity. A reluctance to let the right hand know what the left hand does belongs to no class and to no age. Curious income-tax officials might see the books of Stebbings and be baffled. Inquisitive busybodies, wondering who was behind certain theatrical productions, might discover the name of the gentleman who drew the cheques that paid all the salaries, when the box office failed to supply the needful, and yet hardly guess that the plain "T Smith" that appeared in the south-east corner of the cheque, disguised the identity of a merchant who would never be suspected of such frivolity.

Mr Tupperwill was the repository of many secrets; and if his bank suffered any disadvantage from the possession of so many anonymous clients, it was that current accounts offered a conservative banker very few opportunities for building up big profits. Nevertheless, Tupperwill had his share of general banking business, his pickings of short time loans, his discounts and the other "makings" which add to a banker's revenue.

Usually, he was so engrossed between the hours of a quarter to ten and half past one, that he did not see visitors except upon the most urgent business. So that when his elderly accountant appeared in the doorway with a card in his hand, Mr Tupperwill frowned and waved his hand in protest.

"Not now, my dear man, not now," he said reproachfully. "I really can't see anybody. Who is it?"

"The account that was closed yesterday," said the accountant.

Mr Tupperwill sat bolt upright.

"Amery?" he asked in a whisper.

"Yes, sir. He said he wouldn't keep you more than ten minutes."

Mr Tupperwill pushed back the table lamp by which he had been working – he was rather short-sighted – thrust some papers into a leather folder, and only then took the card and stared at it as though he could read on its conventional surface some answer to the enigma which this call of Major Amery presented.

"Ask him to come in," he said in a hushed voice, and put the Louis Quinze chair in its place.

Amery walked into the room and was received with just that amount of deference and distant courtesy which his position as an ex-client of the bank demanded.

"I have called because I felt that some explanation was due to you, Mr Tupperwill. I closed my account with you yesterday."

Mr Tupperwill nodded seriously.

"It was reported to me," he said, "and I must confess that I was both surprised and – relieved."

A faint smile played about the hard lips of the man from India. "Your relief being due to the unsatisfactory character of the client, rather than the nature of the account, which was a fairly heavy one?"

"It was a fairly heavy one," agreed Mr Tupperwill, "but it was, if you will allow me the observation, mysterious."

"Are not all your accounts mysterious?" asked Amery coldly, to which the banker made no reply.

"I could not escape the feeling," he said instead, "that you were using Stebbing's as a – a makeshift. I am sure you will forgive me if I am in error. But the impermanence of your account was one of its unsatisfactory features."

"It was intended to be permanent," said Amery coolly. "I will make a confession to you – that I opened my account with Stebbing's for a special purpose. I will be even more frank and tell you that it was my intention to engineer an irregularity which would have given me the right to go to the courts for an examination of your books."

Mr Tupperwill gasped at this monstrous confession.

"I now know that such a course would have been futile. In fact, I knew less about banking than I thought."

"You wanted to examine my books?" said Mr Tupperwill slowly, as the hideous nature of the plot began to penetrate. "I – I've never heard anything like it!"

"I don't suppose you have. But, you see, Mr Tupperwill, you live a very sheltered life," said the other. "As I say, when I found that the scheme I had at the back of my mind was impracticable, and moreover, discovered on the same day all that I wanted to know, I removed my account. Tupperwill, who is John Stillman?"

Paul Amery had a fatal facility for making people jump. Mr Tupperwill almost leapt from his chair at the words.

"Stillman?" he stammered. "I – I don't understand you."

"Nobody understands me, probably because I speak too plainly," said Amery. "You carry the account of a man named Stillman; a bigger account than mine, and a much more dangerous one. Stebbing's Bank would survive having me on its list of clients, but Stillman's is one that will tumble you, your fortune and your bank into mud so thick that it will choke you!"

For a second the banker stared at him in horror, and then: "I refuse, I absolutely refuse to discuss the business of the bank," he said, bringing his hand down on the table with a crash. "It is disgraceful… unbusinesslike…how dare you, sir – "

Amery silenced him with a gesture.

"It may be all the things you say, but I tell you that Stillman, unless I am greatly mistaken in his identity, is more deadly than a snake."

"I refuse to discuss the matter," said Mr Tupperwill furiously, as he pressed his bell. "You are talking about a lady, sir; a very charming lady, sir; a lady who, although she occupies an humble position in your office in the City, is nevertheless entitled to my respect, my admiration and my homage, sir."

Amery looked at him aghast.

"A lady?" he said incredulously. "In the City, in my office? Good God!"

THE SPECULATOR

John Stillman, the mystery client of Stebbing's Bank, was Elsa Marlowe! The sinister man could only gaze, speechless, at the red-faced banker. Maurice Tarn's niece! Was she in it, after all?

"You are speaking of Miss Marlowe, I presume?"

"I am speaking of nobody, sir." Mr Tupperwill was hoarse with anger. "You have asked me to betray a sacred confidence: I shall never forgive you."

The accountant was in the room now.

"Show Major Amery from these premises, and under no circumstances is he to be admitted again!"

Amery was still looking down at him.

"Either you have been grossly deceived and tricked, or else you're lying, Tupperwill," he said. "Miss Marlowe has no account with your bank, either in her own or anybody else's name."

"I decline, I absolutely decline, to speak another word. There is the door, sir."

The visitor was about to say something, but checked himself, and, turning on his heel, walked out.

For a quarter of an hour Mr Tupperwill sat simmering in his rage, and at the end of that time had sufficiently recovered to ring for his accountant.

"Bring Mr Stillman's account," he said sharply.

"I was going to speak to you about that, sir – "

"Then don't!" snarled the ruffled banker. "Bring me the account."

A few minutes later, a book was placed before him and opened, and by this time he was something of his urbane self.

"You must forgive my – er – petulance, but Major Amery annoyed me; he annoyed me very much."

He looked at the page before him, and his face fell.

"He's not overdrawn," he said.

"No, sir, he's not overdrawn, but that is all one can say. His speculations have been colossal. Look at these." He ran his finger down a column of figures. "They're all broker's cheques. He has been dealing in Angora Oil: we carried a whole lot of the stock for him, but it fell from fifty-seven to thirteen in a week. I was going to ask you to see Mr Stillman."

"Never seen him yourself?" asked the banker without looking up.

"No, sir; the account was opened with you, and I don't remember that the client has ever been to the bank. I always thought that the cheque signatures looked like a lady's."

"That will do, that will do, Thomas," said Mr Tupperwill testily. "I will write to Mr Stillman myself. So far as I can see, he has lost considerably over a quarter of a million this half year."

He closed the book with a bang and waved it away.

A quarter of a million, he thought with a sense of dismay, and thrown into the gutter!

To Mr Tupperwill, capital was a living thing, and that it could be treated cruelly pained him. A quarter of a million mangled and tortured into nothingness! The thought was frightful. He reached for a sheet of paper and began a letter. Halfway through he read it over with an expression of dissatisfaction, and, carrying it to the fireplace, lit a match and watched the paper burn into curling black ashes. He did no more work that day: he was too occupied with his thoughts.

Toward four o'clock he rang for his accountant.

"I am worried, terribly worried, about Stillman's account," he said. "The truth is – er – unless I have been grossly deceived, Stillman is a pseudonym (from the Greek 'pseudo,' meaning false) for a young lady who was introduced to the bank some years ago, on the assurance that she had inherited a large sum of money."

"Indeed, sir?" said the accountant, whom nothing surprised. "A lady of title?"

"No, not a lady of title," said Mr Tupperwill uncomfortably. "In fact, she holds quite a subordinate – er – position in a London business house. I understood that she was fitting herself for a commercial career and starting, as it were, at the bottom of the ladder. I need not tell you that I deprecate the incursion of the gentler sex into the sordid struggle of commerce, but that is neither here nor there."

"What am I to do if further cheques come in?" asked the accountant, practically. "Mr or Miss Stillman has only the barest balance."

Mr Tupperwill looked up at the ceiling.

"I think I should honour the cheques," he said softly. "Yes, I think I should honour them. Unless, of course, they are for a large sum – an excessive sum."

"I wanted to know, sir," said the accountant, "because I've just had a cheque in for twenty-five thousand pounds, drawn by Stillman, and there's less than fifty to meet it."

Mr Tupperwill went very pale.

STAYING ON

If, obeying his bell, Elsa Marlowe had entered the room of the sinister man and found him standing on his head, she felt she would not have been surprised. He was guilty of such extraordinary behaviour that she felt she was beyond amazement, and was almost resigned even to his impertinent interest in her affairs.

Although several times she was on the point of destroying the letter which he had thrust upon her, she was checked on each occasion by a feeling that in doing so she would be acting disloyally to one who, she was quite certain, had no ill will toward her. That he might be using her for his own purpose, playing her off against Ralph Hallam, she thought was more than possible. But since his revelation, her feelings had changed entirely toward her sometime friend. Even now she could not grasp the extent of Hallam's offence. Occasionally she had read in the newspapers stories of "dope fiends," but the practice had only an academic interest for her. She thought it was unpleasant, and that was all, for she had never been brought into contact with the victims of this vice, and her imagination was of that healthy type which did not dwell upon morbidities.

But though she was ready to endure much, Major Amery's conduct that afternoon was especially trying. Nothing seemed to please him. He snapped and snarled like an angry dog, exploded violently and with the least excuse, and raged through the offices, major and minor, like a devastating wind, leaving elderly sub-managers dazed and breathless, and junior clerks on the point of mutiny.

"He reminds me," said Miss Dame, in a tremble of wrath, "of one of those bullying head cowboys who go around making up to the boss' daughter, and are always punching people or shooting them, till the handsome young fellow arrives that has had a row with his father who's a millionaire, and he comes in and throws a glass of rum in the head cowboy's face – from what I read in the papers, they've got more rum than they know what to do with over there – "

"And what has he been doing to you?" asked Elsa good-humouredly.

"What hasn't he been doing?" asked the wrathful young lady. "A bullying, hectoring hound, that's what he is, a bullying hectoring hound! I'd like my pater to say a few words to him. My pater would just look at him and he'd curl up."

"I'm sure your father wouldn't curl up," said Elsa, wilfully dense.

"I don't mean pater, I mean that woman-worrying vampire! Which reminds me, Miss Marlowe – when are you coming home to have a cup of tea? You haven't seen our new house."

Here was an invitation which Elsa had most successfully evaded for a long time.

"Some day," she said vaguely.

"Of course, we're not your style," said Miss Dame, "but father's a perfect gentleman, and you wouldn't see a nicer houseful of furniture in the West End of London."

Elsa laughed.

"I shan't come to see your furniture, Jessie. Honestly, I'll come just as soon as I can. This dreadful inquest – "

"I understand perfectly, my dear," said Miss Dame, with a tragic look of melancholy. "I know just how you feel. I've seen Pearl Winsome that way often. And as to his nibs – "

A faint sound in the next room, which might have been the creak of a chair, or the tap of a paper-knife against an inkstand, was sufficient to send Miss Dame into hasty retreat.

Elsa was dismissed that afternoon nearly an hour earlier than usual, and she was glad of the extra time, for she wanted to call at the hotel to get her trunks and the little instrument that had given her so much pleasure in the days when she was glad to get away from Maurice Tarn and the everlasting scent of brandy, and catch from the ether the mystery music that came from nowhere, and was miraculously caught on the silk-covered wires of her small frame aerial.

Between the hotel, where she recovered her belongings, and Herbert Mansions, it came to her that a few hours before she had not the slightest intention of remaining the guest of Mrs Trene Hallam a day longer than was necessary. Yet here she was, with her box on top of a taxicab, en route to her home, content to extend her visit for an indefinite period! She did not ask herself the reason for this change of mind: only too well she knew. Major Paul Amery had settled the matter in two sentences. She was almost resigned to his tyrannical will.

Mrs Hallam watched the erection of the wireless apparatus with more interest than enthusiasm, and seemed relieved when the girl told her that she intended keeping the strange contraption in her bedroom.

"It looks dangerous to me," said Mrs Hallam decisively. "All those wires and electricity and things...I should hate to have it around...how does it work?"

But here Elsa was in no better position than the average devotee of wireless.

"You're coming to stay then?" asked Lou, as the girl was fixing the terminals. There was no great encouragement in her tone.

"You asked me to stay a month," said Elsa, a little uncomfortably.

"As long as you like, my dear," and the lady's attempt to enthuse some warmth into the invitation was not wholly successful.

Deep down inside her, Mrs Hallam was annoyed. She hated strangers, and was by no means impressed with one of whom she thought as "Ralph's latest." That she was pretty she was ready to confess, but it was not the kind of prettiness which Mrs Hallam favoured. In Elsa she found no spiritual affinity, though she did not exactly describe her failure in those words, even to herself.

"I suppose you'll spend a lot of your time listening to this thing?" she asked hopefully, and, when Elsa nodded, Mrs Hallam took a kindlier interest in the apparatus. Elsa explained the character of the programmes.

"Opera!" said Mrs Hallam, making a little face. "Opera's all right, but the singing spoils it. I suppose you're looking forward to meeting old what's-his-name again?"

"Mr Tupperwill?" smiled Elsa. "No, not very much."

"You don't like him?"

"I don't dislike him. He seems a very pleasant old man."

"You've made a hit with him, anyway," said the lady brusquely, "and he's got stacks of money. I suppose he's clever, but from my point of view he'd make the Dead Sea look like a soda fountain. I hate that kind of man, who talks about the things you expect him to talk about."

"Then you must like Major Amery?" said Elsa.

A faint tinge of colour came to Mrs Hallam's face, and she shivered.

"When that man dies, I'll go into white," she said viciously. So many people hated the sinister man, thought Elsa, as she finished her unpacking alone. The realisation that "so many people" did not include herself came to her in the nature of a shock.

THE GENTLEMAN FROM CLEVELAND

There was a conference at Scotland Yard, and outside that quaint "informants' door," where shabby men come creeping in the dusk of evening to tell stories to the hurt of those who have mistakenly given them their confidence, two officers were waiting to escort a man who had not yet arrived.

Sir James Boyd Fowler, Chief Commissioner of the CID, had in his office his superintendent and a detective inspector. The hour was short of five, and from time to time Mr Bickerson looked up at the clock impatiently.

"They ought to be here in a few minutes now," said Superintendent Wille, following the direction of the other's eye. "Do you expect this fellow to give you much information, Bickerson?"

"Yes, sir," nodded Bickerson. "He was in London three months before his arrest, and I have reason to believe that he was in very close touch with the amateurs, and possibly with Soyoka's crowd."

"Will he squeal?" grunted Sir James. "That's the question: will he squeal? In four days I've had three letters from the Secretary of State, asking for an encouraging report. Up to date we've had nothing. You're satisfied that Amery is the pea?"

"I was never more sure of anything," replied Bickerson promptly.

Sir James growled something under his breath. He was by nature an intolerant man, and his irascibility was considerably accentuated by the annoyance he was receiving from men higher up.

"Did Soyoka kill Tarn? Do you suggest Amery was in that?" he asked.

"I suggest that if Amery wasn't in it, he was behind it. Everything points to his being our man. His history is enough to damn him. Thrown out of the political service for trafficking in opium, he's either Soyoka or, what is more likely, the real head of the amateurs."

"But you said Hallam was that?" interrupted the superintendent.

"I'm sure Hallam is in it up to his neck – equally sure that, if Major Paul Amery is the big boss, Hallam is in total ignorance of the fact. But that is the way these gangs are worked; there's always somebody right on top, pulling all the strings, directing most of the operations, financing every deal and clearing the proceeds; and there's somebody lower down, under the impression that he's the fellow that's doing it all. Amery is a trafficker in drugs, as slippery as an eel and as cunning as the devil."

"Did you have much trouble in getting Moropoulos over, sir?" asked the superintendent.

"None whatever. The case against him was too thin, and the district attorney decided not to go on with it. The Cleveland police were in cable communication with me, and I had the inspiration to consult Bickerson and cable for the man to be brought over – he's under escort of a Cleveland detective, by the way. I think he'll talk; from the description I've had of him, he seems that kind. And if he talks, I'm going to put these people where I want them. Here's your man."

A uniformed constable hurried across the room and laid a slip before the Commissioner.

"That is he," he said. "Bring him in."

He returned escorting three men, one of whom was a Scotland Yard officer; the second, tall and lean-faced, was evidently the American detective, and the third of the party, a stout and rosy individual, who bore no sort of resemblance at all to a hardened criminal. He looked to be what he undoubtedly had been, the fairly prosperous proprietor of a small store; and though he was a Greek, his voice showed no indication of foreign birth. He bowed genially to the chief, and accepted the chair which Bickerson pushed up for him with a polite little murmur of protest.

"Yes, sir, I am Moropoulos. This gentleman is the chief?" He nodded to Sir James. "Yeh, I thought so. Now I'm going to tell you gentlemen, before we go any further, that there's no squeal coming from me. I've come to Europe because the chief at Cleveland advised me that if I could make myself useful to you, there was a chance of the police on our side dropping the case. Not that they had one, I guess, but that's a matter of opinion. The living I'll not talk about; the dead" – he emphasized the word – "why, I'm ready to say just as much about them as I think is decent. Now, Captain, shoot!"

"By the dead, I suppose you mean Maurice Tarn?"

Moropoulos nodded.

"Yes, sir, I mean Maurice Tarn. I don't know whether he was the big guy, but he was certainly one of them. I had dealings with him; I brought a whole lot of cocaine over from Germany in a specially made box. I guess you found it when you searched his lodgings. It had five wooden trays, one on top of the other – that's what you call them over here, isn't it, 'trays'?"

"I didn't see that," said Bickerson thoughtfully.

"Maybe he burnt it. I'm only just telling you that I brought the box over for him, and I had a long talk with him before I left."

"Did he say anything to you about Soyoka's gang?"

A shadow passed over the pleasant face of the Greek.

"No, sir!" he said emphatically. "It was Soyoka who got me pinched. One of the bulls tipped me off. He said I was invading the territory of his man, which is a lie, for I was the only guy working the stuff on a big scale in Ohio."

"Did you get any hint who this man was?" asked Bickerson.

"He's somebody big in London. An officer – he's got a rank, I guess."

"You've never heard the name?" asked Sir James. "It wasn't by any chance Major Amery?"

"Amery?" repeated the Greek slowly. "Well, I wouldn't just swear to it. All I know is that he was mad at me, and one of his people came along and squealed. Oh, yes," he added frankly, "I had the stuff all right! But they didn't catch me with it. That's where their case broke down. When they raided my parlour they didn't find anything more intoxicating than a bottle of tomato ketchup!"

"Did Tarn have any confederates? You must know that, Moropoulos?" asked Sir James.

"I make a pretty fair distinction between the living and the dead. If any of his friends have died, maybe you'll produce their death certificates and I'll start talking. Otherwise – " he shrugged his shoulders.

The Commissioner and Bickerson exchanged a few words in a low voice, and then the American detective was beckoned forward.

"You're not holding this man, officer, are you?"

The American shook his head.

"No, sir. So far as I am concerned, he is as free as the air; I've only come over as a sort of chaperon."

"It's true, then, what he says?" asked the Commissioner in an undertone. "The case against him has been dropped?"

The officer from Cleveland nodded again.

"Yes, sir. He was a little too quick for us. We thought we'd caught him with the stuff, but we came about five minutes too late."

It was Bickerson who took charge of the Greek, escorting him to the smartest restaurant within walking distance.

"No, sir," said the Greek, "it's never too early for supper for a hungry man – or dinner, just what you call it so long as it's food. That journey from Liverpool was certainly the hungriest thousand miles I've ever travelled. Two hundred, is it? It seemed longer."

"I've taken a room for you at one of our best hotels," said Bickerson, when they had found a table and a waiter. "And if you're short of money, you must let me know. We should like to make your stay in town as pleasant as possible."

Moropoulos shook his head, a gleam of reproach in his eyes. "Listen, baby," he said gently; "they do that much better on our side. Say, they're artists! They'd deceive *me*! You haven't got into that way, I guess. It comes naturally awkward, trying to be my only friend in the great city. I'll pay for this lunch, Bill, just so I can have the satisfaction of telling you that you've heard all the squeal that's likely to pass my lips during my absence from home."

Bickerson laughed, though he was not in a laughing humour.

"There is nothing we want from you," he said untruthfully. "In fact, I don't know that you could add to our information. Hallam we know – "

"Who's Hallam?" asked the other, in bland surprise. "He's half-brother to Stillman, I guess."

"Stillman!"

"Ah!"

The Greek was obviously tickled at the effect the word had produced.

"I thought that would get you. A new one on you?"

"It's certainly a new one on me," said Bickerson, recovering from his surprise. "Who is Stillman?"

The Greek took some time to consider the question, and when he answered he sounded a very definite note.

"Stillman I don't know and have never seen. All I know I got from one of Soyoka's crowd that I used to run with in New York. Stillman is one of their top men, but I guess that isn't half his name. And now I'm through answering questions."

Bickerson was wise enough to drop the question of the dope gangs until the hungry man had finished his supper. But neither the production of the choicest wine, nor the discovery of the most piquant liqueur, caused the Greek to grow any more loquacious. Bickerson escorted him to his hotel, and then went on to call at Ralph Hallam's house.

As the detective put his hand on the bell, Ralph himself opened the door. He was in evening dress.

"Hullo!" he said, a little wearily. "Have you come to see that prescription book?"

"Forget it," said Bickerson amiably. "No, Hallam, I've dropped in to make a final call, and then maybe you and I will never meet, except professionally, in a hundred years."

And, seeing the look of dubiety in the other's face, he roared with laughter.

"When I say 'professionally,' I mean as a doctor and patient," he said. "Can you give me a minute?"

"Come in," said Ralph ungraciously, and led the way into his dining-room.

"Now this is what I want to know from you. You have a pretty good idea of old man Tarn's possessions. Do you remember his having a box with five trays?"

"No," said Ralph promptly – too promptly. The detective viewed him with suspicion.

"Now listen, doctor, there's nothing against you, even if you were a friend of Tarn's and he was a dope runner – as you know he was. Can't you help a fellow with a morsel of information?"

"If I knew I wouldn't tell you. What is wrong with the box?"

"Nothing: it had a false bottom, that's all. And I'm wondering whether the old man might have concealed something…"

He saw a sudden change come over Ralph Hallam's face; his eyes had grown bright with suppressed excitement.

"You're thinking of something pleasant?" said the keen detective, and Ralph nodded.

"Very pleasant!" he said.

He was thinking of a million dollars.

Suppose it were true? Suppose Tupperwill were mistaken? And suppose the money that he saw in Amery's box were really and rightfully the property of the sinister man? And suppose that, in his queer, secretive way, Tarn had taken the money back to the house and had hidden it? Elsa would know where the box was, he thought, as his car carried him toward Herbert Mansions. The balance of probability was that the money was in Amery's possession or at his bank; but there was just that chance, faint and barely possible, but possible. The very thought made him grow hot and cold.

Elsa was in her room when he arrived.

"That lady is certainly a bright companion for me," said his wife ironically. "She sits in her bedroom half the night, with those 'hullo' things in her ears. What is going to happen now?"

"Nothing," said Ralph, "except that we dine with Tupperwill."

Mrs Hallam groaned.

"What morgue does he live at?" she asked. "Ralph, boy, I've given up two dances for you – real jazzy ones."

"Go and call the girl," said Ralph, whose patience in his wife's presence was never far from the breaking point.

Elsa saved her hostess the trouble. She was walking down the passage when Mrs Hallam emerged from the drawing-room, a dainty figure in the new gown she was wearing in honour of the occasion, though she thought it was very dreadful going out at all, and said so.

"You're thinking of Tarn?" said Ralph slowly. "Well, he wasn't so close a relative that it need send you into mourning. You look tired," he added sympathetically. "Have you had a bad day with the ogre?"

She shook her head. Mrs Hallam had left them alone for a moment, and it was an opportunity not to be lost.

"I wonder if you remember, Elsa, whether your uncle had a trunk with a number of trays, fitting one on top of the other?"

She opened her eyes in surprise.

"Yes, I remember it very well, because that particular box is in this house," she said.

For a second his heart leapt, and it required all his will power to hide the excitement under which he was labouring.

"I packed some of my old clothes in it," she added, and his hopes fell.

"Empty, was it?" he asked carelessly.

"Why, yes, it was empty" – she hesitated. "At least, the top trays were empty. One or two at the bottom I could not lift: I found tonight when I was unpacking, that they are screwed to the side of the box, and it struck me that there must be something underneath, for the trunk is extraordinarily heavy, even when it is empty. Why do you ask?"

"There is no especial reason," he replied carelessly, "except that I took a fancy to the old case when I saw it, and your uncle told me that, if I wanted it, he would give it to me."

"You can have it," she smiled, "but you must find me another to take its place."

Then and there he would have cancelled the dinner party and taken the box to Half Moon Street, but it was inadvisable to show so much eagerness, and Mrs Hallam returning at that moment, the subject dropped. A little later, just before they left the house, he found time to utter a warning.

"Don't attempt to unscrew the bottom trays," he said, in a voice low enough to evade his wife. "I have an idea there is something there which – well, frankly, should not be there."

"Do you mean drugs?" she said quickly.

He nodded.

Mrs Hallam's impatient voice called them from the corridor. "Are you coming?" she snapped, and the girl hurried to join her.

"This evening is going to be so entirely wasted," complained Mrs Hallam, when they were in the car, "that I'd just as soon have chloroform right away!"

To Mr Tupperwill, superintending the finishing touches of his little feast, the night was to be one of peculiar significance. He fussed from drawing-room to dining-room; he went up to his own apartment and solemnly surveyed the etceteras which a knowledgeable housekeeper had produced, and which ranged from lip-sticks to cold cream; and whilst he felt that many of these acquisitions were unlikely to be of more service than a first-aid outfit, he had the satisfaction of knowing that nothing had been left undone for the entertainment of his guests.

A trim maid showed the two women into the room, and Mrs Hallam inspected the appointments with an approving eye.

"There's a million pounds' worth of furniture here," she said enviously, surveying the rare Empire furnishings.

Her hand, sweeping over the silk-panelled wall in an effort to price the quality, stopped at the edge of a heavy golden picture frame, that hung, it seemed, a little low. Instantly she divined the reason, and, pushing the picture aside, she saw a circular disc of steel sunk in the wall. Was this the safe that Mr Tupperwill had misguidedly spoken about? Those ineradicably predatory instincts of hers flamed into life. What was the word? – something to do with "peace"; and yet it wasn't "peace." It was a word that meant running – "pace"!

In a mirror she caught a glimpse of Elsa, who was taking of her cloak and in the act of turning. With a quick movement Lou straightened the picture and walked back to the dressing-table her colour heightened, her heart beating a little quicker.

"Look at all that truck," she drawled, indicating the serried rows of pots and dishes on the table. "The poor old fish!"

Elsa laughed softly.

"Poor Mr Tupperwill! He hasn't been used to entertaining women."

"That's a good sign, anyway," said Lou, and then: "I wonder if he's one of those eccentric millionaires that give dinner party presents?"

Pace! That was the word: she was sure of it now. She could hardly tear herself away, but the maid was waiting at the door, and there would be other opportunities. Such a man as Tupperwill would in all probability collect all manner of valuable trinkets: he seemed that sort of man. And one little piece would not be missed. Her passion for easy "findings" was beyond her power to combat. She went downstairs to meet the anxious Mr Tupperwill, resolved to carry away at least one souvenir of a very dull evening.

And a dull evening it proved to be, for the banker was not in his most talkative mood, and reverted to the subject of business and its cares so frequently that Elsa had all her work to conceal her yawns.

"I've had a very trying afternoon," said Mr Tupperwill over the coffee, "an extremely anxious afternoon. In fact, I cannot remember an afternoon quite as full of unpleasantness. Clients can be very annoying."

"I always thought your clients were models in that respect?" said Ralph.

He too had been silent throughout the meal, his mind so completely occupied by the possibilities that Elsa's old box contained, that he scarcely spoke half a dozen times.

"Yes, they are usually," admitted Mr Tupperwill; "but this particular customer I have in my mind has been − very − er − distressing."

Even he was glad when, at the end of a long-drawn-out rubber of bridge, in which Lou cheated shamelessly, the women rose to go upstairs to collect their cloaks.

"I'm afraid I've been extremely boring."

Ralph murmured something as he strolled out to get his coat and hat from the melancholy butler.

"And I intended this party to be quite cheerful," said Mr Tupperwill miserably. "But my usual vivacity…entirely evaporated …entirely."

"I'm sure the ladies have enjoyed themselves," soothed Ralph.

"I hope they have," replied the host, in doubt. "I sincerely hope they have."

Elsa had got her cloak and was leaving the bedroom, when her companion stopped.

"Go down, dear. I won't be a moment." She was stooping over her shoe. "This wretched buckle has come undone."

"Can I help you?"

"No, don't wait," said the woman impatiently. Her hands were trembling with excitement.

Scarcely had the door closed upon Elsa Marlowe than Mrs Hallam crossed the room, pushed aside the picture, and, with shaking fingers, turned the dial, her ears strained for the slightest sound from the corridor. She had a small combination safe of her own and knew its working, and in another second the door had swung open.

She caught a glimpse of a number of envelopes; there were two or three flat cases; but the only valuable in sight was something which looked like a gold cigarette case. She could not afford to wait for a closer search, and, slipping the case into her bag, she closed the safe, spun the dial, and replacing the picture, was descending the stairs before Elsa had reached the bottom.

She saw Ralph's eyes fixed on her with a steady, enquiring, suspicious look. Hallam knew his wife only too well. But she met his eyes boldly, and was gushing over her host before Ralph Hallam could decide in his mind the inward meaning of her flushed cheeks.

Tupperwill escorted Elsa to the car; Ralph and the woman followed.

"You haven't been playing the fool, have you?" he asked under his breath.

"What do you mean?" she demanded in surprise.

"You didn't find any of Tupperwill's jewellery lying loose? By God! if you ever try that with my friends – "

"You're mad," she said angrily. "Do you imagine I would do anything so…"

At that moment they came within earshot of the other two and took their farewell.

"Are you going straight home?" asked Ralph as the car started.

"Where else?" asked his wife. "Have you any suggestions?"

"Let us go to the Mispah. We'll have some supper and dancing, and get the taste of this funereal evening out of our mouths."

He looked at Elsa, and the girl hesitated.

"We needn't go on the dance floor," he said, reading her unwillingness. "We can have supper upstairs in the balcony and watch the people," and reluctantly she agreed.

The Mispah, though the least advertised, is the most fashionable of the London dance clubs, and the floor was covered with dancers when they picked their way through the crowded balcony to the table he had reserved. The girl, to whom this night club life was a novelty, looked, fascinated, at the glittering throng that swayed and moved to the staccato pounding of the orchestra.

"This is what Jessie Dame would call life," she said with a smile. "Poor Jessie! Her one ambition is to mingle with a hectic throng, mainly composed of sinister men in evening dress, and meet the aristocracy on equal terms."

"A base ambition," said Ralph gaily. "There are not many of the aristocracy here, though there are a few. That is Letty Milenko From

185

the Gaiety. That tall man is Lord Sterrer. The name of the scarecrow with whom he's dancing I don't know, although I've seen her here before."

Elsa was gazing speechlessly at Lord Sterrer's partner. She was a woman of about middle height, painfully thin, and on whom clothes hung loosely. Her ears, her throat, her hair glittered with diamonds, and the big hands that lay upon the black coat of her partner flashed and scintillated dazzlingly. As the face came to view, Elsa saw that her eyes were half closed, and that she seemed to be moving in an ecstasy of perfect enjoyment.

It was the romantic Miss Dame!

MAJOR AMERY IS SURPRISED

Jessie Dame! There was no doubt about it, no mistaking her. Jessie Dame, flashing with diamonds, expensively garbed, and dancing on the most exclusively public floor in London!

At first she was sure that she was mistaken. And then…no it was Jessie! As the dance finished, the girl looked up, and Elsa drew back out of sight.

"Is she somebody you know?" asked Ralph, who had observed the effect this strange spectacle had upon her.

"Yes, I know her," said Elsa shortly. "Do you?"

Ralph shook his head.

"I've seen her here once or twice before. She usually comes with a middle-aged man – there he is."

He pointed to a corner whither Jessie was making her way accompanied by her partner. The man to whom Ralph pointed was stout and bald, and to somewhat coarse features he added a sweeping cavalry moustache, suspiciously yellow.

Jessie! The discovery shocked her. She had never imagined that this gawk of a girl, with her foolish chatter of picture heroes and heroines, could lead what was tantamount to a double life. Elsa had always thought of her as, if not poor, at least one who lived in modest circumstances; yet here she was, carrying a small fortune in jewellery, and obviously on terms of friendship with people whom Elsa did not imagine she could know.

She was being snobbish, she told herself. There was no reason in the world that Jessie Dame should not dance at the Mispah Club; less reason that this doting "pater" of whom she so often spoke, should not cover her with jewels. At the same time she felt a strange uneasiness, and could not keep her eyes from the girl whose awkward gestures of animation were visible from where she sat.

Ralph saw that something unusual had happened, but did not for the moment connect the girl's changed expression with the raw apparition on the floor below. He asked her to dance, and when she declined, he was promptly claimed by Mrs Hallam.

"Let me get a dance out of the night, at any rate," she said, and carried him off, leaving the girl alone, not to her regret, for the train of the evening was beginning to tell on her.

She moved her seat so that, whilst free from observation herelf, she had a good view of Jessie Dame. The band had struck up, he floor was again a kaleidoscopic tangle of colours and movement, but Miss Dame, now vigorously fanning herself, did not join the throng, and apparently her cavalier had left her.

Elsa took her eyes from the floor and surveyed the other occupants of the balcony, and then she uttered an exclamation of surprise. Between two pillars was a table at which sat a solitary and detached observer. He was looking at her, and, as their eyes met, he rose and came round the corner of the balcony toward her, an unusually gracious proceeding on his part; his interest in her presence was more unexpected than the actual discovery of Major Amery in this gay spot.

At first she thought he was going to pass her, but he stopped, and, sitting down in the chair recently occupied by Ralph, he looked across to where the long-plumed fan of Jessie Dame was working agitatedly.

"The skeleton at the feast," he said sardonically.

This piece of mordant humour was so typical of him that she laughed.

"I don't often come to the Mispah," he said, "but if I had, and I'd seen that lady before, I should have been saved a very uncomfortable afternoon."

She hoped that others might also have been saved the discomfort of that afternoon, but she took little notice of his remark, thinking that he was still jesting.

"All gay and girlish," he said. "How funny! Somehow I never imagined that lank woman in a setting like this."

"Why not, Major Amery?" she asked, ready to defend her friend, and conscious that she was being something of a hypocrite, since she had experienced exactly the same sense of the incongruous as he was now feeling. "Jessie works very hard, and she's as much entitled to a little recreation as I am – but probably it strikes you as being funny that I am here?"

He shook his head.

"You have been dining with the massive Tupperwill," he said, "and the Hallams brought you on. Besides, you fit. The illuminations on that woman's ears are fascinating."

Every time Jessie turned her head there was a flicker and flash of jewels.

"And all on three pounds a week!" he murmured. "The thrift and economy of a poor working girl fills me with awe. That is Hallam and his wife, isn't it?"

He looked down to where Ralph was threading a difficult way across the crowded floor.

"That is Dr Hallam and his sister-in-law," she said.

"His wife," he corrected, and, seeing her look of blank astonishment: "You didn't know he was married? He hasn't told you?"

Elsa shook her head.

"No, I didn't know," she said simply.

Her mind was in a turmoil. Why had Ralph kept the truth from her? What had he hoped to gain by his deception? As if reading her thoughts, the sinister man went on:

"I think it is a matter of convenience, and, for Hallam, of mental ease. His lady wife has one or two unpleasant hobbies – you haven't lost any small article of jewellery, have you?"

She shook her head, wondering.

"Did you seriously mean what you said the other day – that she was a kleptomaniac?"

He nodded.

"That is the scientific description. Personally, I should call her a sneak-thief, with an itch for other people's property. You need not be shocked: some of our best people suffer from that complaint."

But married! She couldn't understand that. And yet she remembered wondering how it was she had never met his "sister-in-law" before. The reason was plain enough now.

For a second she felt uneasy, but then the humour of the situation came to her, and she laughed softly.

"She was the skeleton at his feast, then?" she asked. Amery's eyes twinkled for a second and grew solemn again. "Or he at hers: I'm not quite sure," he said. "That man with Miss Dame is her father – I suppose you know that? I didn't, until I took the trouble to enquire. You haven't seen him closely, I suppose? You should, but probably you're not interested in anthropology? Pale blue eyes and a very large, fat, straight chin, which usually marks a man with epileptic tendencies. The hair of the moustache extremely coarse – Mantegazza thinks that is a bad sign."

"Mantegazza?" she asked, bewildered.

"He is an Italian anthropologist – one of the few whose conclusions are worth study. The thickness of the moustache hair should be .015 of a millimetre. If it is coarser than that, the man is either a great criminal or a great scientist."

She listened, astounded, as he rattled on, and remembering the uncomfortable moment she had had when he had told her her height and detected the accident she had once had to her little finger, she began to understand that he had been pursuing a hobby.

"You have made a study of these things, Major Amery?"

He nodded.

"Yes, years ago, when I was in the Indian Service, before I adopted the criminal career which is now exercising the minds of Scotland Yard, anthropology was an interest of mine."

She was looking at him intently. Not a muscle of his face twitched; there was no sign of embarrassment or of shame, when he expressed his guilt. And there was no boastfulness, either. He was simply stating a fact, and a fact beyond controversy. The music stopped, there was a clapping of hands, and he waited, his eyes fixed upon Ralph and his wife. Not until the music started again, and he saw the pair resume the interrupted dance, did he speak.

"Do you know the Dames?"

"I know Jessie," she said. "I've never met her father."

"Ever been to the house, I mean?"

She shook her head.

"She's invited me to tea, but I've never gone."

"You should go," he nodded. "And I think I should go very soon if I were you. It is rather a nice house, near Notting Hill Gate; a largish kind of establishment for people of those circumstances, with a fairly big garden, at the end of which is the garage."

"Have they a car?" she asked, open-eyed.

He shook his head.

"I don't know. As a matter of fact, I have not been immensely interested, except that I've seen the house – in fact, I've seen the house of every person holding down a job at Amery & Amery's. The position of a girl who lives with her parents – or parent, for I understand Miss Dame has no mother – is always the more difficult to judge. Her father may be anything or nothing. By the way, you have a black box at home, haven't you, belonging to Tarn – a box with trays?"

He turned so abruptly to this subject that she was surprised into an admission. And then:

"How on earth did you know?" she demanded. "And what is the mystery of that box? You're the second person who has spoken – "

"Only two?" he asked quickly. "Are you sure only two people have asked you about that box? Myself and who?"

"Dr Hallam. You think there is something in that box?" She looked at him gravely, and he nodded. "Drugs?"

"Yes, the drug that dopes the world," he said flippantly. "I shouldn't investigate too closely if I were you, but under no circumstances are you to let that box out of your possession. Here comes your amiable friend, and by the expression on his face I gather that he has recognised me."

"Won't you wait and meet him?"

191

He hesitated.

"Yes, I think I will," he said.

A few minutes later, Ralph came along the narrow balcony, a watchful, suspicious man.

"You know Major Amery?" said Elsa.

He bowed slightly.

"And of course Mrs Hallam you know?" said Ralph.

"Yes, I have met your wife."

Their eyes met in a challenge, and Ralph's were the first to be lowered.

So Elsa knew! Well, she had to know sooner or later, and he would rather she learnt in the present circumstances than any other.

"I have identified the lady of the earrings," he said as he sat down. "She's one of your girls."

"You mean Miss Dame? Yes, she is one of our minor lights."

"You must pay very big money, Major Amery," said Ralph drily.

"Evidently," was the cold reply.

He got up with a little bow to the girl, and, without so much as noticing Lou Hallam, walked back to his place between the pillars.

"What did he have to say?" asked Ralph. And then: "So he told you my guilty secret?"

He tried to carry the matter off with a smile, but he went red under her questioning scrutiny.

"The fact is," he said awkwardly, "Lou and I have never quite hit it off, which was probably my fault. But we've always been good friends – "

"Up to a point," broke in Mrs Hallam. "He told you we were married, did he? That fellow ought to be running the gossip column of the 'Megaphone'!"

A HOUSE IN DISORDER

Amery sat over his third cup of coffee and a cigarette, watching the dancers, long after Elsa had passed, with a little nod and a smile, on her way home. He saw Miss Dame disappear finally, and the first series of lights go out as a warning that the club was closing, and then he came down the marble stairs into Citron Street. It was raining, and the linkman, holding a huge umbrella, lifted his hand enquiringly.

"No, thank you," said Amery. "I'll walk."

He strolled across Leicester Square, through the midnight bustle of Piccadilly Circus, and made his leisurely way up Regent Street. He had not gone far before he was conscious that his movements were under observation. Glancing back, he saw two men, as leisurely as himself, walking in his rear, and smiled quietly.

As he turned into Hanover Square, one of his pursuers quickened his step and passed him, and Amery swerved slightly to give him a wider berth. Hanover Square was a bleak desert; a crawling taxicab was the only sign of life.

He whistled, and the cab came toward him. The door was open and he was stepping in, when a man came round the back of the taxi. It was impossible to see his face; his felt hat was pulled down over his eyes, a silk scarf covered his mouth.

"Good evening, Mr Stillman!" said Amery pleasantly.

As he spoke he gave the impression that he was waiting to meet the advancing man. The words were hardly spoken before, with a quick turn, he had leapt into the cab, slammed the door behind him, and the muffled man faced the black cavity of a pistol muzzle.

"Stillman, I think?" said Amery.

The action had been so quick that the man was taken off his guard.

"I don't know what you're talking about," he said, in a muffled voice. "I'm only telling you to get out and stay out!"

"That sounds familiar," said Amery coolly. "I seem to have used the identical term when addressing a partner, confederate or enemy of yours, one Maurice Tarn. You talk too much!"

The motionless figure on the pavement moved his hand slightly, but, dark as the night, Amery detected the motion.

"Keep your hand down, my friend, or in a minute or two this cab will be carrying your lifeless remains to Middlesex Hospital, and the most brilliant house surgeon will not be able to restore animation. I should hate to put our friend the cabman to the inconvenience of mussing his upholstery."

"Listen," said the man, hoarse with rage. "Life is pretty sweet to you, I guess? If it is, you'll get out of the game. I don't know who Stillman is, but you can't bluff me – I know who you are! There's a heap of correspondence in the bottom drawer of your desk that is very interesting to read – "

Bang!

Amery had been leaning forward to the window, and he caught the glitter of a gun and flung himself back just in time. He felt the wind of the bullet as it passed the bridge of his nose, and before he could recover, the frightened driver had jerked the taxicab forward and was going at full speed round the gardens of the square. Looking back, Amery caught a glimpse of a figure running across the road... On the whole he approved the driver's precipitation.

"I'm going to the nearest police station," quavered the taxi-man, when Amery leant out of the window to give him instructions. "I don't care what you say, I'm taking you to the nearest police station! I'm not going to have that sort of thing happen in my cab!"

And then a hand came round the corner, and in it was a crisp, bright note. By the light of the lamp which illuminated the meter, the driver saw the magic word "Ten" and changed his mind.

"All right; where do you want to go?" he growled.

The sinister man gave directions and leant back in the cab. That was a narrow squeak. He must never take such a risk again.

Usually a light burnt in the passage of his house, visible through the transom, but there was a complete darkness when he put the key in the lock and pushed the door wide open. No sound came to his ears save the ticking of the clock on the stair landing. Feeling along the wall, he found the switch and illuminated the passage.

The first thing that struck him as curious was that the door leading to his study was open, and he had taken a step toward the room, when he heard the patter of feet behind him and turned quickly, to meet the grinning face of Feng Ho. The Chinaman was clad from head to foot in a shining oilskin.

"Inclemency of elements – " he began, and then he saw Amery's face, and asked quickly, in the Cantonese dialect: "What is wrong?"

"I don't know," replied Amery in the same tongue, "but I rather think somebody has been here in my absence."

The Chinaman ran past him into the open study and put on the lights. Amery heard a guttural exclamation of astonishment, and, following the man into the room, saw the cause.

The place was in hopeless confusion. Half the drawers of his desk lay on the floor; the cupboards had been wrenched open, the furniture moved, and a little pinewood cupboard had been emptied by the simple process of tipping its contents on to the carpet.

"Where is Chang? Go and find him," said Amery quickly.

The Chinaman ran out of the room, and presently Amery heard his name called and went towards the voice. Feng Ho was kneeling on the floor by the side of a prostrate figure, so trussed and bound and gagged that he bore no resemblance to anything human. He was unconscious when the bonds were loosened and the steel handcuffs unlocked.

"There's been no struggle here," said Amery, looking round the little pantry where the man had been found.

Feng Ho went to the mysterious region at the back of the house and came back with a basin of water.

"They came through the kitchen," he said. "The window is open."

Amery's European servants did not sleep on the premises the last of these usually left at half past ten, and it must have been after that hour that the burglar made his entrance.

"They have taken my dossier," said Amery, after a careful examination of the strewn papers on the floor.

He pointed to a steel drawer; the lock had been torn bodily from its place, and where the drawer had been was a confusion of splintered wood.

It was curious that neither of the men suggested summoning the police. That idea did not seem to occur to them, and when Feng Ho went back to attend the half-conscious Chinaman, and Amery took up the telephone, it was not a police number that he called.

"It must have been done half an hour ago," said the sinister man thoughtfully, after his telephone conversation had finished and Feng Ho had returned. "Quick work!"

Again he took up the telephone; this time he gave a Mayfair number, and almost immediately Ralph Hallam's voice answered him.

"Is that Dr Hallam?"

"Yes," was the reply. There was no mistaking the voice.

"So you're at home, are you?" said Amery with a smile, and before the answer came he had hung up the receiver.

"Quick work," he muttered. "Help me get this stuff together. Where have you left Chang?"

"I've put him on his bed. He is a little shaken, and not hurt," said Feng Ho, with that curious callousness which so shocks the Westerner. "Perhaps he will live."

"I think so."

Chang not only lived, but within an hour was a very voluble young man, invoking his familiar devils to the destruction of his enemies.

"I was asleep, *tao*," he said frankly, "and I knew nothing until my head was in a bag and my hands tied."

"If you had been awake then, I think you would have been asleep now, Chang," said Amery cryptically.

He spent the rest of the night putting his papers in order, but the most important collection of documents had disappeared.

He knew this before the search began. He had known it from the moment Stillman had spoken. Tomorrow he must be early at the office. There were other things even as important as his dossier, and these must not be found.

THE FOUR BROWN PACKETS

Elsa Marlowe woke up in the middle of the night with a sense of deep trouble. She got up and put on the light, and, sitting down on the bed, carefully analysed her mind to find the cause. Was it the discovery that Ralph Hallam was married? She dismissed that thought as being too absurd for consideration. Jessie Dame? It had certainly disturbed her to find Jessie at the Mispah Club, bejewelled and expensively frocked; but Amery had spoken the truth when he said that working girls were very difficult to place. They might come from homes where families were starving, and none would guess the tragedy behind their smart frocks and their amiability; or they might be the children of well-off people, immeasurably the social superiors of their employers. She had often heard Jessie Dame talk about her "pater," and had dismissed that little piece of pompous Latinity as sheer snobbishness. Possibly Jessie's excess of refinement was based on a consciousness of superiority.

No, it was not Jessie. She was very well able to look after herself, romantic as she was, though Elsa determined that the long-deferred visit to the girl's ancestral home should be made that day, for she was curious to see what kind of home life the girl had.

Certainly it wasn't Jessie. And it was not Ralph. Then what had so depressed her? In a vague kind of way she felt it was Amery, his queerness, his loneliness, and the sinister shadow that her suspicions had thrown over him. He was engaged, she knew, in a business that was both dangerous and unsavoury. He had undoubtedly struck down a comfortable middle-aged banker, for no other offence than that he had talked too much. Cold-blooded, cynical, remorseless, ruthless…and very lonely.

She caught her breath in horror at herself. She had once heard of a man whose formula for winning the love of women was to "treat 'em rough and keep 'em going!" Was she being subjected to this process, and was this the result?

She was wide awake now. Her sense of unhappiness had been swallowed up in the alarm of her discovery. Looking at the clock, she saw that it was four. And then her eyes fell upon the battered box which had so exercised the interest of Ralph and the sinister man. She pulled open the lid, took out the three top trays, and tried again to move the fourth, but it was screwed tightly, if clumsily, and defied her efforts. Lifting one end of the box, she felt its weight. There was something beneath that fastened tray – what?

It was five o'clock when she went back to bed, but not to sleep. She was dressed and had cooked her breakfast before Mrs Hallam's daily maid had put in her appearance. Even now she did not feel the least bit sleepy. A night of rain and storm had been succeeded by a bright spring morning, which stirred something in her heart that was akin to happiness.

"You're early, miss," said the maid, with that touch of resentment which domestics invariably show toward the early riser.

"I'm going to the office early," said Elsa, feeling that some excuse was necessary, and not wishing to have the story of her sleeplessness carried to Mrs Hallam.

It was like Elsa that having, on the spur of the moment, invented an intention of going early, she should find herself, soon after eight, walking up Wood Street and wondering whether the office would be open.

It was not only open, but apparently there were other early callers. She saw two men talking in the doorway, and recognized one as Bickerson. There was no mistaking his well-set figure. His head was turned as she came into view, and he was walking slowly up the street, in earnest consultation with his companion. Before he had turned, she was in the passage and mounting the stairs.

The cleaners had left her room, and she was apparently the only member of the staff on the premises. Fortunately, there was plenty of work to occupy her, and she went into Amery's cold office to collect a card index of addresses that she had promised herself to put in order.

Placing the little box on his desk, her nimble fingers passed quickly over their edges, withdrawing one here, replacing another there, for, neat in other respects, he was the most careless of men, and more often than not it was necessary to search the floor for addresses he had removed and forgotten to return.

The door was ajar; she could hear distinctly the sound of feet on the stairs, and wondered what other member of the staff came so early. And then she heard Bickerson's voice, as two men came into her office. She raised her head and listened.

"He will be here at nine. I would rather the search was conducted in his presence," said the voice of the stranger, and by the respectful tone in which Bickerson answered, it was evident that he was the detective's superior in rank.

"Just as you like, sir. I've not put the warrant into effect before, but the information which came to me early this morning leaves no doubt that the stuff is on the premises. There's a cupboard by the side of the fireplace which I noticed when I called last time."

Elsa listened, breathless. Looking round, she saw the long, narrow cupboard, and remembered that it was one she had not seen the Major use. What was the "stuff"? Should she go out, meet and warn him? That might help, but it could hardly prevent the discovery of the incriminating material, whatever it was, that was behind the small door.

Somebody took a step toward the room, "I'll show you where," said Bickerson.

She looked round, and in a second had passed through the doorway into the little cupboard-like apartment which served Amery as a wash-place and dressing-room. She was just in time.

"There it is," she heard Bickerson say, "on the right of the fireplace. Most of these old-fashioned offices have cupboards in that position. I don't see why we shouldn't open it now, sir."

"Wait till he comes," said the other gruffly, and then the sound of their voices receded.

She came back to Amery's room. They had closed the door behind them when they went out: the key was in the lock, and, without counting the consequences, she turned it and flew back to the cupboard by the mantel-piece. This was locked, and defied her efforts to open. In desperation, she took up the poker from the fireplace, and, with a strength which surprised her, smashed in the panel. The sound must have reached the ears of the men outside, for they came back, and one of them tried the door.

"Who is there?" he called.

She made no answer. Again the poker fell upon the door, and now the panel was so broken that she could see inside.

On a shelf lay four little packets, each about three inches square, and each wrapped in brown paper and fastened with sealed string. She put in her trembling hand and took out the first. The label was partly in German and partly in English, but she needed no knowledge of German to realize that the package contained cocaine.

What should she do? The firegrate was empty. Then she remembered the washing-bowl.

Somebody was hammering on the door.

"Who is there?"

With her teeth set, she ignored all except the pressing problem of Amery's danger. Tearing off the paper cover, she let drop into the basin a heap of glittering white powder. Turning on both taps, she emptied the second and then the others, and, without waiting to watch the deadly drug flow to waste, she came back to Amery's room, found his matches, and, striking a light, burnt the wrappers, watching them turn to black ash. When she returned to the wash-bowl, every vestige of the cocaine had disappeared, and then, and not until then, did she walk calmly to the door, turn the key and open it. A red-faced, angry Bickerson confronted her, behind him an older man, taller and white-haired.

"What have you been doing?" demanded Bickerson roughly. "Why didn't you open the door when I called you?"

"Because I do not recognize your right to give me instructions," she said.

One glance he gave at the smashed cupboard door.

"I see! So you're working with Amery, are you, young lady? It's as well to know that. I suppose you know you're liable to a severe penalty?"

"For what crime?" she asked, with a calm she did not feel. "Looking after my employer's interests?"

"What did you find in there?"

"Nothing."

He saw the charred paper in the fireplace.

"Nothing, eh?" he said between his teeth.

He heard the sound of running water, looked into the dressing room and understood.

"What did you find?" he asked again. "Come, Miss Marlowe, I'm sure you do not wish to connive in the breaking of the law. What was in that cupboard?"

"Nothing," said Elsa doggedly.

She was very white; her knees felt as if at any moment they would give way under her; but she stood up square to the police officer, defiance in the tilt of her chin and in her fine eyes.

"You didn't know she was in that room when you spoke," said the older man with a little chuckle. "Young lady, you've taught a very able detective inspector a lesson which I hope he will not forget!"

Bickerson was now conducting a thorough search of the office. The cupboard on the left of the fireplace was unlocked but empty. He tried the drawers of Amery's desk: they all opened save one, and as he pulled a bunch of keys from his pocket and knelt to open this, the man most concerned in the search walked into the room.

"Looking for something?" he asked politely.

"I have a warrant to search your office," said Bickerson, trembling with anger.

"I doubt it," replied Amery coolly. "Since when have Scotland Yard had the right of searching a City office? I am under the impression that there is an admirable force of police operating in the one square mile of territory known as the City of London; and unless I am mistaken, these gentleman are extremely jealous of their authority being taken from their hands. May I see your warrant?"

He took the paper from the man's hand and read it.

"This is an authorization to search my house in Brook Street, not this office," he said, "and I'm rather surprised that Superintendent Wille connived at this irregularity."

The bigger man started.

"I understood that the necessary permission from the City Commissioner had been obtained," he said stiffly. "You told me this, Bickerson."

"The City detective is downstairs," growled the other. "If Major Amery is so particular as to form, we'd better have him up."

When the third detective arrived, Elsa recognised him as the man she had seen in consultation with Bickerson. He produced the document, and seemed a little piqued to find that the search had already begun. For whilst there is perfect friendship between the police of the guarded City and Scotland Yard, there is, as Major Amery very truly said, a very jealous objection to the Yard men operating east of Temple Bar or west of Aldgate Pump.

"There's nothing to be found here," said Bickerson, after Amery had opened the locked drawer and the City man had made his search. "But it *was* here!" He pointed to the smashed cupboard. This had been the first object on which Amery's eyes had fallen when he entered the room. "There was something there, and this girl has taken it out and destroyed it. I think you will be sorry for this, Miss Marlowe."

"If she is," said Amery coldly, "I will 'phone you."

He did not speak again until the men had left the building, then he turned and surveyed the girl with a new interest. And from her, his eyes strayed to the wrecked cupboard.

"You did that, of course?"

She nodded.

"What did you find?"

"Oh, Major Amery, why do you pretend?" she burst forth. "You know what I found! Four packets of that awful stuff!"

203

"Opium?"

"I don't know what it was; I think it was cocaine. It was white and glistening."

He nodded.

"That was cocaine. Four packets?" He whistled softly. "And you washed them away, did you?"

"Yes," she said shortly, and was preparing to go back to her work.

"That was very good of you." His politeness was almost mechanical. "Very good of you indeed! Four packets of cocaine. German, by any chance?"

"Oh, of course they were German!" she said impatiently. "You know – "

He shook his head.

"I don't know," he said. "I have never had a greater surprise than to learn that there were drugs in this office."

He walked to his desk, gave a little jerk to the edge, and, to her astonishment, the whole of the top slid back, revealing a shallow cavity in which lay a small thin package of papers. These he took out, put in his inside pocket, pulled the top of the desk back in its place, and smiled.

"Did Mr Bickerson, in the course of any unguarded conversation, reveal how he came to know that the cocaine was in my office?"

"No; he said he knew early this morning."

"I see," said the other softly. "Now I wonder how our friend put them there?"

"Our friend – which friend?"

"A gentleman named Stillman," he said carelessly, "who came in before office hours and planted the drugs in my office."

"But – but – " she stammered, "aren't you a dealer in drugs?"

He smiled.

"I have never bought anything more deadly than chewing-gum in my life," he said.

THE CORRECTED LETTER

Elsa could only gaze at him blankly.

"But you are Soyoka! I know…you have admitted that you are!"

His face was expressionless.

"Be that as it may," he said, "I have never bought or sold drugs of any kind, with the exception perhaps of the interesting commodity of which I spoke."

She drew a long breath.

"I can't understand it."

"Don't try," he said.

He walked across to the smashed cupboard.

"Poker?" he asked. "Of course it was the poker. Now just tell me how you came to do it."

In a few words she explained how she had come early, had seen the detectives waiting in the street, and overheard Bickerson and his superintendent talking, and all that followed.

"How very wonderful!" he said, looking at her strangely. "You remarkable girl!"

She coloured under his eyes, felt absurdly tearful, for the reaction had come, and she wanted to get away, sit down and recover her normal breath. He must have seen this, for his old manner returned.

"Ask Feng Ho to come to me, will you, please?"

She went out and found Feng Ho tickling the canary with the end of a long-handled paint-brush, and the Chinaman was inclined to linger, until she said: "Feng Ho, something has happened in Major Amery's office. He wants you at once."

And then Feng Ho moved with some celerity.

It was only a quarter to nine, she saw, when she looked at the office clock, and she was glad for this little respite before the real business of the day commenced. She was feeling weak and shaken, and she would have given anything to have got away from the office for an hour.

An interest in life came with the arrival of Miss Dame, and, observing the fiery hair and the red button of a nose, Elsa wondered if this plainly dressed and unattractive female could have been the resplendent being she had seen on the previous night. The fatigue attendant upon the gay life left no visible evidence, for Miss Dame was as voluble as ever.

"My dear," she said, "who do you think I met downstairs? That Mr Dickerson, the famous sleuth!"

"Bickerson?"

"Bicker or Dicker, it's all the same to, me. Such a nice man! The way he lifted his hat shows that he was meant for something better than a detective. And yet I've known a few good detectives in my time, perfect gentlemen but secret service agents, if you understand? When the plans are stolen – you know what I mean, Government plans about war, where the forts are going to be built and that sort of thing – they get them back. They're younger than Mr Bickerson, though," she added, as though regretting the lost opportunities for romance which the stolid Bickerson might otherwise have offered.

"Jessie, how long have you been a member of the Mispah Club?" Miss Dame dropped the papers she was carrying, and hid her confusion in gathering them together.

"My dear, how you startled me! How did you know I was a member of the Mispah?" she asked, a little self-consciously. "Of course, there's no reason why I shouldn't be. A young girl like me wants to see a little bit of life. But I'm not, as a matter of fact. Pater is a member. Why – did you see me?"

Elsa nodded.

"Yes, I saw you," she said quietly, and Miss Dame tossed her head.

"Well, there's nothing in it, is there?" she asked defiantly. "I mean, a young girl has to live. She can't be a fogey or a stick-in-the-mud. It's quite time enough to settle down when you're older. And if the pater takes me out, well, that's nobody's business. Not that I'm saying you're poking your nose into my affairs, because I'm not. Did you like the dress?" inconsequently. "Of course, the jewels…I borrowed those; they're not real. Yes, they are – they are real, but I…"

She was incoherent, torn between a pride of possession and a fear of the impression she might be creating.

"I don't want you to think I'm not a good girl, Miss Marlowe," she said, with an almost comical attempt at the virtuous. "But my pater is rather well off. I've never told anybody, because they might think it funny that I'm working here for a mere pittance, so to speak. I needn't work at all."

"I wonder you do, Jessie."

Miss Dame was apparently also wondering at her condescension, for she did not answer, and though she opened her lips twice to speak, it was not until the third effort that she offered an explanation which was, on the whole, unconvincing.

"Pater likes me to have something to occupy my time. 'Satan finds work for idle hands,' as the good book says. Pater's rich."

"That's what Major Amery thought," said Elsa, and Miss Dame's jaw dropped.

"Amery?" she squeaked, her face going pale. "My Gawd! he didn't see me? Was he there?"

Elsa nodded.

"At the Mispah – that misery at the Mispah! What did he say, Miss Marlowe? I suppose he thought it was funny?"

"He did rather," said Elsa, speaking nothing but the truth.

But it was not the girl's idea of funniness that she was thinking about.

"I'll bet he did!" said Jessie in a hushed voice, her eyes gleaming redly through her spectacles. "I suppose he's got all sorts of low ideas about me. Did he see pater?"

"Yes, he saw your father."

"Oh!" said Miss Dame blankly. And then, after a long cogitation: "It can't be helped. He didn't ask to see me this morning?"

"No, he doesn't seem to be the slightest bit interested in you this morning," said Elsa with a smile, "but that doesn't mean – "

"I know it doesn't mean anything," interrupted Miss Dame. "He's one of those fly, underhand people, who are always on the look-out for trouble, and before you know where you are, bingo!"

She thought again, and again said that it couldn't be helped.

"I bought it in Shaftesbury Avenue – the dress, I mean – fourteen guineas. It was a lot of money, but you can't get classy robes cheaper than that. Pater collects diamonds; he's in the – in the trade – in the diamond trade, I mean. As a hobby."

She seemed anxious to discover the effect she had produced upon the girl, but more especially upon Major Amery.

"If he saw me with my pater, he would know it was all right, wouldn't he? I mean, he'd know I wasn't one of these fast girls that go round luring men to their ruin?"

Elsa did not laugh, though she was strongly tempted.

"I don't think I should worry what Major Amery thinks," she said soothingly; "and unless he mentions the matter to you, I should not speak about it."

"Hm!" said Miss Dame dubiously.

She made no further appearance that morning, and Elsa was not sorry, for Amery was in a mood of indecision. Usually, his letters to his foreign correspondents needed little or no revision. As they were dictated, so were they signed; except on very rare occasions, when he would scrap a letter and begin anew. This morning he dictated a long epistle, and she was half-way through its transcription when he came into her room.

"You needn't bother about that letter," he said. "Bring your book and I will give you another one."

And then the same thing happened again. She was almost on the last sentence of the second literary effort when he appeared.

"I don't quite like the wording of that letter. Will you come in, and we'll try afresh?" he said.

It was a letter to a Chinese merchant in Shanghai, and dealt, not with shipments of merchandise, but with a mysterious individual to whom he referred as FOI. FOI wasn't quite satisfied with the way things were going. And FOI thought that a little more energy might be displayed at the Chinese end. At the same time, FOI recognised all the difficulties and was deeply appreciative of all Mr T'Chang Fui Zen was doing. FOI was also worried about a man called Stillman, "though," said the letter, "I have been able to locate this gentleman, and hope at an early date to counteract his operations to our advantage." This passage occurred in all three letters, and seemed to be the main theme, though there were endless details which varied in description with each new attempt he made to produce the perfect communication.

"I suppose you get rather bored with typing the same letter over and over again?" he said, as he put his signature to the last of the epistles.

She smiled.

"No; it doesn't often happen, and I'm getting quite used to your ways now, Major Amery. Soon, I think, I shall understand you!"

"And you're leaving on Saturday, too," he mused. Then, catching her eye, he laughed as though he were enjoying some secret jest of his.

He followed her into her room and took a quick glance round.

"Why, of course!" he said. "Though that doesn't explain everything."

She looked up at him.

"Explain everything?" she repeated.

"I was thinking of – another matter," he said hurriedly. Just before lunch, in his abrupt way, he asked her a question, which, like so many of his interjections, was altogether unexpected.

"Where are you going tonight?" he asked.

"Tonight? Nowhere."

She could never lose the habit of surprise at the strange butterfly movements of the sinister man's mind.

"Are you sure?"

"Why, of course I'm sure, Major. I am more especially sure because Faust is being broadcast from the Opera House – and I love the music."

For the first time she saw the man startled.

"Faust? How strange, how very odd!"

"I see nothing very odd in it," she laughed. "I am one of those wireless enthusiasts who love opera – I wouldn't miss a note or a word for anything!"

"How very odd!" he said again. "Faust!"

The oddness did not seem particularly obvious to Elsa, but she knew her man too well to pursue the subject; and, as she might have expected, when he spoke again it was of something that had not the slightest relation to opera or broadcasting.

"Don't forget what I told you about your box," he said, and before she could answer he had gone back to his room, closed the door behind him, and she heard the click of the lock as the key turned.

Elsa frowned. Was he quite…? Men who have lived for many years in hot climates, particularly the climate of India, were strange. She had known an old Indian general who invariably started dinner with a sweet and finished with soup. She couldn't imagine the sinister man doing anything so eccentric, she thought whimsically. But he was…queer.

The luncheon interval gave her an opportunity of going back to Mrs Hallam's flat for a prosaic purpose – to replace a laddered stocking. Mrs Hallam had given her a key, and she went in, believing she would have the flat to herself, for the lady had told her she was going out to lunch. She walked down the narrow corridor, turned the handle of her door and walked in, and then stopped dead, with a gasp of amazement and annoyance.

The black trunk was in the middle of the floor, and opened. By its side Ralph Hallam knelt in his shirt-sleeves, a screwdriver in his hand, and he was busily unscrewing the fourth tray.

RALPH EXPLAINS

He looked up with a start, and went very red.

"Hullo, old girl!" he said, with an uneasy attempt at carelessness. "I thought I'd come and solve the mystery of your box."

"I didn't think there was any mystery about it, Ralph," she said coldly; "and at any rate, I don't know why you want the thrill all to yourself."

He got up, dusting the knees of his trousers, and put on his coat. "The truth is, Elsa, I wanted to save you from what might have been a very embarrassing discovery," he said. "I will say nothing against Maurice Tarn, but I rather think there is something hidden here which would shock you to see."

Elsa's quiet smile he did not like.

"I'm proof against shock, Ralph," she said.

He had lifted the first of the loose trays to replace it, when she stopped him.

"Continue the good work. Don't deny me my flash of excitement – one screw is out and there are only three others."

"You mean you want it opened?" he said uncomfortably. "I should wait if I were you, Elsa. Give me a few minutes alone, and let me be sure there is nothing here you shouldn't see."

Elsa tried to take the screwdriver from his hand, but he pulled it back.

"Leave it," he said. "I'm dreadfully sorry if I've annoyed you, but believe me, I've nothing but your interests at heart."

"Then why not finish your work and let me see what there is to be seen? And please don't distress yourself about shocking me, Ralph, because, if I really am not shockproof, at least I'm on the way to be. Won't you take out the other screws?"

He shook his head.

"No – as a matter of fact, just before you came in I had decided that it was hardly worthwhile."

She watched him as he replaced the trays, pulled down the lid and pushed the box against the wall, where it had been when she had left that morning, and she noticed that he never let go of the screwdriver.

"You're back early," he said. "They tell me you went out early this morning. I suppose Amery has some little humanity left in his system and has let you off for the day? I saw old Tupperwill this morning; he asked after you. Queer devil, Tupperwill! You've made a hit there, Elsa, and I shouldn't be surprised if our stout friend doesn't invent another excuse for a party…"

He chattered on, clearly ill at ease, anxious to go, and yet as anxious to be sure that she should not finish the work he had begun. She decided the matter for him.

"I want my room now," she said, and almost pushed him out.

When she had made her change and come out into the dining-room, he was on the point of leaving.

"Can I take you anywhere? Have you had lunch?"

"Yes, I've had lunch," she said, which was not true.

Her objection to his presence was so marked that presently he began pulling on his gloves.

"You mustn't imagine I had any designs on your property," he said jokingly. "And believe me, Elsa, I am serious when I ask you not to open that box except in my presence."

"Well, open it now," she said. He shook his head, "No, this is not the moment. You will understand why when" – lamely – "well, before you are much older."

When he had gone, she went into the little kitchenette in search of a screwdriver, determined that she would see for herself what he was keeping from her, but apparently tools were not included in Mrs

Hallam's household equipment, and, locking the door of her room and putting the key in her pocket, she went out, to find Ralph, a worried figure, biting his nails on the sidewalk before the mansions. He seemed relieved that she had come out so soon.

"You have a key of the flat: may I have it?" she asked.

For a second he seemed inclined to refuse, and then, with a smile, produced it from his waistcoat pocket.

"Really, Elsa, you're taking quite a high hand to deprive me of the key of my – "·

"Not your flat surely? I shouldn't like to feel that you had the means of entry day and night, Ralph," she said quietly, and for the second time that morning he coloured a deep red.

Refusing his escort, she found a taxi and drove back to a City restaurant, where she had a small lunch, before returning to her work.

The door of Amery's room was still locked, and when she knocked his voice asked sharply what she wanted. A few minutes after this the door was unlocked, and, going into the room, she found it empty.

At three o'clock the telephone bell rang. She took all the calls in her office, and those that were intended for her employer she switched through, after she had first made enquiries as to whether he would accept the call. This time: "Can I speak with Miss Marlowe?" asked a familiar voice.

"Yes, I'm speaking," said Elsa.

"It is Mr Tupperwill. Is Major Amery in?"

She recognized his voice before he told her his name.

"No, Mr Tupperwill, he is out."

"Is it possible for me to see you, Miss Marlowe? It is on rather an important matter, and I am particularly anxious that Major Amery should not know that I have called you."

"I can see you after office hours," she said. "Otherwise, I must get his permission to leave the office."

A long silence.

"Is that absolutely and vitally necessary?" asked the anxious voice of the banker. "I assure you I would not dream of asking you to come without your employer's knowledge unless the circumstances were very urgent; and they are very urgent, Miss Marlowe. I want to see you in the course of the next half-hour."

Elsa considered the possibility.

"I will come," she said, and cut short his thanks by hanging up the receiver.

Amery allowed her more freedom than most secretaries have, and she could have gone out without reference to him; but somehow she was reluctant, on this occasion, to take advantage of the liberty he gave to her. She turned the matter over in her mind and then knocked at the door.

"Come in."

He had returned so quietly that she had not heard him.

"I want to go out, Major Amery, for half an hour."

"Where are you going?" he demanded bluntly.

"Somebody wants to see me…Mr Tupperwill."

"Oh!"

"I don't think he wished you to know that I was going to him: that is rather natural, isn't it? You don't mind?" He shook his head.

"No, I don't mind a bit, but I'm glad you told me. If Tupperwill asks you whether I know where you have gone, you will tell him?"

"Why, of course!" she said in surprise.

"I think I should."

He was the strangest man, she thought, as the 'bus carried her toward Old Broad Street…the very strangest man. Such queer, unimportant details interested him. The big, vital things of life left him unmoved.

THE NEW CHAUFFEUR

Mr Tupperwill's office at the bank was situated on one of the innumerable courts that dive out of Old Broad Street and stagger through a labyrinth of passages to end no man knows where. One foot was on the step leading into the purlieus of the bank when Mr Tupperwill appeared. She had the impression that he had been waiting, for he hurried down to meet her, and, taking her arm in a paternal fashion, led her deeper into the maze of crooked passages that intersected one another.

"This is a short cut that will bring us to Lothbury," he said, leaving the girl without any explanation as to the business upon which he had called her so urgently to the centre of the City.

In Lothbury a car was waiting. She had a glimpse of a bearded chauffeur behind the window of his cabin.

"I haven't much time – " she began.

"I won't keep you a moment longer than is necessary," said Mr Tupperwill urgently.

The driver evidently had his instructions, for in a few minutes they were running through Moorgate Street toward the City Road.

"The matter I want to see you about is so important, so tremendously important, to me, that I simply dared not interview you at the bank. There is, I believe, a young lady at your place named Miss Dame?"

She nodded.

"I have met her once," said Mr Tupperwill, evidently labouring under the strain of a deep emotion. "She was introduced to the bank – do you mind if I pull those curtains?"

There were side curtains to the windows, and, without waiting for her permission, the stout man leant over and pulled them across so as to make it impossible that they should be seen from the street. He followed suit with the curtains on the other side, and then: "For your sake and my sake, I do not wish to be seen consulting you, Miss Marlowe."

"Why on earth not?" she demanded.

"There is a reason, a very pressing reason, which you will understand sooner or later. You know Miss Dame?"

"I know her very well."

"Are you aware" – his voice sank – "that she is a lady of considerable wealth?"

"Indeed I am not," smiled Elsa. "I am under the impression that her father is well off, but that she is only just as rich as he can make her."

"You think that?" Mr Tupperwill bit his lower lip, and maintained silence until they were running through a drab street in Islington.

"Where are we going, Mr Tupperwill? I must be back at the office in half an hour."

He nodded.

"I realize that. Believe me, I shall not keep you a moment longer than is necessary, and the Major will hardly miss you, even if he comes back."

"He came back just as I went out," she said, "and of course I told him that I was coming to see you."

She thought he had not heard this, for he did not answer her.

"He came back just as you were going out?" he said at last. "And you told him, of course, that you were coming to see me? That I should expect you to do. It is a very small point, and one which perhaps would not appeal to the average employee, but I hold it as a maxim that not in the slightest degree should one deceive an employer."

They were now in a street one side of which was occupied by a factory wall, and the other by a scattering of poor houses, except toward the farther end, where there was a yard of some kind, marked by high walls and a gate which was open.

The car swung as though it were going into the gateway, and at that moment Mr Tupperwill sprang to his feet, and, dropping the window with a crash, said something to the chauffeur. Instantly the man righted the machine and went slowly past the gates. Looking through, Elsa saw a little red quadrangle, surrounded on three sides by low buildings which had the appearance of stables.

"Now why on earth did my man do that?" gasped Mr Tupperwill in astonishment. "I don't like it, Miss Marlowe! I don't like it at all. He is a new man who came to me only last week, and – phew!" He mopped his large face. "I'm getting to the stage where I see a plot in the simplest action. I feel as if I am moving in an atmosphere of mystery and danger. In fact, Miss Marlowe, since that outrageous attack was made upon me, I have lost my nerve."

They were now clear of the mean streets and were traversing the principal shopping thoroughfare of Islington, and, as the girl saw with relief, moving back toward the City.

"You wanted to talk to me about Miss Dame," she reminded him.

"Yes, yes, but that incident put everything out of my mind. Miss Dame...yes. A curious girl. And you think she isn't wealthy?" he asked anxiously. "And that if she pretended to be wealthy, she was deceiving me?"

"Deceiving you! Surely she hasn't an account with Stebbing's?" The discreet Tupperwill evaded the question. He was apparently still preoccupied with his suspicions of the new chauffeur, for suddenly he burst forth fretfully: "I don't like it, I don't like it at all! And yet I had the most excellent references with this man."

She laughed.

"Surely, Mr Tupperwill, you're exaggerating a very insignificant incident?"

"I don't know." He shook his head. "I might have been driven into that yard and murdered! You may laugh, young lady. Laughter is the prerogative of youth, but fear is the instinct of age...I must write that down: it is almost epigrammatical."

Apparently, in his agitation, he had decided to drop all discussion of Jessie Dame and her delinquencies, and he left Elsa to piece together the fragments of his disjointed references to the girl.

The car dropped her in Wood Street, and she went back to the office, a little mystified, to find the sinister man sitting before her typewriter, laboriously tapping out a letter with one finger.

"Where is the 'h'?" he asked, without looking up.

She touched the key.

"Had a nice journey? Tupperwill ought to buy a new car."

"How did you know we went by car?"

"Feng Ho saw you," he said. "Did you notice Tupperwill's new chauffeur?"

"I saw the back of his head."

He laughed softly to himself.

"You should take a good look at his neck."

"Why?"

He did not satisfy her curiosity, but, with a shudder, she knew instinctively that behind that pleasant laugh was grim menace.

"What a horrible idea!" she said, shivering.

"Yes, it is, rather. I'm sorry. And yet a murderer's neck fascinates me."

"A murderer?" she gasped.

"I rather think so." He was still tapping his painful way through the alphabet. "That chauffeur killed Maurice Tarn."

JESSIE DAME AT HOME

"At least, that is my view," he said, without looking up from the machine at the white-faced girl. "Where is the 'j'? I can never find the 'j' on these machines. Oh, here it is! Yes, a stalwart man, with a beard and motor-goggles? Beard and motor-goggles are attached – and the beard is really clever. It is fixed to a silk lining that fits his chin as a glove fits your finger."

He was not looking at her.

"Yes, that was our friend," he went on pleasantly. "How far did you go?"

She described the journey, and told him of the curious little incident of the open gate.

"I thought Mr Tupperwill was unnecessarily alarmed," she said.

"Not unnecessarily," Amery answered gently. "Oh no, not unnecessarily! If the car had passed through that gateway, Mr Tupperwill would not be alive at this moment. Or, if he were alive, he would be in such a grievous plight that he would welcome a merciful end."

"Are you serious, Major Amery?"

He looked up quickly.

"I'm afraid I've alarmed you. Yes, I was quite serious."

"But does Mr Tupperwill know the character of this man?" she asked in horror.

"He will be warned before the day is out. You didn't see the chauffeur's face?"

She shook her head.

"No, I caught a glimpse of him. The driver's seat is enclosed in Mr Tupperwill's car, and it is rather difficult to see him. I only noticed that he was a very powerful-looking man, and I thought it strange that he wore a beard. Do you really know him?"

"The chauffeur? Yes, a gentleman named Stillman. A powerful looking fellow, eh? He is all that. What did he want to see you about – Tupperwill, I mean?"

She hesitated.

"There is no reason why you shouldn't know," she said at last. "It was about Miss Dame."

He inclined his head.

"I thought it might be," he said surprisingly.

"What would have happened to me?" she demanded.

"You?" He got up slowly from his chair, slipped the page he was typing from the machine, tore it into four parts and threw it into the wastepaper basket, before he replied: "I don't think anything very bad would have happened to you, but you might have been scared."

"Then only Mr Tupperwill was in danger?"

"In real danger – yes. Danger of life or limb, and that's the only kind that counts. When are you contemplating taking tea with Miss Dame?"

"I don't know. I'm not at all anxious to go."

"Go this evening," he said. " 'The pater' will interest you."

Her anxiety did not prevent her smiling.

"You know how she refers to him, then?"

He walked into his room and she followed. There was one question she wanted settled beyond all doubt.

"Major Amery," she began, "do you remember the night that Mr Tupperwill was attacked?"

"I remember it perfectly."

"You know that I found the weapon in your cupboard?"

"I also know that."

"It was you who struck him?"

He nodded.

"Yes, it was I. That your mind may be set at rest, it was an accident. The blow was not intended for Mr Tupperwill, and I had not the slightest idea that he was within range of my stick when I struck. And now let us forget that very unpleasant incident."

It occurred to Elsa, when she made known her intention, that Jessie Dame was not too pleased at the prospect of entertaining her friend.

"I don't know whether it will be convenient tonight," she said, and Elsa, who was quite ready to accept any excuse for dropping the project, was glad enough to murmur something about "some other evening" and make her escape.

But the visit was not to be postponed. Just as she was on the point of leaving, Jessie Dame appeared, already dressed for the street.

"I've been out to telephone to pater," she said breathlessly, "and he says he'll be very glad to see you. We'll take a taxi home, if you don't mind."

At any other time this extravagance on the part of the romantic young lady would have startled the girl, but the information which she had acquired about the wealth of the Dames made misgiving unnecessary.

The Dames' house was one of a dozen stucco dwellings in a short cul-de-sac off Ladbroke Grove. It had a tiny patch of grass lawn before the house, the inevitable laurel bushes planted near the railings, and the six steps up to the front door, which are peculiar to houses built at that period of Victorian history when English and American architects were apparently obsessed with the idea that London and New York might be flooded at any moment, and that it was necessary to build the ground floors ten feet above the level of the Street.

No sooner was Elsa inside the house than she realised that Jessie Dame was living in a much better style than she had imagined. The room into which she was shown was substantially, even handsomely, appointed, and if it erred at all, it was on the side of lavishness and over-ornamentation.

"I'll tell pater you're here," said Miss Dame, hurrying out of the room, to return after a considerable time with the bald and florid man whom Elsa had seen at the dance.

The first thing that struck her was the accuracy of Major Amery's description. The eyes were pale, the jaw full and fleshy, and the moustache was patently dyed. But for this, and his complete baldness, Mr Dame did not look old enough to be Jessie's father, for his complexion was flawless.

"Glad to know you, Miss Marlowe," he said.

The voice was harsh, like that of a man suffering from a cold.

"I have been expecting you to come over with Jess before. Come and have a look at the house."

He was undisguisedly proud of his establishment, and not until he had shown her over every room and into the immaculate kitchen was he satisfied. To maintain a polite interest through three floors of inspection would have been a tax at any ordinary time, but there was something about this house and the personality of its owner that interested the girl. She could endure the procession from one spare room to another without fatigue, and could honestly admire the economy of the kitchen equipment.

"No expense has been spared," said Mr Dame complacently. "It's a home, as I have often told Jess, that she ought to be proud of and ask no questions…what I mean to say is, that she ought to be content with what she's got. Don't you think so, miss?"

"I certainly do," said Elsa.

Evidently Jessie had moments of curiosity and unease, thought the girl, as she followed the proud owner into the garden.

It was a long strip of land, and it showed the practised hand of a skilled horticulturist. Again no expense had been spared to produce, within the limits of Mr Dame's modest estate, the best effects that money could buy.

"That's the garage," he said shortly.

At the bottom of the garden, running its width, was a one storeyed shed, substantially built, and lighted by two small windows placed just under the overhanging roof. As they looked, the door opened and a man lounged through, carrying a spade. Stripped to his shirt, he was wiping his forehead with a bare arm as he came into the cooler air, and for an instant he did not observe Mr Dame and his visitor. Then, almost at the second that Elsa recognized him, he scuttled back into the shed and slammed the door behind him. Quick as he was, Elsa recognised the labourer.

It was the bearded chauffeur, the murderer of Maurice Tarn!

THE SIGNER OF CHEQUES

Mr Dame had not noticed the incident. At the moment he was drawing attention to the tiny rock garden, and he did not observe that the girl was staring at the shed.

"Is that a garage?" she found her voice to ask.

"Yes, it's a garage," replied Mr Dame shortly. "The entrance is on the other side. There's a lane at the back. You must come here in the summer, miss, and see my roses…"

Had he noticed her white face? she wondered, for the shock had sent every vestige of colour from her cheeks.

Apparently Mr Dame was so absorbed in the pride of possession that he had no eyes for aught to which he could not lay claim, and by the time the tinkle of a bell summoned them to the ornate dining-room, where tea had been laid, she had recovered her self-possession.

"Well, what do you think of your boss, miss?" demanded Jessie Dame's father, nonchalantly pouring half the contents of his cup into the saucer. "A regular mystery?"

Elsa was not inclined to discuss the sinister man with anybody, least of all with an acquaintance of a few minutes.

"They tell me the life he leads you girls is perfectly hellish," Dame went on. "I keep telling Jessie to throw up the job and come home, but she's one of those obstinate girls that will have their own way. Oh, woman, woman!"

Perhaps it was his triteness, or the string of commonplaces, that reminded her for a second of Mr Tupperwill. Except that she liked the stout banker, and disliked this man with his furtive, cold blue eyes, most intensely.

"You have a car, Mr Dame?" she asked, anxious to keep off the subject of Amery.

"I haven't but I'm getting one. I've had the garage built three or four years, but never used it. In fact, I haven't been inside the place for a year."

"Father doesn't like anybody to go into the garage," said Jessie. "He says he won't let anybody enter until he's got a car to see. I wonder he hasn't bought it before."

"All in good time; everything comes to he who waits," said Mr Dame complacently.

When at last the time came for the girl to go, Jessie accompanied her to the sidewalk.

"What do you think of the pater?" she asked.

"He's a very interesting man," said Elsa safely.

"Yes, he's pretty interesting," said Jessie, without any trace of enthusiasm. "I suppose you're going home now? It must be nice to live alone."

Elsa looked at the girl quickly. There was something wistful in her eyes and in her voice, a human quality that momentarily transfigured her. Only for a flash, and then she was herself again.

"Come down and see us any time you want a cup of tea. The pater will be glad to show you over the garden," she said, and, running up the steps, closed the door almost before Elsa had left the gate.

Mr Dame was waiting in the dining-room when his daughter came back to him, and he was carefully carving off the end of a cigar.

"That's her, is it?"

"Yes, that's her. Why were you so anxious to see her, father?"

" 'Why was I so anxious to see her, father?' " he mimicked. "You get out of the habit of asking questions, will you? Now what have you got for me?"

She went to the side table where she had put her attache case when she came in, opened it and took out a few sheets of crumpled paper, which she passed to him.

"What is this?" he demanded wrathfully.

"It was all I could find," she said. "I got them out of the wastepaper basket."

"Didn't he write any other letters?"

"He may have done," said the girl. "Father, I think he's suspicious. Up to now the letters have come to me to be entered in the despatch book before they were posted. This afternoon he kept back all his own letters, and when I sent the office boy to ask for them, he said he was posting them himself in future."

The man scowled from his daughter to the crumpled typewritten sheets in his hand.

"These are all the same letter," he said. "What is the use of them to me?"

"I don't know, father. I've done all I could," said Miss Dame quietly. "I'm sure there are times when I feel ashamed to look him in the face, prying and sneaking as I do; and if Miss Marlowe only knew – "

"Shut up about Miss Marlowe 'only knowing,'" he said gruffly. "What I want to know is, why haven't I got his letters?"

"I've told you," said the girl with an air of desperation. "I can't take them out of his hand and copy them, can I? It was easy when they came to me to be entered, but he's stopped that now, and I'll have to do as I did before – get any scraps I can from the wastepaper basket."

He was reading the letter carefully, word by word, his stubby finger following the lines.

" FOI – what's that?" he muttered to himself. "All right, Jessie, you can go up to your room. Be dressed by seven o'clock and I'll take you out and give you some dinner."

She shook her head.

"I don't want to go tonight."

"What you want to do and what I want you to do are two different things," he shouted. "Get dressed!"

Jessie Dame ran like a scared rabbit, and when, three-quarters of an hour later, she came down to the dining-room, she saw that he was still in his day suit.

"I've changed my mind about taking you out," he said. "You must go by yourself. And sign these before you go."

There were three blank cheques on the table; they were upon Stebbing's Bank, and, taking up the pen, she signed, in her angular writing, "H Stillman," blotted them and gave them back to him.

"Is there nothing else, father?" she asked timidly.

"Yes, there is something else. You'll dine at the Cardinal and go on to the Mispah about half past nine. If anybody asks you where I am, you can tell them that I'm on the premises somewhere. You'll stay at the Mispah till two o'clock. You've always said that you like being with classy people – well, you'll stay with 'em a little later tonight. You understand?"

"Yes, father," she said meekly.

"I don't want you back a minute before two."

"Yes, father," she said again, picked up her cloak from the chair and went out. And none would guess, seeing the misery in her face, that Jessie Dame was sallying forth to the desirable association of classy people.

MR TUPPERWILL SEEKS ADVICE

Long after Elsa had left the office, Major Amery was sitting at his desk, his swift pen covering sheet after sheet of foolscap. He wrote a beautiful clear, almost copperplate hand, and with a rapidity which, in all the circumstances, was remarkable.

He had come to the bottom of the sixth sheet when there was a gentle tap on his door, and, rising, he crossed the floor, turned the key and pulled the door open. It was the night watchman who was in charge of the premises between business hours.

"I beg your pardon, sir; I didn't want to disturb you, but there's a gentleman wishes to see you – Mr Tupperwill."

Amery looked at his watch: it was half past six.

"Show him up, please," he said, and, going back to his desk, put his writing away in a drawer and swung round in his chair to face the door through which Mr Tupperwill presently came.

The banker was obviously ill at ease. He closed the door behind him and stood behind the chair to which Amery pointed, his hands resting on the back, grotesquely reminiscent of a budding politician about to make his maiden speech.

"You will think this visit is remarkable, Major Amery," he began huskily, "particularly since I cannot claim to be – ah – a very close friend, or even an intimate acquaintance."

"I was expecting you to come," said Amery shortly. "Won't you sit down?"

Mr Tupperwill lifted the tails of his frock coat and sat gingerly. "The truth is, I am in such confusion of mind that I hardly know

228

which way to turn, whose advice to seek; and thinking matters over in the privacy of my office, I decided that you, as a man of the world, and a man, moreover, of vast experience beyond my range, would perhaps be able to assist me in forming a conclusion. Major Amery, I am beset by enemies – and if that sounds to you a little highly coloured and melodramatic, I beg that you will bear with me for a little while. The matter which I will ask your patience to discuss affects not only the honour of my name, but the very foundations of my business."

He stopped and licked his dry lips. Amery made no reply; he sat, tense and alert, waiting for what was to follow.

"You were good enough, at a moment when I was extremely angry, to make a prediction, which, alas! seems upon the point of fulfilment," Mr Tupperwill went on. "That prediction, in effect, was that a certain client of the bank would drag me and my business into the mud. I fear, I very greatly fear, that your prediction is within measurable distance of fulfilment. Major Amery, I have trusted a certain person beyond limits that a banker and a business man can safely go. I have been deceived. The bank has been the victim of the grossest duplicity; and now, not only is my fortune, but my very life, threatened, as the result of my stupendous folly.

"Two years ago I was at the head of a flourishing commercial concern, respected and honoured throughout the City of London – "

"Two years ago," interrupted Amery, "you were at the head of a bankrupt business, which was maintained in existence by the falsification of accounts!"

His words fell like hammer blows upon steel,

"Stebbing's has been insolvent for years," he went on remorselessly. "It is your boast that you defied the efforts of the joint stock banks to absorb you. The truth is, that you dare not allow an impartial investigation into the affairs of Stebbing's, knowing well that honest auditors would bring you into the criminal court, and eventually into one of His Majesty's prisons."

Mr Tupperwill did not change colour, but there was a pathetic droop to his lip and an almost tearful entreaty in his eyes, as he blinked stupidly at his accuser.

"I hope that what you say is not true," he said in a hushed voice. "If it is, then indeed I have been more grossly deceived than I imagined, and there has been a conspiracy to deceive me. It is true that I am in a bad way. Certain indiscretions, which came to the knowledge of an unscrupulous man, have placed me in his power. The circumstances I have put down in black and white," he said impressively, "and I have come to you to ask you whether, if that document were placed in your hands, it would be of any service to you or to me?"

"None whatever," said Amery promptly, and Mr Tupperwill's face fell.

"On the last occasion we met, you referred to a gentleman named – ah – Stillman. Now, Major Amery, I wish to avoid unpleasantness; I wish to avoid – ruin! You, knowing so much, can advise me. It may be that this is the last time that you and I will ever discuss this matter, the last opportunity for adjustment."

Amery looked at him steadily.

"There will be other opportunities," he said.

Before the interview ended Mr Tupperwill had something to say.

"I am a man of peace. The violent expressions of human feeling are repugnant, indeed terrifying, to me. I have had one horrible experience, and do not wish that to be repeated."

He touched the scar on his head feelingly.

"And yet I have the sensation that I am drifting into a welter of violence. That I am surrounded by unscrupulous, evil, possibly cruel men, who will not hesitate to wreak their vengeance on me, and I am appealing to you, as a man of action, for help and guidance. Major Amery, a week ago I engaged a new chauffeur. The man came to me with the most excellent credentials; he had a character from the Army, he had eulogistic recommendations from previous employers, and as a chauffeur he is everything that I could desire, except" – he hesitated – "I cannot escape a suspicion that he is not what he seems. The man has come in and out of my house without let or hindrance, and my butler informs me that on one occasion he has found him in my bedroom."

Leaning forward, he went on, in a lower voice.

"In my bedroom is a wall safe, in which I keep a few important papers, a number of trinkets of no especial value, and this morning I missed a small book, containing particulars of my private account. It was not an ordinary book: it has the appearance of a gold case, and was presented to me by my dear father many years ago."

"What is in the book besides your accounts?"

"Nothing. A number of addresses, a few memoranda about our family fortune, particulars of the combination of my safe at the office, my private deposits at the Bank of England, and suchlike."

"If you think this man has stolen it," said Amery with a weary sigh, "why don't you call in the police?"

Mr Tupperwill raised his eyes slowly to the other's.

"You have told me my business is bankrupt; you have taunted me with the fact that I dare not allow independent investigation; you have suggested that there are secrets about Stebbing's which could not be revealed. One or two of those secrets are in that book, Major Amery."

He rose with a long-drawn sigh.

"I fear I have wearied you," he said, "but remember that I am a man torn with anxiety and doubt, a man placed in the most cruel dilemma. Your advice, your help, your co-operation would have meant much to me, and perhaps much to you."

He brushed his silk hat on his sleeve in an absent-minded way, looked thoughtfully at the shattered face of the cupboard by the side of the fireplace, and then, with another sigh and a little bow, waddled out, a picture of dejection and misery.

Amery sat listening to his footfalls until there was silence in the office. Then he lit a thin black cigar and blew a cloud of smoke to the ceiling. A deep frown furrowed his forehead; his expression was one of irritation. Nobody would have guessed that his mind was wholly concentrated upon Elsa Marlowe.

MAJOR AMERY GOES OUT

The church bells were striking seven when he walked out into Wood Street and, reaching Cheapside, allowed three taxis to pass him before he called the fourth.

Before he could put his hand upon the bell of his door it was opened by Feng Ho, who followed him into his study.

"Do you know a man named Jarvie?"

Amery nodded.

"He was arrested this afternoon. He and a man named Samson, at Hull."

Amery nodded again.

"Bickerson is busy," he said. "One supposes that the fall of Dr Ralph Hallam is very near at hand."

"If I had my way he should sleep on the Terraces of the Night," said Feng Ho murderously. They were speaking in the Chinese dialect, the Chinaman standing by the desk, looking down at his master as he went over his letters.

"That is a heavy punishment for folly, Feng Ho."

"For murder, master," said Feng Ho. "For this Hallam killed the old man. Was I not in the room, searching, when he came in? Did I not hear, with my remarkable ears, the 'swiff!' of the knife as it came from his pocket? I think I was a fool to have turned out the lights when I came into the house, but it was very tempting. The control switch is just inside the door below the stairs, and I turned it out because I wanted to make sure whether the old man was awake. If he had been the lights going out would have brought him on to the landing."

"Nevertheless, you're wrong. The man who killed Tarn was Stillman."

The Chinaman clucked his lips impatiently, but made no other comment. He followed his master upstairs, and, while he was in his bath, laid out Amery's dress suit. The sinister man had nearly finished his dressing before he gave his instructions.

"I shall be in Box One – that is the box nearest to the stage. Get me the Listener."

Feng Ho found a small flat black box in a drawer, and, bulky as it was, Amery put it in the tail pocket of his dress coat.

"And a gun," said Amery.

Feng Ho produced from the same receptacle a short, heavy Browning, snapped home the magazine, and, pulling back the jacket, fastened the safety catch.

"This is better," he said.

As if by magic, there appeared in his hand a short broad knife with a lacquered handle. He stropped it tenderly on his palm, and, stooping, picked up a piece of tissue paper that had come out of Amery's collar-box, rolled it into a ball and threw it into the air. As it fell, the knife flickered and the paper ball fell in two parts.

" 'All men fear steel,' " he quoted the old Cantonese proverb with some smugness. "It is silent and swift and very satisfactory."

Major Amery smiled.

"So I should think," he said drily, "but I will take the gun." He pushed it into his hip pocket. "And now get me sandwiches and a glass of Tokay. Have the car in the little street that runs by Covent Garden Market. You'd better be in the crowd before the portico. There is always a throng to see people going into the Opera."

He finished his apology for a dinner, then he took up the telephone and called a Treasury number.

"Is that Scotland Yard? I want to speak to Superintendent Wille."

After a long delay, a voice answered him which he knew was not the Superintendent's.

"Major Amery," he said, in answer to the enquiry.

After another little wait, there was a click, and Wille's gruff voice greeted him curtly.

"It is Major Amery speaking. I have an important statement to make to the police, and I wish to see Mr Bickerson at my house at eleven o'clock."

"What is it about?" asked Wille.

"I think I would rather tell Bickerson. He is in charge of the case."

"A dope story, eh? All right, I'll get in touch with him and send him to you."

"At eleven o'clock," said Amery, and hung up the receiver with a little smile.

The news of Jarvie's arrest had come to Ralph Hallam like a thunderclap, and when it had been followed by a long-distance phone call from Hull, telling him that a second member of the gang had been taken, he was almost panic-stricken. That evening he spent an uncomfortable hour locked in his room, burning papers and small account-books, and it was nine o'clock before he remembered that he had promised to call on Lou, and that she would be waiting for him.

He found his wife fuming.

"I'm supposed to be going to dinner," she said shrilly. "Haven't you got any clocks in your house?"

"Go to supper instead," he snarled. "Where is the girl?"

"In her room," snapped Mrs Hallam, "where she spends all her evenings. Is she staying here for life?"

"She'll be going in a day or two. Come in here."

He opened the drawing-room door and almost dragged her in.

"Now listen, Lou: I'm in a pretty bad way. There is trouble – police trouble – and it will require all my ingenuity to crawl out of the wreckage when my affairs collapse, as they will very shortly. I have a little ready money, but I want a whole lot, and you've got to help me all you can, unless you wish your allowance to drop dead."

"What is all this?" she asked suspiciously.

"Now listen." She saw he was in deadly earnest. "I want you to stay here till eleven o'clock, then you can go out to supper. You were going

to the Mispah, weren't you? There's a late dance. Stay till it breaks —
that will be two in the morning."

She shot a suspicious glance at him.

"I see," she said, and he would have been dense if he had missed
the sneer in her tone.

"No harm is coming to the girl: you need have no fear of that," he
assured her.

"Even that wouldn't keep me awake at night," she said callously.
"But I think you're well advised, Ralph, not to go too far there. She's
got a letter for you."

His mouth opened in amazement.

"A letter for me? What do you mean?"

"The maid found it under her pillow this morning, addressed to
Dr Ralph Hallam, and in Amery's handwriting. On the top of the
envelope are the words, 'To be used in emergency.' You're looking a
little white, Ralph. What has he got on you?"

"Nothing," said the man roughly. "How do you know it is his?"

"If I didn't know, I'd guess," she said coolly. "He put his initials to
the last remark — P A. So I warn you, go slow!"

"I tell you no harm will come to the girl. It isn't the girl I want at
all; it is something else. I've thought it all out, Lou. Suppose I appear
in the middle of the night, she'll think all sorts of things, and when I
say that I just want to look at the box, she'll be glad enough to let me
take it out."

"What is in the box?" she asked curiously. "I looked into it the
other day; the bottom part is screwed down. Do you want me to stay
on till eleven? Is that necessary?"

He nodded.

"It will be better if she thinks you're here. I can explain to her later
that you've gone out. What is she doing?"

"Listening to that darned monkey-box," she said impatiently, and
then: "Very well, I will do as you ask. Do you want anything?"

"Nothing, except a key. She has mine."

She handed him a flat key, and he put it in his pocket. "Wait. Before
you go, I'd like to hear some more about this crash and wreck and

crawling out that you were talking about when you came in. Ralph, what's your game? Are you dope running?"

He nodded.

"How did you guess?" he asked.

"It's the only kind of crime so free from danger that you'd take it on," she said quietly. "Tarn was in it too, wasn't he? I thought so. And is Tupperwill?"

"Tupperwill!" he said contemptuously. "I don't think he's got too much money, but he's straight enough."

She laughed quietly.

"That idea struck me too – I mean, about his having no money. Even if he does have his books bound in gold – "

She checked herself as she saw his piercing eye upon her.

"I peeped into his library when I was there," she went on glibly. "He's certainly a highbrow reader."

She saw him out and shut the door on him, then came back to her bedroom, opened a little drawer and took out a shining gold object, that might have been mistaken for a bloated cigarette case, but was, in fact, a small note-book bound between golden covers. She turned the thin leaves with a contemptuous curl of her lip, and threw the thing back in her drawer. She had taken a lot of trouble and a considerable risk for nothing, and there was certainly more satisfaction in surveying (as she did with pride) a brilliant diamond sunburst that she had acquired during her visit to India.

At ten o'clock she knocked at Elsa's door and went in, without invitation, since she had learnt by experience that an enthusiastic listener-in cannot hear anything but the sounds which are coming from the ether.

Elsa took off her headphones with a smile.

"It is very beautiful. I wonder you don't listen, Mrs Hallam," she said. "Are you going out?"

"I don't know," said Lou mendaciously. "I haven't quite made up my mind what to do. You are all right here?"

"Perfectly," said Elsa. "Please don't worry about me. And, Mrs Hallam, I think I have found a flat for myself. I don't want to inflict myself upon you a day longer than is necessary."

"You're welcome," said Lou Hallam mechanically. "Just stay as long as you like, my dear."

She looked down at the box against the wall.

"Why don't you have that old thing put into my lumber-room?" she asked. "It takes up a lot of space."

"I think it had better stay here until I go," said Elsa, and thereafter the conversation drifted into awkward pauses, the girl anxious to get back to her opera, Mrs Hallam just as anxious to begin her dressing.

At last an excuse came: the telephone bell rang in the dining-room, and Mrs Hallam went out. It was Ralph.

"You might keep your eye on the street outside," he said. "If you see anybody who is apparently watching the house, will you let me know?"

"Are you scared of that?" she asked, and was cursed for her insolence.

When Elsa resumed her listening, she discovered that the broadcasting station had switched over. She listened to weather reports, the latest news, barometer readings and the like.

"In a quarter of an hour," said the voice from nowhere, "we shall switch you over to the Opera House and you will hear the last act of 'Faust.' "

She put down the headphones and took up a book, trying to read. But her mind was elsewhere, as it had been even as she listened to Gounod's masterpiece. There was something very fascinating about the sinister man, but it wasn't the fascination that the spectacle of perversity exercises. She felt that she had penetrated the outer layer of his nature, and had learnt something of the real man which lay beneath. He puzzled her, he frightened her, but he never revolted her. Her keen woman's instinct had vibrated to the fineness of his character, and whatever were his offences, his wrongdoings, she felt he was a good man. It was so absurd a conclusion that she almost laughed.

And yet he was good, and, despite his bearishness, kindly, and, behind his suspicions, trustful. She could not understand him; he was a man who must be taken in the whole, his faults accepted, his delinquencies excused. She wondered how many women had fallen in love with him, or whether any had had the vision to get beneath the unpleasing surface and find something worshipful. Not that she worshipped him, she told herself hastily, or even loved him. She wasn't sure, now that she came to analyse her mind, that she liked him. This was sliding on a treacherous surface, she decided, and took up her headphones in time to hear the burst of applause that followed the opening aria.

The reception was perfect; it almost seemed as if she were sitting in a box within a few feet of the stage. Every note, every delicate cadence, was clearly marked.

Marguerite was singing when, of a sudden, the voice died down, and instead came a hubbub of sound which she could not understand. A voice said: "Go away – get off the stage!" And then another spoke thunderously in her ears.

"Elsa!"

She gasped. It was the voice of Major Amery.

"Elsa, lock your door and barricade it. Admit nobody! Do you hear? Lock your door immediately. You are in the deadliest danger!"

THE ALARM CALL

Almost at the back of his box Major Amery sat, listening, and yet not listening, to the delicious harmonies of the opera. The box next to him was empty. Twice he had opened the little black box, and taken out something which looked like a stethoscope, the disc end of which he had applied to the wall. No sound came from the box, until the curtain had gone up on the last act of "Faust." Then, without the aid of his apparatus, he heard a sound of chairs being moved. Two men had come into the box, and he judged, from the location of their voices, that they, too, were sitting well back from observation. He put the receiver to the wall and listened, immediately recognizing the two voices.

"…she is the biggest card to play. We may be able to pull off a hundred to one chance if you get her…"

The second voice mumbled something, and then:

"…I had thought of that. We can kill two birds with one stone. The stuff is in the box of course? The old man took it away from Stanford's the night before his death and brought it to his place in Elgin Crescent… It is all American stuff, and easy to change, but I must have the girl as well… I have arranged that…eleven o'clock…five minutes to eleven. I believe in working to a timetable."

There was a silence, and at that moment Amery incautiously jerked at the thin wire connecting the microphone with the small battery at the bottom of the black box. The wire snapped. Instantly his capable fingers were stripping the silk covering from either end, and a new junction was made. But when he put the receiver to the wall, there was a silence. He thought for a moment that the battery had gone wrong, and, dropping the earpieces, he stepped out into the corridor and opened the door of the next box stealthily. It was empty!

"Five minutes to eleven!"

And they worked to schedule! He looked at his watch and gasped. It was exactly that hour.

Only for a second did he hesitate. Marguerite was in the centre of the stage, enthralling the silent audience with her glorious voice but he did not see her, did not hear her. All he knew was that, somewhere in London, a defenceless girl was listening-in, and in another second he had leapt from his box to the stage.

Immediately the house was in an uproar. Marguerite fell back affrighted, on the verge of tears; fierce voices called to him from the wings; but he was walking along the footlights, looking for the microphone, and then he found it and, stooping, shouted his warning. In another second strong arms had gripped him and pulled him back out of sight, and he was facing an enraged manager.

"Send for a policeman," said a shrill voice. "He's drunk!"

Two stalwart stage hands were holding his arms; the manager, almost hysterical with rage, was shaking his fist in the expressionless face; and then Amery said: "Take me to your office. I've something to say to you."

"You can say it here!" screamed the theatrical man. "How dare you, you scoundrel!…"

Amery said something in a low voice and the man's expression changed.

"You're probably bluffing, but come along," he said gruffly, and the sinister man followed him to a little office behind the stage.

There was a telephone on the table, and, without asking permission, Amery took it up.

He got through to his objective, and for three minutes he was speaking rapidly, fiercely, whilst the dazed manager listened, dumbfounded. Presently he put the instrument down.

"The way out – quick!"

The manager piloted him down and up stairs, along narrow corridors, and finally into the street.

"I'll help you find your car – do you want any assistance?"

Amery shook his head.

"Herbert Mansions," he said, as he sprang on the footboard and took his place by the driver's side. "Go slow as you go round the corner: I want to pick up Feng Ho. After that, there are no traffic regulations in London for me tonight!"

Elsa heard the words and listened, stunned, for a moment beyond comprehension. It was the voice of the sinister man, warning her to lock her door…she was in danger!

She tore the phones from her head, ran to the door and turned the key, and, as she did so, she heard a rustling sound outside and the handle turned in her hand.

"Who is there?" she asked, affrighted.

And then there came to her ears a scream that ended in a stifled sob, a scream that turned her blood to water.

"Help!"

It was Lou Hallam's scream that rose and died to a gurgle.

She thought she was going to faint, but, calling into play all her will power, she pulled at the box and set it against the door. In another minute the little bedstead had been wrenched across the room and wedged against the box.

"Open, I want to come in," said a muffled voice.

"Who are you?"

"Open the door, I tell you. I won't hurt you. I want the box. Give me the box and I swear to you that I will do no harm."

"Who are you?" she asked again. "Where is Mrs Hallam? What have you done to her?"

She heard a muffled curse, and then the door shook under his weight.

There were two men there now: she heard them in consultation. What should she do? She ran to the window and threw it open. The

241

street below was deserted. There was no escape that way. If she could only see somebody – somebody to whom she could appeal.

Mrs Hallam's flat was on the third floor, and escape from this direction was impossible. Presently she saw a figure crossing the road, and screamed.

"Stop that!" cried a voice from the passage, hoarse with anger and fear. "Stop shouting, or I'll shoot!"

At that moment the panel smashed in, and she saw a pair of eyes glaring at her malevolently and shrank back.

It was just then that the whine of a car came to her ears. She looked out again: the machine had stopped at the door; three men were getting out and were racing up the flagged path to the vestibule. The assailant outside had heard something too.

"Thank God!" she cried wildly.

The man outside heard her voice; there was a rustle of footsteps in the passage, and then suddenly the corridor, which had been in darkness, was illuminated, and she heard a familiar voice.

"Don't move, my friend. Unless you have an important appointment with Peter."

It was Amery!

A door slammed; it was the kitchen door, which was almost opposite her own, and she heard a smothered exclamation of annoyance from the Major. In another second she saw him, through the hole in the door, pass to the kitchen and switch on the lights. She saw that the outer door of the kitchen was wide open and that he went out to a small balcony and peered down. Then he came back.

"Are you all right?" he asked sharply.

"Yes – yes!" she quavered. "I'm quite all right. Have they gone?"

"They've gone all right," was the grim reply. "There is a service lift from the kitchen balcony; I think they slid down the rope."

She was making a feeble effort to remove the barricade, but her strength had suddenly evaporated, and she had to stop twice and sit down, before eventually she removed the final obstacle and opened the door to him.

In the passage by the front door she saw Feng Ho, and a man in uniform, whom she recognised as Amery's chauffeur.

"Feng Ho, get the lady some water," said Amery shortly. "Where is Mrs Hallam?"

She could not speak until the water came.

"I don't know – I thought she had gone out," gasped the girl as she lifted the glass to her lips with a trembling hand, "but I heard somebody scream – dreadfully!"

He left her and walked into the dining-room, turning on the lights. The room was empty. From there he passed to the drawing-room, with the same result.

"Where does she sleep?"

The girl pointed. The door of Mrs Hallam's room was locked, and he rattled on the handle.

"Somebody is there," he said, and flung his whole weight at the door, which burst open with a crash.

He turned on the light and stood for a moment gazing at the sight which presented itself. Mrs Hallam lay half on and half off her bed; her face was blue, her handsome dress was torn, there was blood on her white shoulder, but more menacing was the silk scarf tied about her throat.

In an instant Amery was at her side and had removed the strangling silk.

His voice brought the girl, who, at the sight of the woman's plight, forgot her own weakness. Together they lifted her on to the bed; and whilst the girl searched for brandy at his request, Major Amery made a rapid inspection of the apartment.

In many ways it resembled his own study after the visit of the unknown burglars. Drawers had been opened and their contents thrown on the floor; the dressing-table had been swept clean. For what had they been searching? he wondered. Hitherto he had not regarded Mrs Hallam as a serious factor in the game. And yet this had been no wanton attack; there was a reason behind it. What that reason was, he was determined to discover.

In a few minutes the woman recovered consciousness, staring at him blankly.

"Was it you?" she croaked. "Oh, you devil!"

He shook his head.

"If you mean, was it I that attacked you, I can reassure you on that point," he said. "Have you lost anything?"

With difficulty she got up on her feet and staggered across to the dressing-table.

"The book is gone – that's all, the book!"

"The book? What book?" he asked quickly.

"A little gold book."

A light suddenly dawned on the sinister man.

"Tupperwill's?"

She nodded.

"How did you come to have it? But I can guess the answer. You took it, then?"

She nodded again.

"I borrowed it" – she explained with difficulty.

"I see."

So that was the explanation, and a logical one!

"Now, young lady" – he turned to the girl – "I think we can leave Mrs Hallam for a while. I want to see you in a place of safety. Will you stay here for five minutes and promise not to move?"

She nodded, and the next instant he had disappeared. She guessed, from the direction he took, that he was in her room, and speculated on what took him there. True to his word, he was back in five minutes, carrying a suitcase which she recognized as her own. The thought that he had been collecting her clothes was so odd that she could have laughed.

"I think the Palace Hotel is a very safe place for you tonight," he said.

The girl glanced at Mrs Hallam, who had recovered her normal pallor.

"You had better ring up your husband and tell him – " he began, and then the sound of a key in the front door made him walk into the passage.

Ralph Hallam stood stock still at the unexpected apparition of the sinister Amery.

THE ARREST

"What are you doing here?" he asked harshly.

"The same question might be applied to you," was the cool response. "Really, Hallam, you are the quickest mover I know!"

"Where are you going, Elsa?" demanded Hallam.

"I'll save this lady the trouble of answering you. I'm taking her to the Palace Hotel, where she will be safer."

Ralph saw the light coming from his wife's room and strode down the passage. One glance he gave at the room, its tumbled contents and the pale face of the woman, and then he spun round.

"What is the explanation of this?" he demanded. "You're not getting away with this, Amery."

"Somebody attacked your wife and made their escape as I came in."

"How did you get in?"

Amery smiled.

"I am going to answer no more questions tonight. I haven't the time," he said, and was walking to the door when Ralph stood before him.

"What have you got in that suitcase?"

Amery considered a second, then: "Something over a million dollars," he said coolly, "the property of Miss Marlowe. I found it in the bottom of her box, and I am now about to put it in a place of safety."

Ralph's face went red and white.

"You're not leaving here until you explain…"

"Tomorrow I'll give you an explanation that will satisfy you," said Amery, with a touch of his old irascibility. "For the moment you've got to do some quick guessing. I've warned you once before, Hallam that there isn't room for two crowds in your profession, and you are on the edge of finding how truthful I can be! Get home and lock yourself tight – or, better still, club a policeman and get yourself arrested. The angel of death is abroad tonight!"

Ralph Hallam staggered against the wall and watched the two pass out of sight, like a man in a dream.

Feng Ho was waiting outside the door, and to him Amery issued a word of instructions.

"You will remain here; trail Hallam – I want to know where I can find him."

They passed down the stairs into the deserted street. His chauffeur was turning the car, and opposite the door was a taxicab which had apparently just driven up, for two men stood talking to the driver. Amery's subsequent error was excusable.

"You men come from Superintendent Wille?"

"Wille? I don't know anything about Wille, but we're from Scotland Yard," said one of them unpleasantly. "Are you Amery?"

"That is my name."

"I have a warrant for your arrest, Major."

Amery looked at him incredulously.

"A warrant for me? What is the charge?"

"You hardly want telling that, do you? You'll find out when you get to the station. I have only instructions to take you into custody."

There was a silence.

"There is some mistake here," Amery said. "At any rate, I'll go along with you, but perhaps you will let me first drop this lady at the Palace Hotel?"

The man did not answer but followed him into the taxi, handing the suit-case to the driver, and by the light of a street standard which flashed past, the prisoner caught a glimpse of a long-barrelled revolver in the detective's hand. The man must have known that the weapon had been seen for he said:

247

"I'm giving you a word of advice, Major Amery. Don't put your hand to your hip pocket or you'll be shot. I'm taking no risks with you. And whilst we're discussing the subject…" he pressed the muzzle of the pistol against the other's white waistcoat and, reaching down, drew the Browning from his pocket. Another instant, and a circle of steel snapped about Amery's wrist.

"Hold still or you'll get hurt," said the other man, speaking for the first time.

The voice sounded familiar to the girl, but it was Major Amery who identified the man.

"Can it be 'pater'?" he asked mockingly. "Really, Mr Dame, I've misjudged you – I thought you did no work for a living!"

Jessie Dame's father! Elsa uttered a cry as she too identified the man. What did it mean? Was he a detective?

Amery's next words put the matter beyond all doubt.

"This is a trap and I have fallen right into it," he said, "an old stager like me! Where are we going?"

"You'll find out."

She heard the jingle of Amery's handcuffs, and then a bright light pierced the gloom as one of their captors switched a pocket lamp upon the manacled hands.

"'Perfectly marvellous,' as your daughter would say," sneered Amery. "No precautions omitted, no risks taken, eh? I see we are taking the back street route, and, I guess, a very circuitous one at that, but not to a police station, I gather? Where are we going?" he asked again.

"Wait and find out," growled Dame.

"At least you will allow the lady to leave us?"

Dame guffawed.

"To go to the nearest copper and spill it?" he asked contemptuously. "Have a bit of sense, Major. Besides, we want her."

Of course they wanted her, he remembered. She was to be the hundred to one chance that they were banking on.

With the light on his wrists, there was no chance of ridding himself of the handcuffs, and he knew these characters too well to make any attempt to attract the attention of the very few pedestrians they passed.

They had not a very long distance to go. The car passed up a street composed of a suburban type of house, turned into a narrow opening, and stopped before what looked to be a one storeyed building. The driver of the taxi got down, opened the door, and first Amery and then the girl were led into the darkness.

Scarcely had the cab disappeared carrying Amery and his captors, than Feng Ho flew down the sidewalk and called to the chauffeur who had just drawn up by the cab.

"Where is the Major?" he asked.

"I don't know; I'm waiting for him."

"He came out this moment. Didn't you see him, oh foolish blind man?"

"I saw a man and a lady, but I didn't know it was the Major. Why did he go off in a cab?"

Feng Ho uttered something in Chinese, and at that moment he was joined by the ruffled Ralph Hallam.

"Did you see him go, medical doctor?"

"See who go?" asked the other sourly. "If you mean Amery, I didn't."

He was turning to walk away when Feng Ho seized his arm and poured forth such a stream of voluble, pedantic English that for a time Hallam could not grasp his meaning.

"Who is he?" he asked incredulously.

"They have incarcerated him, I tell you, medical sir," said the Chinaman, in a state of anguish.

"Tell me again what you said – who is Major Amery?"

And, when Feng Ho had finished, Ralph turned to the chauffeur.

"Which way did the cab go?"

"I didn't notice, sir. You can easily find out. Drive up to the end of the road."

It was not until Feng Ho gave the order that the chauffeur obeyed.

At the end of the street they found a policeman, who had seen a cab, which might or might not have been that in which Amery was travelling. When, after five minutes' drive, they overtook the taxi, they found it was empty. Another clue brought as unsatisfactory an ending, and then, when Feng Ho had sent the car in a third direction and had himself elected to walk to the nearest police station, a cab came past, and he saw, by the reflected light of the lamp that was burning inside, a face which he immediately recognized.

It was only for the fraction of a second that he saw the man. The cab was going at a good pace, and there was no time to recall the car. With long, tireless strides, Feng Ho went in pursuit. The machine drove across Bayswater Road, entered a narrow thoroughfare that opened into a square, and then began the ascent of a slight rise.

He was gaining on the cab when there appeared from nowhere four men, two from each side of the road, and without warning they closed in upon him. Gasping and breathless, Feng Ho stood at bay, a knife in his hand. He drove the first man back, but the second caught him under his guard. He did not see the flicker of steel that brought him low, and, with a choking sob, he fell on his knees, and the man with the knife struck again.

"Into that garden, quick!" hissed his assailant who had struck at him.

They lifted the limp figure, and with a swing flung it over the railings. There was a thud as the body struck, and then silence...

"Mind how you step," warned Dame. "Have you got that chain there?"

The taxi-driver pushed past them, and Amery heard the jangle of a chain being passed through what he guessed was a bolt or socket of some kind. Then his hands were seized, something snapped on the connecting chain of the handcuffs, and he was drawn to the wall until the links touched what he found to be a steel bolt through which the chain had been drawn.

"Don't you step anywhere, miss," warned Dame, "or you'll break your neck!"

The door had been shut behind them, but even the confinement of the place could not account for the curiously dead sound of their voices. There was a splutter of flame as Dame's companion lit a lantern candle, and by its light Amery saw that the driver had disappeared.

They were in a brick shed measuring some twenty feet by ten. He could only guess it was brick, because the walls were hung with dark brown Army blankets, and this had accounted for the unusual deadness of all sound. In the middle of this apartment, which was floored with cement, was a deep hole, as near as he could judge some five or six feet in depth, of similar length, and about two feet wide. It had obviously been dug by skilled hands.

"What is that?" whispered the girl.

She was crouching at Amery's side.

"It looks like pater's garage," he said coolly. "You know what this place reminds me of, Dame?"

"I don't want to hear anything from you," growled the man.

"It reminds me of an execution shed. That hole could be made a little wider and a little deeper, a wooden trap, a lever for release, a stout oak beam and a steel winch…it's a horrible feeling to be wakened at six in the morning and be told to dress yourself in the clothes you wore at the trial. I've seen men go mad – better men than you, Dame. Ever read Wilde's poem –

> " '*The hangman with his gardener gloves*
> *Slips through the padded door,*
> *And binds one with three leathern thongs*
> *That the throat may thirst no more*'?"

"Blast you!" screamed Dame, his face livid and in his eyes a great fear. "I'll tear your cursed tongue out if you don't keep your mouth shut!"

Amery chuckled softly. He had to look across his shoulder at the man, for he was held tight to the bolt in the wall.

"Come on, you!" Dame was speaking to the girl, and Amery's eyes glittered.

"You'll look after her, Dame, because, whilst there is a chance of reprieve for plain murder, any aggravation of the crime, anything that turns the jury's mind to loathing – don't forget they have women jurors in murder trials – will make it hard for you and friend Stillman."

"Take her out!" cried Dame hoarsely. "Through that door." His hand was shaking like a man with ague.

"Don't let me go, don't let me go!" she begged, half mad with terror.

"Hush!" His voice was gentle and infinitely sweet. "I love you too dearly to have you hurt. You will remember that, won't you? The 'sinister man' loves you better than anything in life."

He dropped his head down to the white, upturned face, and their lips met, and in that moment of supreme happiness she forgot their dreadful surroundings, forgot the danger in which they stood, was conscious only of the glory which wrapped her as in a sheet of living flame. In another second the arm of the first man was about her and had lifted her bodily to the other side of the shed.

"You go quiet!" he hissed. "If you raise a scream I'll bash your head in!"

Amery's eyes, baleful as a snake's, were on him, and despite his commanding position, the man wilted.

Elsa was struggling to escape from the encircling arm. Her mouth was open to scream, when a big hand closed on her face.

"Help me with her!" snarled the gaoler, and Dame was leaping across the pit, when exhausted nature took its toll and Elsa lay, an inert heap, in her captor's arms.

"She's fainted. Thank God for that!" thought Amery, watching the girl with hungry eyes till the door closed on her, leaving him alone with whom he judged to be his executioner.

IN THE HOUSE OF DEATH

"Now, young fellow" – Dame was almost jocose – "you've got a very little time to live, and that time won't be so full of misery!"

He made no attempt to approach his victim. In one corner of the room was a large barrel, which he rolled near to the hole, and, knocking off the head, turned it over on its side.

A stream of grey dust poured forth and, upending the barrel, he emptied it into a big heap. At the farther end of the shed was a tap and two pails, and Amery watched him as he set the water running. In a little time Dame came back with the pails full, and, making a hole in the centre of the heap, poured water gently into the cavity, stirring it with a spade.

"I gather that you are the Lord High Executioner?" said Amery calmly.

In spite of the man's bravado he was trembling from head to foot.

"No, I'm not," he said. "That's nothing to do with me. I'm going to put you where you won't be found."

"A plasterer? I thought by your face you were a carpenter," said Amery.

The man jumped.

"Who told you that? I was a carpenter. I don't want to talk to you."

He began plying the spade with vigour, throwing in shovelfuls of fine sand, and mixed until the heap was of the consistency of mortar. He paused to rest on the heavy shovel, and, as he did so, the blanket curtain that covered the door bulged, and Amery turned his head, to stare, unafraid, into the eyes of the man who hated him with a hatred that only death could end.

Bearded, tall, with a face still covered with motor goggles, the man called Stillman nodded pleasantly and smiled. And so perfect was the fitting of the beard that even the smile did not betray his disguise.

"Well, Amery, you'll be interested to learn that your Chink is at this moment wishing he hadn't butted into our affairs."

"You surprise me," said Amery with mock politeness.

"He followed your cab – you didn't know that, did you? I'll give him credit, he's some runner! But we caught him at the end of Ladbroke Grove, and he's not the only man that can use a knife."

"So I understand," said Amery. "You are pretty useful that way, as poor old Maurice Tarn knew, if he knew anything. Queer… I thought you were driving the cab. What next?" The bearded man lit a cigarette before he spoke.

"I? Oh, I do nothing. I am the interested spectator. The big man does the big work." He glanced down at the pit, and from the pit to the wet cement. "Dame and I are the first and second gravediggers – merely that."

"What are you going to do with the girl?"

The other shook his head, blowing out a cloud of smoke.

"I don't know. The big man has views about her. She knows a great deal more than is good for us. I suppose you realize that, Amery?"

"She knows nothing. She doesn't even know who I am."

The eyebrows of "Mr Stillman" went up.

"You don't mean that you haven't confided that important particular? Bless my soul, I thought for your safety's sake you would have told her that you were the Chief of the Foreign Office Intelligence Bureau for counteracting the drug traffic, and that they'd brought you over when poor old Bickerson had failed – and did this, moreover, after the thick-headed authorities had taken the trouble to send you to Shanghai, so that the story of your spoof disgrace could come to England and disarm suspicion. I admit you deceived me, but only for a little time. This is the finish, Amery! If I had my way it would be the girl's finish too. It is madness to fool around and leave her alive, but the big man thinks it is necessary, and I've annoyed him so much lately that I dare not protest."

Amery was feeling gingerly at the handcuffs. Once upon a time an Indian prisoner had mystified him by the ease with which he had freed himself from these manacles. A handful of rupees had bought this secret. He was wondering whether he had forgotten the trick.

Suddenly Stillman walked toward him, took a strap from his pocket, and, stooping, buckled his feet together.

"It would be a thousand pities if our friend was hurt by a chance kick," he said.

Amery was trying hard to compress the bones of his right hand, as the Indian had taught him, and, with a sinking of heart, he realised the truth of the Indian's words: "Master, you must practise every day for this trick, or it can never be done."

"What is it to be – a hanging or a shooting?"

"Neither, I should imagine," said Stillman, and glanced at Dame. The man looked sick with fright.

"You'd better go and look after the girl," he said. "I'll wait for the boss – there he is now! Come back in a quarter of an hour. I don't think you need wait any longer."

Glad to escape, the bald-headed man staggered out of the shed.

"I hear nothing," said Amery, his ears strained.

"Feng Ho would have heard," smiled Stillman. "Here he is." Again the blanket bulged, a faint click as the door closed, a white, podgy hand appeared round the blanket, and there came into view the smiling face of Mr Tupperwill, banker and purist.

THE EXECUTIONER

Mr Tupperwill's large, fat face was creased in an expression of pain and distaste. His mild eyes sought the prisoner's, held for a second and then wandered to the deep pit and the heap of slaked mortar.

"Everything has been done as it should have been done," he commented. "It is such a relief to be able to depend upon one's friends! I daresay you yourself have suffered from the inefficiency of subordinates in little matters?"

Amery smiled contemptuously but did not offer to speak. The silence in that room, with its deadened walls and draped ceiling, was so profound that he could hear the ticking of his watch.

"One likes to deal with dependable people, even in the trivial affairs of life." Mr Tupperwill spoke earnestly. " 'Trivial,' by the way, does come, as Trench suggests, from 'tri via,' meaning the three cross-roads where gossips meet."

Again his eyes sought Amery's.

"Theologians, great thinkers, metaphysicians, the brightest minds that science has known, have speculated upon what you so soon will know for certain, Major Amery!" he said, and sighed heavily. "Is there an after life? Who knows? Is it possible that the theory of a future state was born of man's vanity and the preposterous assumption that such perfect creatures as we must, as a reward for our perfection, enjoy another existence which we deny to the common animals?"

As he was talking, he was fumbling in the pocket of his long frock-coat, and when his hand was withdrawn from the folds, it held a thick stick of irregular pattern. Amery recognized it immediately as the sjambok with which the banker had been struck down on the night he and his confederates had made their first attempt upon him, and when Tupperwill, in his anxiety, had incautiously come a little too close to the struggling man.

"This, I think, you know? It was taken from your study a few nights ago, when my friends visited your house, for purposes of – ah – inspection. That stain" – he pointed to the end – "is blood. It is my blood. Observe!"

He bent his head so that Amery could see the angry scar his blow had left.

"My blood is very precious to me," he said, "and has an importance greater than any – as you will learn. With such a weapon as this," said Mr Tupperwill in his even way, "it is possible to beat a man so that he is beyond recognition, to beat him until he dies. I daresay that, considering in your mind the mode of death that I had planned for you, various methods, such as shooting, killing, hanging, perhaps, or something equally painless, must have occurred to you? Even my friends in all probability pictured some such system."

He looked across to Stillman for confirmation. Stillman's attitude was curious. He seemed entirely under the spell of the stout man's eloquence, and had neither eyes nor mind for the prisoner. He was gazing intently upon the banker, hanging on to every word he spoke, his lips moving as though he were repeating, syllable by syllable, all that "the big man" said.

Tupperwill examined the chains and the bolts, tested them by exerting all his strength, felt the handcuffs, the strap about the prisoner's feet, and, as if satisfied with his scrutiny, he stepped across the pit, and, laying down the stick, first placed a handkerchief on the floor, then, taking off his coat, folded and placed this as carefully on the handkerchief. On the top of the coat he laid his shining silk hat, unfastened the heavy gold links about his shirt cuffs and rolled them back until his big arms were revealed.

"You have the smock?" he asked pleasantly.

From where Amery stood he could not see the black coat that hung against the end wall.

"Such as butchers use," said Mr Tupperwill, as he was helped into the long black garment that buttoned from chin to foot. He lifted the lantern and brought it nearer to the prisoner.

"I wish to see what I am doing," he said with a smile, and wetted the palm of his hand. "You are going?"

"Yes, I'll go," said Stillman huskily.

The spell was broken: he could not stay and see what was to follow.

"Perhaps it is as well," said Tupperwill with great politeness. "Happily, I am entirely without nerves. When in ten minutes you return, I shall have gone, and Mr Dame and you will have little to do. Now, Major Amery, are you ready?"

The thud of the first blow came to Stillman's ears as he hurriedly closed the door… He found Dame sitting in the kitchen before a half-emptied bottle of whisky. The man was looking ghastly, was almost in tears, and, when Stillman came in: "Well," he stammered, "is it over? Oh, my God! Oh, my God! You heard what he said about being wakened up in the morning? Did you ever see an execution, Stillman? Is it bad?"

"Shut up, you fool!" growled the bearded man.

He looked back at the door through which he had come. "I've a mind to stop it!" he said between his teeth, and Dame laughed hysterically.

"You dare not! He'd shoot you like a dog. You know him better than I do. Besides, we're both in it. What does it matter? One more or less…"

"He might have used the knife," growled the man. "It is butchery. Where's the girl?"

"In there." Mr Dame nodded to a door leading from the kitchen. "That's the pantry – I've got a bed there. What are we to do with her?"

"Keep her."

"Here!" shrieked the horrified Dame. "She can't stay here! My daughter would find her."

"Then send your daughter away. You've any number of rooms. Dope her with that."

He banged a little bottle down on the table, and the other examined it stupidly.

"Did *he* get that?"

Stillman nodded.

"He thinks of everything," breathed Dame.

"Give her a few drops in her tea," said Stillman, "and she will give you no trouble. The rooms at the top of the house are furnished?"

Dame nodded.

"Put her there. What time do you expect that girl of yours home?"

"Not before two."

The bald man looked up at the noisy American clock that was ticking above the mantelpiece.

"It's only twelve now. My God! Only twelve, and it seems…years! What is he going to do with her?"

"I don't know," impatiently. "He'll fix her tomorrow. She'll not give you any trouble, I tell you. She's quiet enough now."

He opened the door and peered in. There was no lamp in the pantry, but by such light as the kitchen supplied, he saw a truckle bed in one corner and a figure that lay motionless. Closing the door noiselessly, he came back to the brooding Dame. Their eyes went to the clock together.

"Ten minutes," said Dame. "You're going to help me?"

Stillman looked round sharply.

"That is not my business, Dame…don't be a fool. There isn't ten minutes' work in it."

The other licked his dry lips.

"Suppose they trace him? This would be the first place they'd search. They'd see the floor was newly cemented."

"Who is going to trace him – the Chink? You can ease your mind; the Chink's dead. I settled him myself. Look!"

The white cuff under the sleeve was dabbled red. Dame drew a long, sobbing breath.

"Oh, my God, I wish I was out of it!"

"Don't let him hear you," warned the other, "or you'll be out of it in a way that you least expect!"

259

The clock tick-tick-ticked, the hands did not seem to move. They sat dumbly, waiting for the minutes to pass. Ten eternal minutes went at last.

"Come now, do your job," said Stillman.

The man did not move. Fifteen minutes, and then Stillman's hand fell on his shoulder, and he jumped up with a scream. Like a blind man, he staggered down the garden and stood for fully five minutes at the door of the garage, his heart thumping so that it seemed to choke him. At last, gritting his teeth, he pulled open the door. The candle had burnt down to the socket; it spluttered, died, flared up, spluttered again and then went out, but in that brief moment of light he saw the empty handcuffs, and out of the corner of his eye, a figure at the bottom of the pit.

The perspiration streamed down his face; he was sobbing hysterically as, working like a madman, he shovelled the viscid mortar into the pit, covered it with earth until at last it was level.

The rest must wait; he could not stay any longer in the dark, and, flinging open the door, he rushed up the garden, as though the gibing spirit of Paul Amery were at his elbow.

Stillman jumped up as the white-faced man fell in, and catching him as his knees gave way, he dropped him into a chair and poured out a glassful of neat whisky.

"Drink this, you fool," he said. He was almost as white himself as he looked round toward the pantry door.

"I've fixed a padlock – here is the key. Look after her, do you hear?"

The man nodded stupidly.

"You understand? She is to be taken upstairs and kept there she must not be allowed to attract attention in any circumstances."

"Where are you going? Don't leave me alone," whined Dame his teeth chattering, as Stillman made a move to go.

"I'm off to find Tup and tell him that you've settled things And I want to know what is going to happen to this girl. She's important, I tell you."

Another second, and Dame was alone – alone with his ghosts, his fears, the strange sounds of the night that nearly drove him mad, the sough of wind in the chimney, the patter of rain on windows, and above and through all, the consciousness of the dark secret that he must go out with the first light of dawn to hide finally.

He raised the glass to his lips and did not put it down until half its contents were drunk. Then, with a start, he remembered Amery's words, and, dropping his head into his arms, he sobbed like a frightened child.

THE ESCAPE

Elsa Marlowe knew she had fainted, knew this while she was unconscious, knew that something dreadful…horrible had happened, and groaned as she turned on the hard bed. Her elbow came into contact with the wall, and the pain of the blow did much to bring her to complete consciousness. Her head was throbbing, she felt a queer fluttering in her throat, and when she tried to stand up, her knees gave way under her and she fell back on the bed.

And then, in a flood of terror, she remembered. Paul Amery was a prisoner, and they were going to kill him…and he loved her!

She struggled toward where four tiny circles gleamed in the darkness. They were holes cut into the pantry door, and through them she looked out upon a kitchen which at first she did not recognize. A man sprawled across the table, his head on his arms, an empty glass and a nearly empty bottle by his side. Mr Dame! Jessie's father…

She tried the door: it was fastened. Yet, there was hope, for the man was fast asleep, and if she could only find a way of opening he door, escape was assured. She heard his deep snores, and pressed with all her might, but though the door gave slightly, her most strenuous efforts failed to wrench loose the fastening. She was weak, but even if she had been stronger, it might, have been a task beyond her strength to break the stout hasp. There was nothing to do but to wait…and, waiting, torture her mind with thoughts of what would happen to the man in whose eyes she had seen such love and tenderness as she did not dream was in all the world.

262

The thought drove her frantic. Again she threw herself at the door, only to be hurled back bruised and hurt. And then she heard footsteps in the hall, and her heart stood still. There came the sound of feet on the stairs, and then silence…after a while he heard the intruder descend the hall again, and a voice called: "Father!"

It was Jessie Dame!

Was it possible that she was in league with these terrible men?

"Father, are you downstairs?"

The girl had evidently seen a light, for now Elsa could hear her coming down the passage toward the kitchen.

"Father, what is the matter?"

"Jessie, for God's sake!"

At the sound of the terrified whisper, Jessie Dame spun round, ludicrous in her fear.

"Who is that?" she gasped.

"It is I – Elsa Marlowe."

"Where are you? Oh, how you frightened me!" whimpered the girl.

"Don't make a noise. I'm in here."

"In the pantry?" said Jessie, gasping.

"Let me out, please."

Jessie Dame came slowly over, with a backward glance at the slumbering man.

"The padlock is fastened…he'll have the key in his pocket. Did he put you here? Oh, my God, he'll get into trouble! I knew he'd get into trouble!"

She tried to pull the lock loose.

"I'll go and find my key," she whispered, and went out.

She seemed to have been away for an hour, though it could not have been many minutes before she returned, and, creeping on tiptoe to the door, tried key after key, till at last the rusty lock turned and the girl came out into the kitchen, free.

At that moment Mr Dame growled in his sleep and moved.

"Quick, quick!" hissed the frightened girl, pushing her companion into the passage. "He'll kill me if he finds I've done this!"

Even as they were mounting the stairs to the hall, the man awoke. One glance he gave at the open door, and then, with a yell that froze his daughter's blood, he came blundering out into the passage and up the stairs. Jessie was fumbling at the lock, her palsied fingers refusing to function, and Elsa thrust her aside. Just as Dame's head came level with the hall, the door was opened and they fled out, slamming it behind them.

The Street was in darkness. There was not a soul in sight, as they fled toward the main road, Dame, staggering in pursuit, roaring and screaming in a frenzy that was half drunkenness, and half genuine fear of what would follow the girl's escape.

Glancing back as she ran, Elsa saw that she was alone. Jessie Dame, who knew the neighbourhood, had dived into a side turning, unnoticed by her father. The man had shaken off his stupor and was gaining.

And then, as the girl felt that she could not go another step farther, she saw a blessed sight. Crossing the road, visible in the street lamp, a line of helmeted heads, and to her ears came the thud-thud-thud of tramping feet. The night patrols were returning from duty.

Into their very midst she ran, and a stout policeman caught her as she fell into his arms. The night and its horrors faded in a swoon from which she was not to recover till the morning sunlight fell across the hospital bed in which she lay.

THE MORNING AFTER

At eleven o'clock the next morning, Inspector Bickerson walked into the office of his Superintendent and dropped wearily into a chair. Wille looked up from under his shaggy brows and demanded: "Well?"

"Well enough for you, Super," said Bickerson bitterly, "but for me it's hell! What with a lunatic girl's statements and frantic cock-and-bull stories about Soyoka, I haven't stood in one place from five o'clock this morning! According to the telephone message you sent me, the girl stated specifically that Amery was a prisoner, if he wasn't dead, at Dame's house. She's either mad or dreaming," said Bickerson decisively. "I was at Dame's house before eight o'clock. He'd evidently had a real good souse, for he was still far from sober. I went to the garage, and I certainly was suspicious when I saw that there had been a hole in the centre of the garage and that it had been filled in. That looked almost as if Miss Marlowe's story was true. But I had it opened, every scrap of earth and cement taken up – fortunately, the cement hadn't had time to set – and not only was there no sign of a body, but there never had been a body!"

"Marks of blood?"

"None. The floor had recently been washed down, but Dame explained that by telling me that he'd had a clean-out the night before. He explained the hole by telling me that he had been trying to dig a pit for his car, but finding himself encroaching on gas lines and drain lines, he wisely gave it up. My labourers found pipe lines six feet below the surface of the garage."

The Superintendent consulted a memorandum.

"There were no blankets hanging on the walls to deaden sound?"

"No, but there had been. I found a heap of blankets in a corner of the garage."

The Superintendent leant back in his chair.

"Isn't it queer Amery hasn't turned up?"

Bickerson shrugged his broad shoulders.

"I have stopped trying to keep a tag on Amery."

"And this other story" – Wille turned over a pile of paper and found a document – "this suggestion that the head of the Soyoka gang is Tupperwill? Have you seen him?"

"I've just come from him," said Bickerson. "His worst offence from my point of view, is that he is a very loquacious and long-winded gentleman, whose mind is completely taken up with the question of licensing hours and the need for introducing prohibition into working-class districts. I asked him point-blank what communication he had had with the Soyoka people, or if he knew anybody or had any clients on his books who might be Soyoka's agents, and he gave me the impression that I was a harmless lunatic that needed humouring. He said he'd never heard of Soyoka, and I couldn't even get him to understand that he might be under suspicion of being Soyoka himself. I had the good luck to catch him just outside the bank: he had been spending the night at Brighton, he told me, and hadn't been home. When told him I was a police officer, his chief concern seemed to be whether there had been a burglary at his house."

Superintendent Wille's frown was intensified.

"I don't understand it," he said. "There must be something in the story. Here we have Amery's Chinese manager picked up half dead, undoubtedly knifed, and that within a few hundred yards of Dame's house – by the way, how is the Chinaman?"

"The doctor says he's out of danger," said Bickerson, "and will be well in a few weeks. The fellow who stabbed him seems to have just missed touching a vital spot. I admit that *is* queer and I wanted to interrogate Feng Ho, but the doctors will not allow him to be questioned for another day. I'm going round to see the girl Dame.

Apparently she went to the office very early – maybe I'll find friend Amery – "

"Who you still think is Soyoka?" asked Wille.

Bickerson shook his head.

"No," he admitted ruefully, "that was an error into which the cleverest man might fall, and I don't profess to be clever."

Bickerson walked eastward, a preoccupied and, as Superintendent Wille hoped, a chastened man. He found Jessie Dame in her tiny office, and it was not necessary that he should have made a close study of her to see that a remarkable change had come over her. Jessie Dame never had a good colour, but now her complexion was a pale green, and her hollow eyes told of a sleepless night.

"Good morning, Miss Dame," said Bickerson. "What time did you get home last night?" And then by way of explanation: "You know me – I'm Mr Bickerson."

"Yes, sir, I know you," she said quietly, avoiding his keen eyes. "I've seen you here before. I got home at twelve o'clock. I ought really to have stayed out until two, but I was so worried – I mean," she said, in some confusion, "I intended staying out later, but owing to business troubles I came home early."

"That almost sounds as though it weren't true," smiled Bickerson. "What were your business troubles?"

"Oh, the office, and – the way Major Amery goes on and all that sort of thing," said Jessie Dame desperately. "I can't explain."

"You left home early this morning? I was at your home before eight, but I did not see you."

"Yes, I came away very early."

In truth, Jessie Dame had walked the streets all night, and if she was lying now, it was in obedience to the urgent note that she had found waiting for her on her arrival at the office, giving her exact instructions as to what she was to say, and ending with a horrific threat that chilled her blood to read.

"You didn't by chance find Miss Marlowe in your house, locked up in a cupboard?"

For a fraction of a second she struggled to find her voice.

"No, sir," she gulped at last, "and if Miss Marlowe says that I did, she is not telling the truth. I don't know what happened last night," said the girl. "I really don't know! I had one glass of wine and it sort of went to my head."

"You heard nothing about Major Amery being locked up in our garage?"

The green turned to a sickly white. Jessie staggered back against the table.

"Major Amery?" she said hollowly. "Locked up in our garage? What do you mean?"

"I see — you know nothing about that. Didn't Miss Marlowe tell you?"

She was almost eager in her reply. It was such a relief to tell the truth.

"Major Amery isn't here this morning?"

She shook her head, not trusting her voice.

He strolled from her room into the little office usually occupied by Elsa, tried the door of Amery's room and, finding it locked, walked back to Jessie Dame.

"Where is Miss — Miss Marlowe?" she asked jerkily.

"When I saw her last she was at the West London Hospital."

"She — she's not hurt?"

"No, she's not hurt. The doctor thought she could go out today but I doubt if she will."

He had hardly spoken the words before a light step sounded in the passage outside, and he had a fleeting glimpse of a dainty figure as it passed the open doorway.

"That's her!" gasped Miss Dame.

"Miss Marlowe? Impossible!"

He went out and looked after her. Jessie Dame was right. Elsa was hanging up her hat and coat as he walked in to her, marvelling at the extraordinary reserves which women possess, that could enable her to appear after such a night as she had spent, bearing such little evidence of her ordeal. Save for the shadows beneath her eyes and the faintness of the pink in her cheeks, she seemed in no way changed.

She greeted him with a grave inclination of her head, took off the typewriter cover with the assurance of one who expects to be called at any moment.

"Why did they let you out?" he demanded. "When I saw you this morning you seemed more dead than alive."

"I came out because I wanted to come," she said.

"That doesn't seem a very good reason. I suppose you know I've investigated your story?"

"I know; you've already told me."

"I've told you there was no body in the garage, and certainly no sign of murder. Otherwise the particulars you supplied correspond with the position of the building, and certainly there has been a hole in the floor."

She shivered.

"But, as I tell you, there was nothing in the pit but earth and drying cement. I think you must have dreamt this. Hadn't you visited Mr Dame's house the day before?"

"Yes."

"Did you see anything there that suggested a pit to you?"

She looked at him frowning.

"I – " she began. "Why, yes, I saw a man come out of the garage with a spade in his hand."

"Exactly!" he said triumphantly. "I don't know the name of the nervous disease from which you're suffering, but perhaps Dr Hallam will tell you."

"I didn't imagine all I saw last night," she said in a low voice. "You were talking to Jessie Dame; she can confirm my story."

"On the contrary," said Bickerson, "that is just what she wouldn't do! Miss Dame says she did not find you in a cupboard or release you, or do any of the things which you say she did."

THE BANK

For a moment Elsa stared at him incredulously, and then her face changed.

"Of course, poor girl! She's afraid of her father."

Mr Bickerson threw out his hands in a hopeless gesture.

"I'd sooner have any kind of case than this," he said in despair. "A witness with illusions is a nightmare! I don't want to hurt your feelings, but I can't believe you. Major Amery hasn't come?"

"No, I don't think he's come," she said, ignoring the doubt he was throwing on her sanity. She tried the door. "Why, it's locked!"

"Was it locked last night?"

"I don't know. I left before him," she said slowly. Stooping, she looked through the keyhole. "The key is not there. I think I can open it with the key of my door," she said, and this she did.

The office was exactly as Amery had left it. The cleaners had not been able to get in. A few cigarette ends lay in the grate and a half-burnt cigar.

She offered no further information, and after a glance round Bickerson walked out of the room and she followed.

"He is a mysterious fellow," said the detective, "but not quite as – " he was at a loss for a word.

" 'Sinister' is the expression you want," suggested the girl with a faint smile.

"Yes, it is," he said in surprise. "No, he's not as sinister as I thought he was. In fact – " he seemed on the point of telling her something, but changed his mind. "What is that book?" He pointed to a worn leather book that lay on her table.

"The night watchman's report," she said. "He brings it up every morning for Major Amery to see the names of people who may have called, or telephone calls and telegrams that have arrived after office hours."

She opened the book where the blotting paper marked the place, and checked an exclamation.

"Mr Tupperwill came at ten minutes to six!"

For a moment she was so interested that she forgot her audience. "Tupperwill came here?" he said incredulously, and looked over her shoulder. "That is very queer." He spoke half to himself. "I was with Mr Tupperwill this morning, and he told me that he went home from his bank at five o'clock and never stirred out, until he decided, for no reason at all, to spend the night at Brighton, and went down by the nine o'clock train."

Later, after he had made a further round of calls, he reported by telephone to his chief.

"This case grows queerer and queerer," he said. "I've just been talking to Mrs Ralph Hallam, who tells me that she was half killed last night by somebody who broke into the house. Who it was she doesn't know, but the first person she saw, when she recovered consciousness, was Major Amery, and apparently he went out of the house with the girl – Miss Marlowe, I'm talking about."

"That gives her story support," said the Superintendent after a pause. "Was he alone?"

"No, his Chinese manager, Feng Ho, was with him, and apparently Dr Hallam came soon after."

"Is she related to Dr Hallam?"

"His wife," said Bickerson, "but she says he didn't leave the flat until long after Amery went. I've been round to see him, but he's not at home."

Another long pause.

"This case grows queer. Keep in touch with the office, Bickerson."

"I'll do something more than that," said the detective. "I'll watch that girl. There is something about the business that I do not like."

Whether she were watched or unwatched, Elsa Marlowe was indifferent. The hours passed with leaden feet; at every sound she started up; not once, but fifty times, did she open the door of Amery's room and peep in, hoping – praying, indeed – that he would come in in his own, furtive way, and every time she looked she saw nothing but his chair and the blotting-pad, and the bell above her head was silent.

He must have escaped – he must!

Weary as she was, and reluctant to leave the office for fear he should come in, she made a journey back to the hospital to enquire the condition of Feng Ho, and was relieved to learn that he was so far out of danger that she might see him. She was most anxious to learn all she could about his master, for she guessed that this little man would know far more about him, if he were free, than the best detective in the world.

He looked up at her as she came into the private ward which he occupied alone, and greeted her with a grin.

"Perforations of thorax notwithstanding," he said faintly, "scientific bachelor will escape mortality on this occasion."

She read the question in his eyes and shook her head.

"I don't know. When did you see the Major last?"

"Last night, young miss," he said gravely. "Has he not resumed appearance in commercial centres, viz, City of London?"

"No, Feng Ho," she answered quietly.

"Then Tupperwill knows."

"Mr Tupperwill?" She thought he was wandering in his mind.

He nodded.

"Mr Tupperwill is an extremely dangerous character, being connected with Nipponese Soyoka, purveyor of noxious and intoxicating drugs."

"But surely you're mistaken? Not Mr Tupperwill?"

"Yes, young miss. The honourable Major has distinct information. All errors are eliminated."

She could only gaze at him in stupefied wonder. That pleasant bore, engaged in a criminal conspiracy? It was impossible.

"Did you tell Mr Bickerson?" she asked.

"Young miss, eminent detective policeman has not yet interrogated owing to reluctance of medical officials to risk elevation of temperature. Young miss" – his voice was a whisper – "you must exercise great care owing to absence of Major. I desire to call at Major's house and instruct Chang to hasten to me. Give explicit directions, remembering he is a poor, ignorant Chinaman, of dubious parentage and deplorable education."

He seemed so exhausted by this effort that she made no further attempt to question him, and, after exchanging a few words with the matron, she took a taxi to Brook Street.

The Major's housekeeper had not had word of him, nor had his butler.

"Can I see the Chinese servant?"

"Yes, miss," said the housekeeper, "though he doesn't speak much English."

Whether he spoke English or not, the diminutive Chang understood all that she had told him, and took the address and the little map she had drawn, directing him to the hospital, shaking his head to indicate his understanding.

There was no fresh news at the office when she returned. Greatly daring, she had requested one of the sub-managers to take Feng Ho's place, and had deputed another to deal with the correspondence that ordinarily would have been seen by Amery, and she was now free to continue her investigations along the lines suggested by Feng Ho's monstrous and extraordinary charge.

She was sufficiently well acquainted with Mr Tupperwill's habits to know that he would be at the bank until three o'clock, and she remained in the office just long enough to attend to an enquiry that had come through, and which the sub-manager could not deal with, and then she boarded a bus and went eastward.

It took her some time to locate the court in which Stebbing's Bank was situated; then:

"Stebbing's?" said a policeman, looking at her queerly. "Yes, it is round the first court to the left. You a depositor, miss?" he asked with the fatherly familiarity of the City policeman.

"No," she smiled, "I haven't that fortune."

"You're lucky," he said cryptically.

She thought it was a piece of pleasantry, but she turned into the court and saw a small crowd standing before a closed doorway, on which had been pinned a notice. She looked up at the fascia – yes, it was the old-fashioned Stebbing's. But why was the door closed at midday?

Pushing her way through the crowd, she read:

STEBBING'S BANK

The Bank has temporarily suspended payment. Enquiries should be addressed to Slake & Stern, Solicitors, Bolt Street, E.C.

She drew clear of the crowd, bewildered, stupefied by the news. Poor Mr Tupperwill! For the moment she forgot Feng Ho's wild charge, and remembered only the kindliness, the gentle inadequacy of the placid banker. And then she heard somebody speaking.

"…a man named Tupperwill…they said he laid his hands on all the money he could find and went to the Continent this morning by aeroplane."

RALPH HALLAM'S COAT

The failure of Stebbing's Bank was notified to the duty officer at Scotland Yard within five minutes of the notice being posted, and Superintendent Wille despatched an orderly in search of Bickerson. That officer was taking an afternoon doze in his room, the blinds drawn, when the constable came for him, and he hurried to the bureau of his chief.

"Look at this," growled Wille, pushing his paper across the table.

Bickerson read and whistled.

"The City police closed the bank, from information evidently supplied by Major Amery overnight. There is a warrant out for Tupperwill and for the auditors, but Tupperwill seems to have skipped. What time did you see him?"

"At a little before eleven."

"Was he going into the bank? This report says that he hasn't been in the City today."

"I didn't actually see him go into the bank. I left him at the entrance of Tredgers Court, not doubting that he was on his way to his office."

"Did you notice anything unusual about him? Did he look worried or upset in any way?"

"No," replied Bickerson thoughtfully. "I thought it queer that he should have gone to Brighton on the previous night – that struck me as strange for a man of his settled habits. But there was nothing at all remarkable in his appearance or his manner."

The Superintendent read the paper again. It contained a very full description of the wanted man. Then he rang the bell for his clerk.

"Circulate this description to all ports and railway stations, for detention and report. Get Croydon and find if he has left by aeroplane – that is the City police theory. Notify C Divisional Office that his house is to be occupied until further orders. That will do."

"We must wait now," said Wille when they were alone, "until we get the report on which the City police acted. But in the meantime you'd better round up Tupperwill's friends. Do you know any?"

Bickerson considered.

"I've an idea that Hallam was one. If he wasn't a friend, they were certainly on dining terms, and Hallam was a depositor at the bank."

"The doctor?"

Bickerson nodded.

"The man you are getting a warrant for?"

"If Jarvie squeals I shall certainly get a warrant for him, but at present there is no information to go upon."

Superintendent Wille chewed a meditative toothpick.

"Go along and see Hallam. You may learn something about Tupperwill's other friends, and more especially about Stillman. I've heard only the faintest rumour about this gentleman, but he was evidently a client. From the 'phone talk I've had with the Chief of the City police, it seems that Stillman is one of the persons who are wanted in connection with the bank failure. He was evidently a man closely in the confidence of Tupperwill, and I've got a hunch that friend Hallam may be able to put you on to this person. Report here as soon as you're through. I'm having a consultation with the Commissioner this afternoon about Miss Marlowe's story."

"Do you think Stillman is Hallam?" asked Bickerson bluntly.

"I don't know. I have no very definite theory. At any rate, I shall have a clearer idea after you have seen the doctor."

Ralph's servant admitted the detective. His master was upstairs, dressing, he said.

"A late bird, eh?" asked Bickerson, in the friendly tone that had been the undoing of so many innocent and talkative servants.

"Yes, sir, he was rather late; he was out at a dance last night."

"Tell him I'm here."

He had been shown into the study at the back of the house, a small and comfortably fitted room. The windows were open, for it was a mild day, and the window-box, crowded with golden daffodils, caught the early afternoon sunlight.

Bickerson strolled to one of the bookshelves and scanned the titles aimlessly. Then his inquisitive eyes roamed systematically around the apartment. Evidently Ralph had partly changed in the room when he had returned in the early hours of the morning, for his great-coat was thrown over the back of a chair, and one buttoned dress boot was under the table, the other being beneath the chair and hidden by the hanging coat. Without hesitation, Bickerson picked up the coat, slipped his hand into one of the pockets, found it empty, and tried the other. And then something attracted his attention and he carried the coat to the light. One of the sleeves was caked hard with some liquid which had been spilt upon it. He turned back the cuff, and the lighter lining showed a rusty red stain.

Blood! He tried the other sleeve. Here the stain was larger, and extended from the cuff halfway up the inner part of the arm. He picked up one of the boots and whistled softly. It was spattered with stains, and when he scraped them his fingers were covered with dark red dust.

He heard Ralph descending the stairs, put down the boots and waited.

"Good morning, Bickerson." Hallam's voice was expressionless, his face a mask. Instantly his eyes had fallen upon the coat and the boots, and he was waiting.

"Good morning, doctor. I've called to make a few enquiries about Tupperwill. You know the bank has bust?"

Hallam expressed no surprise.

"I didn't know. When did this happen?"

"This morning. Tupperwill has left hurriedly. You knew him very well?"

"Fairly well," said Hallam.

"Have you any idea where he is likely to be?"

"Not the slightest," said the other calmly. "I know Tupperwill only in his home. If he is not there, I haven't the slightest idea where he is to be found."

"You don't know where Major Amery happens to be?" The ghost of a smile hovered at the corners of Hallam's set lips. "He also is an individual who seldom took me into his confidence. Has he disappeared?"

"He has very much disappeared," said Bickerson, and, stooping slowly, picked up the coat. "Had an accident last night, didn't you?"

"You mean the blood on the sleeves?" said Hallam coolly. "There's some on the cuff too."

"Did you cut your finger or something?" asked the detective sardonically.

Hallam laughed.

"How absurd! A cut finger wouldn't make that stain."

"What would?" asked Bickerson sternly.

"Well," – Ralph chose his words carefully – "picking up a wounded Chinaman, who had been knifed by some persons or persons unknown, might make a mess of a man's sleeve."

Bickerson was staggered.

"Was it you who found Feng Ho?" he asked.

Hallam nodded.

"I was one of those who assisted him to the hospital."

Their eyes met.

"The police of the Hammersmith Division made no reference to your being present when Feng Ho was found."

"They must have overlooked me," said the other lightly. "And really, I feel so insignificant in the presence of police officers that I don't wonder! The truth is, Bickerson, I was looking for Amery – Feng Ho and I. He went away suddenly from Herbert Mansions, as his servant believed, kidnapped with Miss Marlowe, who, I am happy to learn, is safe."

"Who told you that?" asked the detective sharply.

"I telephoned this morning because I saw something in the evening paper about a young lady who was found wandering in Kensington."

"You tell that story too, do you, about them being taken away? It is an extraordinary case. Presumably you will be able to account for every minute of your movements last night?"

"Almost every minute," said the other.

"What time did you return home this morning?" asked Bickerson.

Ralph hesitated.

"Whatever time my servant said I came is about accurate," he said. "Somewhere in the region of four – it may have been a little later. As for Tupperwill, if that is really the object of your coming, I am absolutely unable to give you any information. I know nothing about him except that I have an overdraft at his bank and that I've dined with him once or twice. Of his habits and his inner life I know less than you."

He expected Bickerson to return to the question of the bloodstained coat, but, to his relief, the detective made no further reference and left shortly after. He did not report immediately to Wille, but, going to his own room, got through on the telephone to the Kensington police.

"Who found the Chinaman?" he asked.

"Constable Simmons. He was on patrol duty and heard a groan in a garden. Going in, he found the man and had him taken to the hospital on a lorry that happened to be passing."

"No other person assisted?" asked the interested Bickerson. "Nobody named Hallam?"

"Oh no, there was no question about the facts," said the voice of the sergeant on duty. "Simmons and the driver of the trolley were the only people concerned."

"Thank you," said Bickerson, and put the telephone back. "Dr Hallam," he said softly, "you are a liar. And if you're not something else, I'm very much mistaken!"

DAME PASSES

His interview with Wille was short enough. Wille and the Commissioner had discussed Elsa's story, and had decided that further investigation was necessary.

"See Dame and arrest him. You'd better report to the local division: they will send a man with you," were his instructions.

Jessie Dame went home very early that afternoon, in response to the instructions she had had from her father that morning. She was sick with fright as she slowly mounted the steps of that fateful house and rang the bell. Dame opened the door himself, and at first she did not recognize him. His yellow moustache had vanished, and she stared into the face of a stranger.

"Come in," he growled. "You…! You've got me into a mess, you and that… And you've got to get me out!"

"Is anything wrong, father?" she asked, trembling.

"Wrong!" he roared. "Wrong!"

There was no need to ask. His face betrayed the seriousness of the crisis. He almost dragged her into the dining-room. On the table she saw his grip, packed and strapped.

"I'm leaving London at once," he said.

"Where are you going?"

"I'm likely to tell you that, ain't I?" he almost howled at her. "Here is some money." He threw a handful of notes on the table. "Go on to a boarding-house and keep quiet. When I'm ready for you I'll send for you, and you'll come – you understand? You'll tell nobody where I am, if I ever do send for you."

"But, father, what is wrong? Is it serious? Is it about Miss Marlowe?" she whimpered.

"Never mind what it's about: that is nothing to do with you. I'm going at once. If anybody comes, you're to say that you expect me back tonight. And if you tell them that I've taken my moustache off, I'll murder you! You can sell the furniture and keep the money, in case I want it. And – "

There came a sharp rat-tat at the door, and he ran to the window, pulled aside the blinds and staggered back.

"Two 'busies,' " he said huskily, "Bickerson and another man. By God! they wouldn't pinch me!"

Again came the knock.

"I'll go down to the kitchen. Tell them I'm out," he said, and tiptoed down the stairs.

With a fainting heart the girl opened the door and stammered the message.

"He's out, is he?" said Bickerson good-humouredly. "Come, come, Miss Dame, you oughtn't to tell those kind of stories. I want to see him for a few minutes."

"He's gone out, really, Mr Bickerson," said the girl, half fainting with fear.

Bickerson pushed his way past her, walked into the dining-room, saw the grip on the table and smiled.

"Just wait here" – he was speaking to the other man – "I think I can find my way to the kitchen. You watch the stairs."

She stood, petrified with terror, heard the kitchen door open…

Instantly came the deafening sound of an explosion.

"Here, quick!" shouted Bickerson, and the second detective flew down the stairs into the kitchen.

The bald man lay in a huddled heap on the floor, within reach of his hand a revolver, the barrel of which was still smoking.

"Get on the 'phone – there is one here. Call an ambulance and the divisional surgeon, though I don't think he'll be much use. And keep that girl out!" he said sharply.

There was little need to tell Jessie what had happened. With a wild scream she flew toward the open door, but the detective caught her in his arms and carried the struggling, demented girl back to the dining-room.

By the time the police surgeon and the ambulance arrived, Bickerson had made a very thorough search of the man's clothes, and the kitchen table was strewn with the articles he had removed.

"He's dead," said the surgeon. "Suicide — in fear of arrest, I presume?"

Bickerson nodded.

"I hardly saw it happen," he said. "Not having been able to question the girl, I don't know what occurred, but I guess that he saw us from the window of the dining-room — I noticed the blind move." He thought a moment. "It was a lucky shot for that poor, howling female," he added.

Elsa read the news in the late editions of the evening papers. She was inured to shock, and save that her sympathetic heart softened toward the poor girl who had saved her from untold horrors, she had no feeling save an almost savage satisfaction that the man who was in some way responsible for Paul Amery's suffering had gone to his account.

She dared not let her mind rest upon the sinister man and his fate. Again and again she told herself that he was alive. She sat at her table, her hands clasped before her, praying that the bell might ring, and that his sharp voice might call her in to him; and it was only when the evening came, and she found herself alone in the building, that for the first time she broke down and gave way to a flood of passionate weeping.

Her head was aching, her eyes hot and painful; misery was coiled about her heart until it was a pain to breathe; but at last she flung off her sorrow, and, bathing her face, went out, not knowing whither and caring nothing.

"Elsa!"

As she reached the Street a familiar voice called her and she turned. Ralph Hallam was standing on the sidewalk, his debonair self.

"I am not going back to Herbert Mansions, Dr Hallam," she said quietly.

"I know," he nodded. "I've taken a room for you at the Palace. Lou has sent your things there."

The girl hesitated. She had come to regard Ralph Hallam in the light of an enemy. That he hated Amery she knew, and it almost hurt her to accept even this slight service at his hands.

"Thank you," she said simply, and then: "You've heard about Jessie's father?"

"Dame? Yes. He was mixed up in a scandal of some kind, and shot himself when the police went to arrest him."

She walked slowly down Wood Street and he kept pace at her side, well aware that his presence was objectionable to her.

"I'm afraid you think I am a pretty bad egg," he said.

She shook her head.

"I don't know whether you are or not," she answered listlessly. "I'm really beyond caring."

"You don't trust me, at any rate?"

"Why should I?" she asked quietly.

"Will you do me one favour?"

She stopped and looked at him, suspicion lurking in her eyes.

"Will you come to Half Moon Street and let me tell you the whole truth – the truth about myself, and the truth, that I have recently learnt, about Amery?"

She knew the truth about Amery – that he loved her! That was the vital, triumphant truth that eclipsed and obliterated all others.

"I would much rather not," she said. "Besides, there is nothing for me to know about Major Amery. He has already told me."

"Do you know that Amery was a detective – *is* a detective, I mean – " he added hastily, and, seeing that he had startled her, he went on: "Amery is on the staff of the Foreign Office Intelligence Department, and was brought from India to cope with the drug traffic. I never guessed he was working with Bickerson, but he is, Feng Ho told me last night. They say he is the cleverest intelligence officer that has ever served in India. He has been fighting out there with

Soyoka's crowd, and his agents have been everywhere. Sometimes they pretended to be working for one of the gangs, like that man Moropoulos, the Greek, who was a detective from Washington. He has strangled my business; half the crowd I've been working with are under arrest and I expect to be pinched at any moment. It was Amery who put the police into Stebbing's Bank. Tupperwill was Soyoka's principal agent; he made a fortune out of dope, but Amery has finished him! Elsa, I don't know what is going to happen to me, and I may never be able to ask you again to dine. Lou will be there."

Again she hesitated.

"I'll come," she said, "but I must first go to the hotel and unpack."

"You can do that later," he urged.

There was something in his eagerness which she did not understand, and which did not quite fit in with his frankness.

"I will go with you, but I won't stay late. I have a feeling that I'm being a fool, but I'll take the risk."

She did not see the smile that flitted across his face as he helped her into the taxi, but she noticed that he was most anxious to entertain her on the journey to the house, and hardly stopped speaking once…

"Tupperwill, for some reason, wanted to hold you, I think, as a hostage. It may have been just fondness for you, and it may have been a knowledge of Amery's mind. He called you out one afternoon, didn't he, to meet him?"

"Yes," she said, in surprise.

"But he asked you first whether Major Amery was out? He said you were to come at once, but you met Amery before you left, and told him where you were going? Tupperwill had a great little scheme for kidnapping you. The car was to drive into a yard at Islington, and you were to be taken out and held till the night, when you were to be moved somewhere else. But just before the car turned into the gate, you happened to mention the fact that Amery knew, and he changed his plans. Do you remember?"

Then that was the explanation! And Feng Ho must have been following her! Only now she was beginning to realize the care with which the sinister man had surrounded her, and at the thought of him her lips trembled. It was just then they reached Half Moon Street. He jumped out first. As she stepped from the cab, the door opened, and he almost rushed her into the house.

WILLE SAYS "NO!"

Superintendent Wille was by nature a sceptical and unbelieving man. In nine cases out of ten he had found, in the course of a long and interesting life, that his suspicions were justified; and now, as he presided over a conference of minor officials of Scotland Yard, he enlarged upon the creed of disbelief.

"That girl told the truth, Bickerson," he said definitely. "If it was not the truth, why did Dame commit suicide the moment you went to arrest him? And if she told the truth in one particular, she told the truth in another. We have had the statement of Hallam, that he and the Chinaman went in pursuit of the cab which carried away Major Amery and Miss Marlowe. In confirmation, we have Feng Ho struck down in the open street, probably in the act of pursuit; and now we have the suicide of Dame."

"But the girl Dame said – " began Bickerson.

"I'm not taking much notice of what the daughter said. It was her duty to lie on behalf of her father, and well you guessed she was lying!"

Bickerson could do no more than agree.

"The garage, the pit, the threat of murder, the abduction – they all hang together," Wille went on deliberately, "and the fact that there is no body in the pit proves nothing, except that no murder was committed in the shed. It does not prove that it was not committed elsewhere, or that Dame was not privy to the act. We have Dame's record: he was a man with three convictions, and ex-convicts of his mental calibre do not commit suicide to avoid Dartmoor, but to keep

286

their feet off the sliding trap of Pentonville. Therefore, I argue that there has been a murder – somewhere. What is the time?" He looked at his watch. "Half past nine. Do you know where Miss Marlowe is to be found?"

"I believe she's staying at Herbert Mansions," said Bickerson.

"Go along and bring her back here. We will have her story tested in the light of our subsequent discoveries. You boys can hang on," he said to the little knot of detectives, major and minor.

At Herbert Mansions, Bickerson interviewed Mrs Hallam.

"No, she's not here," said that self-possessed lady. "As a matter of fact, my husband took a room for her at the Palace Hotel, and all her trunks were sent there this afternoon."

This statement Bickerson confirmed. The trunks and bags had arrived and had been sent up to Miss Marlowe's room, but she herself had not arrived.

"You're sure?"

"Yes, sir," said the reception clerk. "Miss Marlowe hasn't taken her key yet," and he lifted it down from the hook behind him.

To make absolutely certain, a page was sent to the room and returned with the news that it was not occupied.

"She couldn't very well come in without our knowledge," said the clerk.

Bickerson was more disturbed than Superintendent Wille would have imagined. He remembered there was a night watchman at Amery's office, and got connected up with him at once.

"Miss Marlowe left the office rather late, sir – nearly seven o'clock, I think."

"Did she go alone?"

"No, sir, Dr Hallam was with her. He had been waiting outside the door for the best part of two hours."

He did not call up Ralph, preferring to make a personal visit. It was a long time before his knock procured attention. He saw a light appear in the passage, and Ralph opened the door to him.

"Hullo! What do you want this time?" he asked cheerfully. "Are you taking me for knifing the Chinaman?"

"We'll discuss the Chinaman at another time," said Bickerson coldly, "and then I shall ask you to explain why you lied to me about finding him and taking him to the hospital. At the moment, I want to know something about Miss Elsa Marlowe, with whom, I understand, you were seen at seven o'clock this evening."

"Which is perfectly true," admitted Ralph. "I called for her at the office; in fact, I waited there some time for her."

"And then?" asked Bickerson.

"Then I drove her to Notting Hill. She was going to call on the girl Dame."

"Are you sure you didn't bring her here?"

"Perfectly sure," said Ralph coolly. "Miss Marlowe hasn't been in this house in weeks. My servant is out, or he would support my statement that I returned alone."

His eyes did not waver under the detective's gaze.

"She was seen coming in here," he bluffed.

"Then whoever saw her suffers from illusions," replied Ralph. "I tell you she has not been inside this house. She is probably at the Palace Hotel, where I took a room on her behalf."

With this story Bickerson had to return to his chief.

"She's not at Dame's house," said Wille decisively. "The police are in possession, and Miss Dame has been taken to the home of a distant relative."

They looked at one another.

"I don't like it," said the Superintendent. "Whoever was responsible for getting the girl away last night is taking care of her tonight. Warn all stations, with a full description; patrolmen to be notified that the girl must be detained wherever and whenever she is found. At nine o'clock tomorrow morning all officers concerned in the case will meet me at Dame's house. I am going through that establishment with a fine comb!"

Bickerson went back to his office, leaving the shrewd old Superintendent to make another examination of the papers and money that had been found on Dame's body. He was so engaged when the door was pushed open and Bickerson came in.

"Can I have a warrant to search Hallam's house?" he asked.

"No, you can't," grunted the Superintendent, without looking up, and Inspector Bickerson stared at him.

It was not the fact that he almost pushed her into the house, but the quickness with which Ralph turned, locked the front door and put the key in his pocket, which brought the girl round in alarm.

"Why did you do that?" she asked.

"I have my reasons," smiled the man.

He was deadly cool. Remembering how easy it had been to arouse his anger or reduce him to a condition of helpless embarrassment, she could only wonder what had produced the change of attitude.

"Where is Mrs Hallam?"

"At Herbert Mansions, so far as I know," said Hallam, without shame. "In fact, Elsa, I've deceived you. I wanted you here for another purpose than to discuss my iniquities. The night isn't long enough, anyway, to give you a detailed account of my numerous falls from grace."

The dining-table was laid for two, but she did not attempt to sit down.

"I don't think I'll stay," she said.

"I, on the other hand, am certain that you will," he replied, "and I will tell you why."

He beckoned her out of the room and pushed open the door of the library. The writing-table had been cleared of the paraphernalia which ordinarily littered the cloth. Instead was a typewriter, a thick pad of paper, and a cardboard package of carbons.

"You will spend the rest of the evening in making a very detailed statement about my connection with the amateurs, my knowledge of Soyoka, and a few other particulars with which I will not bother you for the moment. After – "

"After?" she repeated, when he paused.

"You shall please yourself whether you stay or whether you go. Elsa, there are certain things in this house that no man or woman has ever seen, important actualities that Bickerson, at any rate, would give his head to see with his own eyes. In a few days I am leaving England and starting afresh – under another name, of course" – he smiled – "in spite of the failure of Stebbing's Bank. My friend Mr Tupperwill has disappeared, as you probably know. His present whereabouts are a mystery. I can assure you, my dear Elsa, that his disappearance has made no difference to me."

The smile faded from his face and he looked at her moodily for a long time, and then: "Elsa, I wanted you once – wanted you very badly. And maybe it's going to take a long time for you to forgive me – wanting. But somebody wants you more than I – somebody who will not be denied."

He waited for her to speak, but her lips were closed firmly. "Come," he said suddenly, and took her by the arm. She struggled to free herself.

"Let me go – for God's sake let me go, Ralph!"

"I can't. I swear that you shall not be hurt!" Weakened as she was, the grip about her arm was too powerful to be shaken off, and she went with him up the stairs, scarcely knowing what she was doing.

"This is your room," he pointed. "And this – " he turned the handle of the second door which led, as she knew, to his small drawing-room, "is the hiding place of a gentleman who, I regret to say, is for the moment master of the situation."

She shrank back as he opened the door, but he pushed her in. "Here is your lady," he said, and pulled the door tight.

THE PIT

At nine o'clock in the morning a small knot of plain-clothes police passed into the Dames' house and filed into the dining-room. Superintendent Wille was the last to arrive, and with him were two men in labourers' clothing, carrying spades.

Bickerson, who had been in the place half an hour and had already completed his search of the upper rooms, came down at the sound of voices and joined the party.

"You have found nothing?" asked Wille.

"Nothing whatever, except a number of old clothes, and evidence that the place has been used as a sort of headquarters by Dame's crowd."

Wille led the way down into the kitchen. The dark stains of Dame's blood still showed on the floor, but he had a less morbid interest in the place.

"There is the pantry, exactly as the girl described it," he said, and pulled open the door. "And there is the bed."

He examined the door again, tried the hasp and picked up from the floor a padlock in which was a key; from the key hung a ring with many others.

"I agree that Miss Marlowe's story has plenty of corroboration," said Bickerson, a little crestfallen. "In fact, I don't think I've handled this case as well as I might."

"As you had other matters on hand you couldn't be expected to," said the Superintendent gruffly. "I'm not pretending that the case was easy. It wasn't. From the first it has been a Chinese puzzle."

He opened the door leading into the garden and stepped out. "There is the shed at the bottom of the garden; have you got the key?"

Bickerson nodded and pulled out two keys tied with red tape. Wille, taking them from his hand, walked down the path and, swinging open the heavy door, stepped inside.

He looked down at the earth-filled break in the concrete floor and then at the walls.

"And there is the ring bolt," he said. "You saw that? You remember how Miss Marlowe in her statement described the bolt through which a chain was drawn – ?"

He stopped suddenly and touched the wall above the place where the ring protruded.

"Do you see those?"

There were four pear-shaped stains on the brick wall. "They may be blood or they may not. Look, there are others on the floor!"

He went to the door and called in the labourers.

"Open that hole," he said, "and dig down until you can dig no deeper."

They strolled out into the garden whilst the men began their work.

"Do you think Amery is dead?" asked Bickerson.

"I thought so yesterday; I'm not so sure today," was the Superintendent's reply, and then: "Did you have this pit thoroughly cleared?"

"Absolutely. I went down as far as the pipes; beyond that it was unnecessary to go."

"What time did you do this?"

"Early yesterday morning, about eight o'clock."

"And you found nothing?"

"Nothing at all."

"Did you fill in the pit afterwards?"

"Yes," said Bickerson. "Why do you ask?"

"And you locked both doors? Are there any other keys?"

"So far as I know there aren't, but probably there are."

"You should have sealed the doors," grumbled Wille.

He walked up the garden path, stopping now and again to look at one of the flower-beds, or to poke with his stick a heap of loose earth, and he was so engaged when the voice of one of the labourers called him, and he hurried back.

"There is a body here, sir," said the man.

They were crowding round the doorway to look in at the dreadful sight, when Bickerson, turning his head, saw a man coming out of the kitchen – a tall, lean man, with a white bandage about his dark forehead, and a queer, cynical smile on his thin lips.

"Amery!" he gasped.

Amery did not answer, until he came up to the staring group, and then: "Have you found the body?"

Wille nodded.

"I was afraid you had," said Amery. "It is Tupperwill – I killed him! It was an accident. He had me chained up to the wall, and had given me one blow, when I managed to get my hands clear of the handcuffs and struck back at him. Again, by a lucky chance, his infernal stick caught me and almost knocked me out. If I had fallen then it would not have been Tupperwill's body you would be finding! By the greatest good luck I caught him on the point and knocked him backward. His head caught the edge of the pit and he crumpled up and fell."

A long and a painful pause.

"I hope he was dead," he said softly. "I hope he was dead!"

And they knew he was thinking of another dreadful possibility. "You have made a very serious statement, Major Amery," said Bickerson. "You may be able to explain – "

"I'm making another. Put up your hands, Stillman. Put 'em up!"

Bickerson's hands went up; his face had the pallor of death.

"You'll find in his inside waistcoat pocket a most perfectly constructed beard. At the European Bank in Threadneedle Street, Superintendent, you will discover a balance in his name that will stagger you. Crook from the day he put on uniform, to the culmination of his career, when he succeeded in joining the Soyoka gang, there isn't a straight place in his life."

A pair of handcuffs snapped about the detective's wrists, and two of his former comrades hurried him through the house into the car that was waiting.

Wille took the arm of the sinister man, and together they walked out of earshot.

"I got your message last night. How did you finally escape?"

"I mightn't have got away at all, for Bickerson was somewhere in the garden, and I was as weak as a rat from loss of blood. Fortunately, I managed to get the door open that led into the lane, but even here Stillman might have finished what the other devil began, only there was somebody waiting for me – the last person in the world I expected to find."

"Not Hallam?" gasped Wille.

"Hallam it was," nodded the Major with a little wince of pain. "There is another kind of crook. God makes them in many ways. He got me out of the lane, took me home, put me to bed and dressed the injury. There's this excuse for his being a crook, that he's a pretty bad surgeon! But he was good to me, and did it all without any hope that he would escape the consequence of his own misdoings."

"Then Bickerson killed Tarn?" said Wille.

"Who else? It could only be Bickerson or Hallam. Tarn had got a telegram, which came to my office in error. It was from a man who used to be one of Tarn's agents. In the course of that wire the sender was indiscreet enough to mention the name of Tupperwill. Now, here is the curious thing about the Tarn murder. Hallam was scared to death that Tarn intended betraying his crowd, and he got to know that the old man had an appointment that night with Bickerson. In order to stop him talking, knowing something of his habits, he doped the old man's brandy, thinking that that would carry him over till the next morning and make his confession impossible.

"To make absolutely sure, he called on Bickerson, and found that the inspector was on the point of going to his appointment. Now, Bickerson knew that Maurice Tarn was engaged in the dope trade, but I doubt then if he had any intention of injuring him, until he learnt by telephone that Tarn knew the head of the Soyoka gang. He allowed

Hallam to go with him so that, in the event of any trouble, the blame could be shifted. By an extraordinary coincidence, my man Feng Ho had gone into the house that night to make an examination, and switched out the lights in order to test the old man's wakefulness, so that, when they went into the study, all the circumstances were favourable to the commission of the crime. In the darkness Bickerson leant down, felt for the heart and drove the knife home. The blood on his hands could easily be accounted for – he was the only man who had handled the body.

"Two factors occurred to frighten him. The first was the presence in the room of Miss Marlowe, and the second the intrusion of Feng Ho."

"Humph!" said the police chief. "It's a pity Dame committed suicide – "

"Dame was murdered," was the calm reply. "He was shot down by Bickerson as he entered the kitchen, and for an excellent reason! Dame, at a critical moment, broke down, showed weakness which decided his fate."

"Did Bickerson know that Tupperwill was dead?"

The Major shook his head.

"No," he said quietly, "that was the one shock that Mr Bickerson had – that Tupperwill and not I lay in the grave that he had so carefully dug. But he knew that Tupperwill had disappeared, and was scared. That was why he invented the story of having seen the banker.

"There is one favour I have to ask: it is that a suitcase, which you will find in Bickerson's lodgings, should be handed to me intact. I'll tell you frankly that it contains money earned by Tarn and Hallam in the course of their nefarious practice, and I suggest that the money be passed along, because, if it comes to a matter of law, there are going to be a whole lot of complications which would be best avoided."

"What will you do with Hallam? There's a warrant out for him."

"I don't think I should execute the warrant if I were you," said Amery quietly. "I learnt last night one curious thing. Tupperwill, who must have known that Maurice Tarn's money had disappeared, tried to work on Hallam's feelings by telling him that I had the money in a box at Stebbing's Bank. He hoped to induce the doctor to go after me – for Tupperwill and Bickerson knew me for what I was. As to Hallam – the two gangs are broken, and unless I am mistaken, by this time Bickerson is dead."

"Dead!" said the startled Superintendent.

"He carried cyanide tablets loose in his waistcoat pocket," said Amery, "and if he is an intelligent man he will find them before he is searched."

"And now," he said, looking at his watch, "I am going back to my neglected business. I am out of police work for good. From henceforward, point to me as a rising City merchant with aspirations to the Common Council."

It was a glorious morning, and as his cab carried him back slowly through the tangle of City traffic, his thoughts were far away from death and danger, from that hideous night in the Dame's garage, from the pit and the Thing that went down to it. His work was done, the labour of years finished. There might be a trial; there would certainly be an inquest, and he would figure as part of a nine days' wonder. But after that there was work, and a serene future, and a girl into whose soul he had looked.

Ralph Hallam was waiting for him when he arrived.

"Well, was it as you thought?"

Amery nodded.

"Now what of me?"

"Come to my house tonight," said Amery. "I will give you part of the contents of the suitcase, unless friend Wille changes his mind. The remainder I purpose sending to a charity. Miss Marlowe did not come with you?"

"No, Lou told me she was asleep."

Amery bit his lip.

"It was good of your wife to stay with Elsa last night. By the way, are you going to your unknown destination – alone?"

Ralph scratched his chin.

"N-no," he said. "I think I shall make a desperate attempt to be respectable. Lou isn't exactly an inspiration, but she's a warning!"

He was scarcely out of Wood Street, and had crossed Cheapside, when he saw the girl go up the street and pass between the ancient portals.

Of a truth this was a day of wonder and magic to Elsa Marlowe; for in the darkness of the night, in a room where she had expected terror, she had met the face of her dreams, and heard a voice beloved overall, and had felt the strength of the enfolding arms.

The sky above was blue, flecked by clouds as fine and white as the veil of a bride. She came into her office, hung up her hat and prepared the typewriter for a joyous day. And then, before she could sit down, the bell rang.

Her heart was beating at a tremendous rate as she turned the handle and went in.

"Do you want anything – Major Amery?" she asked, breathlessly.

He nodded.

"I want you to kiss me," he said.

She stooped over him and their lips met. Then: "Take this," he said, in that old, gruff tone of his, and with a little laugh she sat down, opened her book. The trembling pencil was making lines of its own, when he began:

> To the Manager of the Monte Rosa Hotel,
> Como,
> Italy.

Dear Sir,

In a month's time I am bringing my wife to Como, and I should be glad if you would reserve me a suite…!

Edgar Wallace

Big Foot

Footprints and a dead woman bring together Superintendent Minton and the amateur sleuth Mr Cardew. Who is the man in the shrubbery? Who is the singer of the haunting Moorish tune? Why is Hannah Shaw so determined to go to Pawsy, 'a dog lonely place' she had previously detested? Death lurks in the dark and someone must solve the mystery before BIG FOOT strikes again, in a yet more fiendish manner.

Bones In London

The new Managing Director of Schemes Ltd has an elegant London office and a theatrically dressed assistant – however Bones, as he is better known, is bored. Luckily there is a slump in the shipping market and it is not long before Joe and Fred Pole pay Bones a visit. They are totally unprepared for Bones' unnerving style of doing business, unprepared for his unique style of innocent and endearing mischief.

EDGAR WALLACE

BONES OF THE RIVER

'Taking the little paper from the pigeon's leg, Hamilton saw it was from Sanders and marked URGENT. *Send Bones instantly to Lujamalababa... Arrest and bring to head-quarters the witch doctor.'*

It is a time when the world's most powerful nations are vying for colonial honour, a time of trading steamers and tribal chiefs. In the mysterious African territories administered by Commissioner Sanders, Bones persistently manages to create his own unique style of innocent and endearing mischief.

THE DAFFODIL MYSTERY

When Mr Thomas Lyne, poet, poseur and owner of Lyne's Emporium insults a cashier, Odette Rider, she resigns. Having summoned detective Jack Tarling to investigate another employee, Mr Milburgh, Lyne now changes his plans. Tarling and his Chinese companion refuse to become involved. They pay a visit to Odette's flat. In the hall Tarling meets Sam, convicted felon and protégé of Lyne. Next morning Tarling discovers a body. The hands are crossed on the breast, adorned with a handful of daffodils.

EDGAR WALLACE

THE JOKER

While the millionaire Stratford Harlow is in Princetown, not only does he meet with his lawyer Mr Ellenbury but he gets his first glimpse of the beautiful Aileen Rivers, niece of the actor and convicted felon Arthur Ingle. When Aileen is involved in a car accident on the Thames Embankment, the driver is James Carlton of Scotland Yard. Later that evening Carlton gets a call. It is Aileen. She needs help.

THE SQUARE EMERALD

'Suicide on the left,' says Chief Inspector Coldwell pleasantly, as he and Leslie Maughan stride along the Thames Embankment during a brutally cold night. A gaunt figure is sprawled across the parapet. But Coldwell soon discovers that Peter Dawlish, fresh out of prison for forgery, is not considering suicide but murder. Coldwell suspects Druze as the intended victim. Maughan disagrees. If Druze dies, she says, 'It will be because he does not love children!'

OTHER TITLES BY EDGAR WALLACE AVAILABLE DIRECT
FROM HOUSE OF STRATUS

Quantity		£	$(US)	$(CAN)	€
	THE ADMIRABLE CARFEW	6.99	11.50	15.99	11.50
	THE ANGEL OF TERROR	6.99	11.50	15.99	11.50
	THE AVENGER	6.99	11.50	15.99	11.50
	BARBARA ON HER OWN	6.99	11.50	15.99	11.50
	BIG FOOT	6.99	11.50	15.99	11.50
	THE BLACK ABBOT	6.99	11.50	15.99	11.50
	BONES	6.99	11.50	15.99	11.50
	BONES IN LONDON	6.99	11.50	15.99	11.50
	BONES OF THE RIVER	6.99	11.50	15.99	11.50
	THE CLUE OF THE NEW PIN	6.99	11.50	15.99	11.50
	THE CLUE OF THE SILVER KEY	6.99	11.50	15.99	11.50
	THE CLUE OF THE TWISTED CANDLE	6.99	11.50	15.99	11.50
	THE COAT OF ARMS	6.99	11.50	15.99	11.50
	THE COUNCIL OF JUSTICE	6.99	11.50	15.99	11.50
	THE CRIMSON CIRCLE	6.99	11.50	15.99	11.50
	THE DAFFODIL MYSTERY	6.99	11.50	15.99	11.50
	THE DARK EYES OF LONDON	6.99	11.50	15.99	11.50
	THE DAUGHTERS OF THE NIGHT	6.99	11.50	15.99	11.50
	A DEBT DISCHARGED	6.99	11.50	15.99	11.50
	THE DEVIL MAN	6.99	11.50	15.99	11.50
	THE DOOR WITH SEVEN LOCKS	6.99	11.50	15.99	11.50
	THE DUKE IN THE SUBURBS	6.99	11.50	15.99	11.50
	THE FACE IN THE NIGHT	6.99	11.50	15.99	11.50
	THE FEATHERED SERPENT	6.99	11.50	15.99	11.50
	THE FLYING SQUAD	6.99	11.50	15.99	11.50
	THE FORGER	6.99	11.50	15.99	11.50
	THE FOUR JUST MEN	6.99	11.50	15.99	11.50
	FOUR SQUARE JANE	6.99	11.50	15.99	11.50

ALL HOUSE OF STRATUS BOOKS ARE AVAILABLE FROM GOOD BOOKSHOPS
OR DIRECT FROM THE PUBLISHER:

Internet: www.houseofstratus.com including author interviews, reviews, features.

Email: sales@houseofstratus.com please quote author, title and credit card details.

OTHER TITLES BY EDGAR WALLACE AVAILABLE DIRECT
FROM HOUSE OF STRATUS

Quantity		£	$(US)	$(CAN)	€
	THE FOURTH PLAGUE	6.99	11.50	15.99	11.50
	THE FRIGHTENED LADY	6.99	11.50	15.99	11.50
	GOOD EVANS	6.99	11.50	15.99	11.50
	THE HAND OF POWER	6.99	11.50	15.99	11.50
	THE IRON GRIP	6.99	11.50	15.99	11.50
	THE JOKER	6.99	11.50	15.99	11.50
	THE JUST MEN OF CORDOVA	6.99	11.50	15.99	11.50
	THE KEEPERS OF THE KING'S PEACE	6.99	11.50	15.99	11.50
	THE LAW OF THE FOUR JUST MEN	6.99	11.50	15.99	11.50
	THE LONE HOUSE MYSTERY	6.99	11.50	15.99	11.50
	THE MAN WHO BOUGHT LONDON	6.99	11.50	15.99	11.50
	THE MAN WHO KNEW	6.99	11.50	15.99	11.50
	THE MAN WHO WAS NOBODY	6.99	11.50	15.99	11.50
	THE MIND OF MR J G REEDER	6.99	11.50	15.99	11.50
	MORE EDUCATED EVANS	6.99	11.50	15.99	11.50
	MR J G REEDER RETURNS	6.99	11.50	15.99	11.50
	MR JUSTICE MAXWELL	6.99	11.50	15.99	11.50
	RED ACES	6.99	11.50	15.99	11.50
	ROOM 13	6.99	11.50	15.99	11.50
	SANDERS	6.99	11.50	15.99	11.50
	SANDERS OF THE RIVER	6.99	11.50	15.99	11.50
	THE SQUARE EMERALD	6.99	11.50	15.99	11.50
	THE THREE JUST MEN	6.99	11.50	15.99	11.50
	THE THREE OAK MYSTERY	6.99	11.50	15.99	11.50
	THE TRAITOR'S GATE	6.99	11.50	15.99	11.50
	WHEN THE GANGS CAME TO LONDON	6.99	11.50	15.99	11.50
	WHEN THE WORLD STOPPED	6.99	11.50	15.99	11.50

Hotline: UK ONLY: 0800 169 1780, please quote author, title and credit card details.
INTERNATIONAL: +44 (0) 20 7494 6400, please quote author, title and credit card details.

Send to: **House of Stratus Sales Department**
24c Old Burlington Street
London
W1X 1RL
UK

Please allow for postage costs charged per order plus an amount per book as set out in the tables below:

	£(Sterling)	$(US)	$(CAN)	€(Euros)
Cost per order				
UK	2.00	3.00	4.50	3.30
Europe	3.00	4.50	6.75	5.00
North America	3.00	4.50	6.75	5.00
Rest of World	3.00	4.50	6.75	5.00
Additional cost per book				
UK	0.50	0.75	1.15	0.85
Europe	1.00	1.50	2.30	1.70
North America	2.00	3.00	4.60	3.40
Rest of World	2.50	3.75	5.75	4.25

PLEASE SEND CHEQUE, POSTAL ORDER (STERLING ONLY), EUROCHEQUE, OR INTERNATIONAL MONEY ORDER (PLEASE CIRCLE METHOD OF PAYMENT YOU WISH TO USE)
MAKE PAYABLE TO: STRATUS HOLDINGS plc

Cost of book(s): —————————— Example: 3 x books at £6.99 each: £20.97

Cost of order: —————————— Example: £2.00 (Delivery to UK address)

Additional cost per book: —————— Example: 3 x £0.50: £1.50

Order total including postage: ———— Example: £24.47

Please tick currency you wish to use and add total amount of order:

☐ £ (Sterling)　☐ $ (US)　☐ $ (CAN)　☐ € (EUROS)

VISA, MASTERCARD, SWITCH, AMEX, SOLO, JCB:

☐ ☐ ☐ ☐ ☐ ☐ ☐ ☐ ☐ ☐ ☐ ☐ ☐ ☐ ☐ ☐ ☐ ☐ ☐

Issue number (Switch only):

☐ ☐ ☐

Start Date:　　　　　　　　**Expiry Date:**

☐☐ / ☐☐　　　　　　　　☐☐ / ☐☐

Signature: ————————————

NAME: ————————————————————————

ADDRESS: ——————————————————————

————————————————————————

POSTCODE: —————————

Please allow 28 days for delivery.

Prices subject to change without notice.
Please tick box if you do not wish to receive any additional information. ☐

House of Stratus publishes many other titles in this genre; please check our website (**www.houseofstratus.com**) for more details.